Praise for Small Pleasures

'The glorious literary equivalent of pulling the duvet over your head... If you admire Tessa Hadley or Anne Tyler (and there are shades of Barbara Pym too), then this is one for you'
Bookseller, Book of the Month

'Clare Chambers is that rare thing, a novelist of discreet hilarity, deep compassion and stiletto wit whose perspicacious account of suburban lives with their quiet desperation and unexpected passion makes her the 21st century heir to Jane Austen, Barbara Pym and Elizabeth Taylor. *Small Pleasures* is both gripping and a huge delight. I loved what she did with the trope of the claim of a virgin birth, and how the hope of a miracle opens the door to love, kindness and hope in an arid existence. This is better than *Eleanor Oliphant Is Completely Fine* and deserves just as much acclaim'
Amanda Craig, author of *The Lie of the Land*

'I adored *Small Pleasures*. It's engrossing and gripping: you want to race on and relish every sentence at the same time. I love the way Clare writes – her wry, subtle turns of phrase, the humour in the smallest of observations, the finely drawn characters. A wonderful book'
Sabine Durrant, author of *Lie With Me*

'*Small Pleasures* is a tender and heart-rending tale that will draw you in from the first page and keep you gripped until the very end. Exquisitely compelling!'
Ruth Hogan, author of *The Keeper of Lost Things*

'*Small Pleasures* is a gorgeous treat of a novel: the premise is fascinating, the characters beautifully drawn and utterly compelling, the period setting masterfully and delicately evoked, and the plot is full of unexpected twists and turns. And oh, the finale broke my heart. I just couldn't put this novel down'
Laura Barnett, author of *The Versions of Us*

'A delicious mystery and a touching exploration of loneliness and desire in cloying 1950s suburbia – a great read'

Sally Magnusson, author of *The Sealwoman's Gift*

'*Small Pleasures* is the best sort of book: full of longing, regret and difficult emotions but leavened with so much warmth and humour it was a joy from start to finish'

Francesca Jakobi, author of *Bitter*

Also by Clare Chambers

Uncertain Terms
Back Trouble
Learning to Swim
A Dry Spell
In A Good Light
The Editor's Wife

SMALL PLEASURES

Clare Chambers

WEIDENFELD & NICOLSON

First published in Great Britain in 2020 by Weidenfeld & Nicolson
an imprint of The Orion Publishing Group Ltd
Carmelite House, 50 Victoria Embankment
London EC4Y ODZ

An Hachette UK Company

1 3 5 7 9 10 8 6 4 2

A CIP catalogue record for this book is
available from the British Library.

ISBN (Hardback) 978 1 4746 1388 0
ISBN (Export Trade Paperback) 978 1 4746 1389 7
ISBN (eBook) 978 1 4746 1391 0

Printed and bound in Great Britain
by Clays Ltd, Elcograf S.p.A

MIX
Paper from
responsible sources
FSC® C104740

www.weidenfeldandnicolson.co.uk
www.orionbooks.co.uk

To Peter

RAIL DISASTER

Rush hour trains collide in thick fog – many dead.

Tragedy struck office workers and Christmas shoppers on the evening of 4 December when two trains collided in thick fog under the Nunhead flyover. The 5.18 from Charing Cross to Hayes and the 4.56 steam train from Cannon Street to Ramsgate had been delayed by the poor weather. Coaches on both trains were packed, with passengers standing as well as sitting.

The Hayes train had stopped at a signal outside St John's at 6.20 p.m. when the steam train ploughed into the rear coach. This was just the beginning of an unfolding disaster, which left more than 80 dead and 200 wounded.

The steam train swung to the side and struck a steel column of the Nunhead flyover, causing the bridge to collapse, crushing two coaches below. A third train, from Holborn Viaduct, was just approaching the fallen flyover, when quick action by the driver brought it to a halt, preventing further catastrophe. The coaches were derailed but no one on board was injured.

The rescue efforts of firemen, police, railway staff, doctors and nurses were hampered by fog and darkness. Worse still, the ruined bridge was in danger of falling further, crushing rescuers and trapped victims alike.

But through the long night of toil the army of volunteers continued to grow, with many local residents throwing open their doors to assist the injured. Eleven ambulances attended the scene, driving casualties further and further afield as nearby hospitals struggled to cope.

Local telephone lines became jammed by worried relatives as news of the accident spread. Hundreds of passengers were marooned in London for the night with the mid-Kent line completely blocked.

Many of the dead and injured were from Clock House and Beckenham. Passengers alighting at those stations were more likely to choose rear coaches because of their proximity to the station exits. It was these that took the brunt of the collision.

Southern Region authorities have launched an immediate inquiry.

The *North Kent Echo*, Friday, 6 December 1957

I

June 1957

The article that started it all was not even on the front page, but was just a filler on page 5, between an advertisement for the Patricia Brixie Dancing School and a report on the AGM of the Crofton North Liberals. It concerned the finding of a recent study into parthenogenesis in sea urchins, frogs and rabbits, which concluded that there was no reason it should not be possible in humans. This dusty paragraph might have been overlooked by most readers of the *North Kent Echo* were it not for the melodramatic headline 'Men No Longer Needed for Reproduction!'

The result was an unusually large postbag of mostly indignant letters, not just from men. One wounded correspondent, Mrs Beryl Diplock of St Paul's Cray, deplored the article's sentiments as dangerous and unchristian. More than one female reader pointed out that such a proposition was liable to give slippery men an excuse to wriggle out of their responsibilities.

There was one letter, however, that stood out from all the rest. It was from a Mrs Gretchen Tilbury of 7 Burdett Road, Sidcup, and read simply:

Dear Editor,
   I was interested to read your article 'Men No Longer Needed for Reproduction' in last week's paper. I have always

3

believed my own daughter (now ten) to have been born without the involvement of any man. If you would like to know more information you may write to me at the above address.

The next editorial meeting – usually a dull affair involving the planning and distribution of duties for the week and a post-mortem of the errors and oversights in the previous issue – was livelier than it had been for some time.

Jean Swinney, features editor, columnist, dogsbody and the only woman at the table, glanced at the letter as it was passed around. The slanted handwriting, with its strange continental loops, reminded her of a French teacher from school. She, too, had written the number seven with a line through it, which the thirteen-year-old Jean had thought the height of sophistication and decided to imitate. Her mother had put a stop to that; she could hardly have been more affronted if Jean had taken to writing in blood. To Mrs Swinney, all foreigners were Germans and beyond the pale.

Thoughts of her mother prompted Jean to remember that she needed to pick up her shoes from the menders on the way home. It mystified her why someone who seldom left the house should need so many pairs of outdoor shoes. Also required were cigarettes, peppermint oil from Rumsey's, and kidneys and lard if she could be bothered to make a pie for dinner. Otherwise it would just be 'eggs anyhow', that old standby.

'Does anyone want to go and interview Our Lady of Sidcup?' asked Larry, the news editor.

There was a general creaking backwards in chairs, indicative of dissent.

'Not really my thing,' said Bill, sports and entertainment editor.

Jean slowly extended her hand to take the letter. She knew it was coming her way sooner or later.

'Good idea,' said Larry, huffing smoke across the table. 'It's women's interest, after all.'

'Do we really want to encourage these cranks?' said Bill.

'She may not be a crank,' said Roy Drake, the editor, mildly.

It made Jean smile to remember how intimidating she used to find him when she had joined the paper as a young woman, and how she would quake if summoned to his office. She had soon discovered he was not the sort of man who took pleasure in terrorising his juniors. He had four daughters and treated all women kindly. Besides, it was hard to be in awe of someone whose suits were so very crumpled.

'How can she not be?' Bill wanted to know. 'You're not saying you believe in virgin births?'

'No, but I'd be interested to know why this Mrs Tilbury does.'

'She writes a good letter,' said Larry. 'Concise.'

'It's concise because she's foreign,' said Jean.

They all looked at her.

'No Englishwoman is taught handwriting like that. And "Gretchen"?'

'Well, clearly this is the sort of interview that is going to require some tact,' said Roy. 'So obviously it's going to have to be you, Jean.'

Around the table heads nodded. No one was going to fight her for this story.

'Anyway, the first thing is to go and check her out. I'm sure you'll be able to tell pretty quickly if she's a charlatan.'

'Give me five minutes alone with her – I'll tell you if she's a virgin,' said Larry, to general laughter. He leaned back in his chair, elbows out, hands behind his head, so that the gridlines of his vest were clearly visible against his shirt.

'She doesn't say she's *still* a virgin,' Bill pointed out. 'This happened ten years ago. She may have seen some action since then.'

'I'm sure Jean can manage without your expertise,' said Roy, who didn't like that sort of talk.

Jean had the feeling that if he wasn't there, the conversation would rapidly turn coarse. It was curious the way the others moderated their language to suit Roy's prudishness, while Jean herself was treated as 'one of the chaps'. She took this as a compliment, mostly. In darker moments, when she noticed the way they behaved around younger, prettier women – the secretaries, for example – with a heavy-handed mixture of flirtation and gallantry, she wasn't so sure.

Jean divided the rest of the afternoon between her Household Hints column and Marriage Lines – a write-up of the previous week's weddings.

....

After a reception at St Paul's Cray Community Centre, Mr and Mrs Plornish left for their honeymoon at St Leonard's, the bride wearing a turquoise coat and black accessories . . .

....

Household Hints was a cinch because these were all supplied by loyal readers. In the early days Jean used to put some of these to the test *before* publication. Now, she took a certain pleasure in selecting the most outlandish.

That done, she wrote a brief note to Gretchen Tilbury, asking if she could come and meet her and her daughter. Since she had provided no telephone number, the arrangements would have to be conducted by letter. At five o'clock she covered her typewriter with its hood and left the building, dropping the letter into the post room on her way out.

Jean's bicycle, a solid, heavy-framed contraption that had come down, like most of her possessions, through generations of the Swinney family, was leaning against the railings. Standing in front of it, too much in the way to be ignored, was one of the typists locked in a deep embrace with a lad from the print room. Jean recognised the girl but didn't know her name; there wasn't much interplay between the reporters and the other departments on the paper.

She had to step around them, feeling rather foolish, to retrieve her bicycle, until they finally acknowledged her and pulled away, giggling their apologies. There was something almost cruel in their self-absorption and Jean had to remind herself that it was nothing personal, just a universal symptom of the disease of love. Those afflicted could not be blamed, only pitied.

Jean took a silk headscarf from her pocket and knotted it tightly under her chin to stop her hair from blowing in her face as she cycled. Then, squashing her bag into the basket on the handlebars, she wheeled the bicycle to the kerb and swung herself onto the saddle, smoothing her skirt beneath her in one practised movement.

It was only a ten-minute ride from the offices of the *Echo* in Petts Wood to Jean's home in Hayes and even at this time of day there was little traffic. The sun was still high in the sky; there were hours of daylight left. Once she had seen to her mother there might be time for some gardening: ground elder was coming in under the next-door fence and menacing the bean rows; it required constant vigilance.

The thought of pottering in the vegetable patch on a summer evening was infinitely soothing. The lawns, front and back, would have to wait until the weekend, because that was a heavy job, made heavier by an obligation to do her elderly neighbour's grass at the same time. It was one of those generous impulses that had begun as a favour and had now become a duty, performed with dwindling enthusiasm on one side and fading gratitude on the other.

Jean stopped off at the parade of shops that curved down the

7

hill from the station to complete her errands. Steak and kidney would take too long but the thought of eggs for tea again had a dampening effect on her spirits, so she bought some lamb's liver from the butcher. They could have it with new potatoes and broad beans from the garden. She didn't dawdle over the rest of her list – the shops shut promptly at five-thirty and there would be disappointment indoors if she returned home without the shoes or the medicine, and utter frustration for herself if she ran out of cigarettes.

By the time she reached home, a modest 1930s semi backing on to the park, her cheerful mood had evaporated. Somehow, in transferring the waxed paper package of liver to her tartan shopping bag she managed to drip two spots of blood on the front of her dust-coloured wool skirt. She was furious with herself. The skirt had not long ago been cleaned and she knew from experience that blood was one of the most tenacious stains to treat.

'Is that you, Jean?' Her mother's voice – anxious, reproachful – floated down the stairs in response to the scrape of her door key, as it always did.

'Yes, Mother, only me,' Jean replied, as she always did, with a degree more or less of impatience in her tone, depending on how her day had gone.

Her mother appeared on the landing, fluttering a blue aero-gramme over the banisters. 'There's a letter from Dorrie,' she said. 'Do you want to read it?'

'Maybe later,' said Jean, who was still taking off her headscarf and divesting herself of her various packages.

Her younger sister, Dorrie, was married to a coffee farmer and lived in Kenya, which might as well have been Venus as far as Jean was concerned, so remote and unimaginable was her new life. She had a houseboy and a cook and a gardener, and a nightwatchman to protect them from intruders, and a gun under

8

the bed to protect them from the nightwatchman. The sisters had been close as children and Jean had missed her terribly at first, but after so many years she had grown accustomed to not seeing her or her children in a way that their mother never would.

'Is there something nice for tea?' Having noticed the paper bag containing her mended shoes, her mother began a slow and wincing descent of the stairs.

'Liver,' said Jean.

'Oh good. I'm ravenous. I haven't eaten anything all day.'

'Well why ever not? There's plenty of food in the larder.'

Sensing resistance, Jean's mother backtracked a little. 'I slept rather late. So I had my porridge instead of lunch.'

'So you *have* eaten something, then?'

'Oh, I don't call that *eating*.'

Jean didn't reply to this but took her purchases into the kitchen and deposited them on the table. The room faced west and was warm and bright in the early evening sun. A fly fizzed and bumped against the windowpane until Jean let it out, noticing as she did so the specks and smears on the glass. Another job for the weekend. They had a woman who came in to clean on a Thursday morning, but she seemed to Jean to achieve very little in her allotted hour, apart from gossiping to her mother. But this was a chore of sorts, Jean supposed, and she didn't begrudge her the five shillings. Not really.

While her mother tried on the newly mended shoes, Jean took off her skirt and stood at the sink in her blouse and slip, inspecting the spots of dried blood. In the curtained dresser she located a box of rags – the earthly remains of other ruined garments – and, using the severed sleeve of a once-favourite cotton nightdress, began to dab at the stain with cleaning spirit.

'What are you doing?' said her mother, peering over her shoulder.

'I got blood on it,' said Jean, frowning as the rust-coloured

9

patch began to dissolve and spread. 'Not mine. The liver, I mean.'

'You messy girl,' said her mother, extending a twiggy ankle to admire her shoe, a beige kidskin pump with a Cuban heel. 'I don't suppose I'll ever wear these again,' she sighed. 'But still.'

The mark was slightly fainter now, but larger, and still quite visible against the grey fabric.

'What a pity,' said Jean. 'It was such a good skirt for cycling.'

She took it upstairs with her to change. She couldn't wear it, but neither could she quite bring herself to consign it to the rag box yet. Instead, she folded it up and stowed it in the bottom of her wardrobe, as if an alternative use for unwearable skirts might one day present itself.

After tea – liver and onions cooked by Jean and a pudding of tinned pears with evaporated milk – Jean weeded and watered the vegetable patch while her mother sat in a deckchair, holding but not quite reading her library book. She would never sit outside alone, Jean noticed, however pleasant the weather, but only if there was company. From the park came the high, bright shouts of children playing, an occasional sequence of barks from the dogs in the street as a pedestrian passed along and the even less frequent rumble of a passing car. By the time dusk fell, all would be silent.

Jean and her mother moved into the sitting room at the front of the house, drew the curtains and switched on the lamps, which gave out a grudging yellowish light behind their brown shades. They played two hands of gin rummy at the small card table and then Jean picked listlessly through a basket of mending, which she had been adding to but otherwise ignoring for some weeks. Her mother, meanwhile, took out her leather writing case to reply to Dorrie's letter. By way of preparation for this task, she reread it aloud, which Jean could only presume was for her benefit, since her mother was already well acquainted with the contents. She did the same thing with newspaper and magazine articles when she was finding the silence of a Sunday afternoon irksome.

Dear Mother,

Thank you for your letter. It sounds lovely and peaceful in Hayes. I wish I could say the same — it's been non-stop here. Kenneth has been staying on the farm — he's got a new manager at last who needs to be 'broken in'. Let's hope he lasts a bit longer than the previous one — now referred to in private as 'Villainous Vernon'. (Mrs Swinney tittered at this.)

I have joined the Kitale Club and it's become my second home while Kenneth's away. There are some real 'types' there as you can imagine. I went to see the Kitale Dramatic Society's production of Present Laughter *on Friday night. Pru Calderwell — the absolute queen of the social scene here — was ever so good as Liz Essendine. The rest of the cast were pretty wooden. I thought I might as well audition for the next one myself if that's the standard!*

We've got ourselves a new black Alsatian pup called Ndofu. We're completely besotted with him. I'm supposed to be training him up as a guard dog for when I'm here by myself but he's such a soppy creature, he'll just roll over for anyone who tickles him.

The children will be home for the holiday in a few weeks' time so I must take advantage of my last few weeks of freedom and get some more tennis in. I've been having some lessons and I'm playing in a mixed doubles tournament tomorrow with a chap called Stanley Harris who is about 60 but madly competitive and throws himself all over my half of the court shouting, 'Mine! Mine!' so I shan't have much to do.

Must dash for the post now. Keep well. Much love to you and Jean.

Dorrie

'She writes a super letter,' Jean's mother said.

'Well that's because she has a super life to write about,' Jean retorted.

These breezy bulletins always left her feeling a trifle sour. Fond memories of their shared childhood closeness were now clouded by resentment at their contrasting fates.

At eight-thirty Jean's mother rose effortfully from her chair and said, as though the idea had just that moment occurred to her, 'I think I'll have my bath.'

Although Jean had occasional misgivings about their domestic routines, and intimations sometimes reached her that other people had a different, freer way of doing things, her mother's bath-night ritual was one she was keen to uphold. Twice a week, on Tuesdays and Fridays between eight-thirty and nine, Jean was mistress of the house, free to do as she liked. She could listen to the wireless without her mother's commentary, eat standing up in the kitchen, read in perfect silence or run naked through the rooms if she chose.

Of all the various liberties available, her favourite was to unfasten her girdle and lie at full stretch on the couch with an ashtray on her stomach and smoke two cigarettes back to back. There was no reason why she couldn't do this in her mother's presence – lying down in the day might prompt an enquiry about her health, no more – but it wasn't nearly so enjoyable in company. The summer variant of this practice was to walk barefoot down the garden and smoke her cigarettes lying on the cool grass.

On this particular evening, she had just peeled off her musty stockings and stuffed them into the toes of her shoes when there was a tremendous clattering from the back parlour, as if all the tiles had fallen off the fireplace at once. Upon investigation she found that a blackbird had come down the chimney, bringing with it an avalanche of soot and debris. It lay stunned in the

12

empty grate for a few seconds and then, at Jean's approach, began to thrash and struggle, battering itself against the bars.

Jean recoiled, her heart heaving in horror. She was quite unequal to the task of either rescuing or finishing off a wounded bird. She could see now that it was a young pigeon, blackened with soot, and that it was perhaps more terrified than injured. It had flopped out of the grate and was beginning to flap unsteadily around the room, imperilling the ornaments and leaving dark streaks on the wallpaper.

Throwing open the door to the garden, Jean tried to wave it towards the doorway, with stiff-armed gestures more suited to directing traffic, until it finally sensed freedom and took off, low across the lawn, coming to rest on the branch of the cherry tree. As Jean stood watching, next door's ginger cat came stalking out of the shrubbery with murder in its eyes.

By the time she had swept up the gritty mess from the hearth, wiped the worst of the marks from the walls and closed the door on the damp, subterranean smell of soot, she could hear the bathwater thundering in the drain outside. She smoked her cigarette standing up at the cooker waiting for the milk to boil for her mother's Allenbury's.

Now that her heart rate had returned to normal she felt quite a sense of accomplishment at having seen off another domestic crisis without having to call on anyone else for help – even supposing there had been anyone to call.

....

Sawdust is excellent for cleaning carpets.
Damp the sawdust, sprinkle lightly over
the carpet to be cleaned and then brush
off with a stiff brush. It leaves no stain on
the most delicate-coloured carpet.

....

2

Number 7, Burdett Road, Sidcup was a 1930s semi in slightly better condition than Jean's own. In the front garden a symmetrical arrangement of marigolds and begonias bloomed in weedless borders on three sides of a neat rectangle of lawn. A matching pair of tame hydrangeas flowered at either end of the low front wall. The brass letterbox and door knocker had been polished to a high shine. Jean, standing on the doorstep, taking a moment to collect herself before ringing the bell, resolved to pick up some Brasso on the way home. It was all too easy to overlook the chores that related to those parts of the house her mother didn't see.

After a few moments a shape loomed behind the stained-glass panel and the front door was opened by a slender woman of about thirty with dark brown curly hair pinned off her face by a tortoiseshell clip. She was holding a balled-up duster and a pair of rubber gloves, which she passed uncertainly from hand to hand before depositing them on the hallstand beside her.

'Mrs Tilbury? I'm Jean Swinney from the *North Kent Echo*.'

'Yes, come in, come in,' said the woman, simultaneously holding out a hand to shake and standing back to let Jean in so it was now out of reach.

After they had negotiated this rather bungled introduction,

Jean found herself ushered into the front parlour, which smelled of wax polish and had the pristine, dead feel of a room that was saved for best.

Mrs Tilbury offered Jean the more comfortable of the two chairs by the window, angled towards each other across a small table.

'I thought you might need to make some notes,' she said. It wasn't so much her accent as the faintly staccato delivery that marked her out as foreign.

'Thank you – I usually do,' said Jean, taking out her spiral notebook and pencil from her bag and laying them on the table.

'I've made some tea. I'll just get it.'

Mrs Tilbury whisked out of the room and Jean could hear her clattering in the kitchen. She took advantage of this momentary absence to glance at her surroundings, evaluating them with a practised eye. Bare floorboards, a tired-looking rug, tiled fireplace, the grate empty and swept. On the piano in the alcove were half a dozen photographs in silver frames. One was a family group, posed with unsmiling Edwardian rigidity, the patriarch standing, his wife seated with a baby in christening robes on her lap, a girl in a pinafore staring glassily into the camera. Another was a studio portrait of a girl of nine or ten with a cloud of dark curls – Mrs Tilbury herself, perhaps – gazing up as if in wonder at something just out of shot. African violets and a Christmas cactus on the windowsill; a tapestry on the wall depicting an Alpine scene with snow-capped mountains and a wooden hut surrounded by fields of wild flowers; an embroidered sampler, reading 'Home Sweet Home'.

Mrs Tilbury came back in carrying a tray on which were two delicate china cups, milk jug, sugar bowl and a teapot wearing a crocheted cosy. As she poured the tea her hand shook a little, jangling the spout against the edge of the cup. Nervous, perhaps, thought Jean. Or just butterfingered with the best china.

Now that she had a proper look at her, Jean could see that Mrs Tilbury was one of those women blessed by nature. She had a clear creamy complexion, a tiny straight nose and slanting blue eyes, which gave her face an un-English kind of beauty. She wore a round-collared top tucked into a fitted skirt.

Jean found herself caught between admiration and envy. She would have liked to wear that style of nipped-in waist herself, but she had no waist to nip. Even as a young girl she had been solidly built. Not fat exactly – portions had never been generous enough for that – but with a straight up-and-down figure, much more like a grandfather clock than an hourglass.

'You're not English?' Jean tried not to make this sound like an accusation.

'No. I'm Swiss. From the German-speaking part, actually. But I've lived here since I was nine.'

They smiled at each other across their teacups and a silence descended while Jean deliberated whether to make more general conversation about Mrs Tilbury's background or to cut straight to the matter at issue.

'We were all very interested in your letter,' she said at last. 'You didn't give much away but it was most intriguing.'

'I expect you have a lot of questions. You can ask me anything. I don't mind.'

'Well, perhaps you could start by telling me about the birth of your daughter.'

Mrs Tilbury clasped her hands in her lap and fiddled with her wedding ring. 'Perhaps first of all I should say that although I was a very innocent girl growing up, I did know where babies came from. My mother was quite strict – she was a very religious woman – and of course there were no boyfriends or anything of that sort; but I was not kept in ignorance. So when I went to the doctor, not long before my nineteenth birthday, feeling tired and my breasts aching, I couldn't believe it when he said I was going to have a baby. Because I knew it wasn't possible – I had never even so much as kissed a man.'

'It must have been a terrible shock.'

'Yes, it was,' said Mrs Tilbury. 'But I really thought, it can't be right. They'll realise they've made a mistake soon.'

'Presumably you explained all this to the doctor who had examined you?'

'Yes, of course. He said the manner of conception wasn't his concern and my surprise did not alter the fact that I was most definitely expecting a baby.'

'In other words, he didn't believe you.'

'I suppose not. He said he had met many girls in my condition who were equally confounded to learn that they were pregnant. But they soon came round to the idea when they realised that their denials would make no difference to the outcome, and he hoped I would, too.'

'What a horrible man,' said Jean with more force than she had intended. 'I despise doctors.'

If Mrs Tilbury was taken aback, she was too polite to show it.

'But of course he was quite right. And he looked after me very well in the end,' she conceded.

'So, when it became clear to you that there was no mistake, how did you account for it to yourself? I mean, what do you think *happened*? Did you think it was a visitation from the Holy Spirit – or some kind of medical phenomenon that science can't explain? Or what?'

Mrs Tilbury spread her hands out in a gesture of helplessness. 'I don't know. I'm not a scientist. I'm not religious like my mother. I only know what *didn't* happen.'

'And how did your parents react to the news? Presumably you had to tell them.'

'My father was dead by this time, so there was just my mother.'

18

'And she believed you?'

'Of course.'

'Not all mothers would be so amenable.' Jean thought of her own mother and had to subdue a sudden surge of hatred.

'But she knew I couldn't have had relations with any man. You see, at the time of the supposed conception I was in a private clinic being treated for severe rheumatoid arthritis. I was bedridden for four months, in a ward with three other young women.'

'Oh.'

Jean was unable to hide her surprise at this revelation. It seemed to provide an unexpected level of corroboration to Mrs Tilbury's account. Her claim had suddenly become much harder to dismiss and to Jean's surprise, she was glad. For reasons that were not just to do with journalistic hunger for a good story, she wanted it to be true.

'I suppose you'd be happy for me to check out all the dates and so forth,' she said.

'Oh yes. I was in St Cecilia's Nursing and Convalescent Home from the beginning of June 1946 to the end of September. It was November 1st when I found out I was pregnant and Margaret was born on 30th April 1947.'

'She wasn't premature or anything like that?'

'No. Late in fact. They had to bring her on because my blood pressure was too high.'

'Mrs Tilbury, do you mind if I ask you a personal question? I'm afraid if we go ahead with this you are going to be asked many personal questions.'

'I understand,' Mrs Tilbury replied, a faint blush rising to her cheeks.

'At the time you went to the doctor, had you not noticed that you weren't menstruating? Wouldn't that have rung alarm bells?'

'Well, it wasn't the first time that there had been a gap.

I was never very regular in that department. Sometimes months would go by.'

The two women exchanged a smile of complicity at the trials of womanhood. Jean was struck by the strangeness of discussing these intimate details over the best china with someone she had only just met. Now that the ice had been broken she decided to press on with other delicate questions.

'It was a brave decision to keep the baby,' she said, although the alternatives were surely braver, involving as they did more suffering for the mother. 'Did you ever consider giving her up for adoption . . . or . . .' She couldn't say the other word aloud.

'Oh no,' said Mrs Tilbury. 'Never that. My mother was a devout Catholic. And she believed the baby was a gift from God.'

'She wasn't worried what the neighbours would think of an unmarried mother? People can be very quick to judge.'

'We were already outsiders anyway.' She stopped suddenly. 'That's Margaret,' she said, her vigilant maternal ear picking up some signal inaudible to Jean.

Only now could she hear the clang of the gate and the scuff of shoes on the path. A moment later the back door creaked open.

'We're in here,' Mrs Tilbury called. 'Come and say hello.'

A girl in a green gingham school dress and straw hat came into the room, flushed and panting from the heat.

'May I go to Lizzie's?' she asked. 'They've got kittens.' She pulled up as she noticed Jean.

'This is Margaret,' said Mrs Tilbury, her face glowing with pride at her own creation. 'This lady is Miss Swinney.' Her Swiss accent rendered it 'Miss Svinny'. 'She works for a newspaper.'

'Hello,' said Margaret, taking off her hat and shaking out her hair. She eyed Jean suspiciously. 'Have you ever met Queen Elizabeth?'

'No,' admitted Jean. 'But I did meet Harold Macmillan, when

20

he was elected MP for Bromley.'

Margaret looked unimpressed. She has probably never heard of Harold Macmillan, Jean thought. And why should she, at ten years old? Jean couldn't help smiling at the delightful resemblance between mother and daughter. She had never seen so disconcerting a likeness between two people who were not twins. In Margaret's cloudy curls and delicate features she could see a faithful reproduction of the pretty child Mrs Tilbury had been twenty years ago. It was no struggle to believe they belonged entirely to each other. If someone else had played a part in Margaret's conception, he had left no visible trace.

'Well, there's no doubting she's yours,' said Jean. 'She's the image of you.'

Margaret and her mother looked at each other and laughed, pleased. The little girl was still young enough to be flattered by the comparison. In a few years, thought Jean, it will be odious to her.

Mrs Tilbury went to the piano and picked up the photograph Jean had noticed earlier.

'This is me when I was just a little older than Margaret is now,' she said, holding it up.

Margaret obliged by assuming the same wistful expression, eyes raised heavenwards. There was nothing to tell them apart, except perhaps that melancholy aura that always seemed to surround the subjects of old photographs.

'Would you mind lending me this?' Jean asked, imagining how the two images might look side by side in the paper. 'We could take one of Margaret in the same pose, if you're agreeable.'

'Yes, of course, do take it,' Mrs Tilbury said.

Really, thought Jean, the woman is so straightforward, it's impossible to believe she is anything other than completely genuine.

'May I go to Lizzie's now?' Margaret wheedled.

Her mother ruffled her hair. 'Yes, all right. For half an hour. But you must do your piano practice as soon as you come back.'

Margaret nodded eagerly, said a polite goodbye to Jean and scurried out of the room.

What a dear little girl, thought Jean with an uprush of longing. Aloud she said, 'You are very fortunate.'

'I know,' said Mrs Tilbury. 'She's an angel.'

The tea had gone cold now but Jean refused the offer of a fresh pot. Now that Margaret was out of earshot they could talk freely again and there was so much more to be said.

'Did they cure you?'

'Who?'

'St Cecilia's. You said you were bedbound for four months.'

'I wouldn't say it was the doctors who cured me. But towards the end I was certainly much better and although I have had occasional flare-ups since, nothing like I had as a child. Since I had Margaret, in fact, my symptoms seem to have almost disappeared.' She waggled her hands. 'If I have been doing a lot of hand-sewing I sometimes feel the old stiffness in my wrists and then I just wear my funny bandages until it goes away again.'

'You're a dressmaker?'

'Yes – I do alterations and repairs and make clothes to order. Wedding dresses and things like that.'

'Goodness. You must be very accomplished.' Jean's own needlework skills were rudimentary and confined to essential mending. Falling hems, dangling buttons. Darning was a particular horror, performed so untidily that her mother had been forced to reclaim the task for herself. 'I could never make a dress.'

'It's terribly simple,' said Mrs Tilbury. 'I could teach you.'

'I'm unteachable,' said Jean. 'I have the school reports to prove it.'

They smiled at each other.

'Does Margaret know about her . . . origins?' Jean asked, struggling for the appropriate word. 'Parentage' seemed to imply scepticism on her part.

'She knows that her birth was special. She calls my husband Daddy, but she knows he's not her real father. I mean he *is* her real father, in the important sense, that he has brought her up and loves her as his own.'

'May I ask what it is you are hoping to achieve by pursuing this investigation? You don't strike me as someone who craves notoriety.'

This was it – the question that had troubled her more than any other. What did Gretchen Tilbury possibly have to gain from exposing her family to public scrutiny? If her case was proven she would become a phenomenon, an object of ravenous and intrusive curiosity to medical science. If she was found to be a fake, her reputation and possibly her marriage would be in shreds.

'I suppose I just read that article in your paper and I thought, Yes! That's me! And I wanted someone to prove what I had always known.'

'But you must understand that our position – mine, the paper's, the scientists', the public's – will be one of extreme scepticism. It's not like a court of law – your word will be doubted until it can be proved true. And I won't leave any stone unturned.'

'I understand that. But I don't have anything to hide so I have nothing to worry about.'

'What about your husband? Is he in agreement?'

'Yes, of course.'

'And he's not putting you under any pressure to . . . prove yourself?'

'No, no. He already believes me absolutely.'

'All the same, I think I'd like to speak to him, if that's all right with you. And even if it isn't,' Jean added, remembering the stones unturned.

Mrs Tilbury glanced at her watch. 'He doesn't get home until six-thirty. He has a jeweller's shop near Covent Garden – Bedford Street. There is a telephone at the shop. We don't have one here.'

Jean turned her notepad to face her and Mrs Tilbury wrote down his name and number in her strange continental script; those crossed sevens and the nines like little gs.

'Thank you,' said Jean, though she had no intention of calling him. She planned to turn up at his shop unannounced. She closed her notebook to signal that the interview was over.

'What happens now?' asked Mrs Tilbury.

'I'm going to contact the geneticist who wrote the original article and ask if there are some tests that can be run on you and Margaret to establish whether or not parthenogenesis took place. You'd need to be able to get up to London. I assume that's not going to be a problem?'

'Will you come with us?'

Jean hadn't considered this far ahead, but she only hesitated for a second before saying, 'Yes, of course.'

The paper would have to live with it. It was her story now and she'd do it her way. Someone else could take over The Garden Week by Week if it got too much. She surely couldn't be the only person on the paper who knew how to prune roses.

'Oh good.'

Mrs Tilbury seemed relieved, as though she was depending on Jean to be some kind of advocate and protector throughout the whole process.

Jean felt the tug of friendship, but it would have to be resisted. If it came to delivering unwelcome news in due course then it was essential to maintain a sensible, professional distance.

3

'So you're saying you believe her?'

'I'm saying I haven't found any reason to disbelieve her. Yet.'

Jean sat in Roy Drake's office, watching him water the desiccated plants on the window ledge. A column of smoke rose straight from his parked cigarette and then rippled into the already dense cloud below the ceiling. While he had his back to her Jean took a sly puff and replaced the cigarette on the ashtray.

'Oh, sorry, have one of mine,' he said without turning round.

Jean gave a start and looked up, their eyes meeting in the reflection in the window.

'Nothing gets past you, does it?' sighed Jean, helping herself to a Capstan from the packet on his desk.

He shook his head complacently. Years ago, during the very worst time of Jean's life, he had come across her weeping in the post room at the end of the day. He had put his arms around her in a fatherly way (though he was not quite old enough to be her father) and without showing any curiosity or distaste, said, 'Come on, old girl.' In the absence of any other comforter she had found his kindness deeply touching. They had never mentioned it again, but it was always there as a thread between them.

'But it can't really be true, can it?' Roy said.

'There have been instances of spontaneous parthenogenesis in fish and invertebrates; not mammals. But experiments on rabbits have proved that it's possible to induce it artificially in a laboratory.'

Roy raised his eyebrows. 'Rabbits? If one mammal why not another?' He had finished with the plants now and spun back to face her in his leather chair.

'It involved quite a high degree of interference – freezing the fallopian tubes – and the failure rate was very high.'

'Poor creatures.' Roy pulled a face. 'How do you know all this?'

'I've contacted the doctor whose article started all this – Hilary Endicott – and she sent me some of her research papers. They weren't an easy read, so I asked her whether or not in her opinion a virgin birth was scientifically possible, yes or no. She got on her high horse and said science wasn't in the business of declaring what was or wasn't possible. All that could be said was that there had been no verifiable instances of spontaneous parthenogenesis in mammals so far.'

'That sounds like no to me.'

'Well, she conceded that she thought the chances vanishingly small, but many new scientific discoveries were once thought impossible and she was interested in seeing what the tests showed.'

'And yet you find her less persuasive than Mrs Tilbury?'

'Yes. No. I don't know. Do you think it's possible to hold two contradictory views at the same time?'

'Perfectly. Religious folk do it all the time.'

'So let's say I think Mrs Tilbury is telling the truth, but I still don't believe in virgin birth, and I see it as my job to close that gap.'

'How do we want to proceed then?'

'Cautiously. I don't want anything to go in the paper until

26

we've got all the test results. If it turns out to be true, it'll be massive, and it's *ours*. I don't want one of the nationals to steal it before we even know whether there's a story. There's no rush, is there?'

'None at all.'

'I wish you could meet her. She looks a bit like Deanna Durbin.'

Roy clutched his heart. 'Now I really am interested.'

'And the little girl is a treasure.' Jean took the silver-framed photograph from her bag and propped it on the desk.

'Is this the daughter?'

'No – it's the mother, but it could be either.'

'And this Endicott woman is keen to get involved?'

'She's keener than keen. She's got a whole team at Charing Cross Hospital who can't wait to get their surgical gloves on them.'

'Splendid.'

'And while they're running the medical tests, I'm going to do a bit more background research to see if the story holds water.'

'Are you going to be able to fit all this in around your regular duties, or are you looking to drop something?'

Roy's tone was neutral, but she knew the answer that was expected.

'No. I'm aiming to fit it all in.'

'Good chap. Everything else all right *chez* Swinney? How's Mother?'

He often asked after her, though they'd never met. Jean had told him some stories of her foibles over the years and he now had her fixed in his mind as a 'character'. If they ever did meet he would be disappointed. She was able to quell any stirrings of disloyalty by reasoning that the 'Mother' described was almost a work of fiction, not unlike the imaginary friends of early childhood.

'Mother is finding the warm weather a trial.'

'But I thought it was cold weather she didn't like?'

'Yes it is. Also windy weather. For someone confined to the house, she has quite particular views on the subject.'

Roy laughed, delighted. 'I imagine her as an orchid.'

'But she will be in a good temper tonight because there are strawberries for tea.'

'Well, give her my best,' said Roy.

4

H.R. Tilbury Jeweller (Second-hand and Antique – Repairs – Best Prices Paid) was in one of those narrow streets north of the Strand, between a tobacconist and a shop selling antiquarian books and sheet music. The name was picked out in elegant gold lettering against the bottle green paintwork.

Through the leaded panes of the door Jean could see that there was just one customer, in conversation with the man behind the counter. She was evidently buying a watch or having a new strap fitted, as she emerged a few moments later, turning her wrist this way and that to see how it looked. Jean waited for her to head up the street before entering the shop, setting the bell above the door jangling.

The proprietor had retreated into his workroom, leaving the adjoining door open and Jean could see him sitting at a bench above which racks of tools were neatly arranged. At the sound of the bell he looked up and laid aside the file he had been holding.

The interior of the shop was tiny. Surrounded on three sides by glass display cabinets, Jean felt as though she filled all the remaining space and was liable to smash something if she made any sudden movement.

'I'm looking for Howard Tilbury,' she said, not quite convinced that the man who now stood before her could be the husband of the pretty young woman with the nipped-in waist and the Deanna Durbin hair.

He was thin and stooped and balding; what remained of his hair was grey. He was dressed on the hottest day of the year so far in a tweed jacket, flannel trousers, hand-knitted pullover, shirt and tie and, in all probability, full-length combinations underneath. But when Jean introduced herself he stood a little straighter and smiled and for a moment didn't look quite so old.

'Oh, yes, you're the lady my wife was telling me about.' They shook hands across the counter and he added with a worried frown, 'Was I supposed to be expecting you today?'

'Not at all. I was just passing, so I thought I'd call in. Could you spare me a moment or two between customers?'

He looked wary but she had intended no irony.

'Tuesday is a slow day for customers. I don't know why. So I mostly do repairs. We could sit in the workshop.' He unlatched the counter top between two cabinets to allow her through.

'If you're sure,' Jean said, glancing back at the unattended valuables in the window as he showed her into the workshop, which was hardly more spacious.

'The bell will ring if anyone comes in and I'll leave the door open.'

Full of apologies for the lack of comforts, he offered her a sagging green armchair in one corner. When she sat in it the arms were level with the tops of her ears, the seat inches from the ground. Her long legs sprawled across the floor between them, as ungainly as a fallen horse. The only other seat, which Mr Tilbury now took, was the revolving stool at the bench where he had just been working. Beside her on a low table was an electric hotplate, kettle, cup, and the remains of a sandwich in a greaseproof paper wrapping and a skinny apple core.

He whisked the debris away and threw it into a waste bin under the bench.

'May I offer you a cup of tea, Miss Swinney?' he asked.

His relief when she declined confirmed her sudden flash of intuition that the used cup beside her was the only one he had and that she was the only visitor he had ever entertained here.

'You and your wife have obviously discussed the *North Kent Echo*'s interest in her story,' Jean began, looking up at him from her disadvantaged position near the ground. 'I wanted to reassure myself that you were comfortable with the idea.'

'That's thoughtful of you,' he replied. 'But this matter is so very much my wife's concern that I take my lead from her. As long as it has no ill effect on Margaret.'

'Yes. Margaret.' Jean shuffled forwards onto the rigid seat edge to gain a few precious inches of height. It was hard to assume any kind of authority with her knees higher than her hips.

'You've met her?' At the mention of her name his worried expression lightened.

'Briefly. I thought her delightful.'

'Yes,' he beamed. 'She is. Quite the best thing that has ever happened to me.'

Jean flipped through her notebook to the pages of scribbled shorthand she had written during her visit to the Tilburys' house in Sidcup the previous week.

'How old was Margaret when you first met your wife?'

'About six months. I came as a lodger to their house in Wimbledon. Gretchen's mother, Frau Edel, let out rooms to bring in money. One of the other tenants had moved out because she didn't like the idea of living with an unmarried mother. It didn't worry me, of course. And then when I got to know the Edels better, they told me Gretchen's story.' He recounted it, at Jean's prompting, all just as Mrs Tilbury herself had described.

'And you never doubted this version of events?'

'No. I know to an outsider it sounds far-fetched. But not if you knew the Edels. I've never had any reason to doubt my wife's honesty. I don't think she's capable of telling an untruth.'

'But unmarried women have very good reason to lie about the circumstances of a pregnancy. Society is so unforgiving.'

'People are quick to judge, that is true. All I can say is she had no reason to lie to me. I made it quite clear that it made no difference to me how Margaret came into being.'

'But she never wavered from her story?'

'Never. And I have to believe her.'

'Presumably you would be happy to see science prove her right?'

'I have never felt the need for any "proof". But if you are asking whether I would be glad, on balance, to know that no other man than me has any stake in Margaret, then yes.'

'And perhaps glad to see any doubters silenced once and for all?'

'I don't know about that,' Mr Tilbury said, flattening the hair on the back of his head with one hand. It was a nervous habit; every few minutes his elbow would shoot out again as he clasped the back of his neck. 'I'm not sure there are any doubters to bother us. Frau Edel died soon after Gretchen and I married, and we moved away from Wimbledon to Sidcup and started afresh as just another couple with a baby. None of our new neighbours knows anything about our past.'

Exactly, thought Jean. So why on earth would you want to risk your privacy now? Instead, she said, 'Are you a religious man, Mr Tilbury?'

'No more, nor less, than most people, I suppose. I don't go to church much, except for weddings and funerals, but I'm glad it's there.'

'Did you marry in church?'

'No. It was easier not to, in the circumstances. Frau Edel's priest wasn't very accommodating.'

'You would think a priest of all people would be open to the idea of a virgin birth,' Jean said.

Mr Tilbury met her glance for the first time. 'They can be rather possessive about miracles, I've found.'

'Was it a long courtship?'

'Four months or so. We were living in the same house, of course, which accelerated things. And Frau Edel was already ill by then so there was a certain urgency for her to see Gretchen safely married, as it were.' There was a pause. 'I know what you're thinking,' he said quietly.

Jean blushed. 'Oh, I'm sure you don't,' she replied.

She had in fact been wondering if she could have a cigarette, or whether the workshop contained material and equipment sensitive to smoke. There was no sign of an ashtray.

'You're thinking a woman like Gretchen would never have looked twice at a man like me if it wasn't for the baby.'

'I wasn't. Really.'

'Well, you're right. She wouldn't. I know that. A woman like her could have had anybody, and I'm certainly nothing special.'

'I'm sure she feels very fortunate to have you,' said Jean, finding this display of self-abasement embarrassing and unwarranted.

To her mind, Gretchen had nothing to complain of. With a mother and a doting husband convinced of her virtue, the woman had already been doubly blessed. And she had Margaret. What more could she possibly want?

The shop bell tinkled and Mr Tilbury stood up. 'Do you mind?' he said. 'Please make yourself comfortable.'

Easier said than done in such a chair, Jean thought, levering herself up to standing and feeling the blood tingle in her numb legs and feet. From the other side of the door came the murmur of voices, male and female. She began to inspect her surroundings, as she always did when unobserved. A lifetime of quiet watchfulness had convinced her that the truth about people was seldom to be found in the things they freely admitted. There was always more below the surface than above.

She opened the topmost of a chest of wide, shallow drawers. It was subdivided into dozens of tiny wooden compartments, each containing a piece of jewellery awaiting repair. There were cameo brooches, engagement rings, bracelets, lockets, all with broken clasps or missing gems, and each bearing a brown paper label, numbered and dated in minute handwriting. In the drawer below were the corpses of numerous wristwatches, their body parts cannibalised for repairs.

Jean picked up a dainty coping saw and touched the pad of her finger against its hair-thin blade. She flinched as the skin peeled apart and blood welled up in the cut. She was still blotting it with her handkerchief when Mr Tilbury returned, holding a sapphire brooch, which he labelled and consigned to the shallow drawer.

Since he had politely declined to notice her snooping, Jean felt a perverse urge to confess.

'I'm afraid I was fiddling with that little saw,' she said, holding out her hand for his inspection and feeling rather foolish. 'I wanted to see how sharp it was.'

He seemed to find this highly amusing.

'Well, Miss Swinney, it's lucky I came back before you decided to test the soldering iron to see how hot it is.'

'I'm very inquisitive, I'm afraid,' said Jean. 'It comes with the job.'

He took down a battered first-aid tin from a shelf and from it took a strip of plaster with which he proceeded to dress her finger.

'Such tiny hands you have,' he said when he had finished. From any other man it might have struck her as a paltry kind of compliment, as if this was the one physical attribute that he could find to praise. But he went on to say, 'You'd make a good jeweller with those delicate fingers,' holding up his own chunky hand in comparison. 'Some days I feel like a bear in boxing gloves.'

'I was just thinking what a satisfying job it must be,' Jean replied, taking her seat again. 'Making and mending people's treasures. I'm far too clumsy to do anything like that.'

'There's nothing very exalted about sizing wedding bands or altering watch straps,' he said. 'But it's my bread and butter, so I can't complain.'

'When you spend all day at a typewriter, the idea of making something real with your hands is very appealing.'

'I'm sure most people would think your world the more exciting,' he replied.

Jean shook her head. 'Fleet Street, maybe. But the *North Kent Echo* is very staid. It makes the front page if somebody breaks into the British Legion and pinches a bottle of gin.'

She thought of the piece she had dashed off that morning to mark National Salad Week:

....

The humble lettuce, if properly dressed, can be the foundation of many nutritious family meals. Try serving with baked or fried forcemeat balls for a crisp new touch . . .

....

'You don't wear jewellery yourself, I notice,' he said.

Jean's hands, wrists and neck were, as always, unadorned.

'No, but not as a matter of principle. I just don't own any. It's not the sort of thing one buys for oneself.' She stopped, conscious that she was straying into territory that was more personal than professional.

35

'I suppose not. Though there's no reason why.'

'And if I did, I would probably never wear it; just keep it in a box and look at it from time to time.' She knew this much about herself.

'That would be a waste. It needs to breathe.'

Jean felt her own breath tighten. This was the most intimate conversation she had had with a man for years.

The shop bell rang again. Jean took this as a signal to leave. She had satisfied herself that husband and wife were in perfect accord over Mrs Tilbury's approach to the *Echo*, and that he had not brought any pressure to bear on her. Of course, it was impossible to know what went on in a marriage behind those neat bay windows, but she had met bullying men before, at work and elsewhere, and Mr Tilbury was quite unlike them.

'I must let you get on,' she said.

He sprang forwards to help her out of the chair. There was a dangerous moment as she took his hand and pulled herself up rather heavily, when their balance faltered and it seemed as though she might topple back and drag him down on top of her. A look of panic passed between them and then he planted his feet more firmly and gripped her hand until she was steady again.

'Goodness, we made heavy weather of that,' Jean laughed. 'I told you I was clumsy.'

'I don't feel I've been much use at all,' Mr Tilbury said. 'But I've enjoyed talking to you anyway.'

'There is one other question,' Jean remembered. 'Your wife said she was in a clinic or sanatorium before Margaret was born. I wondered if she was still in touch with any friends from that period of her life. Or anyone who knew her as a young girl.'

Mr Tilbury considered, his head on one side, but seemed to draw a blank.

'Do you know, I can't think of anyone who comes to mind.

The clinic was down near the coast – Broadstairs, I believe. Before that she was at school in Folkestone. I suppose any friends would have lived down that way. By the time I met the Edels they were living in Wimbledon, and the few people they knew there were recent acquaintances, so I don't know. My wife has friends now in Sidcup, of course. Mothers of Margaret's little chums and so on. But you'd have to ask her about anything further back.'

Jean followed him into the shop where the customers, a young couple, were waiting. Newlyweds, Jean decided, from the way the girl clung to his arm and gazed at him so adoringly. Or perhaps newly engaged and wanting a large and costly ring. Jean hoped so, for Mr Tilbury's sake. As she squeezed past in the cramped space she could feel the happiness streaming from them.

Later, when Jean had cooked mince and potatoes for dinner, and washed up, and watered the garden, she wrote up her shorthand notes of the meeting and underlined the word Broadstairs. Then flicking back to her interview with Gretchen Tilbury she found a reference to St Cecilia's and circled that also. This would be her next focus of enquiry.

There was no urgency, of course. Mrs Tilbury and Margaret were due at Charing Cross Hospital for their first set of tests and observations soon; the results might preclude any further investigations on her part. But she was already looking forward to it. It was quite a few years since she had been to the coast. There was Worthing, of course, in '46, but she didn't count that because of what came afterwards.

Perhaps, she thought, turning her mind firmly to Broadstairs, she might even stay the night and drive home the following day. It took no more than a moment's consideration to dismiss the idea, appealing though it was to imagine waking to the high call of gulls and the shush of waves on sand. It was quite impossible; her mother wouldn't be left, even for one night. The mere suggestion would aggravate her already highly developed sense of helplessness.

Because they depended on Jean's salary to live, Mr Swinney having left neither pension nor savings, she was able to accommodate Jean's absence for the length of a working day, no more. Crises that could be held off between nine and five-thirty were likely to rear up outside of those hours and overwhelm her. Jean, as a rational woman, had always intended to challenge this principle, but time had passed and she never had, and now the habit was fixed.

There had been occasions in the past when she had regretted this. On Friday evenings Bill, Larry, Duncan the picture editor and some of the subs would go over to the Black Horse in Petts Wood for a drink after work. Once or twice they had invited her along, because she was, after all, one of the chaps, but she had declined because she hadn't cleared it with her mother in advance, and now they didn't ask any more.

Now, Mrs Swinney was installed in her wing-backed armchair in the front room, waiting for Jean to help her to wind some wool. She had knitted a pullover to send to Dorrie for Christmas, but it had kept growing and stretching as she worked at it and the end result would have fitted two Dorries standing side by side. Privately, Jean doubted that it ever got cold enough in Kitale to warrant such an abundance of wool, but her mother was adamant. There was nothing for it but to unravel the whole thing, wash and dry the skeins, and start again.

But Jean couldn't seem to settle. Every time she sat down she would jump up again, needing her glasses or remembering some urgent unfinished chore elsewhere. She prowled from room to room, bored and restless, and finally found what she was looking for – an old leather manicure set of pearl-handled implements, with which she began to trim and neaten nails coarsened by housework. This task done, she leapt up again and hurried from the room.

'Where are you off to now?' Her mother's plaintive voice followed her up the stairs.

In Jean's bedroom was a dressing-table drawer filled with things too precious ever to be used. Soaps, cosmetics, perfume, stationery – mostly gifts, or the occasional rash purchase – they had been accumulated and hoarded over many years. The contemplation of these treasures, still pristine in their packaging, gave Jean far more satisfaction than using them ever could. A leather notebook with marbled endpapers and gold-tipped pages was a thing of beauty only so long as its pages remained blank. A lipstick was spoiled the moment it touched her lips – unused, its potential was infinite.

Tonight, though, Jean opened a pot of rich hand cream, releasing a gust of rose-scented air, and drew her finger across the surface with only a faint tremor of regret. As she rubbed her hands together her crumpled skin seemed to soften and uncrease. She knew the transformation was only illusory and fleeting, but for a moment she felt a rare kinship with those legions of women who bother with such things and take pleasure in them.

'What's that smell?' her mother asked on Jean's return. Her nose had become keener lately, perhaps acquiring territory from her hearing, which was in brisk retreat.

'Pink roses.'

'I thought so. You usually smell of the office.' Her mother's face puckered. 'Cigarettes and newsprint and work. I prefer the roses.'

'Well, I haven't been in the office this afternoon. I've been to visit a jeweller's near Covent Garden.'

'Jewish?'

'I've no idea. I didn't ask.'

'I expect so. They usually are.'

'His name was Tilbury. He showed me his workshop where he does all the repairs. It was rather interesting.'

'I should think it was. I wonder if he'd be able to mend this.' She began to drag at the garnet-and-pearl cluster ring on her middle finger, forcing it over her knotted knuckle. 'There's a stone missing.'

'It would be expensive to replace a stone.'

'Well. It's valuable. And it will be yours one day.'

All her geese are swans, thought Jean.

'Don't take it off now – it'll only get lost. I might not be seeing him again for some time, if ever.' But as she said this she felt sure that she would, and soon.

'Shall we wind this wool, then?' she said, drawing up her chair so that they sat opposite each other, knees nearly touching.

From her knitting bag her mother produced the front panel of Dorrie's jumper and unhitched it from its holding pin. It took no more than a gentle tweak to begin the process of unravelling months of painstaking work. Jean held out her arms and watched with secret satisfaction the scribbled wool turning and turning around her tiny, delicate hands.

....

To keep your fingers white and soft, dig your nails into the pith of an old lemon skin after completing any dirty jobs at the kitchen sink.

....

5

The former matron of St Cecilia's clinic in Broadstairs was called Alice Halfyard, for which curious and memorable name Jean was very grateful, as it made the job of tracing her considerably easier. Jean had made enquiries ahead of her visit and discovered that St Cecilia's itself was no longer a convalescent home of any kind but a boy's prep school on the south side of the town, on the Ramsgate road.

Less than a year after Gretchen Edel's residency, the boys' school around the corner had looked to expand into new premises and made an offer for the large Edwardian villa. The patients were sent home or dispatched to other sanatoriums along the coast, and what were once wards and treatment rooms for the sick now held desks and chairs, blackboards and coat pegs.

The headmaster of this establishment, now Anselm House, had a wooden leg and walked with an ebony cane. He offered to take Jean on a tour of the building before showing her the St Cecilia's archive. It was lesson time and the school was quiet; the classroom doors were open because of the heat and as they passed along the corridor the murmured voices within fell silent at the tap and shuffle of his approaching footsteps.

He halted at the last class. The boys rose, as one, with a solemn scraping of chairs. The teacher, evidently accustomed to this kind of unheralded interruption, paused at the blackboard, on which he was drawing what looked to Jean like some terrible monster but was in fact just a flea, greatly magnified.

'This is Miss Swinney, an important newspaper reporter from London,' he said in a rather free interpretation of the facts. Perhaps to the people of Broadstairs, London was a concept that stretched as far as the Medway. 'So we must hope she takes away a good impression of the place.'

Jean gave the room her warmest, most reassuring smile. She would have liked to see how the lesson proceeded.

'That looked rather interesting,' she said, in a half whisper, when they had walked on. 'I wondered if it was an introduction to the poetry of John Donne.'

'I sincerely hope not,' said the headmaster with a frown.

Jean decided it was pain that made him humourless and chose to pity him.

She had taken an early train from Bromley South. The platform was crowded with children in uniform going on a school journey. Two teachers with clipboards were trying to marshal them into lines, while groups of boys kept drifting off to look at a steam engine on the opposite platform.

Jean put her bicycle in the guard's van and chose a compartment near the front of the train. The only other occupant, a woman, glanced up from her book as the door opened and gave her a smile of relief, which Jean understood and returned. She chose a seat in the corner, diagonally opposite, to allow them both the maximum possible space. In her bag was her lunch, an Agatha Christie for the journey, her notebook, of course, and a swimsuit and towel in case there was time to go to the beach.

It was the part of the day she was most looking forward to; she was a good swimmer and in the sea she felt both strong and graceful, a sensation not replicated in the public baths at Beckenham with its chilly tiles and chlorine smell, or indeed on dry land. She had intended to read, but she hadn't opened her book once, preferring instead to gaze out of the window as the dwindling suburbs gave way to the sun-baked fields of north Kent.

After a brief tour of the classrooms, the headmaster took Jean to his office to view St Cecilia's archive, which had lain undisturbed for nearly a decade. He unlocked a wooden cabinet and laid out various ledgers and a photograph album on his desk for her inspection. There were also some artefacts left behind in the move, which no one had ever bothered to reclaim – a kidney bowl, a bedpan, a selection of prayer cards, some leather fingerstalls and a set of callipers.

Jean picked up one of the prayer cards and read:

> *Let nothing disturb thee; nothing affright thee*
> *All things are passing*
> *God never changeth;*
> *Patient endurance attaineth to all things;*
> *Who God possesseth in nothing is wanting.*
> *Alone God sufficeth.*
>
> ST TERESA OF ÁVILA

'May I keep this?' she asked.

'You may take the lot,' the headmaster replied. 'I've no use for them.'

'I suppose the nuns used to give them to the patients,' Jean said, turning the pages of the photograph album and stopping at a staff picture of a group of women standing on the gravel drive in front of the house.

Some were in nurses' uniforms; some in nuns' habits. They were smiling and squinting into the sun; some were even shielding their eyes with one hand, as though unused to posing for photographs.

'I don't doubt it,' said the headmaster.

She wondered whether his distaste was for religion or just the Roman Catholic arm of it.

'Would it surprise you to discover that a miracle had taken place within these walls?' Jean asked him.

'I think my staff feel they perform miracles here daily,' he said with the ghost of a smile.

He does have a sense of humour then, Jean thought. She hadn't intended to give out any more details of the reason for her interest in St Cecilia's than was absolutely necessary, but his lack of curiosity made her talkative.

'A female patient claims to have conceived a child here. Spontaneously, as it were.'

She had his attention at last.

'I should think that unlikely. Other explanations come to mind.'

'Such as?'

'The woman is either deluded or dishonest.'

How ready people are to think a woman they have never met a liar, thought Jean.

'And yet she seems genuine.'

'Dishonest people often do. Are you looking for evidence to discredit her?'

'If it exists, certainly.'

'Well, I hope you find it. I don't like the thought of this place becoming a shrine.'

Jean laughed. 'I must admit, I hadn't considered that as a by-product.'

'We will be besieged by virgins,' he said with a shudder.

You probably think I am one, Jean thought.

'This person here', she said, pointing to a photograph in which a middle-aged woman in a dark dress and white bonnet was seated in the centre of a row of nurses in pale uniforms and starched aprons, 'must be the matron.' She appeared, similarly attired, in several other pictures. 'Do you mind?'

Jean lifted the print carefully from its fragile, tissue-thin corners and turned it over. As she had hoped, some dutiful record keeper had written on the back in brownish ink: L to r: J. Soames, R. Forbes, M. Cox, A. Halfyard, M. Smith, D. Baker, V. (Pegs) Austin, 1946.

'A. Halfyard,' said Jean. 'That must be her.'

'That's a blessing,' said the headmaster, taking the picture from her and replacing it in the album. 'There can't be many of those in the telephone directory. Miss Trevor will have one in her office.'

The secretary was talking on the telephone and simultaneously cranking the handle of a Gestetner machine in full cry when Jean knocked on the open door. She summoned Jean in with a jerk of her chin, without pausing.

'I suppose we could manage modest expenses,' she was saying. 'Though the other candidates are coming from further afield and they haven't asked.'

The air was heavy with the smell of spirit; Jean could feel it stinging her eyes. Miss Trevor continued to belabour the duplicator until the last sheet of blurry violet type had flopped out into the tray. Her desk was buried under cliffs of clutter – books, ledgers, manila folders, box files. And yet in spite of this, at the words, 'Yes, all right, let me take your details,' she flailed helplessly for want of something to write with or on until Jean felt obliged to offer her own notebook and pen.

Having dispatched the caller and straightened her skirt, which had become rather twisted during her exertions, she gave Jean her full attention.

'Do you have a local telephone directory?' Jean asked.

'Somewhere,' Miss Trevor replied, giving the overflowing desk a baleful glance. 'It's not usually like this,' she confided in a lowered voice. 'We've got a bunch of interviewees coming tomorrow and I've just changed offices. Everything's at sixes and sevens.'

'I won't get in your way,' Jean promised. 'I'm trying to track down someone who used to work here when it was a private clinic. I'm hoping she's still in the area.'

The secretary had ducked under the desk and bobbed up again holding a slim yellow booklet with an air of triumph.

'I knew I had it somewhere. What name are you after? Goodness, this type's small.'

Jean began to find her lack of confidence in even the simplest administrative task rather disarming.

'Halfyard,' said Jean. 'There surely can't be many.'

Miss Trevor stopped peeling through the pages. 'Alice Halfyard? Well, I can tell you where *she* lives.'

'You know her?'

'She's a friend of my mother's. She lives in Wickfield Drive — the corner house. You can walk it from here — it's only a mile or so.'

'She used to be matron of St Cecilia's?'

'Yes, that's right. She worked here right through the war up until it closed.'

'I don't suppose you know any of the other people who would have been working here just after the war?'

Miss Trevor shook her head. 'No. I didn't have any connection with the place until the school took over the buildings. I only know Alice because she was a friend of Mother's. I used to call in myself once in a while after Mother died, but I've got out of the habit. I expect she'll be glad of a visit. She's had a rotten life really, but she was always happy to see me.'

The telephone started to ring again and so Jean was able to escape without hearing the detail of Alice Halfyard's rotten life, which Miss Trevor looked all too eager to relay.

It was now midday, so Jean decided to postpone her trip to Wickfield Drive until the afternoon, on the basis that a former matron would surely have strict views on visiting times. She cycled back into town and sat on a bench overlooking the beach to eat her sandwich – Cheddar cheese and the last of the green tomato chutney from the previous year. It had to be made, and once made it had to be eaten, but it gave her no pleasure. I have measured out my life with preserving pans rather than coffee spoons, she sometimes thought.

Down below on the sand were encampments of deckchairs and windbreaks, tiny children toddling in the waves, parents sunbathing, old men with trousers rolled to the knee, a few brave souls jumping over waves. Jean longed to join them, but it would have to wait.

There was hardly a cloud in the sky, which was the deep blue of midsummer, and just the right amount of cooling breeze. Jean had thrown off her cardigan, exposing her winter-white arms to the sun. By evening they would be pink and prickling, and the V of skin revealed by her open-necked blouse would be a fiery red, but for the moment the heat was delicious and comforting.

Her sandwich finished, Jean bought an ice cream from a café on the hill. She was a messy eater at the best of times and this particular treat, a rectangular slab of vanilla ice cream between two wafers, rapidly melting and vulnerable on all sides, presented a challenge too far. Her blouse took a direct hit and she had to eat the rest of the slippery mess leaning over a rubbish bin to catch the drips. Eating in public, something her mother would never do, even assuming she were to go out in public, still struck her as bold and rebellious, adding greatly to her enjoyment.

Number 1, Wickfield Drive was a single-storey cottage on a large corner plot, shielded from the street by overgrown laurels and tall trees, an arrangement at odds with the rest of the houses in the street, which had neat, unfenced lawns running down to the pavement. In Jean's experience, this kind of foliage barrier usually heralded a certain level of dilapidation beyond, but she was surprised to find it concealing a well-tended garden and a pristine cottage. The red tiled doorstep was polished and dustless; the windows, dressed with white nets, were clean to the corners, their paintwork bright and new.

Having buttoned her cardigan to cover the ice-cream spill, untied her headscarf and raked a hand through her flattened hair, Jean pressed the bell. Somewhere inside the house it chimed faintly and a moment later the door was opened by a white-haired woman, dressed as if for midwinter in a woollen dress, housecoat, thick stockings and sheepskin slippers. She was instantly recognisable from the photographs in the St Cecilia's archive, and there was in any case something both authoritative and soothing in the steady gaze now fixed on Jean that was decidedly matronly.

'Come in, I've been expecting you,' she said, then seeing Jean's look of surprise, added, 'I'm not a clairvoyant. Susan Trevor called from the school and told me you were coming.'

Introductions now superfluous, Jean was shown into the back room, which was dominated by an open display cabinet of china dolls. There were perhaps thirty or forty staring down at her with their glassy eyes and still more laid out on the table, amid various rags and sponges, in the process of being cleaned. A fat tabby cat, taking advantage of its mistress's temporary absence, had jumped up on the table and was trampling on the delicate lace dresses as though flattening grass.

'Get down, Ferdie, you tinker,' said Alice, swatting him away. 'You've caught me giving my girls a spring clean,' she said. 'They are a devil for trapping dust.'

'I can imagine,' said Jean, who found the china faces, limp bodies and dead hair, in such quantities, faintly disturbing, and thought collecting them a pitiable hobby for a grown woman. But out of politeness and perhaps overcompensating for her instinctive aversion, she bent over the specimens on the table, murmuring her admiration, and pointed out one in a shepherdess costume, less ghoulish than the others, saying, 'She's rather pretty. What a sweet face.' Was it the dark curls and blue eyes, the faint resemblance to Margaret Tilbury, perhaps, that had directed her hand? she wondered later.

Alice Halfyard was delighted. 'Oh, do you like her? She's my absolute favourite. Such an intelligent expression – for a shepherdess.'

'And the detail,' Jean added, peering at the miniature smocking on the bodice and the tiny covered buttons, marvelling that so much industry should have been expended in dressing a mere toy. Her own clothes were never this well made.

'I dare say you think I'm a silly old woman, playing with her dolls,' Alice said.

'Not at all,' Jean replied, though this was more or less what she did think. 'It's quite a collection – you could open a museum.'

'I keep saying I'm not going to buy any more, but then I pass a second-hand shop and see one looking neglected and I can't help myself. Do you collect anything yourself?'

'Not really,' Jean replied, remembering with sudden disquiet her drawer of unused 'treasures'.

'Well, if you're a newspaper reporter you collect stories, I suppose,' said Alice.

'That's a nice way of looking at it,' Jean said.

Next time she wrote up the Magistrates' Court Reports she would think of herself as a curator of people's stories. Beatrice Casemore of Frant Avenue, Sidcup, who pleaded guilty to stealing a pair of gloves worth 2/11d from Dawson & Co., Drapers. Roland Crabb who was fined 10/- for keeping a dog without a licence. These were her dolls.

'The story I'm collecting at the moment', she added, feeling that the conversation had neatly arrived at its proper destination, 'is about a patient who was at St Cecilia's while you were matron there. If true, it's rather remarkable.'

Alice put down the doll she had been holding and gave Jean the benefit of her attentive, probing gaze. The blue of her eyes was made brighter by a yellowish tinge to the white, not unlike the colour of the doll's porcelain face.

'Go on.'

'I wonder if you remember a girl called Gretchen Tilbury, I mean Edel, as she was then.'

'I remember all my patients,' Alice said, 'so yes, I do remember Gretchen very well. A lovely girl. She suffered dreadfully from rheumatoid arthritis; she was in constant pain, poor thing.'

'Would you call her a truthful kind of person?'

Alice needed no time to reflect. 'Yes, I would. I wouldn't necessarily say that about all the girls at St Cecilia's during my time, but Gretchen was what you'd call a good girl.'

'Did she ever leave the clinic for any reason during her stay?'

'Oh good heavens no. She barely left the bed. It took two nurses to get her up and onto the commode. She really could hardly move.'

'I suppose if I told you the dates she was a patient you'd be able to confirm them?'

'Not from memory,' Alice replied. 'But I have my diaries of the years I worked there.'

This was promising – better than Jean had expected.

'You kept a diary the whole time?'

'Not a *personal* diary. Just a record of the working day – who was admitted or discharged, who had what treatment. If the boiler broke down. That kind of thing.'

'That would be tremendously helpful – if I could read it,' said Jean.

She was already wondering how feasible it would have been for Gretchen to have been impregnated by a visiting boiler repairman.

'You're being very mysterious,' said Alice. 'I hope you aren't going to tell me something has happened to Gretchen.'

'Oh no, Gretchen is alive and well.'

'I'm very pleased to hear it.'

'And the mother of a little girl, who was apparently conceived during her stay at St Cecilia's.'

Alice Halfyard's hands flew up to her throat, coming to rest on her gold crucifix. 'No! That's impossible. Who on earth would have told you such a story?'

'Well, Gretchen herself, and she was as dumbstruck as you. She is adamant that the child was a virgin birth.'

In Alice's pale face Jean thought she could identify the transit of emotions – shock, disbelief, dismay. It was a moment or two before she was able to find her voice again.

'I don't know what to say. It can't be.' She shook her head. 'That child was as innocent as a lamb. She wouldn't have known one end of a man from another. Not that there were any men around the place. The nuns would never have allowed it. *I* would never have allowed it.'

'What about doctors? Surely some of them must have been men?'

'Doctor Reardon was a lady doctor, and a very good one. And Gretchen was on a ward with three other girls – one with the rheumatoid, what was her name? Martha. And Brenda – they didn't like her so much – and poor Kitty in the iron lung. The girls were never alone for one minute. They couldn't sneeze without one of the nuns knowing about it.'

'What about visitors? Fathers, brothers, odd-job men?'

'We didn't have an odd-job man. We had nuns, and very practical they were, too. The families used to visit on Saturday afternoons. Most of the patients lived some distance away, so the parents only came once a week. There was no opportunity for the girls to be alone with a visitor – they were all in the ward together. And the sister was in there too, making sure things were kept calm and quiet for the patients.'

'Did Gretchen have any male visitors?'

'No – just her mother. They were very close.'

'So in your professional opinion, it would have been impossible for this child of Gretchen's to be conceived in the ordinary way?'

'Quite impossible,' said Alice firmly.

Of course you would say that, thought Jean, who had still to decide how she rated Alice as a witness. She seemed an intelligent woman, but those dolls weighed heavily in the balance. She was never going to admit that it was perfectly feasible for a sick and vulnerable young girl to have got pregnant while under her care, but a really unscrupulous person would be looking for an alternative version that deflected blame elsewhere. Jean decided to test her.

'The obvious explanation is that Gretchen is lying and was already pregnant when she was admitted and has somehow falsified the dates.'

Alice shook her head. 'I don't accept that for one minute. She wasn't that kind of girl.'

'But it's the only logical solution.'

'Then you must start to consider illogical ones.'

'You are medically trained. You surely don't believe in virgin birth?'

'It's hard to imagine it here in Broadstairs.' She gave Jean a faint smile. 'But I have seen so many strange things in my career – things that if not miraculous are certainly unexplained – that I have had to accept that there are limits to human understanding. My understanding, at least.'

'I prefer to think that the answers are out there to be discovered, if we try,' said Jean, realising this about herself for the first time.

'Ah, but that's because you're still young,' said Alice. 'You've got time.'

Jean laughed. At thirty-nine, it was quite some years since anyone had called her young. There were advantages to spending one's time in the company of pensioners after all.

'I must get you that diary.' Alice rose to her feet with some effort. 'I might need you to help me.'

Jean followed her along the hallway into a sparsely furnished bedroom overlooking the garden. It contained a single bed, desk and wooden chair with a tapestry seat, and a huge Victorian wardrobe that darkened one entire wall. Though tidy, it had the stale, neglected smell of a room seldom entered. Above the fireplace was a framed photograph of what appeared to be four generations of female Halfyards – ranging from a chubby toddler with flowing curls to a white-haired woman in an armchair. Jean thought she recognised Alice among them.

'My family,' said Alice, noticing the direction of Jean's glance. 'Before the war.'

Jean smiled. The last picture of her own family all together would have been taken at about the same time. But it wasn't out on display, naturally.

'The diaries are in there,' said Alice, pointing to a green suitcase with a rope handle and metal hasps, wedged into the gap on top of the wardrobe between the carved cornice and the ceiling. 'If you wouldn't mind hopping up on the chair.'

Jean did as she was told, feeling a moment's anxiety as the slender chair swayed and creaked under her weight. She pulled the suitcase down, steadying its bulk against her chest before lowering it gently onto the bed, towards Alice's fluttering hands.

Nested inside was a smaller case; inside this yet another. This kernel seemed to be the receptacle for all manner of curious keepsakes – a shabbier, dustier version of Jean's drawer of treasures. As Alice rummaged through the contents, Jean noticed an ear trumpet, a pair of lace gloves, a baby's bonnet, a mouth organ, a coil of brown hair tied up with ribbon, a cricket ball, a music box, snarled-up strings of pearls and chains. Once she had extracted from the core a cardboard box and from this a diary, one of many, identical volumes, it took Alice no time to locate a reference to Gretchen Edel.

'Admitted 2nd June 1946. Discharged on September 28th of that year.'

Jean nodded. It was no surprise to her that the dates confirmed what Mrs Tilbury had told her. Only a fool would lie about something so easily verified.

'What about the nuns that were here at the same time as Gretchen? Are they still in this area?'

'They went back to Ireland when St Cecilia's was sold. To Galway, I believe.'

'That's a pity,' said Jean, dismissing this line of enquiry.

'Campkin!' exclaimed Alice, still browsing through the entries. 'That was the name. Martha Campkin. They were tremendous chums. They'd have chattered all through the night if we'd let them. It often happens with patients stuck on a ward together – especially when they're suffering from the same complaint.'

Jean had only spent one week in her entire life in hospital. She would have given all of her possessions for a friendly soul in the next bed.

'Gretchen never mentioned her,' she said. 'And when I asked her husband if she kept in contact with any friends from that time, he said no.'

'Well, those friendships don't always last on the outside,' said Alice. 'Martha's people came from Chatham, I believe. Whereas I think the Edels lived somewhere in London.'

'Wimbledon,' said Jean.

'People make such promises to keep in touch,' said Alice. 'But they seldom do.' She sounded suddenly wistful. 'The only one who still sends me a Christmas card is Brenda, but she lives in South Africa now.'

'Do you have her address?'

'I do. If you wanted to write to her care of me, I would be happy to post it on.'

'It sounds as though Martha Campkin might be worth talking to as well,' said Jean. 'If I can find her.'

'Her father was a vicar, if that helps.'

'It might.'

'She wasn't as compliant as Gretchen. A bit more spiky, if you know what I mean. But a nice enough girl,' she added loyally. 'And very brave. Nothing we tried ever seemed to work for her.' She held out the little diary. 'You can borrow it for as long as you need. But I'd be glad to have it back eventually. I don't know why.'

'Of course.' Jean realised this was a cue to leave, only now noticing that Alice was looking weary. 'I must let you get on. You've been so helpful.'

'I've enjoyed talking to you, Miss . . .'

'Swinney. Jean.'

'Perhaps you'll come back sometime and tell me the outcome of your investigation. I don't think we get the *North Kent Echo* out here.'

'I'd be glad to.'

'And do remember me to Gretchen,' Alice said as they reached the front door. 'I was so fond of her. And Martha too, if you find her.'

After picking up her bicycle, which had fallen into the laurel hedge, and retying her headscarf, Jean turned for a last look up the path. In the front room, between the parted net curtains,

Alice stood holding the shepherdess doll up to the window. Jean had a horrible feeling that if she waved goodbye Alice would make the doll wave back, and she couldn't bear that, so she just smiled and quickly turned her back.

6

Mrs Tilbury and Margaret were waiting at Charing Cross Station by the ticket office at ten o'clock as arranged. All communications concerning this meeting had been made through Mr Tilbury at the jeweller's shop. Margaret was dressed in her school uniform with satchel and hat, as Jean had promised she would be back in time for afternoon lessons. Mrs Tilbury was wearing a green cotton dress embroidered with daisies and a little white jacket, as though she were going to a summer wedding rather than a pathology lab in a dingy hospital annexe.

Heads turned as she clipped across the concourse in her strappy sandals, perhaps in admiration or just charmed by the likeness between mother and daughter. Jean smiled to herself. Who on earth would choose to wear white for such a trip?

'That's a pretty dress,' she said, almost having to shout over the sound of whistles, the shriek and hiss of shunting trains and the unstoppable flow of announcements from the Tannoy. 'I suppose you are going to tell me you made it yourself.'

'Of course,' Mrs Tilbury replied. 'I make all my clothes.'

They hurried towards the exit, buffeted by the tremendous symphony of noise.

'It fits you far too well to have come from a shop.'

Jean plucked at her own formless garment in brown paisley,

gathering a fistful of surplus fabric at the waist. It had been chosen to withstand the inevitable dust and grime of the city and fitted her across the shoulders but nowhere else.

'I could make one for you, if you like,' Mrs Tilbury said as they halted at the kerb to allow a black taxi to sweep past. 'You could look through my pattern book and choose some material. It wouldn't take me two minutes.'

'I'm sure you have quite enough to do,' said Jean.

'Oh, but I'd like to. It would be my way of thanking you.'

'For what? I haven't done anything yet. And I may still not.'

'You have. You read my letter and took me seriously.'

Let's just see what the scientists turn up, thought Jean as they waited on the Strand for the lights to change. Then we'll see how grateful you are. She had been in correspondence with Hilary Endicott, the author of the original paper on parthenogenesis, and there was now a team of learned physicians at the Charing Cross Hospital eager to meet and measure and test and analyse mother and daughter.

It was clear from some remarks made by Dr Endicott that her colleagues were nothing if not thorough and that six months was but the blink of an eye in the life of a research project. They would be fortunate indeed to have any results before the end of the year. Jean had not yet broken this news to Mrs Tilbury, who seemed to be under the impression that enlightenment was only hours away.

'I'll tell you what,' Jean said. 'If you let me pay your usual rate, I'll accept. But you'll have to choose the style and fabric. I haven't got a clue.'

'That's settled then. You must come round and be measured up, and we'll choose a pattern together. Something fitted. Not too fussy, I think,' she said, squinting at Jean as though already sizing her up.

'Oh dear,' said Jean, sensing mortification ahead.

'Am I going to have an *injection* today?' asked Margaret as they crossed the road, almost borne along by the surge of pedestrians.

The smell of diesel exhaust from idling buses was overpowering here on the Strand. Jean could taste the fumes on her tongue.

'I already told her there may be needles involved,' Mrs Tilbury said.

'No – the opposite of an injection,' Jean replied to Margaret. 'An injection is where they put something into you and a blood test is where they take something out. It won't hurt.'

'I'm not scared,' Margaret insisted. 'I didn't even cry when I trod on a wasp. I haven't cried since I was seven.'

'What happened when you were seven?' Jean asked, feeling that this was expected.

'I was going to be Mary in the nativity, but I got chicken pox so I had to miss it and I cried.'

'That's right,' said Gretchen. 'I made you a little blue costume and then that other girl had to wear it.'

Margaret's face clouded for a moment and then just as suddenly brightened. 'You bought me my Belinda doll to cheer me up,' she said.

Her emotions were so delightfully close to the surface, Jean thought.

'By the way,' Jean said to Gretchen, this mention of dolls stirring a memory of her own. 'I met someone the other day who wanted to be remembered to you. I wonder if you can guess who.'

A flicker of uncertainty passed across Mrs Tilbury's face and a faint blush rose to her cheeks. It took no more than a second for her to master herself and say, 'No, I can't. You'll have to tell me.'

Jean hadn't intended to mention the visit to Broadstairs at all. It seemed somehow indelicate to remind Mrs Tilbury that she was still under investigation. But Jean had noticed her momentary loss of composure with interest. She had someone in mind, then.

'Alice Halfyard. From St Cecilia's. She sent you her good wishes.'

'Oh!' Mrs Tilbury gave a laugh and a little shake of her curls.

Was she disappointed or relieved? Jean couldn't tell; her face was a mask again.

'*Matron*. I never knew her name was Alice. She doesn't look a bit like an Alice. She was always just Matron to us.'

'She remembered you very affectionately.'

'Did she? I was a tiny bit afraid of her.'

'Really? She didn't strike me as very fearsome. She seemed quite . . . motherly.'

'I suppose I was afraid of almost everyone in those days. I was such a timid child. She wasn't unkind but, you know, she was Matron and she didn't stand any nonsense. She once ticked me off for chattering when we were supposed to be having quiet time and after that I was a bit in awe of her.'

'She said you were good friends with another girl called Martha.'

'Oh yes, Martha. I wonder whatever happened to her. And Brenda.'

'You didn't keep in contact with them when you left?'

'Not really. I always meant to. I did go and see Martha once, at her home in Chatham, but it was a long way and when you are back in the outside world other things come along to take up your time.'

'Margaret, for instance.'

'Yes. Everything changes when you have a baby.'

Hearing her name, Margaret perked up. 'Is this the Strand?'

'Yes, darling.'

'If there's time can we go to Simpson's for lunch?'

Mrs Tilbury laughed and squeezed the back of her daughter's

neck. 'Of course we can't. I've made you sandwiches and we have to get you back to school.' She turned to Jean. 'Last year we came up to London for Margaret's piano exam, and afterwards we went to my husband's shop and he took us out to Simpson's for lunch as a special treat. Now Margaret thinks we should go there all the time.'

'Have you ever been to Simpson's on the Strand?' Margaret asked.

'No, I never have,' Jean admitted. Eating out was something other people did. Over the years she had trained herself not to mind.

'I had roast beef and sherry trifle. I didn't get drunk, though.'

'When all this is over I'll take you there to celebrate,' said Jean impulsively and then regretted it.

Who knew how soon and in what way 'all this' would be over, or whether there would be anything in the end to celebrate. And it was reckless to make promises to a child that might have to be broken. They never forgot.

'We're not far from Daddy's shop now,' said Mrs Tilbury, coming to her rescue. She gestured vaguely off to their left. 'Perhaps we can pop in and surprise him afterwards if there's time.'

'Can we?' pleaded Margaret. 'Have you seen my daddy's shop?' she asked Jean.

'Yes, I have, actually.'

'There's a ring in the window that costs *four hundred pounds.*'

'Goodness. I hope he keeps it locked away.'

They had reached Agar Street now and Jean steered them towards a short flight of stone steps leading up to an anonymous wooden door. From the outside, the building looked more like a foreign embassy or a publishing house, but inside the marble lobby was that unmistakable smell, pungent and antiseptic, common to every hospital Jean had ever visited.

A signboard directed visitors to phlebotomy, pathology, X-rays, waiting rooms. A cleaner was working her way slowly down the wide staircase, plunging her string mop into a tin pail of disinfectant and twirling it into the corners before giving each tread a double sweep. There was something almost hypnotic in her rhythmical movements and the clang, slap, swish of mop and bucket. On either side of the corridor swing doors opened and shut with a faint 'whump' of compressed air as nurses and orderlies came and went, moving silently on soft-soled shoes but with a tremendous sense of purpose and urgency. The patients, Jean's party included, tended to walk with less certainty.

At the reception desk two women sat, chatting in low tones and filing a stack of index cards. They continued their conversation until it reached a natural break – a perfectly judged interval designed to signal that they served the public on their own terms – before acknowledging the visitors.

'We're here to see Dr Sidney Lloyd-Jones,' Jean said, bridling.

At the mention of his name the two gatekeepers became instantly deferential.

'Oh yes, Miss Swinney, is it? He said you were to go straight through to his consulting room at the end of the corridor.'

'We're expected,' Jean whispered to Mrs Tilbury. 'That's a good start.'

Dr Lloyd-Jones was a tall, donnish man in his late fifties, with wild hair and smudged glasses over which he peered, blinking, as though dazzled by the manifestation of parthenogenesis-in-the-human-female before him. He shook hands with them all, even Margaret, before summoning his colleague from next door to appraise the resemblance between mother and daughter.

'This is Dr Bamber from the department of pathology,' said Dr Lloyd-Jones as the five of them stood awkwardly in his consulting room like guests at a sherry party. 'He will be doing the analysis of the blood tests. He is a great authority on blood types, so you can have absolute confidence in his findings.' He turned to Dr Bamber. 'A good start, wouldn't you say?'

'It could hardly be better.'

They beamed at each other and then at Mrs Tilbury. Jean had the feeling that they were already sharpening their scalpels, ready to slice her up for microscope slides.

'I suppose it must be a nice change not to have to go to the trouble of curing someone,' she observed.

'This is much more fun,' Dr Bamber agreed. He was the younger, shorter and more personable of the two men. 'Obviously we're very excited. An opportunity like this doesn't come along very often in one's career. It's very good of you to place yourselves in our hands.'

Jean glanced at his hands, which were unblemished by physical labour and almost unmanly in their smoothness.

'Perhaps', Dr Lloyd-Jones said, 'you might take mother and daughter over to phlebotomy for the blood tests and you can answer any questions they may have, while I talk to Miss Swinney.'

As soon as the door had closed on them, Jean said, 'How many other people are going to be involved in these tests? I'm only thinking of the story leaking out.'

'Oh, don't worry about that,' came the reply. 'It's all absolutely confidential. I mean, patients' medical notes are always confidential, but in this case I'm keeping them under lock and key. They will be referred to only as Mother A and Daughter. The nurses will just take the bloods – they have no idea what we are testing for. Dr Bamber will be doing all the analysis himself.'

'I didn't mean to sound distrustful,' said Jean. 'But this is a big story for us.'

'For us too, possibly.'

'I couldn't bear it for one of the dailies to get wind of it prematurely.'

'No indeed. I must admit, I had some concerns when we first spoke about this. But Mrs Tilbury seems a sensible woman and her case is very persuasive.'

'I'm still investigating,' said Jean. 'My first instinct was to believe her. But my second was not to trust my instincts.'

'It will be a blow to you if the blood test results tell a different story.'

'Yes. I've probably overinvested in the whole idea. But it will be worse for Gretchen. Mrs Tilbury, I mean.'

'One has to wonder at her motive. You haven't offered money?'

'Not a penny.'

'A quester after truth, perhaps. Like ourselves. I hope she is not too disappointed.'

'You don't expect her to be proved right?'

'On balance of probabilities, no. But let's not prejudge the results.'

The phone rang on Dr Lloyd-Jones's desk. He answered it and listened for a moment without speaking. Jean could hear the distant bubbling of a male voice on the other end.

'Yes, will do,' he said before hanging up.

'That was Dr Bamber. He wants to talk to the mother without the little girl there for a minute or two. Perhaps you could wander along and entertain her.'

'Gladly,' said Jean.

'It was good to meet you at last, Miss Swinney. Here's to a – I hesitate to say *positive*, so let's just say *interesting* outcome for all concerned.' He thrust an arm across the desk and she allowed her hand to be tugged.

She found Margaret sitting on one of the hard wooden chairs in the phlebotomy waiting room, swinging her legs and reading a health education leaflet about smoking, entitled *The Adventures of the Wisdom Family*. A wad of cotton wool was stuck to the inside of her elbow with surgical tape. The sight of her white ankle socks, smudged with blue where they rubbed the edge of her T-bar sandals, made Jean's heart ache. She remembered her own mother taking out the box of brushes and tins of polish to clean her and Dorrie's school shoes every Sunday evening, and felt a momentary regret that she would never be called upon to perform that solemn ritual.

'I thought it was going to be a comic,' Margaret said, laying aside the leaflet, 'but it's not.'

'We could go and find a newsagent if you want a comic,' Jean suggested. They had passed one on the Strand earlier.

'Why do people smoke?' Margaret asked as they walked back down Agar Street. 'What does it taste like?'

'Strange to say, it tastes exactly how it smells. Of burning leaves. It's unpleasant at first, a bit like drinking tea without sugar, but you persevere and after a while it tastes just fine. And then after another while you can't stop.'

'I'm never going to smoke. Have you ever sleepwalked? I have.'

'No, I don't think so. Where did you walk to?'

'Just into Mummy's room. You're not supposed to wake people up when they're sleepwalking.'

'I'd heard that.'

'They can die. Have you got any pets?'

'No. Have you?'

'I really, really want a rabbit. Or maybe a kitten. But kittens grow up and get run over.'

Jean couldn't help laughing. She was finding Margaret's scattergun approach to conversation and morbid imagination thoroughly entertaining. She felt more than a hint of envy for Gretchen; to have the unthinking love of a daughter like this, to watch her grow every day and know that she was completely yours.

They had reached the newsagent's by now and after some prompting, Margaret shyly pointed out a copy of *Girl*. Her gratitude when she at last had the magazine in her hands was out of all proportion to its value; she was almost vibrating with excitement.

Spontaneous generosity was a new experience for Jean – until today such opportunities had seldom come her way and would probably have gone unnoticed. She and her mother exchanged small, practical gifts at Christmas, of course, but she was a stranger to more ambitious forms of giving. Dorrie had long ago forbidden her from sending anything to Kitale for her or the children. The postage was exorbitant and things were too likely to be impounded at customs or go astray.

It used to give Jean a pang when she passed a shop window and saw some toy or trinket that would have delighted her nephew or niece, and for a while she had ignored Dorrie's injunction and sent gifts anyway. But no word ever came back to say that they had been received and Jean couldn't bring herself to ask, so she had let the habit lapse. Recalling all this now, she felt ashamed of herself.

Beside her Margaret was jabbering away. Jean caught up as she said, 'Have you ever seen one?'

'One what?'

'*Angel.*'

'No,' Jean replied, firmly, and then relented a little. 'But then I've never seen gravity either, but it's there all the same.'

Margaret seemed quietly impressed by this. 'I've never seen one,' she said. 'But I've heard them.'

This was such an unexpected remark, delivered in such a matter-of-fact way that Jean felt her scalp prickle. 'What do they say?' she asked with a sense of unease.

'They don't *say*. They *sing*. That's how I know they are angel voices.'

'Oh. Do they sing hymns?'

'No. Just funny words, over and over. Like gabardine.'

Jean gave a burst of laughter. What sort of practical-minded angel concerned itself with mackintosh fabric? An angel whose mother was a dressmaker, perhaps?

Margaret laughed too, revealing a half-built smile of milk teeth, gaps and new serrated incisors. 'Don't you ever hear voices?' she asked.

'Sort of,' said Jean, treading carefully. She had no intention of encouraging any supernatural claptrap, but there was no need to lay about her with common sense like a great fly whisk. 'But my voices tend to say things like, "That's probably enough cake for you," or "Isn't it about time you wrote to your sister?"'

Margaret was not to be so easily fobbed off. 'Oh, I have those too, but that's not the same. That's just me thinking things. Angel voices are different.'

'I'm sure they're nothing to worry about,' said Jean, though Margaret herself already seemed quite untroubled.

'I'm not worried,' came the reply. 'I like them. Except when they say a word I don't know – then it's annoying.'

'When you say "a word you don't know", do you mean a word you have heard before but don't know the meaning of?'

'No. I mean a word I've never ever heard. Like Lindenbaum. Or phalanx.'

With this conversation, Jean felt herself being tugged, as if by a muddy tide, far out of her depth. How was it possible to hear a voice in your head saying a word that didn't already exist in your head?

'You are much too clever for me,' she said, finding herself repeating, to her horror, a phrase her mother used to say to her and Dorrie to terminate any discussion that threatened to take an unconventional path. It had seemed like a compliment at the time, but it was a door flung shut in their faces, and now she was doing it herself. 'I do like talking to you, Margaret,' she said. 'You are much more interesting than most of the adults I know.'

'Mummy says I ask too many questions.'

'Asking questions is all right. It's a sign of intelligence. How else can you find things out?'

Perhaps it's just loneliness, Jean thought. She needs that rabbit or kitten. She considered other only children she had known; too much in the company of adults and sheltered from the weathering effects of siblings, they often seemed precocious or strange.

Margaret squinted up at her through sweeping eyelashes. 'You're nice,' she said with an air of finality, and Jean, unpractised at receiving compliments, felt herself blushing with pleasure and surprise.

They had reached the foyer of the clinic now and there was Mrs Tilbury emerging from the ladies' cloakroom looking flustered and a little red around the eyes. She had reapplied powder to her nose but the skin beneath was taut and shiny. For an awful moment it occurred to Jean that she may have been worrying where Margaret had gone and fretting herself into a state of anxiety.

'I'm sorry – you must have been wondering where we'd got to.'

'No – I've only just come out.'

'Look, Miss Svinny bought me a magazine.' Margaret held up her copy of *Girl* for inspection.

'That was very kind of her.'

'Has something upset you?' Jean said, lowering her voice. 'Are you all right?'

'Yes, it's nothing.' Mrs Tilbury's voice was bright with self-control. 'I'm fine.'

'Are you sure? They didn't do anything to hurt you, did they?'

'No, not at all. It was all very painless. I was just . . .' She blinked a few times and shook her head. 'So silly of me. I thought it would all be done and decided now.'

'Oh dear,' said Jean.

'But Dr Bamber said this is just the beginning of many tests. It could be weeks or months.'

'I should have explained better,' said Jean, steering her towards a row of chairs. 'I didn't realise there was any great urgency.'

'I just thought it would be settled and that would be that.'

'No, I'm afraid it's a bit more complicated than that. I'm sorry you're disappointed.'

Mrs Tilbury dabbed at her eyes with a dainty handkerchief.

'Is it the travelling up to London that bothers you? Of course we'll reimburse your fares.'

Jean would have to grovel to the waspish Muriel in Accounts. She never surrendered a penny of petty cash without a struggle.

'Oh, it's not that,' Mrs Tilbury gulped. 'I don't mind the journey.'

'I like coming up to London with you, Mummy,' said Margaret, squeezing her mother's hand. 'I don't mind missing school.'

'Dr Bamber said even if the blood tests are a match, it doesn't prove anything. So what's the point in doing them?'

'Well, the blood test on its own can't prove the case *for* a virgin birth. But a negative result – a mismatch – would certainly *dis*prove it. It's just the first step.'

'It makes me feel as though you don't believe me.'

'Whether I believe you or not is not important,' said Jean, who had an uncomfortable feeling that Mrs Tilbury was having second thoughts about the whole business – was in fact looking for excuses to back out.

'It is to me,' came the reproachful reply.

'I don't disbelieve you.' This double negative didn't quite add up to a positive, but it was already further than she had intended to go.

Mrs Tilbury nodded and seemed to gather herself together. 'I'm sorry. You're quite right. I shall just have to let the doctors do their job. I think it's hospitals that make me emotional. Please ignore me.'

'It's quite understandable,' said Jean, and they made their way back towards the Strand, parting company so that mother and daughter could go to Bedford Street to call on Mr Tilbury, while Jean headed to Charing Cross.

The general mood had quite recovered from this hiccup by the time they said goodbye, but Jean found herself turning over the conversation on the way home, puzzled and unconvinced that she had really got to the bottom of Mrs Tilbury's curious impatience.

7

Dear Mrs Van Lingen,

I hope you don't mind me contacting you in this roundabout
way.

Our mutual acquaintance, Mrs Halfyard, has kindly offered
to forward this letter to you, because I am interested in your
recollections of the time you spent in St Cecilia's Nursing and
Convalescent Home between June and September 1946. I am
particularly interested in your memories of a fellow patient,
Gretchen Edel, who conceived a child while a patient on the
ward during that period – an extraordinary occurrence, you will
agree, to have taken place under your noses, as it were.

If you can throw any light on this or recall anything that
may be significant, I would be most grateful to hear from you at
the above address, or you may telephone me during office hours,
reversing the charges.

[Jean blanched as she typed those words, wondering
how she would ever justify this expense to Muriel in
Accounts.]

I should add that it is with Gretchen Edel's full consent that I am conducting this research.

Yours sincerely,
Jean Swinney
Staff Reporter
The North Kent Echo

'Relax. Don't hold yourself in so much or I won't get a true measurement.'

Jean was standing with her arms straight out from her sides as though crucified while Gretchen whisked around her with a tape measure, jotting down figures on a diagram of the female form criss-crossed by many lines. As well as bust, waist and hips, there were apparently other statistics just as vital to be recorded in pursuit of a well-fitting dress. Nape to knee (back); underarm to elbow; waist to knee (front); shoulder to shoulder (back); armpit to waist (side); upper arm (circumference).

Jean was glad she had taken the precaution of wearing her least ancient slip – the best of a bad lot – and some sturdy underwear, which was now corseting the cushion of soft flesh at her belly while cutting into the tops of her legs.

'It's hard to relax when it's so ticklish,' she said, twitching as the tape measure slithered over the silky nylon fabric.

'All done. I think you are a size fourteen in need of some adjustments.'

'That's one way of putting it,' said Jean, reaching for her skirt and blouse. Tact was often the first casualty of Gretchen's imperfect fluency.

They had come upstairs to the room Gretchen used for her

needlework. In one corner stood a dressmaker's mannequin wearing a grey satin evening gown, inside out and held together with tacking stitches and pins. A Singer sewing machine sat at one end of a large cutting table on which an expanse of printed cotton was spread out; tissue-thin pieces of pattern for some unidentifiable garment were pinned in place – strange abstract shapes that seemed to bear no relation to the human form. Jean looked at Gretchen with new respect; there was more artistry and skill than drudgery in this work.

Somehow, without discussion, they had progressed to Christian names now. It was too bizarre to be calling each other Miss This and Mrs That when in this state of undress and intimacy. Jean wasn't sorry to see the back of 'Miss Svinny'.

The invitation had come while she was at work. Howard, at Gretchen's urging, had called her at the paper. His voice sounded faraway and hesitant, and Jean could imagine his reluctance in undertaking this particular errand.

'My wife wondered if you would like to join us for tea on Sunday. She said something about dressmaking. It'll be just us and Margaret – nothing formal.'

Since her last meeting with Gretchen at the hospital she had told herself to maintain a strictly professional distance, avoiding any overtures of friendship in case it clouded her judgement and made a potentially tricky conversation in the future even trickier. But in the face of this stammered invitation, she had caved in and accepted immediately.

The truth was that congenial new acquaintances were too rare a phenomenon to be dismissed. Her colleagues at the paper were pleasant enough company, but only during office hours. They didn't socialise outside work, apart from those Friday pub nights, from which Jean had already excluded herself. Old school friends were married now and scattered, their weekends taken up with family life. A single woman was an awkward fit.

But the Tilburys seemed to like her, to look up to her, even, as someone of influence and importance.

It was impossible not to be flattered and charmed by their interest, to blossom and expand in their company and become the interesting woman they thought her. And besides, there was Margaret, who was either a perfectly ordinary child, or uniquely, miraculously special. Whichever she was, she had stirred in Jean a longing she had thought safely buried.

Having accepted, Jean had now acquired two new problems: how to manage the abandonment of her mother for the best part of Sunday, and how to reciprocate in due course. The solution to the first came providentially one evening as she cycled home from a doctor's appointment. Ahead of her, toiling up the hill carrying several distended string bags of shopping, was Winnie Melsom, an acquaintance of her mother from the days when she used to attend church.

There had been a disagreement about the annual collection of Christmas gifts for the poor children of the parish. Someone had suggested that hand-knitted toys, stuffed with chopped-up nylon stockings, were not hygienic. Mrs Swinney, who had enjoyed making these little dolls, had taken umbrage and stopped attending. She was not a religious woman and had never much liked the services anyway, so it was no great hardship.

Jean pedalled faster and drew alongside Mrs Melsom, who looked up fearfully at this interruption.

'Hello. Why don't I help you with those?' Jean said, slipping down from her bicycle and relieving the struggling woman of her bags, putting one in her pannier and hanging the other two from the handlebars.

'Oh, you are kind,' said Mrs Melsom, who had taken a moment or two to recognise Jean and recover from the idea that she was being robbed in broad daylight. 'I made the mistake of buying rather more than I could carry. I'm glad you came past.'

They continued to walk up the hill together, Jean pushing the bicycle. Mrs Melsom lived in one of the Victorian cottages on the Keston Road, some way further than Jean needed to go. She remembered that there was a daughter, Ann, who lived overseas, like Dorrie. The pain of separation had once been a bond between the two mothers – up to a point. Unlike Dorrie, Ann made regular trips home.

'How is Ann?' Jean asked.

'Oh, very well. I had a letter from her just yesterday. She writes every fortnight.'

'So does Dorrie,' Jean replied, determined to keep their end up, for her mother's sake rather than Dorrie's.

It had been true once, but now even that meagre sacrifice was apparently too much to ask. The Kitale social scene – tennis, cocktails, play-reading – had crowded out even that small act of filial observance. Jean felt the familiar churning resentment and tried to suppress it. It would only give her dyspepsia.

'I've been meaning to call on your mother. I heard from someone, I can't remember who, that she doesn't get out much any more.'

'No. She's not terribly steady on her feet. She's lost confidence, I'm afraid.'

This was not the whole story, but a portion of it that could be offered up to outsiders without embarrassment.

'I wonder if she would like a visit?'

'Yes, she would.' Jean had to stop a note of desperation from creeping into her tone. 'I think she gets a little lonely with just me for company.'

'Perhaps I could pop in at the weekend?'

It had taken very little manoeuvring to get Mrs Melsom to settle on Sunday afternoon as the ideal time. It only remained for Jean to promote the idea to her mother, who might resent the suggestion that she was being babysat. She decided not to mention her own plans until the Melsom visit had been accepted as fact.

Thursday, hair-wash night, was the most auspicious time for such a conversation. Jean's mother was at her most compliant and grateful while having her hair set. She leaned over the sink while Jean rubbed in Sunsilk and rinsed off the lather with a jug of water, and then sat at the kitchen table with a towel round her shoulders and a bag of curlers in her lap. She looked ancient and vulnerable with wet hair, and barely recognisable as female at all. Jean felt her eyes brimming with tenderness as she ran a comb over her mother's nearly naked scalp and resolved to be kinder.

'I met Mrs Melsom the other day,' she said, drawing up a section of hair and teasing it around a pink nylon curler. '*Pin.*'

Her mother passed up a hairpin, wincing slightly as Jean over-tightened it.

'She said she's going to call in and see you on Sunday.'

'Did she? I wonder what she wants.'

'She doesn't want anything. *Curler.* She's just coming to see how you are.'

'Well, you'll have to do the talking. I've got nothing to say.'

This wasn't going as Jean had hoped.

'You've got plenty to say. *Pin.* It isn't me she's coming to see.'

'Well, I don't know why. I haven't seen her for years. Ouch.'

'Sorry. I'll have a yellow one now.'

Jean's mother rooted in the bag and passed up a yellow curler. These were fatter with longer bristles and gripped like a dream.

'We used to be quite friendly.'

'Exactly. It will do you good to have some company. *Pin.*'

'I don't suppose she'll come.'

'Of course she will. It's all arranged. I'll make you a nice sponge.' She winced. The pronoun was a giveaway and Jean's mother pounced.

'Where will you be, then?'

'I'm . . . having tea with the Tilburys. *Yellow, please.*'

'Never heard of them.'

'I told you. The Swiss woman. I'm doing a story about her.'

'On a Sunday? They're never making you work weekends?'

'No. It's a social visit.'

'Oh. Well, I suppose I'll have to entertain Mrs Melsom by myself, then.'

They lapsed into silence, Jean privately jubilant that she had prevailed, her mother suspicious that she had been outmanoeuvred. She cheered up later when her hair was dry and brushed into a neat white cloud and her looks were restored.

'Very nice, thank you,' she said, turning her head one way and then the other to check her appearance in the two hand mirrors that Jean held up fore and aft for her appraisal.

Having completed her chart of measurements, Gretchen produced a heavy catalogue of Simplicity patterns and flipped it open to the section on dresses, inviting Jean to browse. The watercolour illustrations depicted a freakish race of women, impossibly tall and slender, with strangulated waists, foreshortened bodies and elongated legs culminating in archly pointed toes. It was hard to feel anything other than dispirited confronted by this cartoon glamour and Jean turned the pages listlessly.

'I don't know much about fashion,' she said at last. 'You choose – something not too difficult.'

'I don't mind if it's difficult. It's more interesting to make. But I think a simple style is better for you.' Gretchen turned to a page marked with a turned-down corner. 'I think this would look elegant on you.'

It was a fitted shift with a round collar and white piping, and three-quarter length sleeves. It certainly looked very elegant as depicted by the artist, but would surely be less so on Jean's size-fourteen-in-need-of-adjustments frame. However, she was impressed that Gretchen had, without any discussion or prior knowledge of her tastes, singled out from this vast selection something that she herself might have chosen and could imagine wearing with pleasure.

'Yes, it's lovely.'

'Not black, though. Too severe. I think navy blue or green.'

'Yes. Blue.'

'It will be just right,' said Gretchen, closing the heavy book with a sound like gunshot.

But when will I have any call to wear it? thought Jean.

On their way downstairs she couldn't help glancing in at the open bedroom door and was surprised to see two single beds, side by side, neatly made with matching pink-and-green eiderdowns and a narrow channel between, not wide enough to stand in but a chasm nevertheless. She had never come across this arrangement before between married people, except as an alternative to (unthinkable) divorce. Her grandparents had cohabited joylessly in this fashion for decades until released by death, but the Tilbury marriage bore no resemblance to their frosty stand-off.

Outside in the garden, Margaret and her friend, Lizzie, were playing badminton across a chewed piece of net strung between the fence and a plum tree. The court area was delineated by the flower beds to each side, the rockery at one end and the vegetable patch at the other.

Howard was in among the bean rows, taking on the blackfly with a pail of soapy water and a spray pump. His jacket hung over a spade planted in the soil. He was dressed in shirt and tie as if for a day at the office. He gave the two women a wave as they came out onto the little patio, where a table and three canvas chairs had been set out for tea.

'Your garden is immaculate,' said Jean. 'You put me to shame.'

This was not mere politeness; the flower beds were parallel strips of crumbly soil playing host to tame shrubs of varying colours, textures and heights, and neat clumps of annuals in full bloom. The edges of the lawn were fiercely clipped; the leeks and cabbages in the vegetable patch grew in straight lines at perfect intervals.

There was a kind of beauty in this imposition of order, Jean thought. She was a conscientious gardener herself but had never managed to achieve results like these in the few hours a week she could spare for the job. All her time seemed to be spent holding back chaos rather than on these refinements.

'It's all Howard,' said Gretchen. 'We are dividing the chores very rigidly. I'm housework, he's garden.'

'Well I'm both,' said Jean. 'Neither to a very high standard, I'm afraid.'

She couldn't now recall what, if anything, she had previously revealed about her domestic situation, so she mentioned now the fortuitous intervention of Mrs Melsom in making her visit possible.

Gretchen was mortified. 'I had no idea this would be difficult,' she said. 'Your mother would have been very welcome to come too, naturally.'

'That's kind of you, but sometimes it's nice to get away by myself.'

'Of course. Is your mother so very infirm that she can't be left?'

'Not exactly infirm, but she hardly ever leaves the house. She's fine when I'm out at work because she understands that it's a necessity. But outside of that . . . She's never said in so many words, "You mustn't go out and leave me." It's more subtle than that. I feel guilty if I'm out enjoying myself when she isn't.'

'She wouldn't want to stop you having fun, surely?'

'I don't think she really believes in "fun". Not since my

father died.' She had said too much. This was not teatime talk. She ploughed on: 'She's too old for change. Now, it's all about comfort and routine and taking pleasure in tiny treats.' For a moment Jean had a ghastly sense that she was describing herself.

'Routines can be very useful,' said Gretchen. 'Especially if you are trying to run a household. But they have to be'—she drew her hands apart—'*elastisch*.'

Jean laughed. 'A dressmaker's metaphor.' Something about this conversation stirred her memory. Gabardine, that was it. She lowered her voice. 'Margaret was telling me about her angel voices the other day. I didn't know quite what to make of it.'

Gretchen smiled. 'Perhaps it's not so unusual. Children have such imagination.'

'I didn't,' said Jean.

'But to me, Margaret is already a miracle, so this is far from the most extraordinary thing about her.'

'I suppose. I just wanted to check that it was something she had discussed with you.'

'Oh yes. I didn't think it was anything to worry about. They seem very harmless voices.'

'Did the idea of angels come from Margaret herself, or was that something you suggested?'

'That was me,' Gretchen admitted. 'I thought it was more reassuring to imagine that the voices were coming from heaven.'

'The idea of a guardian angel is rather appealing,' Jean agreed. She felt something approaching envy for those who could believe such comforting nonsense.

'It's not so very different from an imaginary friend. And we have all had those. As long as Margaret isn't troubled by it, I choose not to worry.' A wasp landed on her arm and she flicked it away with a polished pink fingernail.

'You are very level-headed,' said Jean.

'I'm sure she'll grow out of it, but thank you for mentioning it. I wouldn't want her to have any secrets from me.'

'Parenthood is quite a minefield.'

'I haven't found it to be yet,' Gretchen said. 'They say the difficult years are ahead.'

They glanced down the garden to where Margaret and Lizzie were chasing the swooping shuttlecock as it caught the breeze. Their high cries of laughter chimed like bells. Presently the two girls gave up, exhausted, and flung themselves down on the grass, panting. It was hard to imagine any turbulent emotions ever clouding their innocent faces.

Gretchen excused herself and went indoors to fetch the tea. Seeing Jean momentarily abandoned, Howard left off his toiling in the vegetable patch and came to join her, carrying a trug of freshly harvested rhubarb, beetroot and lettuce. As a concession to casual wear he had undone his top button and loosened his tie. Now he hastily redid it, leaving a muddy smudge on his collar.

'Would you like to take some of these home with you?' he asked, laying the trug at her feet for inspection. 'We have a glut in some areas.'

'I'd love to,' said Jean. 'I'm very partial to rhubarb.' The crop looked indecently healthy; some of the stems were dark pink and as thick as her wrist. A spirit of mischief entered her and she said, 'I've never seen anyone wear a shirt and tie to weed a vegetable patch before.'

He looked nonplussed for a moment and then smiled. 'Oh, well, I think formal dress shows the slugs and blackfly who's boss.'

Gretchen had appeared in the doorway carrying a laden tea tray in time to hear this exchange.

'Howard is the only man I know who wears a jacket and tie to the beach,' she said as he sprang forward to relieve her of the teapot, which was slipping dangerously.

He endured the women's laughter with a gracious shrug.

'It's a matter of eliminating unnecessary decisions,' he said.

Having put down the tray, Gretchen snapped open a tea cloth and held it under her chin, concealing her upper body. 'Now, what colour blouse am I wearing today?'

Howard looked stricken. 'Pink? White? I'm sure it's very pretty whatever colour it is.'

Gretchen whisked aside the tea cloth to reveal her primrose-yellow blouse.

'I remember now,' Howard said, shamefaced. 'Miss Swinney will think I'm a monster.'

'It's Jean now,' said Gretchen. 'We are not being formal any more.'

Margaret and Lizzie had joined the table. There were only three chairs, so they sat on cushions on the back steps with a plate on their knees.

'Is that a new teapot?' asked Margaret.

'No, it's not new. It's rather old – older than you, in fact,' said her mother, beginning to pour.

'Well, I've never seen it before.'

'It's the one we use when we have visitors,' said Gretchen.

Not completely done with formality then, thought Jean.

'But we never have visitors, apart from Great Aunt Edie, and she gets the brown teapot.'

'How do you know whether or not I have visitors when you are out at school all day?'

This stopped Margaret in her tracks. It was clear that she had never considered the possibility that anything interesting could ever happen to her mother if she was not there to witness it.

'Your mother has all sorts of fun while you are out of the way,' said Howard. 'As soon as she has waved you off to school, she kicks up her heels and out come the best teapots.'

'You're just being silly,' said Margaret. 'Mummy doesn't do

anything while I'm at school.'

This remark was greeted with splutters of outrage by the two women and guffaws from Howard.

'Well, if I do nothing all day I can't have made this *Sachertorte*, so you won't be wanting a piece of it.' Gretchen cut large slices for Jean and Lizzie and then laid aside the cake slice with a sigh. 'Such a pity.'

'I meant you don't do anything *fun*,' said Margaret, batting her long eyelashes. 'Because you are too busy making the best *Sachertorte* in the whole of England.'

'That's more like it,' said Howard, cutting three more pieces.

There was an appreciative silence as they ate.

At last Jean said, 'I've never tasted anything so delicious.'

She had no time or talent for elaborate baking herself and had to satisfy her sweet tooth with toffees that she hoarded in her room or a spoonful of golden syrup on her morning porridge. But this was something special – closer and denser than a sponge, more grainy than a cake, with a delicious nutty sweetness and the bitterness of dark chocolate. As well as the torte there were little meringues filled with coffee cream and crushed hazelnuts, and some slices of dark, dry bread with a thin scraping of butter. The bread was much less to Jean's taste but she ate it dutifully.

After tea was over, the girls returned to their game of badminton, pleading with the adults to make up a four. The breeze had dropped now and barely a leaf stirred. The garden shimmered in the afternoon heat.

'I'm happy to play,' said Jean, who had a former tomboy's love of all sports.

She kicked off her shoes to spare the grass, which had already taken some punishment over the course of the season, with worn patches either side of the net.

'Howard, why don't you and Lizzie take on Jean and

Margaret?' Gretchen suggested. 'You know how hopeless I am. Nobody ever wants me on their side.'

'Come along then, Lizzie,' Howard said, picking up one of the spare rackets and bouncing the heel of his hand against the strings. 'We won't spare you just because you're a guest, you know,' he said to Jean before ducking under the net. 'In this house winning is everything.'

'We don't need any favours, do we, Margaret?' Jean replied, and the little girl shook her head gravely.

She felt inexplicably light-hearted. It was years since she had played, but people who are good at racket sports never lose the skill, and it only took her a few rallies to remember the rhythm of the strokes, and the delicate touch needed to tip the shuttlecock just over the net and no further.

Howard, still in shirt and tie, and looking like no kind of sportsman, was surprisingly deft and agile, retrieving Jean's best shots effortlessly from the back of the court while Lizzie guarded the net. He played a gentleman's game, Jean noticed, never crowding his partner or poaching her shots, or winning an easy point by belting the shuttlecock at Margaret, who was the weakest player. But at the same time, he didn't patronise her by underplaying, making them work instead for every point.

Gretchen had put her feet up on one of the empty chairs and was reading a magazine, occasionally looking up to throw out an encouraging comment, or to adjudicate a disputed line call.

'The vegetable patch is *out*!'

'What if it lands on a rhubarb leaf that is projecting slightly over the grass?'

'That's still out.'

'Not fair!'

Every so often Jean would look up, through a mist of sweat, to see Howard laughing at her exertions as he drove her from corner to corner, and she would redouble her determination

86

to win. They took a game each, but before they could play the decider, Lizzie remembered that she was supposed to be home by five, some ten minutes ago, to go and visit her grandparents in Bexleyheath.

'Just one more,' Margaret pleaded with a child's infinite stamina for pleasure.

'We'll have to save it for another time,' said Howard as all four shook hands across the net. 'But I think a draw the only fair result.' His handshake was brief and businesslike but it sent a jolt through Jean all the same. 'You play well,' he said to her. 'You must have been practising.'

'Not since my schooldays,' she replied. 'I'd forgotten how much fun it is. And how exhausting.'

She was aware of her fiery-red face and the sheen of perspiration on her forehead. Her cotton blouse clung damply to her back. She pushed her sticky hair off her face impatiently with the back of her arm. Up on the patio she could see Gretchen, cool and elegant in primrose yellow, pouring glasses of water for the thirsty players from a crystal jug – another item brought out for guests, no doubt.

'We must have a rematch sometime,' Howard was saying.

She recognised this for a piece of conventional politeness, but Margaret was immediately eager.

'Yes. Tomorrow. After school.'

The two adults laughed, acknowledging the impossibility of a life governed by reckless spontaneity.

'Miss Swinney doesn't want to come over here again tomorrow just to entertain you!' said Howard, ruffling Margaret's hair.

'How do you know? You haven't asked her!'

'Because she has a life of her own to live.'

In fact, Jean could hardly think of anything she would rather do than play badminton with Howard and Margaret.

'But you're *grown-ups*. You can do anything you want to.'

'Where on earth did you get the idea that grown-ups can do what they like?' asked her father with an expression of incredulity. 'Not from me or your mother, that's for certain.'

'They don't have anyone bossing them about all the time,' she said. 'They just do all the bossing.'

In perfect illustration of Margaret's theory, there was a rattling at the side gate and Lizzie's mother appeared, bristling with impatience, to chase up her errant daughter.

'We agreed five o'clock, young lady,' she said, tapping her watch face as Lizzie slouched up the garden to join her.

'See what I mean?' hissed Margaret after the visitors had been waved off.

'That was unfortunate timing,' Jean laughed. 'But adults don't get to do what they want all the time, or even most of it.'

'There's this thing called Duty,' Howard explained.

Whenever Jean pictured Duty it was as a woman, tall and gaunt, with long hair scraped back into a bun, and grey, drooping clothes. For some reason she wore a pair of men's lace-up shoes, the better to kick you with, perhaps.

'It usually means doing the thing you don't want to but know you must,' she said.

'Like piano practice?'

'Yes. Or in my case, mowing Mrs Bowland's lawn,' said Jean, feeling a twinge of disloyalty to poor Mrs Bowland, who would probably be mortified to think her patch of grass had become such a symbol of servitude.

'Or fixing the Wolseley,' said Howard with a grimace.

'What about you, Mummy?'

They turned to look at Gretchen expectantly. She beamed back at them.

'I must be very selfish, or very clever, because I have everything arranged so I never have to do anything I don't want to.'

Jean experienced the same stirring of unease that had first

troubled her at the hospital. While the three of them had been talking she had glanced up the garden and been shocked to see a look of utter desolation come over Gretchen's face when she believed herself unobserved. The fit of melancholy, or whatever it was, had lasted a few seconds; as soon as Margaret called her name, she had snapped to attention, rearranging her features into the brightest of smiles.

Jean took the pause created by Lizzie's departure as the signal that it was time to make her own farewells. Although the Tilburys pressed her to stay a little longer, and Jean was in no hurry to get home, it was deeply ingrained in her that to overstay an invitation to tea beyond 6 p.m. was an affront to all that was civilised and she declined.

She couldn't decide whether the Tilburys were conventional people who set much store by these rules; it was hard to tell with Gretchen being foreign and she struggled to picture how they would spend their evening when she was gone. Listening to the wireless perhaps, or quietly reading the Sunday paper while Margaret played the piano next door. Howard's time was possibly claimed by paperwork from Bedford Street, and Gretchen might withdraw to her workroom and proceed with her pattern cutting. None of these potential narratives quite convinced her; she would have to get to know them better.

'Did you come by bicycle?' Gretchen asked as Jean gathered together handbag, shoes, cardigan and began to reassemble herself.

'No. Bus.'

It had been two buses, in fact, taking the best part of fifty minutes including the wait in between.

'Well, Howard will give you a lift home. The service on Sundays is terrible.'

'I wouldn't dream of it,' said Jean as Howard reappeared from the kitchen with a carrier bag into which he proceeded to transfer the contents of the trug – rhubarb, lettuce and beetroot. 'The bus will be fine.'

'We insist, don't we, Howard?'

'Yes, you can't carry all this like a market porter.'

Their joint determination swept away all her objections.

'And you must come again soon for a fitting,' Gretchen said as she and Margaret stood at the gate to wave her off.

'And to finish our badminton tournament,' Margaret reminded her.

She was clutching this week's copy of *Girl* that Jean had brought her but been too tactful to hand over until Lizzie had left. By way of thanks she had given Jean a shy hug.

Unable quite to bring herself to return the invitation to tea until she had reflected on how her mother was to be accommodated in such an event, Jean said, 'I'll be in touch the moment I hear from Dr Lloyd-Jones.'

It struck her as soon as the words were spoken that this introduction of a business – and, moreover, medical – matter into what was purely a social occasion had sounded a wrong note, but Gretchen didn't seem to notice.

The interior of the Wolseley smelled of petrol and leather and the memory of every car Jean had ever ridden in. She sensed from its pristine condition, polished chrome trims, glossy walnut dashboard and dustless floor, and the way that Howard opened and gently closed the passenger door on her, that he was as proud of his car as Gretchen was of her orderly house.

'Do you drive?' he asked Jean as they set off along empty suburban streets.

'I do, as a matter of fact,' she replied. 'Although I don't have a car. I used to be a driver with the ATS in the war. I was even a driving instructor for a while.'

'Were you?' He gave her a quick sideways glance as if he

was seeing her in a new light. 'I've tried to teach Gretchen but she's terribly nervous behind the wheel. She's happier being the passenger.'

'Most husbands prefer it that way,' Jean said.

'I did try to encourage her. But perhaps not enough,' he conceded.

He took the corner with his foot on the clutch, something she had always told her students not to do, as it meant you were not fully in control of the vehicle.

'I think men like to keep their cars to themselves, so they put it about that driving is harder than it really is. There's nothing to it once you've learnt.'

'There might be something in that,' he admitted.

His hand on the gear stick, brushed against the side of her knee as he changed down coming out of the turn, but he didn't seem to notice, so Jean decided she wouldn't notice either.

'The car is such an incredible thing, don't you think?' he was saying. 'Not just the engineering. I mean the freedom it represents.'

'Privacy too.'

She was thinking that the whole history of human courtship might have been very different without the opportunities it provided for a man and woman to be alone in a confined space. But this was not perhaps an appropriate matter to discuss in just such a setting.

'You work somewhere around here, don't you?' he asked as they approached the Orpington War Memorial.

'Not far,' Jean replied. 'Petts Wood. It's very decent of you to run me home when you could be relaxing in the garden.'

'I never relax in the garden,' said Howard. 'All I see when I look around are jobs that need doing. Anyway, it's a pleasure. I hope you'll come again. It's so nice for Gretchen to have a friend.'

Jean was surprised and a little embarrassed by this compliment. She had considered herself to be transparently the lonely one among them.

'Gretchen doesn't strike me as someone who'd be short of friends,' she said.

'Neither of us is what you'd call sociable,' he replied. 'You're the first person, apart from Aunt Edie, who's been round to tea in ages.'

'We don't entertain much ourselves. In fact, never. So today has been a lovely treat.'

'For us all.'

This conversation, which Jean imagined as a stately dance, proceeding forwards and backwards, towards and then away from real frankness, brought them to her turning. Just as she pointed out the house as the one with the red door, it opened and Mrs Melsom appeared, saying her goodbyes to Mrs Swinney on the threshold. They both peered at the Wolseley with undisguised curiosity as Howard sprang out to help Jean with her bags.

Damn, thought Jean with a sense of annoyance that she couldn't quite account for.

'Well, goodbye then . . . Howard,' she said, testing out the sound of his name for the first time.

'Goodbye . . . Jean.'

....

This week in the garden:
Harvest radishes and beets. Sow lettuce
seed. Spray cabbage with salt water to keep
caterpillars down. Plant out winter greens,
kale, savoys and broccoli. Earth up main
crop potatoes. Feed berries with liquid
manure. Check fruit trees for woolly aphids;
paint any patches with derris.

....

9

Jean had always assumed Chelsea to be a fashionable district of expensive boutiques and cafés and was therefore surprised to discover among its elegant squares pockets of shabbiness and neglect not much better than slums.

Once, when she was a teenager, she had been invited to lunch by her elderly godmother who lived in a mansion flat in Cadogan Square. Given the courtesy title 'Aunt Rosa', though she was no relative but the descendant of a dynasty of Belgian industrialists, she had taken the young Jean by taxi to lunch at the Anglo-Belgian Club in Knightsbridge. They had vichyssoise and rabbit fricassée – terrible, alien food that Jean had forced down with watering eyes and a bulging throat, all the while conscious that this was a huge treat, and of the envy of Dorrie, who had not been included. Not long after this Rosa had died of an aggressive type of cancer and that was the end of fine dining and rides in taxis.

It was possibly the memory of this outing that had informed her decision, now regretted, to dress smartly in her grey wool suit with the fur collar and court shoes. It had not seemed inappropriate in Sloane Square, where she had ducked into Peter Jones to buy a new nightdress for her mother and some florentines, but looked decidedly out of place in Luna Street.

On the corner an abandoned and crippled Ford Popular, sunk onto four punctured tyres, its windows smashed, was being used as a drum kit by three shirtless boys wielding pieces of metal tubing. Further along a football game was in progress in the empty road, a wire-haired terrier yapping and chasing after the ball and dancing around the children's legs. Jean was half inclined to ask why none of them were at school on a Thursday afternoon, but they were a feral-looking bunch, quite likely to swear at her for interfering, and she felt at a disadvantage in her Sunday best.

She had assumed that Martha Campkin was a respectable, affluent Chelsea-dweller, in the mould of Aunt Rosa, but the tall, soot-streaked villa in Luna Street, where she occupied the ground floor, seemed to tell quite another story. As Jean hesitated on the pavement, checking the address in her pocket diary, a shape moved in the basement shadows and a rat slunk out from behind an overflowing metal dustbin. It seemed to be in no great fear or hurry – swaggering rather, Jean thought as she scuttled, mouse-like herself, up the steps to the front door and rang the bell.

Having learned from Alice Halfyard the useful fact that Martha's father was a vicar, it had taken no more than a minute to find his entry in *Crockford's*: Campkin, William Sefton, St John's Rectory, Chatham, b.1903; Keb. Coll. Oxf.; BA, MA Wells Th. Coll.

She had telephoned the rectory on a Sunday afternoon at a time she judged to be safely between the end of lunch and evensong. The voice that answered was soft and tentative, not one that could be imagined carrying from the pulpit, and Jean was surprised when the speaker identified himself as Reverend Campkin. In response to her request for Martha's whereabouts he said with some apology that he was no longer in contact with his daughter, which seemed an astonishing admission for a clergyman.

'I'm afraid I only have an old address for her, but someone there may be aware of her more recent movements. We, unfortunately, are not. She's not in any trouble, I hope?'

Jean was momentarily thrown by this. 'Oh no,' she said. 'Well, not as far as I know. I'm just doing some research into residents of St Cecilia's Nursing Home after the war.'

'Oh, I see. Well, Martha was certainly there. Perhaps you'll remember us to her if you find her. Her mother is not in the best of health.'

Having agreed to this bizarre commission from a complete stranger, she noted down Martha's last known number in Forest Hill.

It had taken her precisely two further calls to track Martha down to her current habitat in Luna Street. The chain of addresses was remarkably short, causing Jean to wonder what, if any, effort her father had made to find her, and what could have caused their estrangement.

When at last she found herself speaking to Martha, whose confident, cultured voice was perhaps another factor in her decision to overdress for the occasion, she didn't mention Gretchen but stuck to her story of interest in St Cecilia's. It was still true, but not the whole truth.

'Yes, St Cecilia's. I was there. I remember it well, particularly the ceiling.'

'What was special about the ceiling?'

'Absolutely nothing, unfortunately. I just spent an awful lot of time on my back staring at it.'

'Oh. I see. Sorry, I'm a bit slow today.'

'How did you find me, anyway?'

'Dogged, journalistic spadework. May I come and talk to you sometime? This is a party line so I can't monopolise it.'

'All right. Any day except Wednesday or Friday. I teach on those days.'

'Thursday, then?'

'Afternoons are better for me. Three o'clock?'

'Three o'clock.'

The door to 16 Luna Street was opened by a tall, striking woman with scarlet lipstick, a paint-smeared smock and a wide floppy skirt. Her dark hair was tied up in a headscarf, not under her chin the way Jean and all normal people wore it but around her forehead with the knot at the front. She peered at Jean's jacket with an appraising eye and asked, 'Is that collar fur?'

'Yes,' Jean admitted, taken aback by this curious welcome. 'Probably fox, but I don't know – it's second-hand.'

'Well, I'm afraid you'll have to leave it out here – I've got a hideous allergy. Sorry to be a bore.'

She was wearing a pair of red backless leather slippers that made a slapping sound on the tiled floor as she led Jean down the shared hallway towards a row of coat pegs. The most notice-able thing about her, however, which Jean was doing her best not to notice as she struggled out of the offending jacket and hung it up, was that she walked with a stick. And her hands and wrists were bound with curious leather splints, leaving just her fingers and thumbs free.

'Would you like tea? It'll have to be black. The milk's off,' Martha said, opening the door to her flat, which occupied the ground floor at the back of the building, and showing Jean into a large, high-ceilinged room.

It was done out as an artist's studio but with a divan against one wall and a couch and coffee table by the window. The space was dominated by an easel, on which was a prepared canvas marked with ghostly lines. A trestle table was covered with buckled tubes of paint, jam jars of brushes, stained rags and crusted palettes. Canvases were stacked in one corner like giant slices of toast. There was a mixture of competing smells,

97

none of them pleasant – turpentine, laundry, a full ashtray and the remains of lunch.

Recognising poverty, Jean produced the florentines from her Peter Jones bag and handed them to Martha, a trifle self-consciously. 'I brought you these.'

A slow, wide smile transformed Martha's pinched face and while it lasted she looked quite beautiful.

'Did you actually? Thank God for you. I haven't had a treat like this for ages. Let's eat them now.' She began to tear at the cardboard packaging before Jean had even had a chance to sit down. 'I'll make some coffee to go with them. I hate tea without milk. Come into the kitchen.'

She waved Jean ahead of her with her walking stick into a long, narrow room in a state of considerable disorder. The sink and draining board were piled with unwashed dishes, while the small table, covered with yellow oilcloth, scorched and melted in places by contact with hot pans, held a pair of leather boots and a tin of dubbin. The tiled walls were streaked with greasy condensation and spatters of oil, these markings increasing in concentration in the vicinity of the hob. On the bowed shelves chipped crockery, dusty jars of utensils and various unappetising packets and tins jostled for space.

Jean proceeded gingerly across the sticky floor, which crunched underfoot from a coating of spilled salt or sugar, past a wooden airer hung with items of female underwear not normally on public display – stout black knickers, ribbed vests and flesh-coloured stockings like withered legs. Even Jean, whose housekeeping efforts never went much beyond the surface of things, was dismayed. Martha herself appeared unembarrassed by or perhaps oblivious to the disarray, humming cheerfully as she hunted for two clean mugs among the debris, giving them a quick wipe on the hem of her smock.

When they were installed once more in the studio with their

coffee and the ripped box of florentines between them, Jean said, 'Do you remember much about your time at St Cecilia's?'

'Yes,' said Martha through a mouthful of biscuit shards. 'I remember it all, apart from those times when I was dosed to the gills with opiates, of course. They couldn't do a thing for me. I was no better when I went out than when I went in. But perhaps the aim never was to cure me – perhaps it was just to provide respite for my parents. I didn't think of that at the time; it only occurred to me later.'

'You don't see your parents any more, I gather,' said Jean, trying to feel her way around this delicate subject.

'How do you know that? Have you spoken to them?' Martha reached for another florentine.

'Only to try and get an address for you. Your father asked me to send you his good wishes.' Something like that. Jean couldn't now recall his exact form of words, only an impression of aloofness that was both unparental and unchristian.

Martha raised her eyebrows. 'Well,' she said. 'That's a turn-up.'

'He said your mother's not in the best of health. That was the gist.'

'Oh hell. I suppose I'll have to get in contact.'

'You might regret it if you don't,' said Jean, now bizarrely cast as an agent of reconciliation between people who were strangers to her.

She couldn't help feeling that this unsought burden of responsibility entitled her to a measure of curiosity.

'Did you have a falling-out?'

'I got tired of their disapproval.' She picked absently at a scab of blue paint on her smock.

'You don't share their beliefs?'

Beneath the crust the paint was still soft and in the space of a few seconds Martha had managed to transfer blue smudges to her coffee cup, skirt and face.

'That's a mild way of putting it. We disagree about everything. Religion, politics, art, life. My life, anyway. They're Edwardians essentially, absolutely at sea in the modern world. They can't help it.'

'The world has changed so much since they were young,' said Jean, somewhat distracted by the mess Martha was making and wondering if she should point it out.

'Not nearly enough in my view,' said Martha, wiping her finger on her sleeve. 'Anyway, what's your interest in St Cecilia's?'

Jean took out her pen and notebook and flipped it to a clean page.

'Do you remember the girls on your ward?'

'Yes. Gretchen, Brenda and poor Kitty.'

'Everyone calls her "poor Kitty",' said Jean.

'Well, she spent about twenty-three hours a day in an iron lung. What a life. And she was still madly religious. You wonder how she could have any time for a God who saw fit to create polio.'

'I'm sure your father could explain the Christian teaching on suffering if you asked him,' Jean replied.

She was beginning to resent having to do without her jacket. Although it was a warm day outside, in here it was mysteriously chilly and behind her back the couch felt damp.

'No, thanks. I wonder if Kitty's still there.'

'Not at St Cecilia's. It's been turned into a boys' school.'

'That's quite a reversal. I don't think I so much as glimpsed a boy all the time I was there.'

'Interesting you say that,' Jean remarked. 'It's Gretchen I'm here about. You were friends, I understand?'

'Yes, briefly. It was a choice between her on one side or ghastly Brenda on the other. Kitty was out of the frame, really.'

'Poor Kitty.'

Without breaking eye contact, Jean began to doodle on her

notepad. It was always the same sketch – a single staring eye.

'Indeed. So what about Gretchen? Is she all right?'

'She's made a rather extraordinary claim, which I'm doing my best to verify, that she became pregnant while still a virgin during her time there.'

Martha put down her coffee cup with a jolt and stared at Jean.

'Seriously?' she said.

'She is deadly serious. And willing to be subjected to all sorts of medical tests to prove it.'

'God. I can't believe she's still going on about that after all this time.'

Jean's pen skated across the page. 'You already knew?'

'Yes – she told me at the time. She came to visit me in Chatham not long after I left the place. She told me then that she was pregnant and that it was a "miracle".'

'What did you *think*? I mean, you were right there when it must have happened.'

'I just assumed she was lying about the dates.'

'Why would you think that? Why would she lie to you – her friend?'

'Why do women lie? To protect themselves, of course.'

This exchange left Jean reeling.

'Do you know, you're the only person I've spoken to who knows Gretchen who has even hinted that she might be lying.'

Martha gave a short rasp of laughter. 'That's probably because you only talked to nice people. You should have come straight to the bitch.'

They were interrupted by the sound of hammering on the front door and the simultaneous ringing of all the bells in the flats.

'Oh, God. That'll be Dennis. His wife has kicked him out and he keeps coming back when she's at work hoping someone else will let him back in. Excuse me a moment.' She unfolded herself from the chair and limped out to the hallway, pulling the door to behind her.

Jean didn't fancy Dennis's chances against Martha, with or without her walking stick. In the distance she could hear raised voices. She occupied herself during her hostess's absence by looking through the canvases propped against the wall. She was confident that Martha wouldn't mind her snooping and might even expect it.

The paintings, chiefly cityscapes of bomb-damaged buildings, derelict churches and patches of waste ground, took Jean by surprise. She knew nothing of art, except what she had picked up from trips to the National Gallery, and had imagined Martha's style to be bold, abstract and incomprehensible. These were, to Jean's inexpert eye at least, old-fashioned, naturalistic and rather pleasing. In each of the scenes a tiny detail provided a note of beauty or optimism among the greyness – a delicate flower growing in a crack in a wall; a rainbow in an oily puddle; a bird nesting in a ruined chimney.

While she browsed, her thoughts kept straying back to Martha's curious assumption that Gretchen was lying to her. It didn't make sense. Why would Gretchen have needed to lie to Martha, her friend, and, moreover, someone who hardly seemed likely to disapprove or judge?

The commotion in the hallway reaching a crescendo, Jean felt moved to investigate. She found Martha and the would-be intruder engaged in a tug-of-war through the letter box, with Martha's walking stick as the contested rope. Perhaps inspired by the arrival of reinforcements, Martha abruptly let go of the handle, which flew back, catching in the jaws of the letter box and sending the assailant tumbling down the steps. She hastily snatched the stick back to her side of the door while he continued to shout abuse at her.

Several of the other residents of the house now began to descend to investigate the row, which was clearly a regular occurrence of no great moment. Having satisfied themselves that it was 'just Dennis', they shrugged and returned to their flats, leaving him raving outside on the pavement.

'Sorry about that,' said Martha, cheerfully, adjusting her headscarf, which had become twisted in the scuffle. 'It's par for the course.'

She seemed quite invigorated by the altercation. Jean felt a rush of affection for her quiet, suburban street, where the only sound likely to disturb the peace might be the whirr of a rotary mower or the jangle of a milk float.

'I was looking at your paintings,' she said. She was going to elaborate but lost courage when she saw Martha's expression darken. 'I like them,' she finished lamely.

'Please don't say any more,' Martha said, holding up a hand as though to ward off blows. 'I hate it when people praise my work.'

'It's better than criticism, surely?' said Jean, feeling bound to defend herself. She had never met anyone quite so resistant to flattery.

'You can't accept compliments and then dismiss brickbats. You have to treat those two impostors just the same. For my own sanity, I choose to ignore them both.' She fiddled nervously with her wrist bindings as she said this, unbuckling and tightening the straps.

'Do you exhibit? In galleries and things?' Jean sensed herself venturing across thin ice again but was unable to stop herself.

'I'm trying to build up a body of work that I feel completely comfortable with.' Martha's tone was brittle. 'It's a hard world to break into.'

'I'm sure,' murmured Jean, retreating to solid ground.

'Luckily, I have my two days a week teaching to bring in enough to live on.'

'It must be difficult to do both.'

'Teaching is a drain on my time and energy. But I'm good at it,' she said, a trifle defensively. 'And on the other days, I paint.'

'Well, I won't keep you any longer,' said Jean. 'I don't want to take up precious painting time.'

'It's all right. The light in here is lousy in the afternoons anyway. So . . . Gretchen.' Martha sat back down and rummaged in the biscuit box, looking puzzled to discover it was now empty. 'I suppose she's married now.'

'Yes, to a nice man called Howard. Not the father of the little girl, of course. Margaret.'

'Margaret. Well, well. I feel guilty for disbelieving her now. But on the other hand, you can't really go along with all that virgin birth twaddle, can you?'

'I'm keeping an open mind,' said Jean. 'Or rather, I'm confident that the scientists will get to the bottom of it. But I'm interested to hear your view of Gretchen.'

'I didn't mean to give the impression that I thought she was a regular liar. I didn't at all. But I don't believe in the supernatural, and she can't have got pregnant during her time at St Cecilia's. We were never alone. You couldn't even unwrap a toffee without bloody Brenda hearing it.'

'That's more or less Miss Halfyard's view. Although she wasn't so hard on Brenda.'

'Matron,' said Martha, shaking her head at the memory. 'She didn't like me much. We had a few run-ins, as I recall.'

'She sent you her good wishes, actually,' said Jean, hoping to shame Martha into softening her outlook. She had observed before that when people said 'so and so doesn't like me', the dislike was usually in the other direction.

'All these people wishing me well,' exclaimed Martha. 'I should be touched.'

Jean recalled Alice's remark about Martha being 'spiky'. Certainly, it was hard to imagine her being good friends with the reserved and decorous Gretchen.

'I suppose you're not in touch with anyone else from those days?'

Martha snorted. 'Hardly.'

'Well, I'm afraid I can't pass on Gretchen's good wishes because she doesn't know I've come to see you,' Jean said.

'Will you be in contact with her again?'

'Oh yes. The medical tests are ongoing.'

'I wonder if you'd give her a little gift from me,' Martha said, fetching a folder from a drawer in the workbench.

Inside was a selection of postcard-sized silk-screen prints of birds, fruit and flowers. Bold, graphic and colourful, they were quite different in style from the grey urban landscapes.

Her bandaged hand riffled through the collection for some time, selecting and discarding different possibilities before settling on a print of a bowl of tangerines.

'That's . . . er . . .' said Jean, remembering just in time the prohibition regarding compliments. 'I'm sure Gretchen will be delighted.'

Fortunately, Martha was preoccupied with trying to find an envelope to put it in and didn't notice or hear. She left the room for a moment, while Jean buttoned her jacket and gathered up her bags. She was wondering whether to replace the florentines on her way home or do without, when Martha returned with a stiff-backed envelope.

'Something for her to remember me by,' she said.

'That's very kind of you,' said Jean, trying to picture the tangerines on the Tilburys' wall between the Alpine scene and the embroidered sampler. 'I wonder,' she said as an idea struck her. 'Do you remember the layout of St Cecilia's well enough to draw me a floor plan?'

'Yes – at least the ground floor, where we were. I never made it upstairs.'

Jean handed over her notebook, turned to a fresh page, and watched as Martha, frowning with concentration, sketched a neat diagram with quick, confident strokes and added her signature with an ironic flourish.

'Thank you,' said Jean, smiling her acknowledgement. 'Now I must leave you in peace.'

She wondered if it would be quite safe to depart, or whether Dennis might be skulking outside, ready to rush the door as soon as it opened, but all was quiet on Luna Street.

'Well, that was more interesting than I dared to hope,' said Martha as they said goodbye. 'You've certainly stirred up the past. St Cecilia's and my parents – all in one day!'

....

Has the stiffening at the back of your house
slippers worn down? I have successfully
repaired several pairs by sewing a piece of
old collar inside. The semi-stiff kind from a
man's shirt is ideal and will prolong the life
of your slippers.

....

IO

There had been some kind of incident at Charing Cross and the station was in confusion. The rush-hour crowds gathered on the concourse, staring at the departure boards, which declined to display any platform numbers, and awaiting an explanation from the tannoy, which had fallen mysteriously silent. Queues had formed at the taxi rank outside as people lost patience. Every few minutes a fresh load of travellers disgorged from the underground would join the throng. A murmur was running around that someone had fallen onto the tracks at London Bridge; incoming trains were delayed.

'If someone jumps in front of a train the driver gets a day off,' the woman in front of Jean was saying to her companion in a tone of great self-importance.

'I never knew that,' came the reply.

'They don't like to put it about,' said the first woman, her words muffling those from the tannoy, which had just crackled into life.

Idiot, Jean thought, clenching her teeth. This sort of complacent pronouncement of utter rubbish made her fume. And now she had missed the announcement. 'What's that?' 'What they say?' people were asking each other, appealing to left and right. There was a flutter from the departure board – Platform 4 for the Ramsgate train – and the crowd surged forwards, the momentum sucking along even those with no intention of going to Ramsgate.

Jean fell back a few paces to escape the general drift, wondering whether her mother would think to reheat yesterday's half dish of leftover cauliflower cheese, or wait helpless and hungry for her arrival, when she noticed a familiar figure ahead. He was struggling to light a cigarette while holding his briefcase and a bunch of yellow roses.

'Howard,' she called, threading through the crowds to join him.

'Hello,' he said, attempting to tip his hat with the hand that still held the lighter and very nearly scorching the brim.

He parked the briefcase between his feet and the flowers under one arm before he could rescue the cigarette from between his teeth and bat the smoke from his streaming eyes.

Jean laughed. There was something reassuring, flattering almost, in his clumsiness.

'Here's a thing,' he said, nodding to the departure board on which the word 'delayed' was prominently displayed. 'Do you know what it's about?'

'I haven't heard anything official. People have been saying someone's fallen on the tracks, but it's probably nonsense.'

'They can't have fallen on all of the tracks,' said Howard reasonably. 'Some of the lines must be running. You need the Hayes train, I suppose?'

'Yes. Or I could take one to Orpington and get a bus, but that will make me very late. Mother will be frantic.'

'Wait here, I'll go and find a member of staff,' Howard said, heading towards the ticket office, which was already besieged by indignant commuters.

Jean's feet were beginning to hurt in her heeled shoes. She thought with some envy of Martha Campkin's red leather slippers and wondered if she would ever be able to carry off such a look. There had been something admirable in her solitary existence in that seedy flat, labouring to produce some artwork of which she could feel proud. Martha hadn't said as much, but Jean was convinced that she hadn't sold or even exhibited a single painting.

At last the public address system coughed and a tinny voice announced the departure of the delayed Sidcup train from Platform 2. There was a corresponding stampede from the crowd on the concourse as the lucky ones hurried towards the train and a general slumping from those left behind. Jean looked around for Howard, wondering if he had heard the announcement, but there was no sign of him. She was debating whether to pursue him to the ticket office to warn him that his train was in and risk losing him altogether, when she saw him. He was weaving in her direction, against the flow, apologising as people elbowed past or knocked into his bunch of flowers.

'Your train's in,' Jean said as he reached her side, looking somewhat buffeted. 'You'd better hurry.'

'I can't leave you here,' he protested. 'You might be stranded for hours. Apparently there's someone on the track between London Bridge and Ladywell. It's caused a hold-up right down the Hayes line.'

'I'll be fine,' said Jean. 'I'll wait for the Orpington train and then get a bus.'

Her heart plunged at the thought of this detour, which would double her journey time. She would have to call ahead and warn her mother.

'Come and get the Sidcup train with me and then I'll drive you home. My car's at the station,' Howard said.

'Oh no, really.'

'Come on,' he urged. 'I can't abandon you here. Gretchen would never forgive me.'

Gretchen's imprimatur, even if only assumed, seemed to give the plan an air of inevitability and Jean followed Howard, dodging and stumbling as fast as she could, through the waiting throng to Platform 2, where the guard was already walking the length of the train, slamming doors. Most of the rear carriages were full, with standing passengers crushed right up to the windows. At last a stationmaster took pity on them and held a door open for them, obliging those already inside to shuffle closer together, grumbling.

Howard handed Jean in first and then hopped in after her, the shriek of whistles reaching a crescendo as the train lurched forwards in a series of starts as though tugged on elastic. Their eyes slid towards the bunch of roses, now limp and battered beyond redemption, and they began to laugh.

'Oh dear,' said Jean, unable to stifle her giggles. 'They don't look at all well. Were they for a special occasion?'

'No, nothing like that. I just picked them up at Covent Garden this morning on a whim. I'll have to have another whim tomorrow instead, because these have had it.'

Lucky Gretchen, thought Jean, to have a husband who brought home flowers on a Thursday evening for no reason.

Around them the other passengers were stony-faced; either disgruntled at having to stand, or guilty and irritable at having a seat that could not be properly enjoyed because of those looming over them.

'If only I had a seat myself I'd offer it to you,' Howard said a little too loudly, or perhaps just loudly enough, as a young man sitting in the middle of the row hauled himself to his feet with an air of resignation and nodded to Jean.

She would rather have stayed where she was, next to Howard, but didn't want to humiliate the young man, who was already looking flushed from his belated gallantry. And besides, now that he had stood up there really wasn't enough room, so there was nothing for it but to clamber past him, apologising, over a tangle of feet, to take his seat.

The windows on both sides were opaque with grime and it was an unfamiliar line, so Jean had no idea where they were. The grey shapes of tall Victorian houses and narrow walled back yards slid past, one street indistinguishable from another. She looked in her bag for something to occupy her – the woman next to her was patiently crocheting, the ball of wool jumping in her lap – and noticed the envelope for Gretchen. She could give it to Howard to pass on and save herself a stamp. She took out her notebook and began to write, in her best Dutton's Longhand, an account of her meeting with Martha.

At Hither Green the compartment emptied a little and Howard moved to the seat opposite Jean. He took a copy of *The Times* from his briefcase and folded it into a small rectangle, to avoid overspreading himself, and seemed to be absorbed in the crossword. But every time Jean looked up he was watching her, unembarrassed, and would give her a smile or raise his eyebrows as if at the length and inconvenience of the journey.

Eventually they had the carriage to themselves and, having finished her note-writing, Jean moved to sit beside him to see what progress he was making with the crossword.

'You haven't done any!' she remonstrated. 'It's completely blank.'

'I don't have a pen,' Howard replied with great dignity. 'I've been doing it blind. When I get home, I'll fill it in just like that!' He snapped his fingers.

Jean handed him her ballpoint with a sceptical expression.

He gave her an unfriendly look and then began to write, at great speed and shielding the page from her inquisitive gaze. A moment later he cast the paper aside, with the word 'Done!' And when she retrieved it she saw he had filled in the grid with the words:

She gave a peal of laughter.

'Here we are,' he said as the train drew into Sidcup station, stopping with a jolt that threw them backwards in their seats. 'I hope you won't be too late.'

'Mother knows I'm up in town this afternoon, but she still gets anxious if I'm even slightly delayed.'

'Is it just the two of you?' Howard enquired, directing her out of the station to the adjoining street where he had left the Wolseley.

'Yes. Just us two. My sister, Dorrie, lives in Kenya and my father died in the war. Like so many.'

'No less a tragedy for you, though,' said Howard.

Jean was usually adept at fielding personal questions and steering conversations onto safe, neutral territory. But there was something about the sanctuary and silence of a private car, where you could talk without having to make eye contact, that made her uncharacteristically open. She was aware that Howard was hardly an appropriate confidant, but he was so sensible and

113

safe and unlikely to do anything at all except sympathise that she couldn't restrain herself.

'I've made him sound like a hero. He wasn't. He walked out on my mother just as the war started. I think he had some kind of breakdown. He'd fought in the first war and survived. And when it looked as though it was happening all over again it was too much for him.'

'I don't think that was an uncommon reaction among veterans of the Great War,' said Howard. 'All that sacrifice for nothing.'

'Yes, but he'd also met someone else. That was the real reason for leaving. He just took off. I don't think the marriage had been happy for some time; it was just duty holding them together.'

Jean couldn't now recall ever witnessing any signs of physical affection between them – hand-holding or the welcoming kiss at the end of the working day – even before the rift. She had assumed this was normal and every marriage the same until she had noticed that her aunt and uncle in Harrogate did things differently: he called his wife Honeybun and never missed an opportunity to pull her onto his lap, or slide an arm around her waist; higher if he thought no one was looking.

'Perhaps he wouldn't have left if it hadn't been for the war. I think he just felt he'd already used up all his luck in the first war and needed to seize a last chance at happiness. And the thing is, he was *right*. It was his last chance.'

'At least he got to choose,' said Howard after a pause. 'Your mother had no choice.'

'Yes – that's it exactly,' said Jean, all her reticence melting before the warmth of his compassionate good sense. 'It was just imposed on her. And even so she felt this terrible shame and guilt, as though it was somehow her fault for not being able to keep her husband.'

'Did she ever speak to you about this?'

'No, no, that would have been impossible. She couldn't talk

about personal things. But I could tell – it was evident in every fibre of her being. The whole purpose of her life was to be a wife and mother.'

They pulled up at the traffic lights on the Croydon road and were able now to exchange a quick smile of understanding on Howard's part and gratitude on Jean's.

'So she leant on you instead?'

'Yes. Heavily. She doesn't have an independent bone in her body – she wasn't brought up that way. You read about these resilient women who raise five children single-handed and take in laundry and slaughter their own pigs and the rest of it. Well, she wasn't one of them. And then before she could even get used to the idea that he'd left her he was killed in an air raid. So it was as if he'd abandoned her twice over. She'd never had the chance to have it out with him and she couldn't even mourn him as his widow because everyone knew he'd already left her.'

This was the hardest thing, Jean thought. On top of losing everything else – her husband, her future, her pension – she had even been cheated of the sympathy that was her due.

'And you've looked after her ever since?'

'More or less. It was clear that one of us girls would have to. Whoever married first would get away. And that was Dorrie.'

The thought of her sister prompted, as always, a mixture of conflicting emotions, principally rancour and envy, but also powerful, protective love, and grief at the distance between them. She gave Howard a brief account of Dorrie's situation in Kitale, trying not to betray too much of her sense of injustice.

'Another abandonment,' was his observation. 'It must have hit your mother hard.'

'Yes. Missing out on the grandchildren. A further blow.'

'Did you ever see your father after he left?'

'Once. I went up to his office to ask for some money. He was a fruit wholesaler at Covent Garden, but he'd let the business get into debt. He was terribly apologetic and ashamed. It was horrible to see – we'd always got on so well before. He said he still loved Dorrie and me, but we were adults now, and he'd met someone else and that was that. He gave me all the cash in the office that he'd been about to bank. It wasn't very much. About twenty pounds.'

'What an unhappy story,' said Howard. 'Men can be very selfish.'

'And yet for the previous twenty years or so they seemed happy. To me, anyway. But who really knows what goes on in a marriage?'

'Who indeed?'

Jean glanced at him but he kept his eyes on the road and his face was expressionless.

'And most men aren't selfish. My uncle paid for Dorrie's wedding and helped us to get our house in Hayes. I thought Mother might be able to make a fresh start somewhere new where no one knew us. She was so ashamed of being deserted; she always felt the people in Gipsy Hill were gossiping and pitying her.

'But then about a month after we settled into our new house, we were at the cinema and a woman in the queue stopped us and said hello. It was one of our old neighbours who had moved around the corner. She was just trying to be friendly, but it was the worst thing that could have happened; Mother stopped going out almost entirely.'

Howard shook his head. 'Does your uncle still help out?'

'He lives in Harrogate, so he's a bit far away. We used to go on holiday there every year, but he's not in the best of health now. Anyway, we manage. My salary pays for the essentials. He still sends us a postal order for birthdays and Christmas.'

At this remark about money – one of the unmentionables

– Jean felt suddenly embarrassed. And yet it was nothing, really, compared to the revelations that had gone before. She was aware of the risk she had taken in unburdening herself so freely, but the relief was so powerful she couldn't regret it.

'I've never discussed this with anyone before. I'm sorry for rambling on.'

'Please don't apologise. I'm honoured that you felt you could talk to me.'

They both stared straight ahead, making what seemed a solemn declaration of friendship without once exchanging a glance. That would have been too much.

'I've just remembered, I've got something for Gretchen,' said Jean, taking Martha's envelope from her bag and laying it on the dashboard. This seemed to break the spell and draw the conversation back to its proper sphere – Gretchen, Margaret, the story, work. 'I met a friend of hers from St Cecilia's today. She wanted me to pass on a little gift.'

'What a nice thought,' said Howard. 'She'll be so pleased.'

Jean's mother was keeping watch at the window as the car drew up outside, a pale, ghostly figure in the unlit room.

'That man brought you home again,' she remarked as the door shut. 'I thought you were going to Chelsea.'

'I did. Look what I brought you.' Jean handed over the Peter Jones bag and smiled as her mother peered inside with a child-like delight in new things.

'A nightdress. Just what I need. Oh, clever you!' She held it against herself, extending one ankle and striking a pose as though modelling a ballgown.

'Very elegant,' said Jean. 'You'll easily be the best-dressed person in the house tonight.'

'Did you get yourself anything nice?' her mother asked and then a shadow of dismay clouded her face. There wouldn't have been enough money for two such treats.

'Oh, I don't need anything,' said Jean, still feeling somewhat raw and exposed from her conversation with Howard, and yet strangely exhilarated. 'Anyway, Gretchen is making me a new dress, so I'll soon be looking quite the thing.'

The feeling of euphoria lasted right through the reheated cauliflower cheese, hair wash and beyond, to the point that Jean even offered to read aloud from her mother's library book, *My Cousin Rachel*. It was the most harmonious evening that either of them could remember.

II

Dear Dorrie,

I know we don't do gifts but I was passing an antique shop in Chelsea the other day and I saw this exquisite little ciggie box and thought of you. I'm going to parcel it up with tissue paper and hope it makes it through customs in one piece.

We're both well. No other news.

Love Jean

Alice's Diary

12 July 1946

M caused a little scene today. She does love a drama. We were hopeful that the antimalarial drugs might work where the antibiotics, injections and diets have all failed. But she has been roaring with pain. Perhaps it would have been better if she had been in a room of her own, but we thought the companionship would be good for them all.

Her mother came to visit this afternoon, bringing a gift from one of their well-heeled parishioners – a bag of four tangerines. Nobody has seen a delicacy like this in years. Sister Maria Goretti said she hoped M was going to share them with the other girls. She meant well but she speaks bluntly sometimes. M said no, she damn well wasn't: B never shares a damn thing.

Sister MG tried (perhaps unwisely) to remove the bag, which split, sending the tangerines rolling onto the floor. M called her an awful name. Sister MG departed in high dudgeon, saying that M wouldn't be able to peel them herself with her bandaged hands, and surely no one else would help her when she was so selfish, ungrateful and foul-mouthed.

The tangerines were still on the floor when Sister Phil came on duty, so she returned them to M's bedside.

13 July

Overnight the tangerines have been eaten. G must have peeled them. I expect they shared them when the other two were asleep. Such an unlikely friendship.

M soiled herself – deliberately, no doubt – to punish Sister MG, who had to clean her up. Later, M complained that Sister MG had handled her roughly; the two are now sworn enemies. It is a bad business.

17 July

B has complained that she is kept awake at night by M and G whispering together. I suspect she feels excluded, poor thing. When I spoke to M and G separately about it, G immediately apologised. M denied it and accused B of making trouble. She would start a mutiny from her bed if she could.

B tried to enlist the support of K, but K, at the far end of the room, says she is not aware of any noise from the other beds. Perhaps the mechanical wheeze of the iron lung masks the noise, or perhaps she was just being diplomatic.

20 August

I have had to have stern words with Sister Phil. It has come to light that she has been less than vigilant in administering the evening doses of painkillers and sleeping tablets. M and G have apparently hoarded them for three days and then taken a triple dose.

When challenged, M explained that it was an attempt to guarantee a deep and painless sleep. On the pill-free nights they distracted each other by whispering through the night. It is a wretched story and my heart goes out to them in their pain, but M is a devil to take a risk like this. I don't believe G is the author of this reckless scheme – she is led along by M.

28 September

G was discharged today. You would hardly recognise her as the same girl who was brought in all those months ago in a wheelchair, so pale and pinched with pain. She left on foot, walking with two sticks, and made a point of thanking all the sisters individually. She is a sweet girl and a favourite with everyone. Her mother had tears in her eyes when she saw how improved she is.

30 September

M has been inconsolable without her friend. B tries to engage her in conversation, now that G is out of the way and she is not outnumbered. But M stubbornly feigns sleep or shouts across her to K. It is a curious thing – I have often observed that the arrival of someone new or the departure of someone established disturbs the equilibrium on a ward, even when that person is herself unassuming and compliant.

Charing Cross Hospital
Agar St
London W1
July 1957

Dear Miss Swinney,

I am writing to inform you that the results of our preliminary blood tests of Mother A and Daughter have established that they share the blood type A1 rhesus phenotype c̄dec̄de and the results of further, more detailed studies show a complete identity of blood groups – see the table enclosed.

We are therefore eager to proceed to the next stage of our investigation, and would be grateful if Mother A and Daughter could present themselves once more at the Charing Cross Hospital Annexe at Agar Street on 21st July at 9.30 a.m. for further tests.

Yours sincerely,
Sidney Lloyd-Jones

Dear Jean,

I have made great progress with your dress and wonder if you would be able to come for a fitting this weekend whenever is convenient for you (and your mother). Perhaps you could ring Howard at the shop to confirm a time.

With good wishes,
Gretchen

12

'What on earth is that?' Jean's mother stood in the kitchen doorway, holding the fragments of a sugar bowl, which she had just dropped on the tiled hearth.

Her mouth was slack with astonishment. As if she had seen a unicorn, Jean thought.

'It's a rabbit,' she replied. 'Surely you can see that?'

The animal sat on the lino between them, nibbling at a pile of outer cabbage leaves. Apart from a black smudge on its nose, now twitching, and one black ear, it was completely white and still small enough to fit in cupped hands.

'Yes, of course. But what is it doing *here*?'

'I bought it from a pet shop today, but I couldn't manage the cage so the shopkeeper said he'd drop it round on his way home this evening. I hope he remembers,' Jean said.

At this disturbance the rabbit hopped in ungainly slow motion towards a thumb of carrot that had rolled just out of reach and Jean's mother flinched back against the door frame.

'It won't eat you, Mother,' Jean laughed. 'They're herbivores.'

'But why on earth did you buy it? We've never had pets before.'

'It's a present for Margaret. She told me she wanted a rabbit or a kitten. I think she's lonely.'

Jean's mother seemed to take no comfort from the fact that the rabbit's occupancy of the kitchen was to be short-lived. If anything, this admission appeared to rattle her even more.

'You can't give someone a live rabbit as a gift,' she spluttered.

'Well, I certainly wouldn't give her a dead one,' said Jean. 'That would be too macabre.'

'Have you checked that her parents want her to have a rabbit? They may have strong objections.'

'No,' said Jean, experiencing a momentary loss of confidence in her brilliant scheme. 'It's meant to be a surprise.'

'It'll certainly be that,' came the tart reply. 'Whatever possessed you?'

'I thought it was a nice idea. It's not a python. It just sits in a hutch eating leftover cabbage leaves until Margaret wants to cuddle it. I can't see any objection.'

'Well, I think you've been very rash,' said her mother. 'It will cause a huge rumpus if you turn up with it unannounced and the parents refuse to take it. The little girl will be terribly upset.'

Jean felt stung by this remark; she had wanted only to make Margaret happy and in her enthusiasm for her own ingenuity she had allowed herself to get carried away. It occurred to her that her mother was describing exactly what would have happened years ago if they had been the unprepared recipients of a gift rabbit. For a moment she was that disappointed little girl; it was unbearable.

'Oh hell, I was only trying to be kind,' she burst out, railing against criticism that she knew was just. 'You had to spoil it.'

Her mother went rigid, blinking in silent protest at this crossing of uncrossable lines. Whatever their divergence of views, raised voices or confrontation was as unthinkable as a knife at the throat.

'It's nothing to do with me,' she said at last in a brittle voice. 'You must do as you see fit.'

Later, after dinner, they sat in the front room together listening to the Light Programme on the radio, friends again. Jean couldn't apologise for her outburst; to do that would only acknowledge the unpleasantness. Better to agree, without discussion, that it had never happened. There were other, established ways to show contrition: an unequal division of the shepherd's pie in her mother's favour; an offer to massage her sore feet; a suggestion that they look – again – through Dorrie's wedding album together.

The rabbit slumbered in Jean's lap on a folded towel and submitted to be stroked. Its weight and warmth were surprisingly comforting, and she found herself half hoping that the Tilburys might refuse to accept it after all.

The shopkeeper had called round with the hutch as promised. It looked larger in a domestic kitchen than it had in the shop, taking up most of the space by the back door. Jean lined it with newspaper and straw, and tied the glass water bottle onto the chicken-wire window with elastic.

For now it had the fresh, green smell of new wood; it would very quickly acquire a less appealing animal scent, which none of the ordinary kitchen smells – Ajax, Gumption, spent matches, cooking – could quite mask. Of course in the normal way it would have to go outside – basic hygiene demanded it – but there was no sense in carting it down to the shed if it was going to a new home in a few days anyway.

'Quite a placid little thing,' Jean's mother conceded on her way to bed.

Not fully committed to touching the rabbit, her outstretched hand hovered just above its head as though giving it a blessing.

'Howard?'

'Yes. Speaking.'

'Hello, Howard, it's Jean Swinney.'

She had a cast-iron excuse for this call, which he was no doubt expecting and which gave her confidence, so her voice was quite steady. Whenever she thought back to their most recent conversation, she felt a mild panic at how much of herself she had revealed. Without the protective distance of the telephone between them she might have been less composed.

'Hello, Jean.'

There was no trace of awkwardness in his greeting, only his usual warmth and politeness.

'Gretchen sent me a note about calling in this weekend for a dress fitting.'

'Oh yes. She said.'

'I'm sorry you've been cast as my social secretary, but she asked me to let you know a suitable time.'

'Of course. I have my pen and paper ready to take dictation.'

She could hear the smile in his voice.

'Shall we say 11 a.m. on Saturday?'

'Very good.'

'And . . . Howard?'

'Yes.'

'I think I've done something a bit rash.'

'Oh?' His tone was suddenly serious. 'Are you going to tell me what it is?'

'I want you to be completely honest.'

'Go on.'

'I've bought Margaret a rabbit. She said she was desperate for a pet, and I was passing the shop and went in and bought one on impulse. It was only when I stopped to think about it that I realised it might be a terrible imposition.'

'Is that all? What a relief.'

'Are you horrified by the idea? Please say. I won't be offended.'

'A rabbit?' he mused. 'What a thoughtful . . . thought. No, I can't say I feel any horror sweeping over me. Quite the opposite.'

'What about Gretchen? Will she disapprove?'

'Do you know, I'm embarrassed to say I have no idea of my wife's views on rabbits. In nearly ten years of marriage it's not something we've ever discussed.'

Jean felt herself beginning to relax.

'Perhaps I should write her a note.'

'Why don't I ask her tonight and if she throws up her hands in horror I'll telephone you tomorrow. If you don't hear, you can assume she's in favour.'

'The last thing I want is to cause any trouble.'

In the months ahead she would remember this remark — so sincerely felt — and marvel at her own innocence.

13

Jean stood once more in Gretchen's workroom, hardly breathing, as the skeleton of a dress, inside out and bristling with pins, was lowered over her head and tweaked and tugged and tightened around her with still more pins until Gretchen was satisfied with the fit. The slightest movement on Jean's part and she was pierced by a dozen sharp points.

'You are losing weight since I last measured you?' Gretchen said with her curious foreign intonation that made questions of statements, pinching the fabric between finger and thumb.

'Not intentionally,' said Jean, flinching. 'I eat less when I'm busy, I suppose. And more when I'm miserable.'

'And at the moment you are overworked but happy?' said Gretchen, lifting the dress carefully, inch by inch, over Jean's head and laying it on the cutting table.

'Yes, that would be about right.'

She was busy because Gretchen's case took up so much of her time that every other moment at work was spent catching up with her regular duties. The reason for her happiness was something she chose not to examine.

The ordeal by piercing over, the two women made their way downstairs to the kitchen, where Margaret was sitting on the floor playing with the rabbit. Her outstretched legs formed the fourth side of an enclosure made up of the wall, the wooden dresser and a vegetable rack. She was in a state as close to ecstasy as could be imagined.

'I'm going to call her Jemimah,' she said.

No follow-up call had come from Howard to discourage the gift of the rabbit, which had left Jean with the problem of how to transport the hutch to Sidcup. She had half hoped that Howard would foresee her difficulty and offer to come and fetch it, but this had not happened, and so she had been forced to order a taxi – almost doubling the cost of the gift. The driver had helped her to carry it to and from the car, earning every penny of his shilling tip. Between them they had threaded it down the narrow passage at the side of the Tilburys' semi and into the back garden, Jean skinning her knuckles on the brickwork as she stumbled.

All the expense and inconvenience proved worthwhile, however, when Margaret was summoned downstairs for the unveiling of the surprise. The expression on her face, as suspicion and curiosity gave way to rapture, made tears spring to Jean's eyes. The little girl was almost quivering with excitement as she flung herself at Jean and hugged her.

As Jean patted her heaving shoulders, she realised too late that this might well be the greatest, happiest moment of Margaret's childhood, the one that she would always remember. By rights it belonged to her parents, but she, Jean, an interloper, had appropriated it for herself.

She understood, now, her mother's misgivings and could hardly bring herself to look at Gretchen, expecting to see in her face some signs of resentment. Gretchen, however, seemed oblivious to these nuances, showing only a generous pleasure in her daughter's happiness and needing no credit for it.

'Wasn't that kind of Jean,' was all she said.

There had been no sign of Howard in the house or garden,

though the Wolseley had been there in the driveway. It was only when Margaret said something about Daddy building a run for Jemimah when he got back from work that Jean remembered that of course for jewellers and other shopkeepers Saturday was a working day like any other. She felt a jab of disappointment, which quite unsettled her.

It had not just been for the pleasure of seeing Margaret, then, that she had set off that morning with such a light heart. Ever since that conversation in the car, when she had poured out her disappointments and frustrations to Howard as though she had known him years rather than weeks, she had found herself thinking about him in idle moments, more than was allowable or wise. She would have to watch herself.

As this visit had to be incorporated into her morning errands, which still had to be done, Jean couldn't linger once the dress fitting was completed, even though Gretchen invited her to stay and share their lunch of cheese on toast. She had promised her mother that this afternoon they would go through her winter wardrobe and sort out any items that needed spot cleaning or mending, and bag up anything especially threadbare for the Church jumble sale.

As they said their goodbyes in the hallway, Gretchen became suddenly serious and confiding.

'You've been so thoughtful to Margaret and I know she likes you very much . . .'

'Oh, it was nothing, really,' said Jean, wanting no reminders of the rabbit. 'Buying a pet is easy. The hard work of caring for it will be all yours.'

'Well, I'd like to think you would be a friend to Margaret. If anything happened to me. I'd be glad to think you would be someone she could turn to.'

'Why should anything happen to you?' Jean asked, alarmed by the dark tone of this conversation. 'You're not ill, are you?'

'No, no, of course not,' Gretchen laughed. 'Look at me!' She flapped her arms and made a little jump on the spot as if that somehow demonstrated rude health.

'Why do you say that, then?' Jean insisted. 'Did something come up in the blood tests to make you concerned?'

'No, not at all. I promise. I was just thinking that it's a shame Margaret doesn't have any aunts or godmothers and that you seem to understand her so well. That's all.'

'Of course, I've become very fond of Margaret and I'd be very happy to be a . . . special friend to her,' said Jean, flattered but still uneasy.

'I think you'd be a good influence – someone she could look up to and respect. Girls don't always like to take advice from their mothers. And perhaps mothers don't always give the best advice.'

Touched by this sudden acceleration in their friendship, Jean found herself tongue-tied. The idea of spending more time with Margaret, becoming perhaps a secular godparent, or unofficial 'auntie', who might be permitted to take her on outings and spoil her, was everything she could have hoped for.

Mistaking her hesitation for reluctance, Gretchen said, 'Perhaps I'm asking too much, too soon.'

'Oh, not at all,' Jean stammered. 'I was just thinking, perhaps, with your permission, I could take her out now and then, to museums or concerts, if she was interested in that sort of thing.'

She remembered her 'aunt' Rosa, the rides in taxis and the alarming food and the sense of being singled out for special treatment.

'That would be lovely.'

'I could even take her to the *Echo*, to see how a newspaper is made.' She warmed to her theme, dismissing in her enthusiasm the looming obstacle of her mother, which lay like a boulder across her path. 'Perhaps not the paper,' she conceded, remembering the lively language of Bill and Larry and the subs. 'But if you and Howard ever need a babysitter so that you could go out together sometime, then I could do that, too.'

Gretchen smiled. 'All of those things,' she said. 'I think it's a wonderful idea.'

14

'You seem cheerful lately,' said Roy Drake as Jean swept into the editorial meeting, early for once, and deposited her pile of papers on the desk. 'Is anything the matter?'

'Very funny.'

'You have a spring in your step. And a new dress, if I'm not mistaken.'

They were the first to arrive and had the room to themselves; otherwise he would not have commented.

Jean gave a model's twirl. 'Thank you for noticing. It's couture, you know. Not off the peg.'

He raised his eyebrows.

'Mrs Tilbury made it for me. She's an expert needlewoman as well as a Virgin Mother.'

'Hmm. Accepting gifts from 'sources'. That'll have to go before the board.'

She laughed.

'Very smart, anyway.'

'It's amazing the difference it makes when something actually fits.'

Howard had dropped the dress off, wrapped in tissue paper, while Jean was still at work.

'That man came round with a parcel for you.' Her mother

had described the incident with a slight pursing of the lips, but she had relented when she saw the workmanship. It was so beautifully made – not a raw edge to be seen, French binding on every seam – you could have worn it inside out. 'You'll be wanting to save it for best,' she remarked.

'I don't have any *best* to save it for,' Jean replied. 'I'm going to wear it to work.'

At the meeting, the main subject for discussion was the change in layout, moving the entertainments, listings, marriage lines, household hints, gardening, Pam's Piece, features and fashion to the middle pages (displacing 'news from the estates' and motoring). This would then form an eight-page section, aimed chiefly at women, which could be detached from the main body of the paper. It was felt that this would enable couples to share and enjoy the *Echo* more harmoniously. The postbag was split between those who viewed all change with hostility (the majority), those who approved of the principle of the supplement section but had alternative suggestions for its content based on their own preferences, and those (few) who were in favour of the new layout.

After some debate it was decided to proceed as planned. Time, Roy's argument ran, would deal with the opponents of change. The new and threatening would become the old and familiar in due course. The second group's needs were too diverse and conflicting ever to be successfully addressed. That left the third and smallest group to carry the day.

The matter settled, it was Jean's turn to give an update on Our Lady of Sidcup, as Larry styled it. Her frequent absences from the office had been noted and Roy felt the rest of the team deserved a report on the progress of the medical investigations.

'You might remember, but we approached this story with some scepticism,' Jean said, 'imagining that it would be quite quickly dismissed.'

Heads nodded. Most of those present had in truth imagined that this is exactly what had happened, weeks ago, and were surprised that the story was still live.

'I've investigated the woman's claims and interviewed various people connected with her during the crucial period, and I can't find anything that undermines her version of events. For what it's worth, I find myself inclined to believe her. What is more significant, though, is the results of various tests that she and her daughter have had at Charing Cross Hospital to try to prove beyond doubt that parthenogenesis – that's virgin birth to you – occurred. And, so far so good.'

She was aware as she spoke that her colleagues had grown quiet and attentive. During the debate on the new layout there had been the usual distracted fidgeting, fiddling with pens and lighters, the grinding out of cigarettes, but they were all now focused on her.

'The blood tests were compatible, and,' she looked down at her papers to the most recent letter from Dr Lloyd-Jones, 'I'm quoting the doctor here – in the "taste test", both mother and daughter could taste phenylthiocarbamide at exactly the same threshold value of 2.54 mg per litre. This is significant. In the saliva test, both mother and daughter were "non-secretors" and produced identical titres after treating their saliva samples against an anti-A antiserum.'

'Does this amount to proof?' asked Bill.

'Not 100 per cent.' She referred back to her notes. 'The probability of this kind of agreement if there was a father involved is less than 0.01 per cent. There is one more serum test and then if they pass that, the clincher is a skin graft, but obviously they wouldn't proceed with that if any of the previous tests failed.'

'The really persuasive thing as I understand it', said Roy, entering the discussion for the first time, 'is that Mrs Tilbury presented herself as an example of a virgin mother, before she was aware of the results of these tests and not the other way around.'

'Yes, exactly,' said Jean.

'Does the lady herself know the outcome of the tests now?' Larry wanted to know.

Jean nodded. 'She's been kept informed at every stage. The doctor leading the project was adamant that results should not be withheld from her.'

'What's to stop her, having proved her case at our expense, so to speak, running off to one of the nationals with her story? Has she signed any kind of exclusivity contract yet?'

'No,' said Jean. 'It's not necessary. She isn't the least bit interested in money or notoriety.'

'She might be,' said Larry. 'If she knew how much was available.'

'I've built up a relationship with her. She trusts me and I trust her. However,' she turned to Roy, 'if you think it's necessary, I'm prepared to ask her to sign something.'

Roy looked at her over his glasses, considering.

'But,' she went on, 'I think it would bring the issue of money to the foreground and possibly damage our relationship, so I'd be against it on those grounds.'

'I agree with Larry up to a point. It's not much to ask. But on this occasion, I'm going to trust Jean's judgement.'

'Thank you,' said Jean.

'What about the medics? Are they sound?' Larry asked.

'They are already operating under a code of patient confidentiality,' Jean assured him. 'They know that eventually the research will be theirs to publish and own if it has any scientific value. And unlike us, they don't expect everything to be done by yesterday.'

'Suffice to say that in their cautious, academic way they are intrigued,' said Roy.

'So they ought to be,' said Bill. 'It's a hell of a story.'

'All credit to Jean,' said Larry, and there was some appreciative thumping on the table, which she hushed with a raised hand.

'We're not there yet, folks.'

'While we're showing appreciation,' said Roy, 'honourable mention also to the new tone of Pam's Piece.'

'Why, what's happened to it?' Bill wanted to know.

'It's warmer, more reflective,' said Roy.

'As you'd know if you ever actually read the paper,' said Jean to general laughter.

He was lazy, she thought. Cut corners and did the absolute minimum, but he was always affable, quick to put his hand in his wallet, and for that reason you couldn't dislike him.

Later that afternoon he wandered over to her desk, where she was at work on a new Pam's Piece entitled 'The Unofficial Aunt'.

'Me and the lads are going over to the Black Horse for a quick one after work if you're interested. It's young Tony's birthday.'

Young Tony was the new photographer. Jean had spoken to him only recently about taking some pictures of Gretchen and Margaret. He was only twenty-five or so and bounced as he walked as though in sprung shoes. (Old Tony was one of the subs. An alcoholic, he never went to the pub.)

'I know you generally like to get home, but I thought I'd ask.'

'Sorry,' said Jean. 'It's my mother. But thanks for asking.'

It was even less possible now: all opportunities for recreational absences had to be carefully preserved for the Tilburys.

15

Jean was up a stepladder in the front room, re-hanging the curtains, when she saw Mrs Melsom approaching the house. It was one of those jobs that should have been done in spring but was somehow always neglected until late summer. The red damask drapes, heavy with dust, had been hung over the washing line and shaken and brushed before being left to convalesce in the fresh air for a few hours to rid them of their stale smell.

'That tiresome woman,' her mother said, looking up from her letter writing. 'What does she want?'

'Why do you say that?' Jean asked, hopping down from the ladder. 'She's perfectly nice.'

Tiresome or not, she was Jean's best chance of achieving a few hours of freedom at weekends, if only her mother would be more agreeable. Since that first visit, Jean had tried to cultivate Mrs Melsom's acquaintance on her mother's behalf by calling round with a bag of runner beans from the garden, on the pretext that they had a glut.

'It was so kind of you to come and sit with her; Mother enjoyed it so much,' she had said, hoping to prompt a repeat offer.

She didn't realise that her mother had already – so soon – taken a dislike to the poor woman, but it was entirely predictable. Even before she had made herself a recluse, she had a history of taking up new friends and then discarding them, usually over some imagined slight. Her fallings-out were swift and permanent; the casualties numerous. The rift with the church knitters was only one example.

Mrs Melsom stood on the doorstep wearing a faded summer dress and a crushed straw hat, holding a Pyrex bowl of raspberries.

'I brought these for your mother,' she said. 'She mentioned how much she likes them and ours have done well. We've more than we can eat.'

'That's very thoughtful of you,' said Jean, accepting the bowl. 'Won't you come in?'

'Who is it?' came her mother's fluting voice.

Jean glared at her mother over Mrs Melsom's straw-hatted head as she showed the visitor into the front room.

'Look, Mother,' she said, holding out the raspberries for her inspection as though they were an offering to pacify a peevish deity. 'Isn't that kind?'

'They'll do nicely for tea,' her mother conceded, screwing the cap back on her fountain pen.

She was a fussy eater and liked her little treats. Mrs Melsom had, perhaps unwittingly, hit on the surest way to gain her approval.

'Hello, Mrs Swinney,' Mrs Melsom said in that artificially high, bright voice used to address the hard of hearing or imbeciles. 'I see you're doing your paperwork.'

'I have a mountain of letters to write,' the old lady replied, tapping her notepad.

Jean blinked in surprise. Apart from Dorrie, her mother's only other regular correspondent was an old friend in Toronto. The protective barrier of ocean between them had saved this from going the way of other relationships.

'The problem is thinking of things to say,' she added, the mask slipping for a moment. 'When you don't do much.'

'Well, I was wondering if I could tempt you out of the house on Saturday,' Mrs Melsom said, casting a wary glance at Jean. 'The Mothers' Union are doing a strawberry tea at the village hall. The handbell-ringers are giving a little concert and there'll be a bring-and-buy. It should be rather a nice afternoon.' She put her head on one side.

Jean's mother looked momentarily panicked. 'Oh, I think it might be too much for me,' she said.

'Of course it won't,' Jean exclaimed. 'It sounds lovely.'

'We'll find you a comfy seat – you don't have to make conversation if you'd rather not.'

Jean couldn't now remember if she'd briefed Mrs Melsom about her mother's social anxieties, or whether this was something that had become apparent during their tea together.

'It's the walking,' her mother said, shaking her head firmly. 'I'm not steady enough.'

'My husband will take us in the Riley,' said Mrs Melsom. 'Door to door.'

'There,' said Jean. 'What could be nicer?'

'Well I suppose if you're coming, too,' said her mother.

This wasn't the outcome Jean was hoping for.

'The invitation is for *you*, Mother,' she said, shooting Mrs Melsom a supplicating glance. 'It would be so good for you to get out of the house.'

She hadn't wanted to use this form of words. Nothing that was presented as being 'good for you' was likely to hold much appeal. She almost wondered whether it would be worth enduring a strawberry tea and bring-and-buy just to induct her mother gradually into a new world of extramural activities. But the immediate possibility of a free Saturday was too tempting.

'Well, you think about it and let me know,' Mrs Melsom said.

Jean felt the prospect of liberty slipping away. If she didn't settle the matter now, with Mrs Melsom still here providing additional traction, the battle would be lost.

'You might find you enjoy yourself. And it will be something to tell Dorrie in your next letter.'

Her mother wagged her hand as though waving a white flag. 'Oh, all right. If you're so set on it.'

Mrs Melsom, to her great credit, refused to take offence at this ungracious response but beamed as though on the receiving end of a huge favour.

I will make it up to you somehow, Jean thought. She had no great confidence in the long-term success of the experiment. It was too much to hope for that her mother might make and keep a friend, and find some source of entertainment or comfort beyond herself and their four walls.

'I suppose you'll be off gallivanting with your new friends while I'm out,' said her mother astutely as soon as the door was closed on the visitor. 'They seem to be making quite a project of you, for some reason.'

'If I am "gallivanting",' said Jean, magnanimous in her victory, 'surely it's better I do it while you are out having fun yourself than when you are on your own here.'

'*Fun?*' said her mother with a kind of shudder. 'A lot of silly women more like.'

'I'm sure they're not all silly. Mrs Melsom is perfectly decent.'

'As long as they don't try to get me on some kind of committee. You know what those churchy women are like when they get their claws into you.'

Jean laughed. 'You do exaggerate! It's the Mothers' Union, not a pack of wild beasts.'

'I didn't see you volunteering to get involved.'

'I'm not a mother,' Jean said.

16

....

Pam's Piece

THE UNOFFICIAL AUNT

Can there be any category of women more derided
than the maiden aunt? Having missed out on marriage
and motherhood owing to a post-war shortage of men,
she is regarded as both comic and tragic. Prudish and
easily shocked, suspicious of anything modern, fond of
cats and the local curate, she is to be pitied but also
mocked. She dithered in the margins of literature like
Jane Austen's foolish Miss Bates, until Agatha Christie
raised up Jane Marple to be her heroine – the maiden
aunt's natural nosiness and apparent harmlessness
making her an ideal detective.

But there is a new breed of unmarried women at
large now – modern, educated women with money
and careers of their own – and hard-pressed parents
are reaping the benefits.

These women have the time and energy to be 'unofficial aunts' to their friends' or neighbours' children.
What could be more rewarding and mutually beneficial?

The young person acquires a wise counsellor and confidant, unburdened by parental expectations. The childless woman enjoys a fleeting taste of the joys of parenthood and acquires a greater understanding of the younger generation. The parents gain some time for their own pursuits. Everybody wins!

....

The jaunty notes of Rondo Alla Turca filled the church of St Mary le Strand, the vibrations from the piano rattling the flowers in the slender wooden plinth below the lectern. Left over from the previous week's wedding, Jean thought, fanning herself with the printed programme. They had walked through a mush of paper confetti at the entrance. Beside her sat Margaret, swinging her legs, encased in white socks and navy T-bar sandals, in time to the music. On her lap was a bag of toffees. Jean had taken the precaution of unwrapping them all beforehand so they wouldn't rustle. Now, they had softened and fused in the heat, and were proving difficult to prise apart.

Her father had taken her to just such an afternoon concert when she was a girl. She hadn't enjoyed the music much then – and didn't now, in truth. It was the experience of a special day out with just her father that was precious to her in its rarity. A piano recital had seemed a good idea to inaugurate these outings with Margaret – something to encourage her in her music lessons – but she sensed the little girl was bored.

It was rather a long programme and the pews were hard. The rest of the audience were mostly even older than Jean – regulars, perhaps – and there were no other children. She would probably rather be back home playing with the rabbit, Jean thought. Perhaps this is not a treat to her at all but an awful chore, to be suffered to please her mother. And yet when she had arrived at the house in Sidcup at midday to pick Margaret up she had found the little girl dressed in her best clothes, in a state of eager expectation.

Gretchen herself seemed almost equally excited on their behalf and Jean felt a momentary twinge of guilt that she was being excluded from their adventure.

'Will you be all right without me, Mummy?' Margaret asked as they were about to leave, her voice suddenly serious.

'I will try to cope as best I can,' Gretchen laughed, kissing her daughter's shiny cheek.

'If you get lonely there's always Jemimah.'

'Thank you, I'll bear it in mind.'

There was a brief pause after the Mozart before the Rachmaninov while the pianist left the transept to gather herself together, perhaps, or have a drink of water. The air was dry and dusty; particles shimmered in the shafts of light from the high windows, catching in the throat.

'Is it over?' Margaret whispered over the applause in a voice that seemed to carry more hope than regret.

Jean stood up, gesturing Margaret to follow her, and they crept out of the pew and down the aisle, slipping through the heavy west door into the dazzling sunshine and sudden clamour of the street.

'I'd had enough, hadn't you?' Jean said when they were safely away from the silent precincts of the church.

She had never walked out in the middle of a recital or any other kind of performance before and felt almost dizzy at her own daring. Even if you weren't enjoying yourself it was still a waste, and therefore a sin against thrift – the only kind of religion Jean practised.

Margaret nodded. 'I liked that last tune but it was quite long.'

'You could play like that one day, you know.'

Margaret shook her head, screwing up her face in horrified denial.

'That woman in there was once just like you – learning her scales, doing her practice; she wasn't born playing like that.'

'I don't like playing in front of people. As soon as people start listening I make mistakes. I like singing. You don't have to make the notes; they're already inside you.'

She was full of these charming and unexpected comments – at once innocent and profound. Questions seemed to bubble up out of her, prompted by anything or nothing. 'Do you think Jemimah likes me? I mean, do you think rabbits can actually like people?' 'When you look at the sky do you think you see the same colour as me?' 'If you've had one baby does it mean you can definitely have another one?' Jean wasn't sure how to answer this last one without getting into complicated matters of human fertility, far beyond her remit as unofficial aunt. Given Margaret's own curious provenance, it was safer to say, 'Not always. Babies don't always come along when you want them to.'

They walked along the Strand in search of refreshment. Margaret was carrying a small shoulder bag – a child-sized version similar to one used by Gretchen – swinging it at ankle-height. Now and then it caught Jean on the back of the leg.

'That's a dear little bag,' said Jean, sidestepping to avoid another swipe. 'What do you keep in it?'

Margaret hoisted it over her head and across her body like a postman's sack before opening it up to display the contents.

'Handkerchief, purse, toffees, notebook, pencil.'

'What's the notebook for?'

'It's for when the angel voices say a word I don't know, so I can write it down and look it up later.'

'Oh,' said Jean. She hadn't meant to ask about her voices. Gretchen had said it was best to make nothing of it, but the matter had come up quite naturally. 'Have you heard from them lately?' She might have been asking about a penfriend or distant relative.

'They've been a bit quiet since I got Jemimah. I think they're jealous.'

'Possibly,' said Jean, struggling to imagine the human weaknesses of these phantom whisperers. Perhaps it was just loneliness speaking. Perhaps Jemimah really might be a 'cure'.

Margaret took out the spiral notebook and flipped it open at the most recent entry.

'Administrator, malfeasance, ormolu,' she read, stumbling over the syllables.

'Good heavens. I'm not sure I understand all of those words myself,' said Jean, wondering again how Gretchen could accept this bizarre phenomenon with such equanimity. If it was down to her she would be all over it until she had these 'angels' under a microscope. 'You'll have a splendid vocabulary if this keeps up.'

'My teacher Mrs Garpitt said I've got a reading age of thirteen,' Margaret replied.

Jean could tell she was desperate to tell someone of this accolade but at the same time embarrassed to be thought boastful.

'At least, I'd say,' said Jean. 'Shall we have tea at Simpson's? I've got a terrible thirst after all those toffees.'

She was rewarded with a broad smile.

The waiter showed them upstairs to the ladies' dining room, to a table on the far side of the large, high-ceilinged room, at some distance from the concentration of other diners. Jean had a suspicion they were being put out of the way and was rather gratified when Margaret pointed towards a group of elegantly dressed women near the window and said in his hearing, 'That was where we sat last time.'

It was some years since Jean had eaten anywhere smart and she had to hide her surprise at the prices – five shillings for a slice of strudel!

She ordered a pot of tea with scones and jam and Margaret chose a strawberry millefeuille from a trolley of pastries, with a glass of milk. The sight of the strawberries reminded her of her mother and she wondered how she was coping in the village hall. Her stomach gave a squeeze of anxiety at the prospect of the recriminations that might follow an unsuccessful afternoon.

The scone when it arrived was warm, crumbly and scented with rose water. It came with a dish of strawberry jam and some double cream whipped almost to butter. I could easily make these at home, Jean thought, but I never do. She would always rather be in the garden than in the kitchen in the summer. Margaret was deconstructing her millefeuille, eating it from the top down, one layer at a time.

'You could just attack it with a fork,' Jean suggested, observing her struggles.

'But all the insides will squish out,' said Margaret. 'It is lovely, though.' She rolled her eyes appreciatively.

She had managed to get cream all over her fingers and a smudge of icing sugar on her cheek. It was a delight to Jean to witness her childish pleasure in things; that interlude between the dawning of consciousness and the onset of self-consciousness was so brief. Margaret was now ten; there were perhaps two more years at most.

'What would you like to do after this?' Jean asked, helping herself to more tea. An art gallery might be pushing things. You could have too much culture.

Margaret looked shy. 'Shall I tell you what I'd like to do most?'

'Yes, please do.'

'I'd like to go and surprise Daddy at his shop.'

'Oh.' This wasn't what Jean had been expecting and she had no ready excuse to hand, so she said, 'Well, all right. If that's what you'd like. But if he's busy with customers we'll have to keep out of the way.'

When the bill came, Margaret produced a small beaded purse from her shoulder bag and tried to give Jean a shilling.

'Mummy gave me some money to pay for things,' she said.

'Oh no,' said Jean, laughing. 'That isn't how it works at all. This is my treat.'

Margaret accepted this as she did all of Jean's utterances and dropped the coin back in her purse.

It was only a short walk to Bedford Street and Jean felt her spirits lift at the first glimpse of the bottle green shop front and the gold painted sign. A Silver Cross pram was parked on the pavement outside; a baby in a blue knitted romper was kicking vigorously at his blankets and chewing on his fist. One cheek was fiery red with toothache. Jean and Margaret stopped to chatter to him until the mother emerged from the shop next door and bore him away.

Howard was in conversation with a man by the till and didn't notice the visitors peering through the window. Even when they opened the door, setting the bell jangling, it was a second or two before he recognised his own daughter, and then his face broke into a smile of surprise and pleasure.

'I don't know what she'd like,' the customer was saying, peering helplessly at the velvet trays of necklaces and bracelets laid out on the display case. 'They all look much the same to me.'

'Perhaps this lady can advise you,' said Howard, indicating Jean. 'She can bring a feminine perspective.'

The man, who was in his late twenties, perhaps, with a haircut of military severity, looked at her with helpless gratitude.

'But be warned, she has very expensive taste,' he added.

'That is quite untrue,' Jean assured the customer, who was now looking rather confused. 'I know next to nothing about jewellery. But I can tell you which one I think is the prettiest.'

She indicated a delicate silver bracelet, dotted with moonstones – the cheapest of all the exhibits, though this was not, for once, a consideration.

'I like this one,' said Margaret, pointing a nibbled finger at a more ostentatious and costly ruby pendant.

'That's lovely too,' Jean agreed, realising that she had hardly done Howard a favour by recommending the one with the modest price tag.

'Yes. Perhaps a ruby,' the young man said. 'I think it sends the right signals.'

Howard's lips twitched and Jean looked away, feigning sudden interest in a display of gentlemen's wristwatches.

'There are actually matching earrings,' said Margaret. 'You could get those, too.'

'Good heavens, Margaret,' said Howard. 'I'm afraid this young lady is my daughter,' he explained. 'And therefore not an entirely disinterested party.'

'Quite the saleswoman already!' said the man, and almost seemed persuaded to take them until it occurred to him that he couldn't now be sure whether his fiancée had pierced earlobes. The fact that he couldn't remember this detail troubled him. 'You'd think I'd have noticed a thing like that,' he said, shaking his head as Howard polished the ruby pendant and put it in a velvet box.

The box went inside an elegant green bag with handles of satin ribbon. Jean felt a surge of envy for this unknown young woman, soon to be the recipient of such a lavish gift. Although she could not imagine any circumstance in which she would be able to wear a ruby pendant, it would be an exciting addition to her drawer of treasures.

Margaret was staring with unembarrassed interest as the man produced four new five-pound notes from his wallet and laid them on the counter with what was almost a shiver of reluctance. Jean could sense his anxiety at parting with such a large sum of money all at once. It would take her nearly a month to earn it.

'Well done, you two!' said Howard when the customer had

gone on his way, carrying the dainty bag a trifle self-consciously, having failed in his attempt to squash it into his pocket. 'That's the best sale I've made all day.'

'I take no credit,' said Jean. 'I don't think I have any knack for selling.'

'I'm not sure I have, either,' Howard admitted. 'Which is unfortunate.'

'I think to be a convincing salesperson you have to be a spender yourself. I'm far too careful.'

'I used to like buying toys, but now I've got Jemimah I don't need anything else,' said Margaret piously.

'Oh yes, Jemimah's been a great success,' Howard said to Jean. 'I can't think how we got by without her. Now, we just sit around bitterly regretting the wasted rabbit-less years.'

Jean smiled. He had such a droll way of speaking that it was a pleasure to be teased by him. She thought again of their first meeting; how awkward and unimpressive she had found him, and how unworthy of his pretty young wife. Now, she felt the good fortune was all on Gretchen's side. He was by some stretch the nicest man she had ever met.

It also occurred to her that his first impression of her might not have been especially favourable. She had no illusions or anxieties about her own lack of physical beauty; her ordinariness, in fact, grew less irksome with every passing year. It had been dispiriting to be plain at twenty, but by forty it hardly mattered. Time had caught up with most of her prettier contemporaries and those with the most to lose seemed to feel its depredations the hardest.

The arrival of another customer, a woman whose immaculate hair, hat, gloves and fashionable suit, seemed suggestive of a promising combination of wealth and vanity, signalled to Jean that it was time to depart. Affecting the air of satisfied shoppers, she and Margaret slipped out with a discreet goodbye.

'I wonder if Mummy's been all right,' said Margaret, twirling her handbag as they walked down Bedford Street in the direction of Charing Cross. 'She promised she'd make *spitzbuben* for tea.'

'What's *spitzbuben*?'

'They're jammy biscuits.'

'I've learned so many new words today,' Jean mused. 'Ormolu. *Spitzbuben*. I shall need a notebook of my own to keep track of them.'

'You must decide where you want to go on our next outing,' said Jean as they approached number 7, Burdett Road. 'Maybe the zoo, if you haven't been recently?'

'I'd like to go swimming,' Margaret said. 'But only if you come in the water with me. It doesn't count if you just sit on the side and watch.'

'I'm happy to go swimming,' said Jean.

'Mummy doesn't like it, so we never go.'

Maybe it was something to do with being Swiss and land-locked, Jean thought. Although there was surely no shortage of lakes.

She offered this theory to Margaret, who considered it judiciously and then said, 'No. She just doesn't like getting her hair wet.'

At first it seemed as though there was no one at home. The side gate – the usual point of entry – was bolted, but when they rang the doorbell and peered through the stained glass, there was Gretchen coming down the stairs towards them with a basket of ironing under one arm.

'You're all hot,' said Margaret, disengaging herself from her mother's welcoming hug.

'Sorry,' she replied a little breathlessly, fanning herself with the skirt of her pinafore. 'I've been busy.'

'Did you make the *spitzbuben*?'

Gretchen's face fell. 'Oh no. I didn't. I got caught up with other things.'

Margaret screwed her face into the most furious knot of displeasure.

'I'll make them this evening, when I've done the ironing,' her mother promised.

'But I wanted to give Jean one.'

'Poor Mummy,' said Jean, feeling that Margaret was being rather unreasonable. Spoilt even, though it pained her to think the word. 'She's been slaving away all afternoon while we've been out having tea at Simpson's.'

'Really – Simpson's? Margaret, you little monkey! You hardly need *spitzbuben* as well.'

Margaret looked suitably sheepish. She was a good-hearted girl really, thought Jean, and was easily corrected.

'And we called on Daddy at the shop. We helped him to sell a ruby necklace for twenty pounds!'

Gretchen glanced at Jean. 'Oh, did you? That's a nice idea. I bet he was surprised to see you.'

Jean hoped it was apparent that the nice idea had been all Margaret's, but it would have been making too much of it, she felt, to raise the matter. She couldn't linger anyway; there was her mother and the post-mortem of the strawberry tea to be faced, so she said goodbye to Margaret, who was eager to get outside and commune with Jemimah.

As soon as the two women were alone though, it was Gretchen who brought it up again.

'I'm so glad you went to see Howard,' she said. 'He likes you very much, you know, and it's so good for him to have a woman friend to talk to.'

She was so emphatic in her approval that Jean began to suspect her of meaning quite the reverse. It was funny, too, that Howard had described the benefits of Jean's influence on Gretchen in much the same terms. She remembered her mother's jealous remark: 'They seem to be making quite a project of you, for some reason.'

17

September 1957

Dear Jean,

*I wonder if you would be free to come on a little family
outing next Sunday to Howard's Aunt Edie near Maidstone.
We go every year to harvest her apples and cobnuts. She has
a wonderful garden for tennis and a picnic and it's always a
lovely day out.*

I do hope you can join us.

With good wishes,

Gretchen

The day after this letter arrived saw Jean once again paying
court to Mrs Melsom. She took with her a gift of runner beans
and tomatoes from their own vegetable patch, and some plums
and redcurrants, which Gretchen had foisted on her the week
before. Mrs Melsom was out in her front garden, kneeling on
a hassock filched from the church to weed the flower beds. At
Jean's approach and in spite of her protestations, she hauled
herself up to standing using the garden fork.

'I've a little favour to ask,' Jean said as soon as the offering of
fruit and vegetables had been accepted. 'I'm away for the day
next Sunday and wondered if you'd be able to just look in on

Mother at some point. She doesn't seem to take to anyone but you.' She almost blushed at her own shamelessness.

Mrs Melsom wiped soil-dusted hands on her skirt and leaned on the fork for a moment to recover her breath.

'Of course, dear. I was only saying to Mr Melsom that we should take her out for a drive in the Riley one day.'

'Well, that would be wonderful. She had such a lovely time at the strawberry tea.'

This was not too violent a distortion of the truth. Mrs Swinney had not been nearly as critical of the event as Jean had feared, declaring it, 'Bearable, I suppose.'

'Did she? I'm so glad. I wasn't sure. I thought it might have been a bit noisy for her, but she seemed to enjoy the strawberries.'

'Oh yes, there's nothing wrong with her appetite,' said Jean, wondering if Mrs Melsom was hinting at a degree of over-indulgence. Although keenly alert to her mother's faults, it still pained Jean to think others might notice and judge them.

It was left with Mrs Melsom to discuss with her husband the possibility of a drive out into the countryside on Sunday. Jean went home with her usual unsettling combination of a light heart and a heavy conscience, made heavier by her dawning awareness that the impetus behind these plans and schemes was, above all else, the thought of seeing Howard.

On the appointed morning, Jean's mother, having been briefed and coached into a positive frame of mind for most of the previous evening, woke after a poor night's sleep and seemed about to cry off the outing. It took all of Jean's patience and encouragement to cajole her into compliance, until at last she was dressed and brushed and painted and loaded into the Riley, as though into a tumbrel for her final journey.

When Jean arrived at the Tilburys', Howard was on the

driveway, pumping up one of the tyres on the Wolseley, while in the kitchen Gretchen packed a picnic basket with enough food for ten hungry men. Veal and ham pie, chicken, chopped-egg sandwiches, the infamous *spitzbuben*, split scones, Aunt Edie's favourite *zopf* bread – a Swiss plaited loaf that was one of Gretchen's specialities – and tomatoes and plums from the garden.

She was wearing one of her own creations – a cotton lawn sundress with a gathered skirt in a bold poppy print. Jean, who had inferred from the invitation that manual labour and tree climbing would be required, was dressed in twill trousers, a short-sleeved shirt and gym shoes.

'I feel a bit of a scruff,' she said. 'I thought I'd be shinning up tree trunks.'

'Oh, I always leave that to Howard and Margaret,' said Gretchen. 'But you look fine. Aunt Edie's very informal.'

Margaret wandered in, clutching two tennis rackets and looking whey-faced and queasy; quite unlike her ebullient self. She watched her mother's preparations for a minute or two without enthusiasm.

'I can't find any tennis balls and I've got tummy ache,' she said.

'The balls are in the cupboard under the stairs,' said Gretchen. 'I saw them there the other day. Are you all right?' she added, taking in her daughter's wan expression. 'You're very pale.'

Margaret responded to this enquiry by dropping the tennis rackets and bolting from the room with a hand over her mouth. The sound of pounding feet on the stairs was followed moments later by distant retching.

The two women exchanged looks of alarm and Gretchen hurried to investigate, leaving Jean standing in the kitchen feeling spare. The outing would surely not go ahead now, postponed for another day, requiring another favour from Mrs

Melsom, pushing Jean's level of indebtedness even further into the red.

Howard came in from the driveway holding out hands smudged with grease.

'All set,' he said. 'Tyres pumped. Oil and water topped up. Tool kit in the boot. How are things coming along in the catering division?'

'There's been a setback,' said Jean. 'I think Margaret's been sick. She said she was feeling poorly and then rushed upstairs.'

'She didn't eat her breakfast this morning,' said Howard. 'I thought that was odd. Poor old Maggie.'

Gretchen rejoined them, looking harassed. 'Well, she's not going anywhere,' she said.

'Poor thing,' said Jean, trying to master her own disappointment at the cancellation of the trip, in the face of Margaret's greater misfortune. 'Is she all right?'

'An upset tummy, I think. I've put her to bed. What a pity – it's such a lovely day, too.'

'I'd better run down to the call box and see if I can get hold of Aunt Edie,' said Howard. 'Postpone for another day.'

'Oh, you can't let her down at the last minute,' Gretchen protested. 'She'll have been to all sorts of trouble. And the apples have got to be picked. You two go – I'll stay here with Margaret.'

'But that's such a shame for you, Gretchen,' said Jean. 'Why don't I stay with Margaret?'

She felt she knew the little girl quite well enough by now to make this offer. Since the trip to Simpson's they had had two subsequent outings – once to the swimming baths at Beckenham, where Jean had shown a commendable willingness to get her hair wet, and once to the Swinneys' house, where they had made cinder toffee. Both events had passed off successfully and even Jean's mother, initially suspicious of any new acquaintances, had conceded that Margaret was a 'dear little thing'.

'Oh no. I wouldn't leave her when she's unwell. You two must go. The picnic's all made and Aunt Edie will be so disappointed if no one turns up.' She looked from Jean to Howard, beaming with pleasure at her sacrifice.

Jean felt a flutter of uncertainty. Was Gretchen really packing her off for a jaunt with her husband?

As if reading her thoughts, Gretchen said, 'You can put up with Howard for a day, can't you, Jean?'

'I'll try not to bore her to tears,' said Howard humbly.

'And Aunt Edie is tremendous company. You'll love her.'

'She won't think it odd – her nephew turning up with some strange woman?' Jean remarked.

'Oh no. She's a game old bird,' laughed Gretchen.

She continued to wrap packets of sandwiches in greaseproof paper and tuck them into the already full hamper as Howard washed his hands at the sink.

'We surely won't need all this food now?' said Jean, aghast. 'You must keep some of it for yourselves.'

'Well, Margaret certainly won't be eating anything,' said Gretchen, finally consenting to remove one slice of pie and a tomato from the banquet.

Having satisfied herself as to the sufficiency of the provisions, she fastened the buckles on the basket and began to scurry around collecting together the remaining equipment for the outing. Wooden crates for the apples, picnic blanket, tennis rackets and balls were all soon stowed in the boot of the Wolseley and they were ready to go. Gretchen seemed quite invigorated by her efforts on their behalf and almost eager to see them off. Either she was relieved to be ducking out of an irksome family duty, which seemed most unlikely given her apparent enthusiasm for the outing, or . . . Jean was at a loss.

Even now, as the car was reversing out of the driveway,

Gretchen came running after them, brandishing a wide-brimmed straw sun hat, which she passed through the front window to Jean.

'You'll need this or you'll burn,' she panted. 'It's going to be a scorcher.'

As they drove off, at Howard's usual sober pace, Jean could see Gretchen's diminishing figure in the wing mirror, waving goodbye and then turning back to the house, almost with a skip.

Even as an idle daydream, Jean had never dared to imagine an opportunity like this – to be alone with Howard for a whole day, with the complete and cheerful approval of Gretchen. She could hardly believe her good fortune.

It was warm and stuffy in the car, and Howard wound down his window, resting an elbow on the car door.

'Tell me if it's too breezy for you,' he said, glancing at her hair whipping in the wind.

A silence descended – the not entirely comfortable silence of two shy-ish people who feel bound by politeness to make conversation but can think of nothing brilliant to say.

They proceeded for some miles, lost in their own thoughts, until at last Jean said, 'I'm sorry, Howard. I'm very poor company. I'm no good at small talk.'

'That's all right,' he replied. 'Neither am I. We shall have to make do with big talk, or no talk at all.'

This seemed to break the spell of awkwardness and they exchanged a smile of relief before turning back to face the road ahead.

'Your wife is very unselfish,' Jean said. 'Most women would have been bitterly disappointed to miss a day out like this.'

'Yes. Gretchen's a very uncomplaining sort. And she'd do anything for Margaret, of course. She's what you call "a devoted mother".'

'Did you ever think of having more children?' Jean asked.

'You seem to be making such a good job of parenthood.'

If it was an impertinent question, Howard gave no sign of taking offence.

'At one time,' he replied. 'In the early days we thought it might be nice for Margaret to have a brother or sister. And I think Gretchen assumed I would want a child of my own, so to speak. That was never a concern for me – I feel Margaret is as much mine as any child could be.'

'Of course.'

'But it didn't happen. And somehow Gretchen wasn't surprised. I don't think she ever really believed she could have a child in the normal way.'

'She's still young enough,' said Jean. 'She's not even thirty.'

'But I'm not,' said Howard. 'And Margaret is too old now for a new baby to be much of a playmate.'

'I suppose so.'

'And in any case, it couldn't happen now,' Howard said. His voice was barely audible above the noise of the engine.

'Oh.' Jean remembered the single beds and the gap between them – close enough for hand-holding, but no more – and blushed.

'Gretchen and I haven't had that kind of relationship for some years now.'

'I'm sorry. I didn't mean to pry. You always look like a perfect couple to me.'

'Is there such a thing? I doubt it. But yes, we get along very well in our way.'

'Gretchen is absolutely devoted to you,' Jean insisted.

'Has she said so?'

'She doesn't need to – it's perfectly obvious.'

She realised as she said this that it wouldn't do. What could she really know of Gretchen's feelings, when she could hardly bear to interrogate her own?

'I don't doubt that she loves me – like a brother, or a favourite uncle.'

'Oh, more than that, surely!'

'Perhaps I'm exaggerating, but only a little. Not like a wife, anyway.'

'Some men might take that as a licence to stray.'

'No doubt. But it would be shabby behaviour, in my view.'

'In any case, who can know what other wives are like? Or husbands, for that matter. Your . . . arrangement may not be unusual.'

'You are very wise, Jean, but I sincerely hope you are wrong in this instance.'

'Why?'

'Having experienced a proper marriage – if you'll allow that there is such a thing – at the beginning, I can only say that it would be a great pity if many people had to settle for what is a pale imitation.'

'Some of us have to settle for far less than that,' Jean retorted with some warmth. She wasn't sure any more whether she was agreeing or disagreeing with him; it was as if he had taken a sledgehammer to a stained-glass window. 'Companionship and affection and family life – these things can't be easily discounted.' She was aware that her voice was shaking. It was both a relief and a kind of torture to speak frankly for once.

'You are quite right. I'm not blaming Gretchen, by the way. I blame myself. I often wonder if she'd have done better to wait until she met someone she could fully love. But I was there, on the spot, so to speak, when there was a certain amount of urgency to provide Margaret with a father and a respectable upbringing. Her mother certainly thought so.'

'You're not suggesting she was pressured into marriage against her will?' Jean protested. 'Nobody who has seen you together could possibly think so.'

'No, no, nothing as brutal as that. She accepted me gratefully, but now I think I did her a disservice in proposing when she was so vulnerable and her mother was dying. It was hardly a free choice.'

'You talk as if the good fortune was all yours. Because she is young and pretty. But she is lucky to have you, too. Kind, decent men are scarce.'

Of course he was better than just kind and decent, she thought – words that hardly stirred the soul. He was the best man she knew and Gretchen the luckiest woman. But this could not be said.

'Are they?'

'In my experience.'

She could call to mind only three – Roy Drake, Dorrie's husband, Kenneth, and Howard himself. Even her own father had fallen short in the end. To her dismay she found her eyes beginning to smart, and she turned away and stared out of the window at the green hedgerows until she had mastered herself. It wasn't sadness that prompted the threat of tears but a general sense of emotional fullness that always accompanied any attempt to discuss her inner life.

'I'm sorry to hear that, Jean,' Howard said. 'I'm sure you deserve much better.'

'I don't know about that. I probably got exactly what I deserved. I seem to be attracted to precisely the sort of man who isn't husband material. Not my husband, anyway.' She gave a hollow laugh.

'I hope I haven't upset you,' he said. 'I felt I could talk freely to you. I don't know why.'

'You can. I'm glad you did.'

'I suppose you give the impression that you don't judge people.'

Jean had never thought of herself in this light before;

sometimes, in fact, she caught herself out in some act of lofty disapproval and felt ashamed. Howard's confident assertion of her goodness made her the more determined to live up to it and be the broad-minded, tolerant person he thought her. I love him, she thought with a kind of wonderment. I never intended to, but now I do. The relief of admitting it to herself and accepting it as a fact that couldn't be dismissed or changed was like throwing off chains.

'Well, thank you. That's a nice thing to say,' she said, keeping her voice steady.

It seemed impossible that he wouldn't notice her transformation, but he just gave her a quick smile and kept his eyes on the road, as a sensible man would.

They had left the suburbs behind now and were driving through the Kent countryside of sunken lanes and hedgerows tangled with honeysuckle and brambles and teeming with butterflies. At Shoreham, a stream ran through the middle of the village. A gang of children was wading bare-legged in the water with jam jars and nets; they turned as one and stared after the car with tribal hostility as it passed over the bridge.

The house was on the edge of the village, in a large, unkempt garden consisting mostly of shaggy lawn, with fruit trees and beds of straggling wild flowers. Beyond the trees a rustic tennis court had been shaved into the grass.

Aunt Edie was reclining on a wooden sunlounger, swathed in shawls in spite of the heat, which by now was shimmering, intense. She was drinking cider from a bottle and reading a Dashiell Hammett. It was hard to see exactly what she looked like, as her face was so crowded; as well as a yellow sun visor, she was wearing a pair of modern cat's eye sunglasses over her regular spectacles and had a large sticking plaster across her nose. An elderly spaniel lay at her feet, stirring itself to aim a few dutiful yaps at the visitors before slumping back beside her.

'Hello, Auntie,' said Howard, bending to kiss her powdery cheek. 'This is Jean,' was the extent of his explanation for Jean's substitution for his wife and daughter, and all that Aunt Edie seemed to require.

'You'll be thirsty, I expect. Help yourself to cider – you know where it is,' she said, waving an arm towards the open back door.

While Howard went to fetch the drinks, Jean spread out the woollen blanket on the tussocky grass and sat, cross-legged, awaiting interrogation, but her hostess was serenely incurious. Jean was glad now of Gretchen's sun hat, as there was no shade where they sat and the trees were quite useless in this regard, with their lowest branches dipping almost to the ground. She was grateful, too, for the element of concealment, in case her recent upsurge of feeling was readable in her face.

'I like your get-up,' Aunt Edie said, laying aside her book and peering at Jean over both sets of glasses. 'Very practical. I've never worn a pair of trousers. Do you think it's too late to start?'

'Not at all,' said Jean. 'I think you'd look elegant in trousers.'

'Useful for cycling, I should think.'

'You're not still roaring around the village on your bicycle?' said Howard, catching the end of this exchange as he returned with two bottles of cider. 'I thought you were going to get rid of it after your accident.'

Aunt Edie's hand strayed to her bandaged nose. 'I admit, I was a bit shaken up. But I've decided I can't quite do without it. It's so useful for going to the library and so forth.'

'Aunt Edie was in a collision with a horse trough,' Howard explained. 'It was the trough's fault, apparently.'

She swatted him with Dashiell Hammett and he laughed.

'I wish my mother was as intrepid as you,' said Jean.

She took a long swig from her bottle and gasped as it tore at her throat. It was strong and fiery and like no cider she had ever tasted.

'My aunt is one of a kind, I'm afraid,' said Howard. 'Comparisons are futile.'

'Where are the gorgeous creatures today?' she asked, registering at last the change in personnel.

'Margaret was taken poorly this morning, so Gretchen has stayed behind to look after her. Both send their love.'

'I have some bits and pieces for them. Don't go home without reminding me. I've been having a clear-out.'

'Oh dear,' said Howard, who had evidently been the beneficiary of this largesse before.

'Well, it will all be yours to deal with one day,' said his aunt. 'I'm just trying to cull as much as I can now.'

'Oh, you'll outlive us all, surely.'

'I will not,' she replied tersely. 'If you think I'm going to become one of those ancient old crones with a whiskery chin you can think again. I've got a loaded pistol in my bedroom. I shan't tell you where in case you try and get it off me. But I'll be using it when the time comes.'

'You'll probably miss and shoot the paperboy or someone,' said Howard mildly.

Jean was finding this exchange quite stimulating. She couldn't imagine such a conversation arising at home. Her mother shrank from any mention of death with violent superstition, as if to breathe his name was to invite him in. She took another tentative sip from her bottle and shivered.

'Is this last year's cider?' Howard asked, noticing Jean's struggles. 'It's stronger than I remember.'

Aunt Edie took the bottle from him and rolled her eyes. 'You've picked up the apple brandy, you clown. You'll both be pie-eyed.'

Jean lay back on the blanket and began to giggle. She felt quite light-headed.

★

It took them two hours to strip the trees of all but the most unreachable apples, which were left for Aunt Edie to gather as they fell. She wasted nothing: the best unblemished fruit was wrapped in newspaper, packed in crates and kept in a cool stone shed for use over the winter. The second best would be given to friends, exchanged with neighbours for potatoes and beans, donated to the village school, made into pie filling and bottled or kept for imminent consumption. The windfalls and damaged apples were sent to the farm for pressing.

Tree climbing was a new and exhilarating experience for Jean. With no brothers or male cousins, she and Dorrie had never been introduced to rowdy outdoor games. They had spent their childhood in a second-floor flat in Gipsy Hill; by the time they moved to the house and garden in Hayes she was already an adult. Aunt Edie's trees were perfect for a beginner, with a framework of accessible branches radiating like spokes from the trunk to provide steps and handholds.

Jean scrambled up as high as possible, made bold by brandy, until the boughs were too slender to take her weight. From her perch she dropped apples down to Aunt Edie, who was much nimbler than her previous prostration on the lounger had seemed to promise, and adept at catching them in a shawl tied around her waist. Chester, the spaniel, quivered and panted at her side.

Howard, with a basket contraption on his back, tackled the clusters of fruit on the outermost branches using a stepladder and fishing net. The cobnuts, being altogether less fragile, were thrown, shaken or knocked into the long grass, and then gathered into piles with a leaf rake and shovelled into hessian sacks.

For Jean, anaesthetised by fierce sun and strong drink, the whole experience took on a misty, trance-like quality. When she finally climbed back down to earth she was surprised to notice her shirt torn and her bare arms striped with scratches. She had felt nothing.

Howard was astonished to learn that she had never eaten a cobnut, a deficiency he was determined to put right. While she unpacked the picnic, stepping uneasily into Gretchen's role, Howard disappeared indoors and returned with a dish of salt and some nutcrackers.

'A cobnut has many layers,' he said with great solemnity, 'and you have to unwrap them all to reach the prize. Observe.'

He stripped off the leafy outer case, cracked and discarded the shell, scratched off the woody skin and then finally rubbed away the inner membrane to reveal the kernel, naked and marble white. This he dipped in salt and presented to Jean on his open palm like a pearl on a cushion.

'So much effort for such a tiny morsel,' said Jean. 'Even worse than peeling a grape.'

'There are no shortcuts,' Howard insisted. 'You have to remove every layer or it tastes bitter.'

Jean crushed the polished, ribbed nut gently between her teeth, allowing the flavour – a combination of buttery sap and new wood – to fill her mouth.

'It is lovely,' she sighed. 'But you would tire of peeling them long before you tired of eating them.'

'It's self-limiting,' Howard agreed. 'You could hardly gorge on them. But that's part of the appeal.'

He continued dutifully preparing a little mound of these delicacies for Jean and Aunt Edie to share, taking none for himself.

'Gretchen has gone quite mad,' Aunt Edie protested as Jean plied her with veal and ham pie, chicken, *zopf* bread, sandwiches and tomatoes from the hamper. 'Does she think she is feeding the whole village?'

'This is only half of it,' Jean said. 'You need to leave room for the cake and biscuits.'

'I have a horror of waste,' said Aunt Edie with some asperity. 'I can't help it.'

'Well, Gretchen has a horror of want,' said Howard. 'Years of doing without take people in different ways, I suppose.'

Jean felt a fresh surge of love for Howard for having defended Gretchen so tactfully against a mean-spirited remark, even when she was not there to appreciate it. It was the essence of the man, she thought, and absolutely typical of her twisted bloody luck that the very quality she admired most in him – loyalty to his wife – was the one that put him forever out of her reach.

He lay beside her on the blanket, defending the hamper from incursions by Chester and stroking the spaniel's silky ears. There was something intimate about sharing this bed-sized space; he felt it too, she was certain. The heat had stolen their appetite and they could hardly do justice to the picnic. Out of respect for Margaret, Jean forced herself to try one of the *spitzbuben*, a pair of biscuits sandwiched with jam, which attracted a trio of persistent wasps. Having dispatched these pests with a rolled napkin, Howard removed the remains of the food to the cool of the pantry.

'I may fall asleep,' Aunt Edie said to Jean while he was out of earshot. 'But I expect you two will be able to entertain yourselves one way or another.'

Jean wondered if there was any undertone to this remark and looked up sharply, but the old woman's expression, as far as it could be read behind its scaffolding of spectacles, was neutral.

'It's a pity Gretchen and Margaret couldn't come,' she said firmly. 'They're such fun.'

Aunt Edie stared at her. 'Margaret is an angel, of course, but for all her charms one would hardly call Gretchen *fun*.'

She shut up smartly as Howard reappeared and closed her eyes. Jean thought she must be shamming, but within seconds a faint purring came from her parted lips.

'I see you've been keeping Auntie entertained,' said Howard, picking up one of her trailing shawls and draping it across the top of the sunlounger so that it shaded her face.

'She was finding me scintillating company right up to the point where she fell asleep,' Jean replied, fanning herself with Gretchen's hat. There was no breeze and the air was like molten metal.

'Let's find some shade,' Howard suggested, helping Jean to her feet. 'We could play tennis if it was a bit cooler, but I think it might kill me if you make me run around like you did on the badminton court.'

'I seem to remember I was the one doing the running.'

'The return match is very much overdue.'

They walked between the fruit trees to the far end of the garden, past the shorn rectangle of tennis court, marked out with white paint.

'Who laid this out?' Jean wondered aloud. 'Not Aunt Edie, surely?'

'She has an admirer in the village called Wally Noakes. He's about eighty but he does various manly jobs like pumping up her bicycle tyres and mowing the lawn now and then, in exchange for . . . I don't know what.'

'I do like her,' said Jean. 'She's very determined and spirited. She doesn't play the dotty old woman.'

'I'm glad you like her. She's the only blood relative I've got.'

'What will happen when she's too old to manage by herself? Will you have her to live with you?'

'I don't know. I suppose that would be up to Gretchen.'

Howard had clearly never considered the matter. Care of the elderly was a woman's business, thought Jean, and not something men allowed to clutter their minds.

'Perhaps she'll get some kind of nurse to live in. Or maybe she really does have a pistol hidden among her corsets.'

Beyond the tennis court at the furthest boundary of the garden was a stone bench, freckled with lichen, beneath a wooden arbour. An elderly wisteria gripped one of the weathered uprights in its coils and formed a canopy of leafy fronds, offering a pool of shade. Howard produced a clean handkerchief from his pocket and seemed about to lay it out on the bench for Jean's benefit, but she shook her head; her trousers were already scuffed with grass and bark, her shirt torn and grubby.

The bench was narrow; even when they sat at opposite ends the gap between them was barely a hand's span. Less, Jean thought, than the gap between two single beds. Howard offered her one of his cigarettes, lit with a match rasped along the rough stone, and they smoked in silence for a few moments.

Jean felt something dangerously close to happiness stealing over her; a realisation that there was nowhere else she would rather be, and nothing she wanted that she didn't already have. But the moment of perfect contentment was no sooner acknowledged than it began to recede; already she was outside the moment, chasing it into the past. The silence continued, well beyond the point where it was comfortable.

'Gretchen and I were discussing you the other night,' Howard said at last.

'Oh, really?' said Jean, blinking at him through the smoke.

'We agreed that you were a good thing.'

She laughed. 'Why thank you. I'm not sure about being a thing, but I'm glad I'm a good one.'

'You've stirred us out of our routine.'

'I have? I thought it was the other way about.'

'Surely not. Your job must be infinitely various.'

'No – it's remarkably repetitive. The same pages to be filled each week. It wasn't really interesting at all, until Gretchen.'

'Well anyway. Our paths crossed and we're the better for it.'

'Yes.'

For a minute Jean allowed herself to contemplate an alternative reality in which they had never met and her life consisted of no more than the *Echo*, Mother, house, garden for all eternity. Considering the thousands of insignificant chances and choices and paths not taken that had led to their meeting, it was nothing less than a miracle.

'It's been a lovely day,' she said, inadequately.

'It's not over yet. There's a game of tennis to be played first.'

Jean had cooled down somewhat and was in any case happy to fall in with anything Howard suggested.

'I suppose you're going to pretend you haven't played since schooldays,' he said as they warmed up with a few gentle groundstrokes.

'It's quite true,' Jean replied as the ball glanced off the edge of her racket and away into the long grass. 'But what I lack in practice I make up for in competitiveness.'

'You would never tactically lose out of politeness?' he enquired, lobbing another ball gently into her half.

'Never,' she replied. 'I wouldn't think it polite to hand someone a victory they didn't deserve.'

'Even a child, like Margaret, who might need the encouragement of a victory?'

'Children are a special case. But I'd rather teach her well so that she'd soon be good enough to win fair and square.'

'Well then, let's play and give each other no quarter.'

Howard won two sets easily without needing to exert himself. Jean only hit her stride in the second set, managing to get a few first serves in and hit an occasional winner, but by that time she was too hot and breathless to play on. When she looked at her watch she was surprised to see that it was nearly five. The hours in Howard's company had sped past. It would be six before they reached home even if they left now. She felt duty tugging at her with its remorseless grasp.

Seeing her glance at her watch, Howard said, 'This might be a good time to make a move. If we get caught up with tea we could be hours.'

'Yes,' Jean agreed, both grateful and despondent. 'There's Margaret to think of.'

'And your mother.'

Jean nodded. 'I won't forget today.'

This was no idle remark. In the days ahead she would think of little else, replaying their conversation and luxuriating in every remembered detail of their surroundings.

'We must hope there will be others,' said Howard.

'Yes, why not?' said Jean, knowing exactly why not.

The absence of Gretchen, so unexpected and fortuitous, could hardly be depended on in the future, but this was not something that could be said, or even thought, by anyone with a conscience.

They rejoined Aunt Edie, who had been woken by the arrival of Mr Noakes bringing a basket of eggs and a jar of honey, in return for which he received a box of the second-best apples. He had brought a folding canvas fishing stool with him, perhaps accustomed to being offered no seat, and was now perched beside the sunlounger, displacing Chester, who had been bribed with a mutton bone. They were holding hands and leaning towards each other but jerked apart as Jean and Howard approached. Aunt Edie seemed quite flustered in his presence, her previous languor deserting her.

'This is Mr Noakes, who I might have mentioned,' she said. 'He looked after me when I came off my bicycle.'

'I'm very pleased to think you are keeping an eye on her,' said Howard.

'It's a privilege,' said Mr Noakes, looking at Aunt Edie with misty devotion. 'I would do more if she'd let me, but she's very independent.'

'He's been very good to me,' she replied. 'I don't know what I'd do without him.' She squeezed his hand and this time she didn't let go.

'It comes to something when your 83-year-old aunt makes you feel you're playing gooseberry,' said Howard when they were on their way.

Alongside the remains of the hamper, four crates of apples and a sack of cobnuts were stacked in the boot. On the back seat were the promised spoils of Aunt Edie's clear-out – a musquash cape, a satin evening dress and three pairs of shoes last fashionable in 1920 for Gretchen; a jewellery box of tangled chains, broken strings of pearls and coral bracelets for Margaret. To Jean she had given an emerald pin brooch missing one of its stones.

'I'd always assumed she found him a nuisance, but apparently not.'

'They certainly seem delighted with each other,' Jean agreed.

'I've never seen her so flirtatious,' said Howard. 'It made me feel quite uncomfortable. I don't know why.'

'Perhaps you feel they are too old for that sort of thing.'

'Maybe. It seems a bit undignified. But romance shouldn't be the preserve of young people, should it?'

'No, certainly not.' Jean felt the injustice of any prejudice that might one day apply to her and was determined to smite it. 'I'm sure inside they feel the same emotions as an eighteen-year-old. The yearning for approval and love doesn't change. The ageing body is just cladding.'

'You put it so nicely,' said Howard. 'And imagine if dignity was all we had to look forward to in old age!'

They drove in silence for a while through the sunken lanes with exposed tree roots and overarching branches – great cathedrals of beech and oak with their vaulted roofs of sunlit green.

'If you leave me that brooch I'll mend it for you,' Howard said finally. 'It needs a new stone.'

'You don't need to go to any trouble,' said Jean. 'It's fine.'

'It's no trouble,' he replied, shaking his head. 'I'm a jeweller. Anyway, I'd like to. It's one thing I can do for you.'

'In that case, thank you.'

'Aunt Edie's gifts are kindly meant but often more trouble than they're worth. I dread to think what Gretchen will have to say about that fur. And the shoes.'

'The silk dress will probably be all right. She'll be able to turn it into something fabulous.'

'She will be too busy making strudels.'

'Likewise.' They had insisted she take one of the crates of apples, enough to last all winter. 'Although the English equivalent in my case. Turnovers, perhaps.'

There were still hours of daylight left and yet there was a melancholy sense of approaching dusk and the fading of a perfect day, which brought tears to Jean's eyes. Tomorrow she would be back at her desk, writing Pam's Piece and Household Hints and the Garden Week by Week. There was no possibility that circumstances would align themselves in just this way again to allow her another similar outing with Howard. It would survive only in memory; to be taken out and turned over now and then, like one of the treasures from her dressing-table drawer.

They had reached Shoreham now; even after so many hours the children were still playing in the stream. One of the girls – no more than eight or nine herself – was carrying a huge baby on her hip, staggering under the weight of him. They looked just the sort of scruffy, neglected children Jean would have been forbidden to play with or even approach when she was young, and even now they exerted a powerful fascination. She took a deep breath, which emerged as a sigh, and Howard glanced at her.

'Are you all right, Jean?' he asked. 'Have I said something to upset you?'

'Oh no, of course not. I was just giving in to introspection.' She forced her face into a smile, but it was effortful and rigid and would have fooled no one, least of all Howard.

After a moment or two he said, 'My wife has a theory. Everyone has a secret sorrow.'

'Really?' She managed a laugh that sounded more like a sob. 'What's yours?'

'I've already told you mine.'

'Oh. I see. Then what is Gretchen's?'

She recalled now that occasion in their garden – her stricken face when she believed herself to be unobserved.

'I don't know. Perhaps the counterpoint of mine. But it's you I am interested in. You never told me yours.'

'I have had it drummed into me not to dwell on my disappointments.'

'Who is this stern drummer?'

'My mother, I suppose.'

'Does she live by this creed herself?'

'She certainly never talks about things in that way. But you could hardly call it a success.' She gave a brief, bitter laugh.

'Well then?'

'You might think badly of me.'

'Jean, I don't think there's anything you could tell me that would alter my opinion of you.'

'You're the first person I've ever told,' she said, blushing from both the warmth of his compliment and the enormity of what she was about to do. It violated every code that she had been brought up to live by, but the urge to tell him was unstoppable. Decorum, secrecy, self-control were all blown away by the force of this need to confide. 'It's a funny coincidence really, but around the same time Gretchen discovered she was expecting

Margaret, I found out I was pregnant, too. Only in my case it was more of a disaster than a miracle.'

Howard said nothing, his eyes on the road.

'So I did that terrible thing that unmarried women do when they can't keep the baby.'

'Did you do it yourself or go to an abortionist?' There was no disapproval in his voice, only curiosity and sympathy.

'I went to this woman in Stockwell. She made me lie on an old door resting on a couple of trestles. It had blankets over it but I could tell it was a door because it still had a handle – digging into my side.'

Even at a distance of over a decade she could still remember every detail about that day. The street was called Southville, in a part of London that was unfamiliar to her and that she had never since visited.

He had drawn her a map with a casual efficiency that suggested previous experience. Union Grove, Paradise Road; even the street names had mocked her. The left-hand side of the road was a bomb site – a pair of surviving shops stood out from the rubble like old teeth; carboys from an old factory spilled out onto the pavement.

'You're lucky to be alive,' said Howard.

'I remember there was a dead fly on the mantelpiece – it seemed like a terrible omen. But the woman was so matter-of-fact about everything. She said, "I've done this many times and it'll soon be over and you can get on with your life. I've never lost a girl yet."

'I was so naïve; I thought she'd just flush it out and it would all be gone, but it wasn't like that. I had to go back home to my mother and pretend nothing had happened, and then in the middle of the night the cramps started.'

She had crept to the lavatory, carrying the towel she used to protect the bed sheets. As she lowered herself onto the seat there was a sensation of something bursting and a torrent of blood, and clots like raw liver hit the sides of the bowl.

'Oh, Jean. What an awful experience.'

'My mother found me on the floor. She was very good – she must have called the doctor. He'd been quite kind to her after my father died, but he wasn't kind to me.' *I know what you're about, young lady. If it wasn't for your mother, I'd see you prosecuted – you and the person who did this to you.* Even in her state of near delirium Jean had felt the burning shame of his judgement and the injustice that she had to bear it alone. 'He seemed to take great pleasure in telling me that I'd probably never be able to have another child.'

Howard shook his head and his hands clenched the steering wheel, but he didn't interrupt.

'We moved not long after that, so that was the last I saw of him, thankfully.'

'Had you ever considered keeping the baby? The father wasn't willing to . . . take responsibility?'

'No. He wasn't really . . . available, as it turned out.'

'Married already?'

'Oh yes. Anyone but me would have worked that out straight away. He had a wife and children. I wasn't even his only girlfriend.'

They had used to meet in the White Swan in Crystal Palace, not far from the Swinneys' flat in Gipsy Hill. If Frank was early, which he seldom was, he would wait inside enjoying a pint until she arrived. More usually he was late and Jean, who was not comfortable sitting alone in a pub, would stand outside, checking her watch and fretting. Sometimes, more often than she liked to acknowledge, he failed to turn up at all.

'He did pay for the abortion, though.'

'Is that the best you can say for him?'

'Pretty much.'

He had finally turned up at the pub after an absence of three weeks, when she had almost given up. 'Hello, lovely lady,' he said and, registering a certain brittleness in her response, 'You're annoyed with me, aren't you?'

'I was worried when you didn't show up. Twice.'

'Silly girl.'

He had kissed her fiercely – it was the sort of kiss designed to stop a woman from talking and there was no passion in it. They'd left the glow of the pub and crossed into the park, past the stone scars of the old Crystal Palace.

'What did you want to go worrying for?'

'Because I'm pregnant.'

She had watched the words land on him like a woman's blows – a nuisance but doing no real damage.

'How can it have happened?'

'It must have been at Worthing, when the thing came off inside me.'

That trip to the coast had been the high point of their relationship, really, never to be repeated.

They came to a bench, still damp from earlier rain. He spread out his newspaper for her to sit on, accepting the wet seat as his due. With the small change of decent behaviour he had always been generous.

'How did you meet?' Howard asked.

'He came to the door one day selling insurance. I mean, I assume he *was* an insurance salesman. It's hardly something you would invent to impress. I can't even use the excuse that I was young and innocent. I was twenty-nine. I really ought to have known better.'

'It must have left you with a very low opinion of men,' said Howard.

'Oh, I don't know about *men*. It took me a couple of years even to revise my opinion of Frank – I was so infatuated. I only knew I'd finally recovered when I saw him from a bus window on Piccadilly and didn't feel a thing. There was a time when I'd have jumped off a moving bus to chase after someone who merely looked like him. You see, Howard, I wasn't always the sensible woman you see today.'

'I'm only sorry you had to live through it all to become her.'

She gave him a grateful glance. Never before had she considered that all these experiences that had nearly demolished her had built her into something better.

'Thank you for listening. I'm sorry for going on.'

They were crossing the common now and nearly home. Jean felt a weightlessness; the deep relief of the confessional.

'You didn't *go on*. I'm glad you could tell me.'

'My only regret is the baby. She'd be ten now.' Jean blushed. 'I don't know why I say "she".'

The reflective silence that followed this remark lasted the few minutes that remained of the journey.

18

....

Pam's Piece

With orchards and gardens bursting with delicious Kentish apples, now is the time to fetch out those favourite recipes. Spiced Apple Cake is simple to make and a nice change from a pie. It works well served warm with custard, or cold with a cup of tea in place of a traditional fruit cake.

3 apples, peeled, cored and sliced
2 tsp golden syrup
1 tbsp butter
1 tsp ground cinnamon

Sponge mix:
4 oz butter
2 tbsp golden syrup
4 oz caster sugar
2 eggs
4 oz self-raising flour
1 tbsp milk

Simmer the apples with the syrup, butter and cinnamon for a few minutes until tender but not mushy. To prepare the topping, soften the butter and golden syrup in a bowl over a basin of hot water. Remove from the heat and beat in the sugar and eggs. Fold in the flour, adding milk to give the consistency of lightly whipped cream. Place the apple chunks in a greased tin or ovenproof dish and pour over the topping. Bake at Gas Mark 4 for 25 to 30 minutes until the sponge is golden brown and springy to touch.

....

Jean pulled the sheet of paper from her typewriter and added it to the pile. She now had enough apple recipes to make a page and could personally vouch for every one, having tested them all in her own kitchen over the previous weeknights. On the corner of her desk sat an open cake tin displaying the unclaimed remnant of a batch of turnovers. Even the greediest of her colleagues, the beneficiaries of all this experimentation, could no longer be tempted and passed her desk with averted eyes.

The phone rang. Locating it under a drift of foolscap, Jean heard the clipped voice of the telephonist announcing, 'Mr Tilbury for you.' It was not unknown for him to call her at work – at Gretchen's suggestion this was sometimes the way arrangements were made or confirmed – but it was the first time they had spoken since their visit to Aunt Edie's nearly over a week ago now.

Remembering the intimate and confessional tone of their last conversation, Jean was suddenly shy and full of regret. Until now she had never told anyone about the abortion. Her mother knew, of course she did, but had chosen not to know and it was never spoken of, not in the hospital, or later when Jean came home to convalesce, or ever since.

Dorrie, who had left for Kitale two months earlier, was no longer available for sisterly confidences and it was hardly the sort of news for a letter. And now, having kept her own counsel for over a decade, she had settled on the one person in the world she wanted to impress. The heat and the apple brandy must have fogged her judgement.

There was no time to subdue the fluttering of panic; the switchboard operator had already connected him.

'Hello, Jean, I hope I'm not disturbing you,' came his familiar diffident voice.

'Not at all,' she replied. 'I am typing up apple recipes and very ready to be distracted.'

'Apples?' he said. 'Whatever gave you that idea?'

'I have to take my inspiration where I find it.'

'Well, speaking of the spoils of that afternoon, I have fixed that brooch of Aunt Edie's and wondered if I could drop it off on my way home.'

'Do you mean here?' She remembered that Thursday was his half-day at the shop.

'Yes, I meant the office – if that's convenient?'

'That would be fine. It's very good of you.'

'My pleasure. I'll be there in about an hour.'

She hung up and fanned herself with her notebook, relieved that she had handled the conversation without betraying any inappropriate pleasure at the prospect of seeing him.

For the last few nights she had been troubled by insomnia. The dark thoughts that woke her at 3 a.m. and chased away all hope of sleep until just before dawn issued from a strange form of guilt. Not the conventional kind, for past wrongs regretted, but anticipatory guilt, for things that might yet be done.

Since Howard had told her that he and Gretchen no longer had a sexual relationship, Jean had allowed herself to imagine what it would be like to make love to him herself. Or rather, to be made love to, since even in her fantasies she was always the pursued, not the pursuer. She was able to square this with her conscience by reasoning that a) the mind cannot be policed – thoughts will roam where they will; b) she had no intention of revealing or acting on her feelings; c) there was no betrayal of Gretchen involved in these fantasies, since she had apparently renounced any sexual interest in Howard.

At ten to two, Jean went to the ladies to check her appearance in the small mirror tile above the washbasins. She combed her hair and re-powdered her pink cheeks and nose. She wore no other make-up – previous experiments with cosmetics had always made her look painted and clownish, and they were now consigned to her drawer of treasures, to be admired as artefacts but never deployed. In her general appearance, however, she felt more confident than usual, as she was wearing Gretchen's dress, which always prompted compliments.

She was drying her hands on the broken roller towel when the door opened and one of the secretaries came in, red-eyed and wretched-looking, and plunged into a cubicle, slamming the door. Jean recognised her as the pretty one who was often tangled up with the lad from the print room.

In the weeks and months after Frank's desertion Jean herself had cried in that very room and would have been grateful for a kind word from a motherly female colleague. Even so, she could not bring herself to be that woman and ask the weeping girl what was wrong, but slipped out of the washroom, leaving her to her private misery.

On the forecourt, a reason for the girl's distress became apparent. The lad from the print room was in huddled conference with the newest recruit among the secretaries. She had her back to the wall and he was standing over her, whispering in her ear and brushing strands of hair away from her face in a gesture of ownership.

Jean glared at them as she passed and then felt ashamed. We are all fools, she thought.

Howard was waiting just outside the gates, standing by his parked car. Jean was aware that any self-consciousness on her part could very well set the tone for all future encounters. It was vital to behave normally, whatever that meant. Howard himself showed no signs of awkwardness.

'Sorry to have dragged you away from your desk,' he said, producing a green velvet pouch from his inside pocket and handing it to her. 'It just seemed easier to come here.'

Jean loosened the cords and tipped the slender gold pin into her palm.

'You'll notice I've done something a bit devious,' he said, turning it over so that she could see the design. He had a craftsman's pride and interest in the details of his creation, which she found touching. 'It used to have two emeralds either side of an opal, but one of the emeralds was missing, so I switched it around, so you've now got two opals around a single emerald. It's easier to replace an opal.'

'It's lovely, Howard. You would never know it had been repaired. You must let me pay for the stone – and your time.'

'Out of the question. I'm only making good an otherwise quite useless gift from my aunt.'

'I'll always think of her when I wear it,' Jean said.

She pinned it to her dress, meeting some resistance from her bra and petticoat before the job was done.

'Is that the frock Gretchen made?' Howard asked.

'Yes. It's by far my favourite – she made it so beautifully.'

'It suits you very well.'

'People always admire it.'

Jean noticed the way he had managed to praise her appearance while at the same time acknowledging Gretchen, to demonstrate that there was nothing furtive in his compliment.

They were still standing, somewhat provisionally, on the pavement, now and then having to stand aside for other pedestrians and in full view of the large upper windows of the editorial offices. Out of the corner of her eye Jean could see Muriel from Accounts gazing down at her with undisguised curiosity.

'I'm keeping you from your lunch,' said Howard, following the direction of her upward glances.

'Not really,' said Jean.

She had now missed the trolley, which delivered sandwiches and cake and tea to the offices, and would have to go to the bakery in the high street instead. Their conversation, so natural and open at Aunt Edie's, now felt stilted and evasive. It was no mystery: by confiding in each other they had set up a false intimacy, which excluded Gretchen and placed them in a perilous position of near conspiracy, from which she could sense Howard retreating. His reference to Gretchen was his way of signalling his rededicated loyalty.

'Howard,' said Jean quietly. 'All those things I told you about myself. I didn't expect you to keep anything secret from Gretchen. You mustn't think . . .'

He put his hand on her arm and shook his head so urgently that she stopped.

'Don't,' he said. 'We don't need to say anything. We understand each other perfectly as it is. There's nothing to be said. Or done.'

For a moment their gaze held and Jean could read in his unhappy expression all that he was feeling and at the same time the impossibility that he could ever act on it, or even speak of it. But it was enough.

'Nothing,' she promised, her heart singing as she watched him get in his car and drive off, home to his wife.

19

Dear Miss Swinney,

I am taking the unusual step of writing to you regarding the ongoing tests on Mother and Daughter. They failed to attend the scheduled appointment for the serum protein electrophoresis test and Mother has not responded to my follow-up letter of enquiry.

I wonder if you could use your influence to iron out whatever seems to be the problem and reassure her that this procedure is very simple (for the patient at least; the analysis is rather more complex, but that is our business), requiring no more than a blood sample. All of us involved in this experiment are very excited by the findings so far and keen to press on as far as the science will take us.

If hardship is an issue, we may be able to assist with travel costs. Perhaps that is also something your newspaper might consider.

I await your early response.

   Yours,

      Dr Stewart Bamber

They met as before under the clock in the ticket hall at Charing Cross. Jean noticed with dismay that since their last meeting Gretchen had a new short haircut, which suited her but made her look a lot less like Margaret. For the purpose of a striking portrait of mother and daughter to accompany her story, dissimilarity was not ideal.

It took her a moment or two to subdue an attack of wholly unreasonable indignation that she had not been consulted. Howard had so thoroughly displaced Gretchen in Jean's consciousness lately that she was almost surprised to be confronted with the origin and purpose of their meetings.

Since receiving Dr Bamber's puzzling letter, it had taken her an inordinate amount of time to bring matters to this point. Previously, appointments had been arranged by calling Howard at the shop; this time Jean preferred not to use him as an intermediary unless absolutely necessary. In any case, it was Gretchen she needed to talk to in order to discover what lay behind this fresh resistance to further tests. The only solution seemed to be to call on Gretchen uninvited and hope to find her at home.

Accordingly, at eleven o'clock on a Monday morning, an hour when Jean judged Margaret and Howard would be out and Gretchen most likely working at her dressmaking, she left the newspaper office and caught the bus from Petts Wood to Sidcup. It was late September; the trees still wore their summer colours and the fogs of autumn were only a distant threat, but the air was cool and damp. The Tilburys' elderly neighbour was polishing the tiles of her doorstep with red wax; she sat up and nodded at Jean as she opened the gate.

'Mothers' meeting?' she enquired, which struck Jean as an odd and rather rude comment, so she said, 'Hardly,' and gave a thin smile in reply.

The side gate was locked, so Jean pressed the doorbell for just longer than was polite and waited, rehearsing various phrases of friendly concern, which turned to frustration as it became apparent that they would not be needed. Never without a notebook and pen, Jean wrote a brief message and posted it through the letterbox:

> Dear Gretchen,
>   I called to see you this morning for a chat, but no luck. I will try again tomorrow at the same time. I hope there is nothing amiss.
>   Jean

She was at the end of Burdett Road, walking briskly to burn off her irritation at a wasted journey, when she heard her name. Turning, she saw Gretchen hurrying towards her, pulling a cardigan over her dress. Even now she looks lovely, Jean thought. You could call on her uninvited on a Monday morning and still not catch her with nails unpainted and hair unbrushed.

'I'm sorry,' Gretchen panted as she came within range. 'I was in the bathroom and I came down to find your note.' She was holding the crumpled page in her fist. 'Is anything the matter?'

'Not with me. I was going to ask you the same thing,' said Jean. 'You missed your appointment with Dr Bamber; he wrote me a rather peevish letter when you didn't reply to him.'

Gretchen shook her head impatiently. 'Well, I couldn't make that date. Margaret was still a bit off colour from that sickness. I thought I'd told Howard to phone and cancel it, but perhaps I didn't. Anyway, I don't understand why they couldn't use the blood from the first tests.'

'Well, I gather this electro . . . whatever it's called . . . is quite elaborate to run. You have to fast overnight and the blood needs to be analysed within a day of sampling. I don't understand the exact process, but . . .' She tailed off. This is what you signed up for, she wanted to add. You approached us, not the other way around. Instead, she shrugged. 'I was worried that something

188

might have happened to change your mind about the whole business.'

'No, no, nothing's *happened*. I'm just tired of being poked and prodded and not believed. It's all taking so long.'

Jean felt a rising impatience. She bit down on a number of sharp retorts. There was nothing to be gained by growing irritable and everything to be lost. She needed Gretchen's co-operation far more than Gretchen needed her.

'Look, I know this is difficult for you,' she said, mastering the temptation to expound upon her own frustrations. 'If there is any way I can make things easier for you, please tell me. You know I believe in you, Gretchen. And for what it's worth I think Dr Bamber does, too. But science has no business with beliefs. There are only two more stages left now – this serum test and a skin graft. And then it's done.'

'All right. I'm sorry. I didn't mean to be an awkward patient. I'm grateful for all the trouble you've gone to.'

'There's no need for gratitude,' Jean replied crisply. 'We're all on the same side.'

Low, rolling clouds were gathering and a few fat drops of rain hit the pavement between them. Jean wondered if Gretchen would invite her back to the house so that they could conclude their discussion inside, but she showed no sign of it.

'Phone Howard and tell him when the next appointment is and we'll be there,' she promised, lifting the back of her cardigan up over her head to protect her hair.

'I can tell you now,' said Jean, bridling at the high-handed way Gretchen treated Howard as her secretary. 'This Friday morning. I'll meet you at Charing Cross at nine. Don't eat or drink anything except water overnight.'

The matter settled, they parted, the rain coming down in earnest now. Gretchen ran back up the road with her arms over her head, while Jean trudged to the bus stop with a vague sense of dissatisfaction that had almost nothing to do with her having set off that morning without an umbrella.

Now, as they embraced in the ticket hall and made their way out onto the Strand with Margaret between them, the irritable mood of their previous meeting seemed to have been forgotten. By way of experiment, Jean was wearing the emerald and opal brooch pinned perhaps incongruously to the lapel of her shabby mackintosh. She was curious to know whether or not Howard had made a secret of this gift of jewellery; its symbolic value seemed to depend on this factor. However, as soon as the two women had greeted each other, Gretchen had peered at it and said, 'Is that Edie's old brooch? Howard's done a jolly good job. It looks as good as new now.'

'Yes,' said Jean, both disappointed and relieved. If the gift's romantic significance was somewhat diminished, Howard's integrity at least was not. 'It was so kind of her – and him.'

'Aunt Edie's an absolute menace with her so-called presents,' Gretchen retorted. 'They're always broken or incomplete, so you end up spending money you can't spare on something you never wanted in the first place. I sent those awful old shoes straight to the jumble.'

'What about the fur coat?'

'I'm keeping that,' Gretchen conceded. 'It smells of camphor but you never know.'

This time when they reached the annexe in Agar Street the receptionist had evidently been briefed to look out for them, as they had hardly crossed the threshold when Dr Bamber himself appeared and swept them away to his office. A coal fire was burning in the grate and his desk was covered with open books and papers. It was more like the study of a busy academic than a medical practitioner.

'It's very good of you to come all this way again,' he said

smoothly, stirring the coals and sending an avalanche of ash through the grate. He aimed his smile at mother and daughter. 'How are you?'

'Hungry,' whispered Margaret, who had been introduced only that morning to the concept of a fast and was not impressed.

'Then let's not waste any time – as soon as we have taken the bloods there will be tea and toast.'

A spark flew out of the fire and landed, smouldering, on the hearthrug. Dr Bamber stamped on it with his shiny brogues.

'I'm sorry we missed our appointment,' said Gretchen, tugging off her white gloves one finger at a time and tucking them into her handbag. 'I hope it didn't put you out.'

Dr Bamber batted her apology away. Jean was aware of a subtle shift in the balance of power in Gretchen's favour. At their first encounter the men of science had treated her with a certain polite loftiness, the presumption being that she was at best a curiosity and at worst a charlatan. Gretchen had been diffident and grateful for their expertise. With the evidence of each successive test, however, their interest and her status had grown. Now, apparently on the brink of being proved a phenomenon to rival a unicorn or a mermaid, she seemed to have developed a queenly indifference to the whole process. It was most odd.

'Perhaps you could explain to Mrs Tilbury how this test works. I'm concerned that she's being treated rather like a laboratory rat.'

'Oh, surely not,' Dr Bamber protested.

'I didn't put it quite like that,' Gretchen said, smoothing his ruffled feathers. 'I only felt I was being kept somewhat in the dark.'

'Then we must provide illumination.' He picked up his fountain pen and began to fiddle with the cap. 'There's nothing I like more than talking about my field, but most patients find the detail rather dull.'

'Maybe Mrs Tilbury should be considered more of a volunteer than a patient. Since she's not unwell.' Jean's distrust of doctors, even the helpful ones, was never far from the surface.

'Of course. What we are doing is a serum protein electrophoresis test. Serum is the liquid left behind when the red and white blood cells have been removed from the blood. It contains proteins – albumin and various globulins, alpha, beta, gamma. These carry different electrical charges and they will move in fluid to display a distinctive pattern. We usually use this test to diagnose disease, but in this case we are only interested in *comparing* the two patterns – yours and Margaret's – for any variation.' He beamed. 'So all we need is a small sample of blood from you both and we can get to work.'

'I see,' said Gretchen serenely. 'Thank you.'

Margaret's brow had been furrowed with concentration while this explanation lasted. Jean couldn't help wondering if the angel voices, keen curators of esoteric vocabulary, were filing *globulin* and *electrophoresis* away for another day.

There was a tap on the door and, as if she had been awaiting some secret signal, a nurse appeared to take mother and daughter to the phlebotomy department.

As soon as Gretchen and Margaret returned from the lab, Dr Bamber's secretary appeared with the promised refreshments. With only three chairs and two slices of toast between four people, there was no chance of a convivial tea party developing. As non-fasters, Jean and Doctor Bamber abstained from toast, and he drank his tea standing up, looming over the three visitors, rocking back and forth on his heels in his awkwardness.

Gretchen, in any case, was not disposed to linger. She drank her tea quickly, gave half her uneaten slice of toast to Margaret and started to button her jacket as a sign of readiness to depart. Outside on the pavement, she turned to Jean with the unmistakable hesitancy of someone about to ask a favour.

'I wonder. Tell me if you think it is a bit of a cheek.'

'What?' said Jean.

Gretchen looked at her watch. 'I've got a few errands to run while I'm up in town. It seems a bit of a waste not to do them while I'm here, but Margaret really needs to get back to school.'

'No, I don't,' said Margaret. 'It's English comprehension and I'm already the best at that anyway.'

'You can't keep having days off.'

'You'd like me to take Margaret back to school?' said Jean, recognising from her own dealings with Mrs Melsom that there was a tendency for the petitioner in these situations to rely on inference. 'It would be a pleasure.'

The work was piling up on her desk; pieces unfinished, pages unfilled, deadlines advancing . . . But never mind. She would take it home with her and catch up when her mother was in bed.

'Oh, *would* you? That would be so helpful.' She took a pen and a notebook from her handbag and began to scribble directions. 'It's only five minutes from the station.'

'I know where it is,' said Margaret with dignity. 'I bet I could get there by myself from here.'

'Yes, I'm sure you could. But there are some peculiar people about.'

'I bet you are just going to sneak off and have lunch with Daddy without me,' Margaret said, and from Gretchen's blushing denial it almost seemed to Jean that she might be.

'I'm not. I promise.'

Having satisfied herself that Margaret's satchel contained her packed lunch and an explanatory note for her teacher, Gretchen set off along the Strand at a brisk trot, her new short haircut swinging.

Never throw away an old plastic mackintosh.
The hood cut off will make a useful toilet bag.
The large back panel may be used to line a
suitcase to ensure safety from damp should
the case get wet when travelling.

20

In late October Jean booked a week's leave to take her mother away to the coast. In previous years they had been in the habit of going up to Harrogate to stay with Jean's aunt and uncle for a week. They were the last link with her father's side of the family and even after all these years her uncle still seemed moved to try and compensate for his brother's desertion. He would give Jean the use of his car for day trips and never allowed them to pay for anything while they were his guests.

However, his health had been declining in recent years, a combination of emphysema and blocked arteries leaving him with poor breathing and mobility. Jean's aunt had made it clear that they could no longer play host, but he continued to send twenty pounds for Christmas and birthdays. These generous gifts represented Jean's mother's only source of spending money.

For the last few years then, they had been forced to resort to the more costly option of hotels and boarding houses. These trips used to take place in early September, when children were back at school and resorts quieter. This summer, however, Jean had been engrossed with the Tilburys and the weeks had slid past. It was now nearly autumn and nothing was arranged.

Her mother made no reference to this oversight, and some-how her silence on the topic had allowed Jean to avoid tackling it, but it was one of those nagging thoughts that returned to plague her during bouts of sleeplessness. Lying awake at 3 a.m. when nothing practical could be done, she would burn with guilt at her own indolence and procrastination, and vow to call in at the travel agent in Petts Wood at the first opportunity. By morning she would have forgotten.

The truth was, these holidays were never much of a treat for Jean, involving as they did unbroken exposure to her mother's considerable needs, dislikes and eccentricities, which seemed to increase in proportion to their distance from home. However, she knew that her mother looked forward to these trips, and complaining about the weather, the food, the mattress and the journey was for her no small part of the pleasure. Jean was also aware that the process of hawking someone infirm and nervous from taxi and train and bus to hotel was getting more difficult with each passing year, and that the tradition, once allowed to lapse, might never be revived.

Finally, it was the discovery that the Tilburys themselves were going away for a short break to the Forest of Dean that persuaded Jean that she would not be missed, so she booked two rooms at the Stanmore House Hotel in Lymington. The timing was convenient: the results of the electrophoresis serum test had shown a perfect match between mother and daughter, and a skin graft had been performed from one to the other.

Dr Lloyd-Jones's expectation was that if Margaret was indeed the product of parthenogenesis, she would comprise no genetic material not originally from Gretchen and the graft from daughter to mother would take. If the new skin started to shed it would suggest the presence of at least one incompatible antigen, implying the existence of a father. All that remained was to wait and see whether or not the skin was rejected by its new host.

In the days before their holiday, Jean had worked long hours with obsessive focus and pace to clear her desk and produce pieces in advance for the following edition. As well as her regular pages, she compiled a recipe section to mark National Soup Week, and in a nod to falling temperatures, wrote a light-hearted column celebrating the vest. It was a while since she had found time for any serious gardening to use as the basis for her column, so she resorted to calling in at Oaklands, the garden supplies shop opposite the church, and interrogating the owner for his seasonal tips.

She left Roy Drake the telephone number of their hotel in Lymington in case of any developments in the matter of the skin grafts and he promised to pass on any news without delay. Dr Lloyd-Jones had told her not to expect anything to happen in her absence. Mother A and Daughter were not expected to have their dressings removed until their return from the Forest of Dean. A definitive result was likely to take weeks rather than days.

All the same, it was with a sense of reluctance, quite at odds with the holiday spirit she had been trying to instil in her mother, that Jean boarded the train at Waterloo. At the first effortful tug of the engine she had sighed so gustily that her mother had glanced up in concern and asked if she felt unwell.

'No, not unwell. Just the usual anxiety that I've overlooked something,' she said.

'It will do you good to get away. You work too hard at that job. Always dashing around.'

Jean refrained from pointing out that without her wages – the fruits of all this inconvenient 'dashing around' – there would be no holiday. Instead, she took silent refuge in her notebook, reviewing the transcripts of her initial interviews with Gretchen, Howard, Alice and Martha, the floor plan of St Cecilia's and her jotted observations since. One page was divided into two columns headed Virgin Birth +/-:

+	−
H's confidence in G's honesty	*M's assumption G was lying*
A's assumption G is truthful	*G's impatience – why now?*
My first impressions	*G's hidden sadness – irrelevant? –*
Blood test	*but shows ability at concealment*
Taste test	*Drugged sleep – opportunity?*
Saliva test	*But timing is wrong plus Kitty?*
Serum test	*Brenda?*

Her mother, opposite, was crocheting another lace doily, the porridge-coloured circle turning and growing quickly under her hands like potters' clay. They had dozens of these at home, little puddles of string under every vase and lamp and ornament, with still enough to fill an entire drawer in the sideboard.

As she watched, her mother glanced up at her and quickly down, the light catching her glasses and turning them to dazzling mirrors, and it occurred to Jean with a jolt that she had no idea what colour her mother's eyes were. She must have known once, but it was years – a decade, perhaps – since they had made proper eye contact.

They had both been witnesses to each other's disappointments and tragedies, but it had always been understood by Jean that it was weak and shameful to dwell on them and so their conversation never strayed far from the surface of things. Sometimes Jean had the sensation that they were adrift in a perilously overladen boat; a moment of emotional turbulence would be enough to capsize them.

Her mother put down her crocheting and removed her reading glasses, blinking hard to bring into focus the Surrey countryside as it flowed past: neat farms, tamed hedgerows and ploughed fields of crumbled soil.

Grey, Jean thought with surprise. They are grey.

Dear Dorrie,

Mother and I are at Lymington for a week's holiday. The picture on the front shows the high street. Our hotel is on the right with the pillars. It is low season and very quiet, which suits us. There is a pretty cobbled street of quaint shops leading down to the harbour, which looks across to the Isle of Wight. We sit and watch the boats for hours.

The walk up is a bit of a challenge for Mother, but yesterday an old boy in a Bentley took pity on us and gave us a lift back to the hotel. She has talked of little else since. On Monday we took a coach trip to Bucklers Hard, a charming row of fishermen's cottages leading down to a river. We have been lucky with the weather so far.

Love to Kenneth and the twins.

Jean

Dear Margaret,

By the time you read this we shall both be back home, but never mind. I hope you are enjoying the Forest of Dean and that Jemimah is behaving herself at Lizzie's. We are staying in a place called Lymington on the edge of the New Forest, which is in fact very old. We could see wild ponies from the train on our way down.

Our hotel has a resident cat, who has her own favourite armchair in the lounge. If you leave your bedroom door open she comes slinking in and goes to sleep on your pillow.

There are at least half a dozen tea shops within walking distance of our hotel and we try a different one each day. None can quite compete with Simpson's – or home-made spitzbuben.

Your friend,

Jean

Towards the end of the week the weather changed and a series of fronts swept in from the west bringing wintry rain, which kept Jean and her mother indoors. They rose as late as permissible and after a cooked breakfast moved into the lounge, where they played rummy and read the selection of out-of-date magazines. There were a number of other residents, similarly marooned by the bad weather, but the room was large and the arrangement of furniture – remote islands of wing-backed armchairs around low coffee tables, separated by vast expanses of carpet – did not encourage them to mingle. By silent consensus, everyone kept to the seats they had originally claimed, exchanging in passing no more than a nod or smile of fellow feeling at the perversity of the English climate.

Among the mostly elderly clientele were a mother and daughter about ten years older than the Swinneys. The old lady was plump and moon-faced, hard of hearing and lost in confusion. The daughter was thin and round-shouldered with skin ravaged by eczema. The corners of her mouth sagged, and her drooping cardigan, raw, ringless fingers and darned stockings spoke eloquently to Jean of self-denial. In the quiet of the lounge, above the swishing of magazine pages and the slap of playing cards, Jean could hear her patiently answering the same bewildered questions over and over.

'We're just waiting for the rain to pass . . .' 'No, we've had lunch. We're just waiting until it's stopped raining . . .' 'When it clears up. Then we'll go out,' the daughter said, raking the flaming skin of her arms with chewed nails.

Jean's mother, who enjoyed trying to listen in on the conversations of other guests and felt entitled to comment on anything overhead, said, 'She needs to stop scratching. It'll get infected.'

The woman glanced up and blushed.

'Mother!' Jean hissed in reproach, shrinking behind the wings of her armchair.

The room was so very hushed that most people spoke only in whispers, leaving the disinhibited few, of whom her mother was one, brutally exposed.

'If this weather's in for the week we might as well go home tomorrow,' one of the other guests was saying to her husband in a low voice.

'That lady's had enough,' Jean's mother commented, causing several heads to turn.

In one corner an old man in green tweeds had fallen asleep over his tea. The cup and saucer rattled perilously between his fluttering hands as it rode the gentle rise and fall of his stomach like a small boat on a rolling sea.

'Can you hear snoring? I can hear snoring,' her mother remarked as Jean dived to rescue the cup before it deposited its contents in the old man's lap.

On her way back to their island, Jean caught the eye of the downtrodden daughter and they exchanged rueful smiles, but this moment of shared experience gave her no great comfort. Instead, it provided a glimpse of a future that was anything but rosy. 'I'm not like her,' she wanted to announce to the room. 'I have a career and colleagues who respect me, and there is a man who admires me and knows my worth!' But these certainties had lost some of their bite here, so far from home, and Jean felt something close to panic the next morning when they awoke again to the clatter of rain at the window and the prospect of another day of enforced idleness.

In a fit of desperation, she booked them at the last minute onto a trip to Beaulieu, even though neither of them had any great interest in motoring.

Through the misted windows of the coach the New Forest was a bleak landscape of beaten gorse and clumps of tattered trees under leaden skies. Jean's mother had got her feet wet on the short walk across the pavement to the pick-up point and this was now the focus of much grumbling. Jean herself, who had been holding but not benefiting from the umbrella and was thoroughly bedraggled, hunched in her seat and smoked furiously.

At Beaulieu, her mother could not be persuaded to leave the bus. It was too wet and cold; the prospect of walking even a few steps defeated her.

'I'm quite happy here looking at the view. You go,' she urged Jean, who needed no prompting to seize a few moments to herself.

She strolled around the shed of vintage cars with the line of other visitors, enjoying the temporary respite from her mother's stream of comments. Loneliness made some people withdrawn in company, she thought, but others like her mother grew vocal when given an audience, spilling out opinions and observations without any thought for how they might be received.

The allotted hour was longer than was really needed to view the small motorcar collection and those few rooms of the house open to the public, but Jean was in no hurry to return, savouring the silence and the opportunity to wander unencumbered. Her mother had a way of clutching and leaning on her arm as they walked, as if liable to topple over at any moment and determined to take Jean down with her if she did.

When she made her way back to the bus at the appointed time, she found it ready to depart, the engine running and the other passengers waiting and restive. She stumbled down the aisle to her seat, raked by disapproving looks.

'I thought something must have happened to you,' said her mother. 'Everyone's been waiting.'

It had grown cold in the bus with the engine off and she had shrunk inside her coat, the collar up to her ears.

'I'm not late,' Jean whispered back, offering up her watch face in evidence. 'Everyone else was early.'

It would have been easy enough to apologise, but she was too mortified.

The driver took a circuitous route back through Brockenhurst and Sway, 'to enjoy the scenery', he said mirthlessly over the whine of the windscreen wipers and the machine-gun rattle of rain on the metal roof. Between the fug of cigarette smoke within and the boiling skies without, the picturesque views stood no chance.

'Well that was a disappointment, I must say,' was Jean's mother's verdict as the guests trooped back into the hotel, shaking out their umbrellas, filling the lobby with clouds of vapour and a mushroomy smell of wet mackintosh.

This remark prompted general agreement from the company. They began to exchange other reassuring banalities about the weather and the risks of off-season travel until the icy reserve of the past few days was thoroughly melted and they moved into the lounge as a united band, grumbling cheerfully. Later, Jean's mother would describe it as the best day of the entire holiday.

The exertions of the outing must have exhausted her, as she went to bed early. They had eaten their last meal in the dining room – tomato soup, fishcakes with sauté potatoes and peas, and sherry trifle – and played cribbage with a retired bank manager and his wife who were part of the Beaulieu contingent. It emerged in conversation that they lived less than thirty miles away in Blandford Forum and had been coming to the same hotel every year since the end of the war. Jean, for whom seven days in the place had seemed an eternity, found herself depressed and repelled by their complacency.

They had never been to London and had no desire to go. They had heard it was overrun with traffic and Teddy boys and they wanted none of it. Other manifestations of progress, the television and the motor car, were given equally short shrift. The first was a threat to family life; the second was a blight on the countryside and a menace to public safety.

It occurred to Jean to wonder why such sworn enemies of motoring had settled on a trip to Beaulieu, but she was too polite to challenge them. Besides, their opinions were delivered with the sort of assurance that has never experienced dissent and might not even recognise it. Instead, simmering inside, she began to formulate a Pam's Piece on provincialism, which would of course be unprintable but soothed her bad temper.

In Jean's mother they had found a somewhat anarchic soulmate; she was inclined to agree with everything they said but occasionally misheard and ended up roundly seconding a quite contrary viewpoint. More than once Jean had to step in and politely steer her back on track. It all made for effortful conversation and Jean was relieved when her mother, wearied by the day's novelties, declared herself ready for bed.

'Well, they were a very nice couple,' she said on her way upstairs, taking Jean's grunt for agreement. 'It's a pity we didn't get to know them at the beginning of the week.'

Once Jean had overseen her mother's lengthy preparations for bed, from the discreet vantage point of her adjoining room, and satisfied herself that she was settled with her hairnet in place and a Georgette Heyer to soothe her to sleep, she made her escape.

The storm had blown away leaving a ragged sky and it was warmer now than during the day. A few wounded shreds of cloud blew across the moon, which lit up the street with its great wax face as Jean walked down towards the quay enjoying the last cigarette of the night.

A group of working men was just emerging from the King's Head, boisterous with drink, as she approached. They greeted her with beery good humour, dragging each other out of her path with exaggerated gallantry that was closer to mockery than good manners. Jean, who was used to being outnumbered by inferior men, refused to be intimidated.

'Good evening,' she said briskly, causing general convulsion.

'She said "Good evening!"' one of them called after her departing back.

The harbour was quiet, the small boats gently nudging and dipping in the moonlight. Across the Solent the Isle of Wight was visible as a dark mass, Yarmouth a scatter of lights at the shoreline. Jean sat down on a bench to enjoy the view and let her thoughts roam in the direction of Howard, wondering where he was and if at this very moment he might be outdoors and looking at the same stars.

She was aware of somebody coming to stand behind her, a little closer than was polite, and turned to see the confused old lady from the hotel. There was something odd about her appearance; it took Jean a moment or two to realise that she was wearing a nightdress and carpet slippers under her coat. Her bare legs were tracked with ropey purple veins.

'Hello,' said Jean, looking around for the daughter. 'You've come out for some fresh air like me.'

'No,' came the reply.

'Will you be all right getting back? It's a fair walk.'

The woman stared at Jean with mystification and a degree of hostility. 'I suppose you're going to tell me you're Nora. Little tart,' she added.

Her prospect of a quiet half-hour dashed, Jean surrendered to the responsibility of getting the old woman safely back. For a moment, stung by the irony that she had exchanged the modest demands of one geriatric for the much more urgent needs of another, she had considered leaving her to it, but there, a few feet away, was the black oily water plucking at the harbour wall.

'I'm going back now. Shall we walk together?' Jean offered her arm.

The woman allowed herself to be guided away from the quayside and up towards the town, their progress impeded by her tendency to stop every few paces and turn, stiff-necked, towards Jean with some new query.

'Who the hell are you?' she would say. 'You look like Nora but you don't smell like her.'

As the elegant pillars of the hotel came into view at last the fretful figure of the daughter appeared on the steps, casting anxious glances up and down the road. She swooped on them, almost frantic with relief and reproach.

'Oh, Mother, where on earth have you been? I've been out of my mind. I only left her for a minute to get some clean towels. Oh, you are the limit. Thank you so much,' she babbled.

'I found her down on the edge of the quayside,' said Jean, who felt the matter of tragedy narrowly avoided warranted a mention.

The daughter rolled her eyes. 'You are kind. I can't thank you enough. Now come on, Mother. You're as cold as ice.'

The old lady, who up to this point had been meekly linking Jean's arm, suddenly wrenched herself free and gave her daughter a terrific shove, sending her sprawling onto her back, and stomped past her into the hotel.

For a moment it seemed as though the fall had knocked her out or worse, as she lay motionless, crumpled up against one of the pillars with her skirt up over her knees. Presently, however, she gave a moan and drew her legs towards her, raising her hand to explore the back of her head for damage.

Jean squatted beside her, an embarrassed onlooker in a domestic drama that had now become horribly public.

'Are you all right? Do you need a doctor?'

From behind her hands the woman gave a muffled sob.

A young couple, out walking their dog, had now stopped to offer assistance; Jean had a sudden fear that they might assume the woman was drunk. At this angle and in this state of dishevelment she did look quite unlike the respectable spinster of previous days.

'Do you need some help?' the man asked, tugging at the dog,

a fox terrier, who was now pulling on the lead.

'She's had a nasty fall,' said Jean, feeling that the real story of maternal violence was hardly hers to relate. 'I'll look after her. We're both staying at the hotel.'

Shrugging their assent, the couple moved off, giving Jean a doubting backwards glance.

The woman had shuffled herself into a sitting position against the pillar but made no move to get up.

'Will you let me help you in?' Jean said, putting a tentative hand on her arm. 'I'll bring you a cup of tea or something.'

At this gesture of kindness, tears filled her eyes and rolled down her face.

'That was quite a bump. Does she often do this?' Jean asked.

The woman nodded, sniffling. 'She's so strong. She'll kill me one day. If I don't kill her first.'

'Oh, surely not,' said Jean. 'You are so patient with her.' She held out her hands and lifted her to her feet, noticing, as the wide cardigan sleeves fell back, arms smudged with bruises.

'I wish one of us was dead. I don't care which.'

'You mustn't think like that. Is there no one who can help you with looking after her?'

An idiotic question, Jean knew, because it was the sort of thing people said to her, as if she wouldn't have already considered the idea, if such a person existed.

Once vertical, however, the woman seemed to master herself, straightening her clothes, now streaked with grubby water from the pavement, and mopping her face with a balled-up handkerchief.

'I'm quite all right now, thank you,' she said, looking anywhere but at Jean. 'I'm sorry to have been a nuisance.'

'Won't you let me get you a cup of tea or something stronger?'

'No, thank you. I must go and see to Mother. She'll be wondering where I am.'

Wincing, she straightened up and proceeded into the hotel.

21

Dear Miss Swinney,

Thank you for your letter, which has just reached me after a considerable delay. It went to my old address and I'm afraid the new tenants have only now got around to sending it on. It was not the only piece of mail they had been sitting on. Most annoying. Anyway, it made interesting reading and stirred up plenty of memories — not all of them good.

I do remember Gretchen. She was rather quiet but very pleasant. Unfortunately, I didn't get to know her all that well because there was another girl — Martha — in the bed between ours who was a bit of a bully and very possessive. She used to get quite sulky if Gretchen tried to be friendly to anyone else but her. I had to wait until the nurse was giving Martha a bed bath with the curtains drawn and then I would creep round to have a chat with Gretchen, because I was the only one who was well enough to get out of bed.

The two of them were as thick as thieves. You could hear them whispering at night — not especially quietly — when they couldn't sleep. I had to put cotton wool soaked in olive oil in my ears! Martha got into terrible trouble at one point for persuading Gretchen they should take triple the dose of sleeping pills. One of the nuns accused her of attempting a suicide pact, but of course it had been going on for weeks, so it was nothing of the kind. I think it was just attention-seeking myself.

I must admit to being a bit taken aback by your suggestion that Gretchen fell pregnant while at St Cecilia's. Under the noses of Matron and the nuns, not to mention the rest of us on the ward? I can't see how it could possibly have happened. I didn't keep in touch with Gretchen after she left, but I used to get a Christmas card from Kitty, the fourth girl on the ward. She was stuck in an iron lung for her polio and we got quite friendly because I could get up and chat to her. I think she appreciated the company. No doubt you have already tracked her down as she's in your part of the world, but in case you haven't here is her address:

> *Miss K Benteen,*
> *The Grange,*
> *Locksbottom,*
> *Kent*

I don't know if she'd be able to add anything to my reminiscences.

Please remember me to Gretchen, and to Matron, who was always very kind to me, and give them my best wishes.

Yours sincerely,

Brenda van Lingen

This letter, which was awaiting Jean on her return from Lymington, sent her hurrying back to Alice Halfyard's diary, with a guilty jolt that she had allowed her focus on the investigation to slip. But the positive outcomes of the various medical tests had made her complacent and her emotional involvement with the Tilburys had distracted her.

There, on 20 August, was the reference to the deliberate

overdosing of Gretchen and Martha, confirmed now by Brenda as a regular occurrence and not the one-off event Alice had believed it to be. She checked the dates against Margaret's birth – 30 April. She had not been premature, so conception must have occurred some time between early July and the beginning of August. The possibility that for at least some of those nights she had been all but unconscious seemed too much of a coincidence to be ignored. Clearly, Martha and Brenda would have heard nothing, for different reasons, but Kitty?

Jean felt a certain reluctance to pursue the fourth member of this curious fellowship but knew that she must. It was pure squeamishness – a fear of confronting serious illness – that made her hesitate and while she delayed, something else happened that threw all other plans into confusion.

22

'That man's here again.'

Jean's mother was standing at the front-room window, counting in the sacks of coal as they were carried past to the bunker in the back garden, convinced that it was only her vigilance that kept tradesmen honest.

'What man?' Jean asked, but her heart had got ahead of her, already knocking at her ribs.

On the street outside, just beyond the dray from Hall & Co., was the green Wolseley. Howard sat behind the wheel, motionless, for so long that Jean wondered if he might be about to change his mind and drive off.

They had been back from Lymington for a week and there had been no communication from the Tilburys apart from a postcard from Margaret of the Forest of Dean. She had described a visit to a ruined abbey and her frustration at not being allowed to swim in the river because of the dressing on her skin graft.

Work had claimed all of Jean's attention; she had been too busy catching up after her absence, and chewing over the contents of Brenda's letter, to feel more than a trace of uneasiness at the silence, but here was Howard now, calling unannounced on a Monday evening. He showed no sign of moving and in any case it would be easier to talk away from the inquisitive gaze of her mother, so Jean hurried up the driveway, drawing her cardigan around her against the chill evening air.

He looked up as her shadow darkened the window and gave a wan smile, then reached over to open the door.

'Is everything all right?' Jean asked as she slipped into the seat beside him, convinced now that it wasn't.

'Gretchen has run away.'

She stared at him in astonishment, momentarily lost for words. Of all the many varieties of bad news that were possible, this one had not occurred to her.

'What do you mean? How? Where?'

'I mean she's left home. She doesn't want to be married to me any more.'

There was a roaring, whooshing noise in Jean's ears and the rushing sensation that comes just before a faint. But she didn't faint, of course.

'No. Surely not. What about Margaret?'

'Margaret is away on a school journey, so she doesn't know yet. Which is no doubt why Gretchen chose this week to leave.'

'I can't believe it, Howard. She must be having some kind of breakdown.'

'Maybe. Though she seems quite collected.'

'But you've just been on holiday. Did something happen while you were away?'

'Oh no, it's been going on much longer than that.'

Jean was aware of her mother, having dismissed the coalman, peering at them through the front window, in agonies of curiosity.

'Shall we drive?' Howard asked.

'Yes, do.'

It was easier to talk while moving, with eyes on the road ahead.

'Do you know where she's gone?'

'Chelsea, I believe.'

A confused sense of dread, a foggy state of both seeing and not quite seeing, which had assailed Jean from the start of their conversation, now gave way to awful clarity.

'Oh, God,' she said, sick with guilt as if she had deliberately conspired in the betrayal. 'Martha.'

'I think I always knew,' said Howard. 'Not about Martha herself, but that her aversion wasn't just to me but to all men. It ought to make it easier. But it doesn't.'

They were driving through the common now, towards the countryside, with no declared aim other than to keep moving.

'I didn't know they had even made contact. Gretchen never said.'

'That little painting of the tangerines that you brought back – it had Martha's address on. I knew Gretchen had got in contact and been to visit her – once – but I thought nothing of it. A reunion of old friends, that sort of thing. But they've been meeting in secret since.'

'This is all my fault,' said Jean. 'It was me who brought them back together. I never imagined.'

She had a sudden memory of the three of them, Howard, Gretchen and Margaret in the garden; badminton and afternoon tea, dressmaking and piano practice; the ordinary miracles of family life that she had blundered into and destroyed. It had all been an illusion; the real Gretchen was not the happy house-wife with the sunny smile but the other one with the stricken expression, guarding her painful secret.

'No one is to blame,' Howard said. His hands on the steering wheel clenched and released. 'Except perhaps me for going ahead with the marriage when I knew that she didn't love me the way I loved her. Suspected it anyway.'

'Howard, you are too hard on yourself,' Jean protested, tears springing to her eyes.

'She told me she had never really stopped loving Martha, even though she never expected to see her again.'

'That was cruel of her.'

'She didn't mean it to be. She said she loves me too, and I believe her.'

'But what about Margaret? Gretchen would never do anything to hurt Margaret and she must know this surely will.'

'She's beyond reason. Her feelings for Martha have driven out all other considerations.'

'But people deny their feelings all the time,' Jean said. 'Isn't that what parenthood is all about – sacrificing your happiness for your children's?'

'I suppose she would say that's what she has been doing these ten years – and she can't do it any more.'

'You are so reasonable, Howard. You should be raging and storming and demanding that she comes home.'

'I did try a version of that,' he admitted. 'But it's hard to rant at someone who is already on their knees, weeping their apologies. I felt like a brute.'

This image of Gretchen, abject and pleading, was too much for Jean.

'Don't,' she said with a sense of guilt that was out of all proportion. 'This is all my doing. I've brought this chaos into your lives.'

She felt a powerful and irrational hatred for Martha, her filthy kitchen, her pretensions to art, her scarlet lipstick, her scheming. And as she contemplated the wreckage of this once happy marriage, a dark corner of her soul registered that Howard himself was now, if not legally, then at least morally free, and her heart bounded with selfish joy.

'Well, if she's gone to stay at Martha's she won't stick it for long. The place is a slum,' she said with uncharacteristic spite.

It was impossible to imagine the poised and fastidious

Gretchen at home among that clutter.

'Really?' Howard's face fell and Jean immediately regretted her remark. Of course it hardly flattered him to know what a reduction in circumstances she was running to. 'I just can't imagine her being happy there,' Jean added lamely.

The sky was darkening and they were passing Biggin Hill now, the airfield on their left, following the same route they had taken to Aunt Edie's, weeks ago when life was straightforward. It seemed as though Howard might drive all night if she let him.

'Is there anything I can do that might help? Anything at all?' she asked, conscious that her intervention so far in the Tilbury marriage hardly recommended her for the role.

'She'll need money,' Howard replied. 'I wouldn't like to think of her struggling or dependent on . . . someone else.'

'Only you would think like that.'

'I wonder if you would go and see her, give her some cash and check that she is all right. I know she won't want to face me. I don't even have an address for her.'

'Of course. If you think she'll see me.'

'She'll have to see someone. Margaret comes back on Saturday. She needs to be told.'

'Poor Margaret,' Jean burst out. 'This is desperate.'

Howard pulled over to the side of the road. In the pool of light from a street lamp his face looked pale and waxy. He flipped open the glove compartment and took out a stiff white envelope addressed, with touching formality, in his neat hand-writing, to Mrs H. Tilbury. He passed it to Jean.

'It's just twenty pounds. Of course there's more if she needs it. I didn't put in a letter. I started one, but . . .'

'I'll go tomorrow morning,' Jean promised.

'What about work?'

'You and Gretchen *are* my work.'

Chimneys can be kept reasonably clear of soot if potato parings mixed with a little salt are burned in the grate at least once a week. This will form a glaze inside the chimney and prevent it from becoming clogged.

23

'Where are we with this Virgin Mother story? It seems to have been dragging on for months.' Roy Drake shifted, wincing in his swivel chair as Jean explained the unwelcome developments in the Tilbury story. He had pulled his back at the weekend digging his allotment and pain was adding to his displeasure.

'None of the tests so far have proved the involvement of a father. They've done the skin grafts – now they're just waiting to see if they take.'

'You'd think these doctors could work a bit faster. If they treated their patients in this leisurely fashion they'd surely all be dead.'

'I didn't realise it would all be so time-consuming.'

'It was supposed to be an Advent miracle story. It's nearly November and we're still nowhere.'

He tossed her his Capstans and they sat for a moment recuperating in silence as the first hit of nicotine worked its magic.

'Things have got a little more complicated. Mrs Tilbury's . . . left home.'

Roy's eyebrows shot up. 'Found herself another fellow?'

'Oh no,' said Jean, relieved that on this point she had not been required to lie.

Although she looked up to Roy and admired him more than

anyone she had ever worked with, still she could not bring herself to expose the details of Gretchen's defection to his sharp, journalistic eye. Unlike her, he had no feelings of loyalty to the family and might think this development fair game. To her mind it would be unthinkable if the real story of Margaret's mysterious origins was eclipsed by a sensational sex scandal. It would be awful for Gretchen, of course, but her sympathies now lay firmly with Howard and Margaret. It was them she had to protect at all costs.

'It just makes it awkward to get hold of her at the moment, but I'm sure it's only temporary.'

'Do you think it's the pressure of all these investigations?'

'I'm sure it hasn't helped. It's on my conscience.'

'You can't blame yourself for the way things have gone. She came to us. And every marriage has its fault lines.'

'I suppose so. But she hid it so well. It makes me wonder what else she's been hiding.'

The paradox was that while Gretchen's sexuality made it more likely that she had never had relations with a man until Howard, her dishonesty made her a less credible witness.

'I see. You think she might have been hoodwinking us all along?'

The phone on his desk rang and he silenced it with a twitch of the receiver.

'I only know that I feel a bit less confident in Gretchen personally, and yet test after test has vindicated her.' She gave him an apologetic smile.

'Well, get out there and do some more digging. It's not too late. And take a word of friendly advice from an old man. Keep the husband at a distance while this plays out. Newly abandoned men tend to look for consolation wherever they can find it.'

Jean felt herself reddening under his scrutiny.

'Don't tell me he's already . . .'

'No, no, nothing like that,' Jean insisted, her blush deepening.

He expressed his relief by blowing out a long plume of smoke.

'He's the most decent, honourable type you can imagine – apart from you, of course.'

'I'm glad to hear it. I'd begun to wonder whether there wasn't something more personal in your commitment to this story.'

A shadow darkened the room. Muriel from Accounts stood outside the glass-panelled door with a sheaf of invoices. Roy raised an open hand to indicate five minutes and she retreated.

'Well, there was. Is. But it was the whole happy family thing. I wanted a little of what they had. And they were so willing to share. Even Margaret.'

'The little girl.'

Jean nodded. 'I thought I'd buried all those maternal feelings long ago, but . . .'

Roy Drake, father of four, placed his large freckled hand on her shoulder. 'It's all right, old girl. I understand.'

24

Jean's first visit to Luna Street had been in summer. Children had been playing football and vandalising cars on the street, and babies had been put out to air in their prams on doorsteps. On a cold Tuesday morning in late October it was deserted. Frost still glittered on the pavement on the shaded side of the street.

The slanting autumn sunlight exposed the smeared windows of number 16. A glass panel was missing from the front door, a piece of plywood nailed over the gap in the sort of temporary repair that was likely to become permanent. It was not the only house in the street to boast this sort of improvisation.

As she had walked from Sloane Square, Jean had caught a glimpse of herself in a shop window and was dismayed to see reflected there a stooping, middle-aged woman in a shabby mackintosh, with unstyled mousey hair, neither straight nor curly and streaked with silver. This image of round-shouldered drabness was quite at odds with Jean's sense of herself as a brisk and respectable working woman, and reminded her why she generally avoided mirrors.

Drawing herself up straight, she now rang the doorbell and after a long delay heard the slap of approaching feet. It was Martha who answered. She was wearing a belted dressing gown as though just out of bed, but her face was made up, her hair tied back in that charlady bandana.

'Ah,' she said by way of welcome. 'I thought someone would be along sooner or later.'

'It's Gretchen I've come to see.'

'She's not here at the moment, but come in anyway.'

Martha led the way down the passage and into the studio. The doors to the kitchen and bedroom were – perhaps strategically – shut against the intimate evidence of shared occupancy. There were already touches of Gretchen about the place – the dead plant replaced with a jam jar of fresh flowers, the floor swept, the clutter corralled if not exactly tidied. They sat as before on the low couch, but this time there was no offer of coffee and no gift of florentines.

'Do you know when she'll be back?'

'No. She comes and goes as she pleases. She's not a prisoner, you know.'

'I never imagined she was. I've brought her some money. From her husband.'

Martha raised her eyebrows, clearly not expecting this degree of compliance.

'Well, that's useful,' she conceded.

Jean had taken the envelope from her bag but kept hold of it, reluctant to surrender it to anyone but Gretchen.

'You can leave it with me. I won't steal it, if that's what you're worried about.'

'I was hoping to talk to Gretchen herself.'

'She doesn't want to talk to anyone.'

'I can imagine. But there is a conversation to be had about Margaret, sooner rather than later. Do you know what she intends?'

'I expect she'll want her here.' Martha shrugged as if it was a matter of no great moment, one way or another.

'There is scarcely space here for a child,' Jean said, feeling that there was something surreal in this discussion, conducted without any of the relevant parties present.

'We might need to find somewhere bigger at some point, I suppose.'

'She is due back on Saturday.' Jean's voice gave a squeak of impatience. Martha's nonchalance was beginning to rile her.

'I know you don't approve of me, Jean,' Martha said, folding her long legs under her on the couch. 'I'm used to it. People have disapproved of me as long as I can remember.'

'One can hardly "approve" the break-up of a family,' Jean replied stiffly.

She hated being aligned with the forces of narrow-mindedness and conservatism, even though that was where she felt most at home. She had quite admired Martha at their first meeting and she was intrigued rather than alarmed by lesbianism. As a touchstone, she imagined her mother's opinion – and rejected it. She would be disgusted – therefore, Jean chose not to be. But none of this could be said.

'She was mine before she was his,' Martha was saying.

'But now there's a child to consider.'

'I *meant* the child.'

Jean blinked, confused.

'She was named for us, you know. Martha and Gretchen.'

Jean was utterly unprepared for this and had no idea what to say.

'No, I didn't know.'

In the silence that followed this exchange a pin-drop of sound came from behind the closed door. It was less than a breath, but Martha's quick glance confirmed that she had heard it, too.

'She's here, isn't she?' Jean said.

Martha hesitated, on the edge of a denial, and then the bedroom door opened and Gretchen stood there. Her loveliness was never off duty and she wore it like armour today.

'It's all right,' she said to Martha, who had sprung up, as though to her defence. 'I want to talk to Jean.'

There was something defiant in the tilt of her chin.

'Do you want me to stay?'

'No, I'd like to talk to her alone. You go.'

Gretchen squeezed Martha's hand and waited until she had swept up a purse and keys from the table and left, closing the front door behind her.

'Oh, Gretchen,' was all Jean could say.

'Don't be angry with me, Jean,' she replied with downcast eyes. 'I can't help it.'

Without the fortifying presence of Martha she looked much less assured.

'I'm not angry, Gretchen. It's nothing to do with me. Even Howard's not *angry*.'

'Dear Howard.' She perched on the edge of the couch as though not quite at home. 'Is he all right?'

'Well, I don't know about "all right",' Jean replied. 'He's very concerned about Margaret. And you. He asked me to give you this.'

She handed over the envelope and Gretchen opened it in front of her, shaking her head as she counted the money.

'He's very generous,' she said. 'I didn't expect anything.'

'Do you really mean to leave him and live here?'

'Yes.'

'And what about Margaret?'

Gretchen seemed nonplussed by this question.

'Well, she'll be here too, of course, with me. Where else would she be?'

'But school? Will she have to leave her friends and start somewhere new — around here?' Jean waved an arm to signify the hinterland of Luna Street.

'Oh no, I don't think so,' said Gretchen as if this was the first time she had given any thought to the matter. 'She's in her last year – it would be too much upheaval. I'll take her back to Sherwood Park each morning on the train and pick her up. I think that'll be best. Don't you?'

'Best?' Jean echoed, struggling to adjust to this new casual, thoughtless Gretchen. 'No, what would be best for Margaret is what she already has.'

Gretchen flinched as though Jean had flung a glass of water in her face.

'But I can't,' she said in a stricken voice. 'I've never loved anyone but Martha. All these years with Howard – I tried, I really tried. And it's not fair on him, either. He deserves some-one who can love him properly.'

For an uncomfortable moment it occurred to Jean that all along Gretchen had been auditioning her for the role of Howard's comforter; coaching her, finding excuses to throw them together – the thought revolted her. She shook her head.

'You can't really be suggesting that you are doing this for Howard's benefit. He is heartbroken.'

'Don't say that,' Gretchen pleaded. 'I can't bear to think of him unhappy. But I can't lose Martha again now that I've found her.'

'That's what I don't understand. If you wanted to find Martha you could have done it years ago. She's not been in hiding. It took me no time at all.'

Gretchen shook her head at Jean's simplicity.

'It wasn't finding her that was the problem. It was proving myself. And you did that for me.'

'Oh?'

Through a mist of incomprehension, a distant gleam of light.

'When I found out I was going to have a baby I went to see her in Chatham at her parents'. I thought of the baby as ours – it had come to me while we were in St Cecilia's together. I thought she was the one person who would understand. But she wouldn't believe me. She thought I had been with a man and nothing I said would persuade her.

'We had a terrible row. I said I would prove my innocence one day and she would have to kneel at my feet and apologise. Then she told me to get out and shut the door on me, and I never heard from her again until this summer, when you went to visit her and told her you believed my story.'

'So all this was for her?' Jean said.

'When I saw that article in your newspaper it seemed to call out to me. I thought if you could prove I was telling the truth, my picture might be in the paper and Martha would see it and feel sorry for all the things she said.'

'I see.'

'It hadn't occurred to me that I might see her again. I assumed she would have forgotten me and found someone new. I just wanted her to know the truth. That was all.'

'And did she?'

'Did she what?'

'Kneel at your feet and apologise.'

Gretchen laughed, embarrassed. 'Well, not exactly. Martha's not really the kneeling kind.'

I bet she isn't, thought Jean.

'But she believes me, and that's what matters.'

'And do you think you'll be happy here? And Margaret?'

Jean cast a disparaging eye around the room. Even Gretchen's efforts to make the place more homely could not disguise its seediness.

'I know it's rather crowded and messy, but that's because Martha works so hard. But I can help her to make it nice. And if I'm happy, Margaret will be happy. I'll explain it to her. She and her friend Lizzie are inseparable. I'll explain that it's the same for Martha and me – she is my best friend and we have to be together. She'll understand.'

'You make it sound so simple.'

'It is – why can't it be? I love Martha and I love Margaret, but I love Howard too, and even you, Jean. Especially you, because you brought Martha back to me.'

Jean received this declaration with a stony face.

'I've trusted you and defended you against people who assumed you were a liar or a fantasist. And all this time you were deceiving me.'

'I wasn't!' Gretchen's voice was shrill with protest. 'Everything I told you about Margaret's birth is true. I never lied about that.'

'You were playing a different game. And you haven't been honest. How can I know what to believe?'

'Can't you be happy for me?'

'I'm more concerned for Margaret's happiness.'

She had gone too far, trespassing on a mother's territory. Gretchen blinked, wounded.

'I've always put Margaret first in everything,' she said, the words thick with stifled tears. 'You can't accuse me—'

'I'm sorry,' said Jean. 'I spoke out of turn.'

She was only now beginning to realise that her own relationship with Margaret was in jeopardy – dependent as it was on Gretchen's good will, which could be withdrawn at any moment. The thought of being frozen out, replaced by Martha as unofficial aunt, was too much to bear. But Gretchen was not in a vindictive mood and seemed to crave only approval. She took Jean's hand between hers and squeezed it.

'We're still friends, aren't we?'

Jean nodded.

'And you'll look after Howard, won't you? He admires you so much.'

'I don't suppose I shall have any reason to see him if you are no longer living there,' Jean said, in part to test out her suspicion that Gretchen had deliberately thrown them together in order to ease her own escape.

'Oh, but you must! He has so few friends. Will you give him a message from me?'

'I think you need to talk to him yourself. About your plans for Margaret. I can't do that for you.'

'But it was so painful last time. I can't bear it.'

'You must. May I give him this address?'

'Yes, I suppose so. Will you give him my . . . love . . . or whatever you think.'

At the scrape of a key in the lock, which signalled the return of Martha from wherever she had been waiting out this interview, Gretchen immediately stood up and Jean sensed herself dismissed.

The two women stood shoulder to shoulder on the front step to wave her off, or perhaps, Jean thought, to block the doorway against her return. She left with a strengthening resolve. Gretchen had forfeited all claim to Howard through her own recklessness and engineered his friendship with Jean for her own selfish ends. There was no need for any agonies of conscience on her part.

If he reached out to her in his loneliness, she would be ready.

25

Dear Howard,

I went to see Gretchen today as you asked. She was grateful for the money and touched by your kindness. I tried to make her see reason but, as you said, she seems set on this path. She was of course full of anguish at the thought of having caused you pain, as well she might be. She sent her love and will contact you soon — tomorrow — to discuss plans for Margaret.

Her address is 16 Luna Street, Chelsea.

You are in my thoughts constantly. If I can be of any further help you have only to ask.

Your friend,

Jean

Having laboured over this note for far longer than its brevity warranted, Jean tore it up and started again. It had made her sound needy and emotional and a little too eager to step into Gretchen's shoes.

Dear Howard,

I have been to see Gretchen today and given her the money, for which she was grateful. She sent her love and will contact you soon about her plans for Margaret. Her current address is

16 Luna Street, Chelsea.
  I hope you are well, in the circumstances.
  Yours,
    Jean

She was surprised and disappointed to receive no reply, even to acknowledge her effort, and as the days passed she began to wonder if she had all along misread his feelings for her. But she had surely not mistaken the connection between them. It had been there in that pledge of silence when he had given her the emerald brooch weeks *before* Gretchen's desertion. He couldn't now be bound by vows that had been so violently broken.

Each night before bed she would take the brooch from its velvet pouch and contemplate its careful and loving workmanship. Then she would close her eyes and replay the still-fresh memories of the day at Aunt Edie's, when their love was unspoken, real and perfect. Tomorrow, perhaps, he will call, she thought, like any lovesick girl, but tomorrow came bringing nothing.

'What's wrong with you? Are you going down with something?' her mother said, watching Jean prod listlessly at her dinner of roast heart and mashed swede.

'I don't know,' she said, laying down her fork, the food untasted.

The least squeamish or fussy of eaters, tonight she found the sight of lambs' hearts, the valves and chambers still visible in all their anatomical detail, suddenly repulsive. Her throat bulged with the effort of not retching.

'I think I'll just have some bread and marge.'

She stood up and wrenched open the refrigerator door, feeling the gust of cold, sour air on her hot cheeks with relief.

'I wonder if you're going through the change,' her mother mused. 'It takes some women badly.'

'I'm not even forty,' Jean said into the fridge, her teeth gritted. 'Surely not.'

'You've not been yourself since Lymington.'

Jean, who took pride in her ability to conceal unruly emotions, could still on occasions be surprised by her mother's acuity. She was not, then, as inscrutable as she liked to think.

'I suppose I was a bit out of sorts,' she conceded, scraping margarine across the heel of a white loaf. 'The weather didn't help.'

'You haven't seen much of those friends of yours lately. The Jews.'

'They're not Jews. I said he was a jeweller. Gretchen's a Catholic, I think. Lapsed.'

'Them, anyway. I wondered if you'd fallen out.'

'They've been away.'

Although the temptation to talk about the Tilburys in any context was almost overwhelming, and it would have been a pleasure just to say Howard's name aloud, she felt an odd instinct to protect Gretchen from the criticism that would surely follow. And she had no wish to expose Howard to either pity or scorn, the only foreseeable responses to his predicament. So she said nothing and the moment for confidences passed, unused.

'Perhaps you need a day in bed with a hot-water bottle,' her mother suggested, her remedy for every kind of feminine complaint.

'I can't take any more time off work,' Jean replied. 'It mounts up.'

'You are probably worn out from looking after me. I'm sorry I'm such a nuisance.'

'Oh, you're not really,' said Jean, moved by her mother's forlorn tone. She gave her freckled, knobbly hand a squeeze, noting the contrast with her own small, delicate fingers. 'Don't say that.'

'At least I'm not as bad as that old dear at the hotel.' She cheered up at this recollection of someone else's greater misfortune. 'If I ever get like that you must put me in a nursing home.'

'You know very well you'd hate that,' Jean replied, unable to take much comfort from the comparison. As far as she was concerned, the only thing that divided them was the distance of a few years.

'Well, I don't want to become a burden.'

'Don't think like that. We get along all right, don't we?'

'I try,' her mother replied ambiguously. 'If you're not going to eat that, I might as well have it.'

She steered the lamb's heart onto her plate with the tip of her knife.

'Please do,' said Jean, looking away to avoid witnessing the first incision.

'Perhaps we could have a fire tonight, now that the clocks have gone back. I made some spills.'

They usually tried to wait until All Souls' Day before lighting the first coal fire of winter – once having succumbed there was no going back until the following March – but there was a chill to the newly dark evenings now. They had held out longer than most of their neighbours; Jean had noticed the chimney pots smoking on her way back from work for the past few days.

'I don't see why not. The bunker's full.'

'It's a good thing the chimney's swept and ready.'

As every year, her mother insisted on getting the sweep round in spring rather than waiting until autumn when the prices might have gone up. She took some pride in this sort of foresight, paying in advance for a far-off future benefit. To Jean's mind it took a particularly dark outlook on life to greet the arrival of warmer weather by making preparations for the onset of winter.

After dinner had been cleared away Jean filled the coal scuttle and set the fire going with a base of newspaper spills. They settled down together to listen to Paul Temple on the Light Programme – her mother's favourite. The glamorous Steve, with her creamy voice and her chauffeur and butler and her pre-dinner cocktails with Sir Graham Forbes of Scotland Yard, was like no journalist Jean had ever met, and seemed in fact to be a complete stranger to the typewriter. It was hard to imagine *her* cycling through the rain to Petts Wood to write a column about prolonging the life of your dusters with paraffin or stiffening a petticoat with sugar water.

She found her attention wandering, soothed by the melli-fluous voice of Marjorie Westbury as Steve, imagining, just a few miles away, Howard alone in the house in Burdett Road preparing a simple supper for one. She supposed he could cook, although she had seen no evidence of it. Gretchen had always seemed to be the proper *hausfrau*, with her *Sachertorte* and her *zopf* bread. Perhaps he would stay up in town after closing the shop and eat out, at some cheap establishment in Soho, with nothing to hurry home for.

This picture of Howard, standing at the stove stirring a pan of scrambled egg, or trudging the streets in the cold and dark, was so persuasive that it made her eyes smart. It struck her as monstrously unfair that Gretchen should be enjoying her free-dom and the pleasures of a new lover, while she and Howard, out of some misguided sense of decorum, remained aloof and lonely. Even though she has betrayed him, he won't betray her, she thought sadly. He would never be – what was the word he had used? – 'shabby'.

These melancholy reflections were interrupted by the strains of *Coronation Scot* heralding the end of Paul Temple. Her mother, drowsy from the heat of the coal fire, opened her eyes, blinked and said, 'Very good.' If challenged, she would deny that she had been asleep but would be unable to furnish Jean with any details of the plot.

'Oh, I don't bother about the story,' she would say. 'I just like their voices.'

Jean went out to the kitchen to make her a mug of Allenbury's and to smoke her last cigarette of the day, noticing on her way an envelope on the front doormat. It had not been there earlier. She picked it up, her heart clubbing in anticipation as she recognised the neat slanted handwriting and the stiff white envelope that she had recently delivered to Gretchen.

Patience, she thought, laying it aside while she put a match to the stove and measured a mugful of milk and water into a saucepan. Bad news could wait, and good news improved with keeping. She lit her cigarette from the hob and at last sat down at the kitchen table to open her letter:

> *7 Burdett Road*
> *Sidcup*

Dear Jean,

Thank you for your kindness in going to call on Gretchen. She has telephoned me as promised and we are agreed that I will have Margaret on Sundays, and the rest of the week she will stay with her mother in Chelsea. Margaret was naturally a little confused and upset by the new arrangements, but children are resilient creatures and she seems to be bearing up.

The house is very quiet without them and I find myself working later, and sometimes sleeping at the shop to avoid returning to it. Obviously, something must be done in time to address the inequality in our living standards, but Gretchen is in no hurry for any further upheaval and so we proceed as we are for now.

One unfortunate by-product of this unhappy situation, dear Jean, is that a certain awkwardness has crept into our friendship

*and that I regret more than I can say. I quite understand if
you feel uncomfortable in my company now that Gretchen is
not around, but I want you to know that in your company I
always feel only pleasure and comfort and perfect ease.*

*In short, I would very much like to see you and wonder if
you would be able to meet me for lunch on Saturday in town.
There is a decent place near the shop. If you prefer not to meet,
there is no need to reply – I will be at the shop all day anyway
– but I hope you will think our friendship is sturdy enough to
survive a crisis that was not of our making.*

Yours,

    Howard

Jean sat so long at the table rereading these words in a daze
of happiness that the milk boiled up all over the hob, into the
gas jets, and left a burnt ring on the bottom of the pan. But
that was fine, because there was no chore in existence that
could dampen her spirits now. He wanted to see her. Life was
suddenly beautiful, precious and full of meaning. She cleaned
the hob and made a fresh mug of Allenbury's, and when it came
to bedtime astonished her mother by throwing her arms around
her and squeezing her tightly.

26

THE JOY OF POST

In our increasingly hectic lives, and with more and more of us having access to a private telephone, the art of letter writing may soon be in danger of dying out. This would be a great pity, as a thoughtful and well-written letter can bring immense pleasure to the recipient, and can be revisited again and again in the way that a phone call cannot. There is nothing quite like the sound of an envelope landing on the doormat and the thrill of recognising the handwriting of a dear friend or distant relative.

The telephone is a shrill and demanding taskmaster: 'Deal with me now!' it shrieks, like a fractious toddler. Whereas a letter may be read and replied to – or not – entirely at the convenience of the recipient. And at only 3d for a postage stamp, providing carriage from Land's End to John o' Groats if necessary, there can hardly be a cheaper or nicer way of making someone's day.

How many of us, though, restrict our letter writing

to dutiful thank-you notes, seaside postcards or annual bulletins at Christmas? It shouldn't be impossible to set aside half an hour a week to devote to correspondence. It will not take long for the habit to become ingrained and the effort will be rewarded many times over when the replies start coming in. Everybody stands to gain – except perhaps the overburdened postman!

....

Dear Howard,
I'm so glad you wrote. Of course I'll come.
Your friend,
Jean

The next three days passed in a frenzy of industry and efficiency both in the office and at home. Ashamed of having let her work on Gretchen's story lapse, she decided to rededicate herself to the investigation, finally taking the initiative to write to Kitty Benteen to arrange a meeting, using Brenda's letter as an introduction.

She also telephoned Anselm House Prep School, Broadstairs, to ask if she might visit again, after school hours, to get a more thorough look at the former wards. (In this manner she hoped to bypass the headmaster, who she felt was less likely to indulge her.) Susan Trevor, the secretary who had been so helpful on Jean's first visit, was about to go on leave to have an operation but made an appointment for the week of her return.

Optimism was a new mood for Jean, and it gave her energy for work and enthusiasm for even the dullest household chore. In the evenings, after dinner was cooked and eaten, she would launch immediately into some long-postponed task – clearing out the larder, resewing worn sheets sides to middle, polishing the brass door handles, switching to winter drapes.

236

'Why don't you have a rest?' her mother would bleat from her armchair at nine o'clock as Jean dragged the furniture into the middle of the room to sweep behind it, slamming the Ewbank into the skirting board, or jumped up on a chair to wipe cobwebs from the picture rails.

'I don't need a rest; I'm fine,' Jean would call as she whisked past, convinced that if she did everything at double speed she could trick time into hurrying to meet her.

On Friday she left work a little early in time to call in at Deborah's (Ladies' Fashions of Distinction) and bought herself a claret-coloured wool dress with a pleated skirt, which she had seen on a mannequin in the window. Gretchen's dress, although perhaps more elegant, brought to mind too forcefully its absent creator and was therefore ruled out. Claret was a much bolder choice than her usual safe grey or navy and she wondered if it would provoke raised eyebrows indoors.

The only area in which Jean had failed to triumph was achieving a leave of absence for the afternoon. She had taken a detour past Mrs Melsom's on her way to and from work, but they were evidently away. There was no Riley in the driveway, and the curtains upstairs and down were half drawn, and the letter box taped shut – measures more likely to attract burglars than to repel them, in Jean's view.

Her hope rested on the fact that it was some while since she had gone 'gallivanting' on a Saturday and on her week-long tour of duty in Lymington, for which she felt some credits were due. Even so, she was not confident enough to bring up the matter much in advance, leaving it to the morning itself to present it as a *fait accompli*.

'I haven't seen that before,' her mother observed as Jean appeared at breakfast, a trifle self-conscious in the claret-coloured dress. 'Is it new?'

'Yes. I bought it at Deborah's yesterday.' She swished the skirt to and fro to show off the pleats before covering it with an apron to protect it from splashes.

'Very smart. What's the occasion?'

'Nothing special.' Jean turned her back and began to busy herself at the hob preparing porridge. 'I'm meeting a friend in town . . . if you can manage without me for a few hours.'

'Oh. I daresay I can. You won't be out all day, I suppose.'

'No. Just lunch. I'll be getting the midday train. If there's anything you need I could pop into Derry & Tom's afterwards.'

This was a tactical move, turning it from a jaunt into an errand. But her mother was not so easily played.

'I don't think so. Who's the friend? Anyone I know?'

Jean sighed. She had no appetite for the conversation that would surely follow, but she couldn't tell the kind of lie that might need elaborate embroidery in the future.

'Howard,' she conceded.

'On his own?'

Here we go, thought Jean. 'Yes, on his own.'

'Goodness, how modern. Where's his wife? Doesn't she have something to say about this?'

'She's in no position to, since she has left him,' said Jean in a crisp voice.

'Oh.' Her mother drew out the lone syllable – rich with inference – almost to snapping point. 'Well, be careful. That's all I'll say.'

Jean flopped the porridge into two bowls and set them down on the kitchen table with some force.

'Quite unnecessary. I'm not in any danger.'

She could feel her cheeks burning. No one else had the power to rile her in quite the same way. When Roy Drake had cautioned her in almost identical terms it had seemed only old-fashioned and endearing. From her mother it was poison.

'He's still a married man, remember.'

238

'We are just having lunch. I don't see why I should have to forfeit his friendship just because his wife has run off.'

'It's none of my business,' was the wounded rejoinder, and they proceeded to eat their porridge in silence.

Before she left for the train, Jean went to Harrington's to buy a small piece of beef for Sunday, and picked up potatoes and vegetables from the farm shop opposite the church. She couldn't do any dirty housework in her finery, so she contented herself with ironing and folding the laundered sheets and towels, putting some elderly tea towels to soak in borax, intending to deal with them on her return. Then she made her mother a ham sandwich for lunch, which she left on the side, covered with a linen napkin.

The wintry atmosphere of breakfast had not quite had time to thaw when Jean set off. Their disagreements and subsequent reconciliations always followed a pattern: sharp words; withdrawal for sulking and licking of wounds; silence; frosty civility; concessions on both sides; resumption of friendly relations. On this occasion they had reached the stage of frosty civility and they parted with a cool, 'Goodbye then, Mother.'

'Oh. Are you off? Goodbye.'

And then Jean was hurrying down the hill to the station in her smart shoes that pinched, a brisk wind whipping the fallen leaves around her ankles and tugging at the flaps of her drab mackintosh, which was shielding the claret-coloured dress from the threat of showers.

Howard was in his workshop when she arrived. Through the shop window she could see him in profile framed in the doorway. He was quite absorbed, applying solder to the sawn edges of a silver ring with pointed tweezers, biting his bottom lip with concentration.

It was less than five months since she had first set eyes on him here and yet she found it impossible to recapture the critical detachment of that meeting, when he was just an unremarkable, oldish man who meant nothing. Now, there was no one to compare to him; when he looked up from his work and broke into a smile of welcome it filled her with joy and wonder.

She had worried about this moment: the navigation of hellos and goodbyes was fraught with hazards. But with Howard there was nothing but warmth and kindness and the certainty of some feeling not yet declared, but even so accepted and returned.

'I've missed you,' he said simply when he stood beside her on the pavement, having shut up the shop and turned the sign to Closed.

'Likewise.'

'Are you hungry?'

'No. Not even slightly.'

'Me neither. But never mind. Let's at least go somewhere we can sit and compare our symptoms. Come on.'

He walked briskly down Bedford Street, Jean just keeping up. After a few turns she was quite disorientated, with no idea where they were in relation to the shop or the Strand, or anywhere else. It was a strange and liberating experience to surrender all autonomy and be guided entirely by someone else.

Presently, he stopped outside a small Italian restaurant with pots of standard bay trees guarding the door. Its front window was no larger than that of the jeweller's shop. Inside, however, was a mysteriously spacious dining room, lit by candles in wax-spattered wine bottles. Jean had the impression of polished wood and checked tablecloths and the lively clamour of lunchtime trade.

The proprietor greeted Howard with the familiarity due to a regular customer and showed them to a corner table. It was only on stopping to make way for what turned out to be her own advancing reflection that Jean realised that one whole wall was made of mirrors and that the restaurant was only half the size that she had first assumed. She was glad to take off her coat at last, but Howard was no more aware of her smart new dress than he had been of her dowdy mackintosh. I could have worn anything, she thought, with dawning relief, and he wouldn't have noticed or cared.

Without being asked, the waiter brought them a little dish of shiny green olives, a new experience for Jean, who discovered that she liked the idea of them much more than the flavour. They seemed to hail from the same world as Paul Temple and cocktails with Sir Graham and yet tasted like the smell of old gym shoes. More to her liking were the long twigs of salty bread in paper packets, which provided something to do with nervous hands while waiting for the menu.

They ordered minestrone soup and grilled sardines, which they agreed was enough for their impaired appetites, allowing for the possibility of dessert.

'Are you all right, Jean?' Howard asked as she shifted to one side and then the other.

'Yes. I'm just trying to avoid my reflection over your shoulder. It's very disconcerting. I was trying to move so you'd block the view.'

Howard smiled at this, but obliged by adjusting his seat. 'Some women would take it as an opportunity to preen.'

'My mother used to say the Devil would creep up behind me if I stared at myself for too long. I used to run past mirrors with my hands over my eyes.'

'The lies they told us.'

'I could never lie to a child like that,' Jean said with sudden warmth. 'Could you?'

He considered. 'I'm trying to remember whether I ever have. I don't think so. Although recent conversations have certainly been testing.'

'Oh dear. How is Margaret? I often think of her.'

'It's my day to see her tomorrow, so I'll find out. I pick her up from Luna Street at ten and take her back at six, so the whole day is ours.'

'Have you been inside?'

'No, I prefer not to. But Gretchen comes to the door and it's all very . . . cordial.'

His face clouded and Jean could tell that the maintenance of this civilised behaviour was not without effort.

'What will you do tomorrow?' she asked, tearing open another packet of breadsticks, showering the table with crumbs.

Howard was fiddling with a packet of Lucky Strikes.

'She wanted to go swimming, but she can't because of keeping the dressing dry. So we're going to drive down to Aunt Edie's and have a bonfire in the garden. You could come if you like,' he added, suddenly hopeful.

'I can't leave Mother two days in a row,' said Jean, pierced with regret. 'It sounds fun, though.'

Always her mother, the obstacle to any such spontaneous act.

'She was quite taken with you – Edie.'

He offered her the last of the olives and she took it to please him, wondering if like tea without sugar it was a taste that came with practice.

'I can't imagine why. All I did was guzzle her apple brandy and almost pass out on her lawn!'

They laughed at the memory – that day seemed long ago now, chased into the past by the dramas of recent weeks.

'That wouldn't necessarily have counted against you.'

The waiter arrived with the soup and they ate for a while in silence.

'Have you told her about . . . Gretchen?' Jean said presently.

'Yes. I couldn't keep anything from her; she's far too sharp.'

'Was she very shocked?'

'No – nothing rattles Aunt Edie.' He laid down his spoon and looked at her. 'In fact, she said: "Gretchen was never going to make a Tilbury. That other girl would have been much more suitable."'

'Girl.' Jean shook her head. 'I'll be forty next month.'

'Then we must do something to mark the occasion. There are few enough reasons to celebrate, so we must seize them where we can.'

'We've never made much of birthdays,' said Jean. 'My uncle in Harrogate sends me a postal order and I get a card from Dorrie, but that's about it. Perhaps I'll exert myself and bake a cake.'

She remembered as she said this that baking was another area, along with not being forty, in which Gretchen had the advantage.

They finished the soup and the waiter brought them grilled sardines, crisp and crusted with salt and quite unlike the limp and soggy tinned fish that Jean was used to. She had expected potatoes and vegetables as a matter of course, but none were forthcoming and Howard didn't seem troubled by this omission. Instead, she ate the sardines unadorned by anything but a squeeze of lemon and was surprised to find them not only delicious, but also quite sufficient. She wondered how her mother would react if she took to serving an unaccompanied slab of fish or a pork chop for dinner.

Howard tried to persuade her to have dessert, but she was comfortably full and conscious of passing time. Instead they had coffee, dark and silty in dollhouse-sized cups, with a hard almond biscuit, which seemed likely to fetch out a tooth and had to be abandoned for a cigarette instead. Everything about the meal was foreign and unsettling, suggesting that there were, just possibly, different ways of doing things. It was with some surprise that when they emerged once more it was to the fog of a London street rather than a sunny Italian piazza.

'I suppose I must be getting back,' said Jean, already squaring up to the emptiness that would take hold of her when they had said goodbye.

'Must you so soon?' said Howard as they loitered under the restaurant's awning. 'I could swear you only just arrived. Time does strange things when we're together.'

'And when we're apart,' Jean agreed, daring to look him in the eye as she said this.

'Let's walk for a bit,' he said, taking her hand. 'With a bit of luck we'll get lost in the fog.'

Just a few minutes more, Jean promised herself, and then I'll go home. She could feel the pressure of his hand, gently squeezing hers as they walked through the milky greyness. Other pedestrians, appearing as distant smudges, loomed into focus briefly as they passed before being swallowed up again.

'Where are we going?' she asked at last.

'I don't know,' he admitted. 'I just know that if I stop walking, you'll leave.'

'But you know where to find me again.'

They had turned into a narrow street, empty of cars, and walked the length of it before realising it was a dead end, leading nowhere but to the back stairs of restaurant kitchens and a high brick wall at the rear of a theatre. There were empty wooden crates and steel dustbins on the pavement and in the gutter carrot tops and bruised cabbage leaves and other detritus of a fruit and vegetable market. As if given courage by their solitude, he drew her towards him and they stood pressed together for a moment.

'I must go,' Jean said, laying her head on his shoulder.

'I know.'

'Will you stay at the shop tonight?'

'Yes – there's a camp bed in the workshop. It's like a bed of nails but it's better than the empty house.'

'You must miss her terribly. I wish I could help.'

'You do help.' He put his hands on her shoulders and moved her away so that he could look at her. 'May I see you again soon?'

'Of course.' She laughed lightly to disguise a bubbling up of emotion that might embarrass them both. 'You can call me at the paper. Or at home, but of course that's not so private. And now I really must go, only I don't know where I am.'

She looked at her watch and gave a yelp of alarm. Four o'clock. It would be five, perhaps later, before she reached home. She could imagine the reception that awaited her.

Howard led her through the foggy streets to the Strand, where the traffic was crawling along, inch by inch, the headlamps creating cones of milky light, and they said a hasty goodbye.

The train was even slower than usual, stopping at stations for so long it almost seemed it must have broken down before lurching off again at a stately pace, never quite gathering speed. But even her guilty anxiety couldn't quite take the shine off the day. The memory of it was all still there to be taken out of its box and inspected from every angle later.

Out in the suburbs the fog had dissolved, leaving just a gauzy halo around the street lamps as Jean toiled up the hill from the station, her smart shoes biting with every step.

She could tell as soon as she came in sight of the house that something was not right. There were no lights on, even though dusk had fallen, and the front room curtains were still open. She fumbled and jabbed her key at the lock with clumsy hands.

'Mother, where are you?' she called into the cold and unlit hallway, but only the hollow scraping tick of the grandmother clock came back in reply.

A chilly draught licked at her ankles and she traced it to the open back door. Peering out into the twilit garden she saw a row of white tea towels swinging stiffly on the washing line and her mother, a pale shape, stretched out on the grass below as though asleep.

27

The arrival of an ambulance in the Knoll on a Saturday evening brought the neighbours to their windows. Jean was conscious of this silent audience gathering to watch the unfolding drama as her mother was carried up the driveway on a stretcher. Their curiosity would have to go unsatisfied for a while longer.

Jean had crouched beside her on the lawn awaiting the ambulance, having fetched her a blanket, a pillow for her head and a hot-water bottle. The ground was damp and her hands icy.

'I'm glad you're back,' she croaked, looking up at Jean with watery eyes. 'It's terribly cold out here.'

She had been trying to peg out the tea towels – those damned tea towels! – that Jean had left to soak rather than risk splashing her new dress. Somehow in reaching up for the line to hang up the last one she had lost her balance and toppled forwards. There was a raised lump on her forehead, puffy with fluid, and pain everywhere that made movement impossible.

Tears leapt to Jean's eyes as she imagined the frightened cries for help going unanswered while she was dawdling in the fog with Howard. But, at the same time, the clamorous inner voice of self-justification kept up its pleading: why was her mother out in the garden on her own, troubling herself with laundry – a chore she would never bother to attempt while Jean was on hand? And now she probably had a broken hip and double pneumonia, either of which would be enough to carry her off, and it would be all Jean's fault.

The thought of losing her mother, source of so much resentment and self-sacrifice, caused her heart to gallop in frantic denial. How would she tell Dorrie? How would she live out the rest of her years – an orphan – in the empty house?

It was only a short journey to Bromley & District Hospital and the ambulance man, at the head end of the stretcher, kept up a flow of reassuring chatter, even though the patient was unable to respond with more than a blink and a flutter of her fingers.

'She will be all right, won't she?' Jean whispered, from the foot end, when at last she could bring herself to meet his eye.

'Oh yes,' he said with massive, beaming confidence. 'She's tough as old boots, aren't you, Mother?'

Standard-issue reassurance that did for everyone not yet deceased, no doubt, but Jean was grateful for it.

On arrival at the emergency department her mother was borne away and Jean felt herself dismissed. The smell – nauseating gusts of sickness, rubber, disinfectant and cooking – still made her queasy. Her recent happier visits to Charing Cross Hospital with Gretchen and Margaret couldn't quite efface those earlier grim memories of being a patient herself.

In the waiting room, half a dozen people, relatives of other recent casualties, similarly abandoned, sat gazing into space. Occasionally, a door would open and they would sit up hopefully as a nurse appeared and then slump back again as she passed through without breaking her stride.

In one corner an elderly clergyman was trying to cough discreetly into a handkerchief, his lungs bubbling and crackling. Opposite Jean was a young man, with quiffed hair and a cigarette behind his ear, dressed up as though for a night out. He seemed hugely self-conscious and ill at ease, his neck red with embarrassment, one foot tapping uncontrollably. Jean remembered the awkwardness of youth and pitied him.

One woman was attempting to distract a grizzling infant with nothing but a door key on a leather fob. Within seconds its potential to fascinate was exhausted and the child's whining redoubled. The woman stood up, hauling him onto her hip, and began to pace.

'He's not mine; he's my daughter's,' she announced with a pre-emptive glare.

The young man looked up and Jean recognised him now as the Romeo from the print room. She nodded at him and he nodded back, but not before she saw a flicker of alarm cross his face — a fear of being acknowledged in public by a middle-aged woman. Jean sighed. The cigarette behind his ear reminded her that she had smoked her last one with Howard at lunchtime, a lifetime ago. The realisation that she had none left and tomorrow was Sunday brought on an unassailable craving.

Leaving the hospital, she crossed the road to the pub. It was dark outside and cold, too, after the heated fug of the waiting room, and she shivered in her thin mac. The pub was bright and crowded with drinkers enjoying their Saturday night. Jean bought twenty Players. Even though she often ran out and had no intention of giving up the habit, she couldn't quite bring herself to buy in bulk. It seemed to demonstrate too hubristic a faith in the future.

By the time she got back to the hospital a nurse had appeared and was calling her name. Her heart lurched in fear, but the news was reassuring: her mother had been admitted to the geriatric ward and was drinking a cup of tea. She was cold and bruised but otherwise uninjured. There were signs of a chest infection, which needed monitoring.

'Can I see her? Does she know I'm here?'

The nurse looked at her watch. 'Visiting hours are over now.

You can come back tomorrow at three.'

'All right. Will you give her my love?'

The nurse smiled and turned to the next name on her list.

Jean was letting herself into the house for the second time that day when her neighbour Mrs Bowland came hobbling up the drive to intercept her.

'My dear, is there any news of your mother?' she asked with her head on one side in an attitude of concern. 'I saw the ambulance.'

She must have been sitting by the window all evening, hoping for a tragedy to feast on, thought Jean, and then felt unworthy. Her mother was not popular in the street, having frozen out all early attempts at friendship, but the Bowlands had certainly tried, so perhaps her sympathy was genuine.

'She fell over in the garden earlier and gave herself a bit of a knock. Nothing broken, apparently,' she replied, finding herself adopting the same brisk tone as the nurse.

Now she wouldn't need to bother telling the other residents of the street. Once one knew, they all knew.

'Well, it's so easy to fall at our age. And it rather knocks your confidence,' Mrs Bowland remarked.

'Oh dear – she never had much of that to begin with,' Jean said.

Once inside, the door closed, she felt suddenly weary and sat down hard on the stairs. It was nine o'clock; she had eaten nothing since those sardines at lunchtime and her stomach growled. There was a time when the prospect of an empty house would have been precious beyond imagining; a whole evening to spend or waste in solitude just as she chose. But she was too tired and anxious to enjoy it and her feet so sore from walking in shoes that pinched that she could think of nothing more luxurious to do than collapse on the couch and examine her worries, one by one.

28

When Jean arrived on the ward the following afternoon for visiting time she found her mother sitting up in bed with an expression of rapt concentration on her face as she eavesdropped on the whispered conversation taking place at the next bed.

'Shh!' she said, cutting off Jean's greeting. 'I'm trying to listen.'

'Well hello to you, too,' said Jean, relieved to see her mother's spirit undimmed by her surroundings.

She had brought with her a carpetbag containing slippers, shawl, the brushed-cotton nightdress from Peter Jones and a tablet of lavender soap delivered that morning by Mrs Melsom. News of the accident had spread via the Bowlands to the congregation of St Mary's, at which Mrs Melsom was a sideswoman. She had hurried around directly with her gift, wrapped in blue tissue paper.

'I always think it's nice to have something to put under your pillow to mask the hospital smell,' she said, pressing it into Jean's hand. 'I know your mother likes lavender.'

Does she? thought Jean, ashamed to realise that she knew nothing of these preferences. But she was touched by the gesture – one of those small, untrumpeted acts of kindness, passed from person to person, that bind a community together.

'Soap? Funny thing to bring,' said her mother, laying it aside unopened.

'How are you today? Nothing broken, they say.'

'If you believe that you'll believe anything. Look at me!' She threw the bed sheet back with surprising strength and lifted her cotton gown to reveal a livid purple bruise from hip to knee – and much else besides.

'Yes, well, cover yourself up,' said Jean, flustered, replacing the sheets.

It was something she had noticed before about people in hospital; in the face of illness and shared quarters they rapidly abandoned all modesty.

'It's agony, I might tell you,' her mother remarked.

'It looks it. Do they give you anything for the pain?'

'Probably. I don't know. It's a madhouse.' She leant, wincing, closer to Jean and spoke from the corner of her mouth. 'There was a man in here last night – going from bed to bed. He put his hand right under the covers. I soon sent him packing.'

For a moment or two Jean was quite dumbfounded, speechless with outrage.

'A man? On the ward? Why didn't you call out or say something?'

Her mother gave a scornful laugh. 'No one would believe me . . . Anyway, then there was a sort of fire drill, and we all had to get up and go outside in the rain in our nothingness. What a performance.' She chuckled to herself at the memory.

Jean looked around at the other occupants of the ward – comatose, heavily bandaged, intubated or otherwise immobilised – and caught up at last.

'Goodness. Quite a night, then.'

'I'll say.'

All the same, she felt obliged to mention her mother's remarks to the matron before she left.

'She seems a little confused.'

'They all get like that. It's the diamorphine.'

Jean smiled, not altogether reassured.

'She thought she'd been interfered with. By a man.'

Matron shook her head. 'She also thinks Queen Mary is in the bed opposite.'

'It must be so distressing – perhaps she'd be better off without the diamorphine.'

Matron looked at her over her glasses. 'You only say that because you are not in pain.'

Jean accepted the rebuke. 'How long will she be in here, do you think?'

'I can't say. At the moment she can't even use the commode.'

The look in her grey eyes was neither stern nor kind but some combination of the two – a calm, unassailable confidence that she was in charge and knew what was best. It was oddly soothing and reminded Jean of someone; she had been in the presence of this phenomenon before, but she couldn't now recall where.

She went home feeling somewhat disconcerted by the conversation with her mother. Something about it kept tweaking at the edge of her mind, refusing to reveal itself, as she prepared her dinner of cheese on toast. It was there as she washed up her single plate and knife and fork, and as she sat at the kitchen table to write a brief letter to Dorrie explaining about the accident and that there was no cause for alarm, but she couldn't coax it into view.

The next day when she arrived for evening visiting hours after a long day at work, she found her mother slightly worse.

Someone had brushed her hair back off her face, destroying what was left of the curl, and giving her a severe and somewhat masculine appearance, which would have horrified her if she had been able to see it. Looking around, Jean noticed with dismay that the other patients had been treated to a similar grooming regime and now looked like members of the same androgynous tribe.

She was thankful that there were no mirrors within range. For a recluse, her mother had always been particular about her appearance, fretting over her diminishing looks, taking great comfort from her remaining advantages – slender ankles, straight teeth – and frequently reapplying lipstick and powder, even though there was no one but Jean to appreciate it.

Today her confusion was deeper, robbing her of confidence and causing her to retreat into silence, with occasional bursts of chuckling. Enquiries as to what was amusing her produced the mysterious one-word explanation – 'Badgers'. She seemed fascinated to the point of obsession by the woman in the opposite bed, an unlikely source of entertainment, as she was mostly asleep and snoring. If a nurse approached, momentarily blocking the view, she would crane her neck and wave her imperiously out of the way in case she missed something important. Jean, by contrast, she barely noticed.

The sister on duty expressed surprise when Jean mentioned her concerns. From their point of view, Mrs Swinney was an ideal patient – placid and untroublesome, grateful for small attentions, where others were restless and obstreperous.

'But she's not herself,' Jean protested. 'She was perfectly sane when she arrived. Now she hardly knows who I am.'

She remembered with shame her previous irritation with her mother's irksome habits and predictable conversation. What trivial dissatisfactions these now seemed.

Sister looked disappointed. There was a hint of reproach in her voice.

'I'll tell the doctor what you've told me. But *we're* all really pleased with her progress.'

Jean cycled back to the empty house and a supper of beans

on toast. She was getting used to having the place to herself and a little flexibility was creeping into her routines. Her evening meal could be anytime and consist of anything – bread and jam if she fancied it – and bath night could be whatever night she chose. She could listen to the gramophone player, the wireless, or neither without any negotiation and after nine o'clock.

By the time she returned from the hospital in the evening it was hardly worth lighting a fire, so she took a hot-water bottle up to bed instead and left the grate unswept. In an exceptionally bold act, she threw out the threadbare brown rug from the sitting room, which had come with them from the flat in Gipsy Hill with the rest of their belongings. Jean had always hated it, because it curled at the corners to trip the unwary and darkened an already dark room.

She replaced it with a pale blue carpet from Nash's of Orpington in a defiantly impractical shade that matched nothing. Its newness was a dazzling reproach to its surroundings, which now looked evermore tatty and forlorn. But it was difficult to enjoy even these small liberties untarnished by feelings of guilt and remorse, while her mother was so lost and strange.

In those undisturbed evenings she turned back again to Alice Halfyard's diary, rereading the entries covering the dates when Gretchen had been a patient, and then idly – and because she rather enjoyed Alice's brisk prose – reading on into the days and weeks beyond. Gretchen's place in the ward had been taken by a girl called Ruth, who was being treated (unsuccessfully) with ultraviolet light therapy for psoriasis. There were occasional references to someone called V, who Jean was unable to identify among the other inmates or staff and whose symptoms were only alluded to in vague terms.

19 September
V not tolerating the new drugs. V excitable.

6 October
V worse than ever today.

This awakened Jean's curiosity and she re-read the entire diary
to see if there were any other mentions. There was just one
entry from May – *before* Gretchen's arrival:

24 May
Startled to find V waiting for me today in the rain.
Absolutely soaked through like a faithful dog. I managed
to conceal my alarm.

But there was no record of an admission or discharge date,
which puzzled her. V had clearly been a long-term patient
throughout the period of Gretchen's residency and yet none
of the girls had ever mentioned her. Jean decided to query
this with Alice herself and made several attempts to telephone
her, during office hours and in the evening, but there was no
reply.

Howard, and the memory of their lunch and that strangely
intimate walk in the fog, was never far from her mind. He had
said he sometimes slept at the shop, but when she tried ringing
there one evening there was no answer, so she assumed he was
back at home. Calling him during the day was problematic in
a shared office of shameless eavesdroppers, so she sent a brief
note, thanking him for the lunch and explaining about her
mother's accident.

The following evening, Friday, on her return from the hospital, she was contemplating, without enthusiasm, the range of
tins in the larder and wondering what manner of meal might
be conjured from sardines, new potatoes and oxtail soup, when
she heard the flap of the letter box. The fact that the sardines

had already brought to mind the Italian restaurant and Howard himself sent her hurrying to the door. On the mat was the now-familiar white envelope. She tore into it without waiting.

Friday, 8.30 p.m.

Dear Jean,

I have just come home to find your letter with the news of your mother.

I am so sorry that our afternoon should have ended so unfortunately and that you had to deal with it alone. I will not ring the doorbell in case you have company, but I will wait at the end of the road for half an hour or so, in the hope that you receive this in time and want to talk.

Yours,

Howard

Jean snatched up her keys and flew from the house, realising at the end of the drive that she was still wearing her apron and slippers. She tore the apron off and stuffed it into the hydrangeas; the slippers could not be helped and Howard was the last person to mind or notice.

There was the dark shape of the Wolseley parked at the top of the road. The headlights blinked in welcome at her approach. The passenger door was open; she jumped in beside him and they clasped each other awkwardly across the handbrake.

She was aware of the bristly tweed of his jacket against her cheek and his unique scent – a combination of soap, tobacco and wool and the oily metallic smell of the workshop. Strength and comfort streamed from him like a warm current. She felt, as always in his presence, a deep sense of relief. Now she was perfectly safe.

They disengaged from their somewhat contorted embrace and looked at each other. In the shadows cast by the street lamp outside his eyes were black and unreadable.

'My friend,' he said in a kind of wonderment, taking her hand and kneading it in his. 'You're here.'

'Yes.'

'I don't know what I'd have done if you hadn't come. Waited all night, perhaps.'

'I'm just glad I didn't miss you.'

'I would have come sooner if I'd known you were by yourself all this time. I've been kicking around at home with nothing to do but think of you.'

'Same here.'

'What a waste.' He put her hand up to his lips and kissed it.

At the tap of feet on the pavement they moved apart instinctively, guiltily. The passer-by was a stranger to Jean, a commuter, with overcoat and rolled umbrella, returning late from the station. If he had glanced into the car he would have seen a plain middle-aged woman in slippers and an even older man with thinning hair and heavy-rimmed glasses – such unlikely objects of passion, he could hardly have guessed at the longing that flowed between them.

'I wish . . .' Howard began and then stopped.

'What?'

'I was just thinking, I wish I'd found you years ago.'

'You make me sound like a lost glove,' Jean laughed.

'Well that's a good image. The missing half of a pair.'

She had come running out of the house without a coat and it was cold in the car with the engine stilled and the darkness pressing at the glass. He noticed her shivering.

'We could go somewhere warm. A pub, if you like?'

She shook her head, recalling those evenings spent in the White Swan with Frank while he drank himself into a good mood and then out the other side again.

'We have two empty houses between us,' she said. 'Surely

there's no reason for us to skulk in the car? Why should we be lonely?'

And yet the guilt was there between them like an unwanted third person, interfering, spoiling everything.

'No reason at all,' he agreed. 'Just say which you prefer.'

Jean imagined Mrs Bowland stationed at the front room window, observing and judging, and her defiance faltered.

'Yours,' she said.

He nodded. 'Mine, then.'

Only a faint yellow glow leaked from the curtained windows in Burdett Road. All was still.

'Everyone's back in their hutches,' Howard whispered as he let them into the house.

Jean felt a momentary tremor of unease at this act of trespass, but then he switched the lamp on in the hallway and the feeling vanished with the darkness. He led her into the sitting room and turned on the gas fire, which emitted a bluish light and a high-pitched whine and sudden, dramatic heat. She had never seen this room before, with its armchairs and television set; as a guest, she had been ushered into the front parlour, upstairs to the workshop for a dress fitting or into the garden.

They kissed, for a long time, gently at first and then less so. Then Howard pulled away and, holding her face, said, 'Will you stay tonight? I don't think I can bear to take you back home.'

'In Gretchen's bed?'

'No. In mine.'

She remembered the single divans with their matching bedspreads and the chilly chasm between them.

He mistook her hesitation and said, 'Or here,' and before she could correct him, he dashed out of the room and upstairs. Moments later he reappeared dragging a quilted eiderdown and blanket, which he spread out in front of the gas fire.

'All right. Just here,' she said. 'Now, kiss me again.'

He knelt down to undress her, his shaking hands fumbling over every button and zip and hook, until she was naked in front of him. Then he stopped and looked up at her with a troubled expression.

'I haven't done this for seven years. Will you forgive me if it goes badly?'

Jean laughed, amazed at her own boldness in displaying her body while he was still fully clothed. It was the strangest feeling, placing herself in someone else's power with complete confidence. There was nothing she wouldn't do for him.

'Well, I haven't done it for longer than that. But it doesn't matter, as long as we're kind.'

And so even though they were unpractised, they were kind and that made it all right. And afterwards they lay for a long time pressed together, her head on his shoulder, his hand stroking her hip while the night deepened around them. There was no urgency to move apart; morning and work were a long way off.

Jean remembered how Frank could never lie still with her for one minute once the loving was over but would sit up, light a cigarette and start scrabbling for his clothes in one impatient movement. She'd thought it was something all men did.

'Are you tired?' Howard asked, kissing her hair. 'You can sleep if you like.'

'No – I'm wide awake,' said Jean, not wanting to waste a moment of their time together in mere sleep.

They shifted into a sitting position with their backs to the couch, the eiderdown gathered around them, and she confessed that she had had no supper and was hungry. So he made them tea and toast, which they ate there on the floor, and when he noticed that she was shivering he fetched a soft woollen shawl for her shoulders.

'It's not Gretchen's,' he said. 'It's one of Aunt Edie's cast-offs. She's never worn it, I promise.'

He had a gift for anticipating her vulnerabilities and reassuring her before she was even aware of them.

'You know all my thoughts without my saying them,' Jean replied. 'Am I really that transparent?'

'Let's see,' said Howard, gazing into her eyes with a frown of concentration, his lips moving slowly as he pretended to read.

'What does it say?' she laughed.

It was so easy and natural to talk nonsense when your love was returned.

'It says, "I would like to come back and do this again tomorrow and possibly the next day."'

'More or less,' she agreed.

'Why shouldn't we?' he asked, more serious now. 'We are not hurting anyone, are we?'

'No. But, Howard, we won't tell Gretchen, will we? I'd feel so awkward.'

'I can't see that I'd have any *occasion* to tell her. But I don't see any need for deception.'

He was right, of course. Dishonesty could never bring peace of mind. Always he was there just ahead of her, with that lantern of decent behaviour.

'I just feel guilty somehow, for stepping so quickly into her shoes. Her bed, I mean.'

'She was never *in* her bed!' he protested, gathering her in his arms again. 'But whatever you say.'

'Did you really never make love with her? Even in the beginning?' Jean asked.

'Of course, at first. But I could tell she didn't like it – it was just something she felt she had to do, with gritted teeth, so to speak. Which made me feel like a monster. So I gradually stopped asking and the intervals got longer and one day I

260

realised that it had been more than a year and it sort of dawned on me that we would never make love again.'

'It was selfish of her to marry you, knowing that she couldn't love you properly.'

'The thing that hurt most was being made to feel that my desires were unreasonable for all those years. Gretchen always insisted that sex was unimportant and meant nothing to her, but that wasn't true. As soon as Martha reappeared, suddenly her desires trumped everything. Her "natural feelings" couldn't be suppressed for five minutes, but I'd had to suppress mine for years.'

He still loves her, Jean thought with a tightness in her throat of swallowed jealousy.

'I understand', she said in as steady a voice as she could manage, 'that she's still your wife and your feelings for her won't change overnight. I do understand that.'

He looked at her with concentration and amazement.

'You are generous, Jean,' he said, kissing her again, 'but you don't need to be. It's you now.'

'It's you, too,' she said.

A feeling of peace swept over her as if she had reached the end of a long journey and could now rest.

'I sometimes wondered . . .' she said, drawing him to her so that he lay back with his head in her lap. He looked at this angle and without his glasses quite different, a stranger. 'Whether Gretchen was trying to engineer things to throw us together. Did you ever think that?'

'It's possible. Something like it happened once before with Margaret's first piano teacher. Gretchen always made me take her home and seemed to find ingenious ways of leaving me alone with her. It was as if I was being given permission to stray. All unspoken, of course. But I wasn't the least bit attracted to the piano teacher. Or she to me, I might add.'

Jean looked sceptical. The idea that someone could be indifferent to Howard struck her as highly improbable. The woman must have been some kind of imbecile.

'I didn't think I'd made much of a first impression on you myself,' she said.

'You were rather businesslike and brisk with your notebook,' he smiled. 'And then you cut yourself on my coping saw.'

'Yes. I'd forgotten that. You complimented me on my hands.'

'Did I?' He picked one up and turned it over with an appraising glance. 'They are rather pretty. I never imagined you'd be putting them to such good use.'

Jean burst out laughing.

'I don't think I began to notice you properly until that day you came to tea and we played badminton.'

'Now you are making fun of me.'

'Not at all. You were such a good sport.'

'That was a lovely afternoon. And I went home envying your perfect marriage.'

'Ha!'

There was a silence as they separately reflected on the unravelling of that illusion.

'And then I bumped into you at Charing Cross,' Jean went on, 'and you insisted on seeing me home. You were so funny; I didn't want the journey to end, even though we hardly spoke. That was when it started for me.'

'I remember. But it was at Aunt Edie's that I fell in love with you. I think it was when I saw you sitting in the apple tree. But I couldn't say anything.'

'You didn't need to. I felt it, too.'

'The next day was so grey and empty. I was like a child on Boxing Day – all the magic over.'

For Jean it was pure pleasure to reminisce about the painful separation from the safe haven of rapturous togetherness. The sense of security and confidence was quite new to her. All of her dealings with Frank had been tinged with fear − fully justified, as it turned out − that she bored him; that she would do something to incur his anger; that he would leave her for someone younger or prettier.

Howard let out a sigh and rubbed his eyes with the heel of his hands.

'You look sad,' she said. 'Or worried.'

'Because I've so little to offer you.'

'I don't need anything. I just know that when I'm with you I'm happy, and when I'm not I'm miserable. That's all.'

'Will you come back again tomorrow?'

'As soon as I've been to the hospital. They might send Mother home soon and then I'll be confined to barracks again.'

'Then we must make the most of the time we have.'

The thought of her mother, alone and bewildered, made Jean's crowded heart quail within her. The freedom to spend her nights with Howard was entirely provisional upon her mother's continued absence. Jean now found herself in the invidious position of wishing her ongoing ill health and a slow recovery. When she tried to visualise the future any more than a few days ahead there was no certainty, only fog.

29

The crooked tines of the rake made a tinny rattle as they combed the wet grass, drawing the leaves into a copper mound. Jean, defended against the autumn weather by wellingtons and windcheater over her oldest outdoor clothes, was spending her Saturday out in the front garden catching up with neglected chores.

In the last week the horse chestnuts and Canadian oaks in Knoll Park had given up the last of their leaves. Great drifts of them had blown into the Swinneys' driveway and were plastered over the front lawn and banked up against the garage doors. Jean had filled the metal dustbin five times and five times carried it down to the compost heap. She had already taken down the withered runner beans, dismantled their bamboo skeleton, stored the canes in the shed for the winter and dug over the earth. The rhubarb had been mulched and the onions weeded and treated to a dressing of soot.

In the kitchen a cherry cake was cooling on the rack. She would glaze it later and take it with her to Howard's for tea when he came back from work. She had hardly spent any time at home for over a week now, returning only briefly to collect the mail and clean clothes for work.

Mrs Bowland had waylaid her on the first of these flying

visits, ostensibly for news of Mrs Swinney; also to query the pints of milk left out on the doorstep overnight.

'Oh, I've been staying with a friend,' Jean said, cursing herself for overlooking this detail.

'We wondered if everything was all right', said Mrs Bowland, 'when you didn't come home.'

'Yes, quite all right, thank you,' said Jean, refusing to be probed. 'Although Mother is still not quite her old self.'

There had been a few days of what appeared to Jean complete and irreversible derangement, during which her mother entirely failed to recognise her, mistaking her variously for the ward sister, Queen Mary and a pickpocket bent on stealing her wedding ring. She had lost all sense of time and place, with no inkling of where she was or how long she had been there. The mystery of her circumstances didn't appear to cause her any anxiety and her hallucinations – badgers romping up and down the ward – amused rather than alarmed her.

Although Jean found these developments troubling, she couldn't help noticing that losing her wits had greatly improved her mother's mood and general demeanour. She was infinitely more cheerful now than at any time in recent memory. Jean's prayers for her recovery had a flavour of St Augustine's plea for chastity. *Please, God, make Mother better, but not yet.*

Jean carried the last bin load of leaves to the compost, swept the drive and returned the rake and broom to the shed, and not a moment too soon. There was a growl of distant thunder as she crossed the lawn and a few fat drops of rain began to fall.

Howard would be back from work at six-thirty and there was liver and bacon for dinner and then the cherry cake. They would sit together on the couch holding hands and listening to his jazz records on the gramophone. Then they would go upstairs and climb into Howard's single bed together, ignoring that abandoned one just beyond the gap, and make love, because you never knew what was around the corner and when something might come along to put a stop to it.

Now, though, she had a couple of hours before she was due to cycle over to the hospital for visiting time, just long enough to ice the cake and have a hot bath – on a Saturday afternoon! She had just weighed out the sugar when the doorbell rang. Mrs Bowland again, she thought with a sinking heart. Stretching her face into a patient smile, she opened the door.

Margaret stood on the doorstep, red-eyed, her coat bulging oddly as she clutched at her chest. A fine mist of raindrops was caught in her curls like dew on a web.

'Margaret! What are you doing here?' Jean exclaimed, glancing up and down the road for evidence of Gretchen or some other companion.

Belatedly, she took in the child's bedraggled state and the bulge, now revealed to be a struggling Jemimah.

'I've run away,' Margaret said, sniffing noisily and hoisting the rabbit into a more manageable position. 'I didn't know where else to go. Daddy's at work.'

It was some weeks since Jean had seen her and the resemblance to Gretchen, and the doll-like beauty of her face, struck her all over again.

'Come in, come in,' she replied, her mind racing at this new development. 'Have you come all this way by yourself?'

'Yes. With Jemimah. She was all right at first, but she got a bit wriggly. And then it started to rain.'

'How on earth did you find your way here?'

'Mummy takes me to school every day so I know how to get trains and I remembered that you lived near the station from that time I came to make cinder toffee. I know your address from sending you a postcard. So I asked the lady in the newsagent in the station. She hadn't heard of you, but she'd heard of the Knoll.'

They had advanced no further than the hall during this exchange.

'Let's go and put Jemimah down and then you can tell me why you've run away,' Jean suggested, wondering what Margaret would have done if she had not been at home, as was very nearly the case. The thought made her feel quite dizzy.

In the kitchen, while Jemimah hopped around the lino, exploring her new domain and shunning the wizened carrot supplied by Jean from her depleted larder, Margaret took off her wet coat and rotated her aching arms with relief. She had also been carrying a shoulder bag, which she now unpacked onto the table to reveal her beaded purse, toothbrush, notebook and a sack of dried rabbit food. As a running-away kit, it struck Jean as touchingly inadequate.

Jean made her a glass of hot milk, cut a slice of cake and then fetched the least threadbare of their towels to put around her shoulders.

'Now, what's all this about running away?' she said at last as she patted dry Margaret's hair.

'I hate Martha,' said Margaret, her pretty face crumpling into a frown.

'Hate's a strong word,' said Jean, silently rejoicing.

'Well, she hates me, too.'

'I'm sure she doesn't. Who could possibly hate you?'

'She won't let me bring Jemimah in the house for even *one minute* because she's allergic to fur, *she says*. So I have to play with her out in the back yard in the cold. And there's not even any grass. It's horrible.'

'Oh dear.'

'And I have to sleep on a fold-out bed in the room where Martha does all her painting and it's really messy and smells of paint. But if *I* make a mess I get told off.'

'Have you told your mother how you feel?'

'She doesn't understand. Martha's all nice when she's around. But if Mummy goes out she just ignores me.'

Margaret took a sip of milk and wiped her top lip on her sleeve.

'One time when we were on our own I said, "You don't like me, do you?" and she said, "I haven't decided yet. I don't *dis*like you."'

Her rendering of Martha's low, cultured voice was uncannily, almost cruelly accurate.

'Oh, Margaret, I don't know what to say. What can I do to help you?'

The girl blinked hard to try and hold down the first hot prickling of tears.

'I wish we could just go back to the way things were,' she burst out. 'With Daddy. It was better before.'

Jean put a tentative arm around her shoulders and, meeting no resistance, gathered her into a hug. She could feel the bones of her back, fragile and birdlike, beneath the wool of her cardigan as she sobbed.

'Don't cry,' she pleaded, powerless to offer any real comfort. 'Everything will be all right.'

But this was an assurance not hers to make and, as one of the chief beneficiaries of the fractured Tilbury marriage, she felt its hollowness.

At last Margaret's tears were cried out and she consented to mop her flaming face with a cool facecloth. This outpouring of emotion and moisture had fogged the kitchen windows.

'Good heavens,' said Jean, 'much more of this and we'll have to build Jemimah a raft.'

Margaret had recovered sufficiently to giggle between gulps and sniffs.

'Did you tell anyone where you were going?'

'No. I just sneaked out.'

Jean imagined Gretchen, frantic at the discovery and combing the streets. She would have to be telephoned and reassured at some stage, but would it really hurt her to taste a little fear, if it opened her eyes to the cost of her emancipation?

In the end it was Howard she rang, leaving that other, more difficult phone call to him. Margaret was adamant that she wanted to go home to Burdett Road. It was agreed that he would pick her up after work; Sunday was their day together anyway. The rest would have to be negotiated with Gretchen. Margaret's main concern was Jemimah.

'Where is she going to sleep tonight? I had to leave the hutch behind.'

Howard promised to bring a stout cardboard box home from the shop; he would spend the evening fashioning some form of temporary rabbit-proof accommodation. It was impossible for Jean to speak openly with Margaret bobbing about beside her and interjecting every few seconds, and the anguished pauses in the conversation were heavy with unspoken regret for their abandoned plans.

Noticing that Margaret was starting to shiver in her damp clothes, Jean offered to run her a hot bath – the one she had intended to take herself but would not now need. She filled it a little deeper than the scant three inches that was her usual allocation and dug out another of their elderly towels from the airing cupboard. It was only at moments like these, when she saw her belongings through another's eyes – even those of an uncritical ten-year-old girl – that she was ashamed of how shabby they were. There was a crust of limescale around the neck and snout of the tap, and a green streak running down the enamel from the overflow to the plughole. The ancient lino, though clean, was cracked and ridged.

'I'm sorry, it's probably not as nice as your bathroom at home,' Jean said.

Having lived there all week she knew quite well that it wasn't.

'That's all right,' said Margaret kindly, beginning to peel off her jumper. 'It's better than Luna Street.'

Jean left her to undress and returned to the kitchen, where Jemimah had been shut in with a saucer of the chaff from Margaret's running-away kit. She washed up the milk pan and cut herself a slice of the cherry cake – Howard could take the rest when he came – then sat at the table gazing blankly at the crossword in the Saturday paper while brooding on these latest developments.

If Margaret moved back home permanently that would put an end to staying overnight with Howard, even before her mother's eventual discharge from hospital, which would only frustrate matters further. It was a mess.

Her ruminations were interrupted by a cry from above. Jean bounded up the stairs, her heart thudding in alarm. Margaret stood in the steamy bathroom, naked apart from her sturdy white knickers. She was craning to catch sight of her back in the mirror. A patch of raw pink skin the size of a postage stamp was visible just above her waistband.

'I tried not to get it wet but it just came off,' she said, holding out the towel to Jean to reveal a jellied smear of dead skin – the mortal remains of Gretchen's rejected graft.

Good uses for sour milk. Linoleum or floorcloth washed with sour milk comes up brighter than with water. Sour milk also makes a good bleach for discoloured white fabrics. Wring out articles in water, place in a bowl and cover with sour milk. Leave for forty-eight hours. Wash thoroughly and the articles will be snow-white.

30

The coal fire in the grate was banked up and glowing a volcanic orange; the discussion in the room was no less heated.

Enthroned behind his massive desk sat Dr Lloyd-Jones. On the other side of the room – and the argument – were his colleague Dr Bamber, and Hilary Endicott, whose article quoted in the *Echo* had prompted Gretchen Tilbury's original letter. Jean sat quietly, listening to the debate and taking notes.

'I think we can at least say that given the results of the serological tests, it has not been possible to disprove the claim by Mother A. Is that fair?'

Dr Lloyd-Jones alone persisted with this naming convention, though all in the room knew her identity.

'No, it most certainly isn't. You asked me what criterion would satisfy me that parthenogenesis had taken place and I told you – a successful skin graft from child to mother. This hasn't been fulfilled and therefore the mother's claim is disproved. It's quite simple.'

This was Hilary Endicott, formidable in tweed suiting and brown brogues. She looked as though she would be more at home on a highland grouse moor than in a laboratory, but she had in fact come up that morning from her mock-Tudor mansion in Surrey. Jean, who was both taller and older, nevertheless felt dwarfed in her presence.

'I think the significance of the skin graft is less decisive than you allow,' said Dr Lloyd-Jones. 'It is regrettable, for instance, that we didn't perform an autograft as a control.'

'Well, indeed,' said Dr Endicott.

'Another possibility', Dr Lloyd-Jones went on, ignoring this barb, 'is that one of the antigens that gave rise to the incompatibility might be recessive and only present in the daughter.'

'The skin graft test was not equivocal. It failed in both directions.'

'But all the evidence from the blood and serum tests is consistent with parthenogenesis.'

'Among other possibilities,' put in Dr Bamber. It was his first contribution to the debate so far.

'Such as?' asked Jean.

If she had to be the one to break the news to Gretchen she wanted to be able to understand as much as possible of the detail. She had naïvely assumed that the tests would provide irrefutable proof one way or another, that science would drive out all ambiguity, but it seemed that even the three most closely involved could not agree.

'Well, consanguineous mating, for instance.'

'You mean incest,' Jean protested, offended by both the idea and the jargon. 'There's never been any suggestion . . .'

'It's just a for instance,' he replied, holding out his hands in a gesture of appeasement. 'I know nothing of the personal background. I am talking as a scientist.'

'This would need to be excluded as a possibility even if the blood types of mother and daughter were very rare,' added Dr Endicott. 'But they are not, which makes the probability of – let's call it *coincidental* – consanguinity the greater.'

'Surely' – Dr Lloyd-Jones' face was red, the broken capillaries on his cheeks and nose blossoming in the heat – 'where the mother presents herself as an example of a virgin birth without any foreknowledge of the confirming blood test results, the validity of her claim is greatly increased?'

'It is persuasive, certainly, but it is not proven,' said Dr Bamber. 'It would be useful to know, for example, how many – if any – cases there are of wholly segregated women – in prisons or asylums, say – reporting the phenomenon. None, as far as we know.'

'If we had data for the number of recorded women-lifetimes without any instances of parthenogenesis that would give us some basis for an estimate of probability,' Dr Endicott added.

'All this is very fascinating,' said Jean, raking a hand through her hair in frustration. 'But where does it leave Mrs Tilbury? I feel she's been led up the garden path with all these tests and now even you so-called experts can't look at the results and come to a consensus. What am I to tell her?'

'I'm sure it's disappointing for you,' said Dr Endicott. 'You would have liked a more explosive outcome. But perhaps if she is made to understand that the medical results do not support her claim of parthenogenesis she might be prepared to change her story.'

'Never,' said Jean. 'She has too much invested in it.'

She thought of Martha – arch-sceptic – and wondered how she would react to the news. It was hard to imagine her coming down on the side of blind faith. And even harder to imagine Gretchen admitting to the commission of a colossal fraud. Jean, her confidence in Gretchen now fatally damaged, and compromised by her own involvement with Howard, was beginning to wish the story dead and buried. Any publicity generated by publication could escalate to engulf them all in a very unwelcome scandal.

She felt the blood rising to her cheeks in anticipation of the embarrassment in store. The failure of the three scientists to agree might yet work in her favour. An inconclusive result was hardly the bombshell Roy Drake had been hoping for. Maybe if she played her hand carefully he might be persuaded to park the story indefinitely.

31

Jean thought it only fair to brief Roy Drake before the editorial meeting. His disappointment and possible displeasure would be easier to bear without an audience.

'It could hardly be a worse outcome,' she said. 'We're no closer to the truth than we were on day one. The story's completely dead.'

She watched him drop three sugar lumps into his tea and stir it with the arm of his spectacles.

'But you haven't been able to disprove her claim by any other means?'

'Well, no.'

'You don't sound very certain. I thought you said she was sincere and genuine?'

'Yes, I did,' Jean stammered, aware that she was not being entirely sincere and genuine herself. 'I've allowed myself to get distracted by . . . domestic matters, and I stopped digging and questioning. I've been a lousy journalist.'

Roy raised a hand – a faint gesture of demurral, perhaps – but did not contradict her.

'It would have been interesting to see her reaction to the failure of the skin graft.'

'I wasn't there unfortunately. Dr Lloyd-Jones said she pleaded with him to rerun the experiment. Which he wasn't prepared to do. He didn't seem to set as much store by it as the other two.'

'Even so, it's still an interesting story.' He glanced at his watch; the meeting was due to start in five minutes. 'So, we haven't got solid scientific proof. But, equally, we haven't been able to crack her testimony. We could still run it as an unsolved mystery – 'The Strange Case of Gretchen What's-her-name' – without making any claims that are untrue. Here are the facts – let the public decide.'

Jean quailed. Let the public decide? One might as well throw her to the wolves.

'The marriage has broken down. I'm concerned about the effect of publicity on the child – if one of the nationals gets hold of it.'

'Their marital difficulties are hardly our problem,' said Roy. 'She approached us, not the other way round. And divorce is not the scandal it once was. We've invested a lot of time in this and it's an unusual story of legitimate interest to our readers. And if one of the nationals does pick it up, so much the better. That's always been the hope, hasn't it?'

'But without the scientific proof . . . ?'

'Wasn't one of the doctors still open-minded?'

'Dr Lloyd-Jones. He said . . .' Jean opened her notebook and flipped through the pages of Dutton's Double Speed Longhand to the phrase underlined three times. 'It has not been possible to disprove the claim.'

'Splendid. We can use that. Maybe publication will bring some other experts, or even witnesses, out of the woodwork.'

'I still feel uncomfortable.'

Roy shook his head. 'You'll get over it. We can run it the first week of December. Nice feature for Advent. Get young Tony to do some photos of mother and child.'

'All right,' said Jean, defeated. 'I'll get in touch with Gretchen.

I've been putting off talking to her because I thought we might be spiking the story altogether.'

She reddened as she remembered the other reason why she had been avoiding a meeting.

'Good man. Anything else you need to discuss?'

'No, that was all. Thank you.'

She stood up to leave, feeling outmanoeuvred, the result of her own dishonesty and evasion.

'I meant to say you're looking well lately. More . . . *sprightly*.'

'Sprightly?' Jean's face fell.

'No, that's not the word. Relaxed. Healthy. Blooming.'

He was overdoing it now, Jean thought, to compensate for *sprightly*, the preserve of ageing spinsters, immemorially unloved and yet still, somehow, mobile.

'You've done your hair differently.'

'Oh well, I just used a hairdryer for once.'

'Anyway, it suits you whatever it is.'

'Perhaps I'm more relaxed now that Mother's a little better.'

'That's very good news,' said Roy Drake, who had made regular and sincere enquiries about her health, and even sent her a basket of exotic and out-of-season fruit from Harrods – a luxury she had been too unwell to appreciate.

The previous week had seen some improvement. Penicillin prescribed for a urine infection seemed to have cleared a clouded mind as well. For the first time, Jean had been recognised and welcomed. Conversation had proceeded along rational and predictable lines. The delusions of recent weeks were forgotten.

Although greatly relieved by these developments, Jean couldn't help wishing that her mother's memory loss might have been more discriminating. Those dutiful bedside vigils, on top of a day's work, eating into her precious time with Howard, had all been wiped away along with the pickpockets, Queen Mary and the badgers. And soon, perhaps in a matter of days, she would be home and Jean's brief taste of freedom would be over, every absence a matter of negotiation and forward planning.

To complicate matters further, Margaret, in a reversal of the previous arrangements, was now living with Howard at Burdett Road and spending weekends with her mother in Luna Street. This solution was accepted by all parties as the most practical and conducive to Margaret's happiness. She could now walk to and from school with Lizzie, as she had been accustomed to before her removal to Chelsea, and remain at Lizzie's until Howard got home from Bedford Street.

Once, in the guise of unofficial aunt, Jean had joined father and daughter for dinner, but the awkwardness of taking Gretchen's place at the table was too much and she never repeated it. She had been unable to exchange so much as a glance with Howard that might betray them, and then withdrawn in lonely frustration to her empty house.

While this situation lasted, Saturday night to Sunday morning was the only opportunity she and Howard had to be together. From the moment they said hello – clinging to each other in the hallway as soon as the front door was closed – time, which had dawdled all week, now hustled them along towards goodbye again. They didn't go out; the pleasure of small acts of domestic intimacy – sharing a bath, preparing a meal side by side at the stove, putting clean sheets on the bed, smoking the day's last cigarette in the garden while they looked at the night sky – these were all still delightful.

'Stop, don't move,' Howard said once as they half sat, half lay on the couch, Jean's head in his lap. 'Listen.'

The record had finished and there was nothing to hear apart from the rasp of the needle on vinyl.

'What?' said Jean.

'It's happiness. Can't you hear it?'

She put her hand up blindly and found his. 'Yes,' she said, in a whisper, because happiness was shy and easily scared off.

He no longer mentioned Gretchen, either wistfully, which would have been awful, or bitterly, which would have been worse. Jean knew that didn't necessarily mean she was never in his thoughts. A decade of marriage was not easily effaced. But he was not the kind of man who took any pleasure in stoking female insecurity.

The only regrets he expressed were that he hadn't met Jean earlier and been able to love her for longer. At moments like these, and in the afterglow of lovemaking, when Jean felt Gretchen thoroughly vanquished, she thought perhaps it didn't matter even if he did still love his wife a little. In her triumph she could afford to be generous.

32

The Grange, home of Kitty Benteen since the closure of St Cecilia's in 1947, was a large and rather grand detached house in an acre of wooded garden set well back from the road leading between Keston and Locksbottom. Jean had cycled past the end of the driveway and its high walls on her journey to and from work for nearly a decade without ever giving it a glance.

Brenda van Lingen could hardly have known, when she included the address in her long-delayed reply from South Africa, just how very close to Jean's 'part of the world' it was. Now, as Jean wheeled her bicycle up the gravel drive between the dripping laurels, she felt a tremor of fear and anticipation at the thought of coming face to face with the final member of the foursome.

She arrived punctually, as instructed by Kitty's sister and chief carer, Elsie, with whom the interview had been arranged over the telephone. Jean had been given to understand that Kitty looked forward to the stimulus of new visitors and would be disappointed if kept waiting.

'Is she able to talk comfortably?' Jean asked, embarrassed by her own ignorance.

She had seen pictures of iron lungs in the newspapers and imagined the confinement a living death.

'Talk? Lord, yes, I should say so,' Elsie laughed.

'May I bring a gift? Flowers or something?'

'Perhaps not flowers. Pollen makes her nose run, which is no fun when you can't wipe it.'

In the end Jean settled on a jar of hand cream, liberated from her drawer of treasures. Elsie had confirmed that this would be quite suitable. Though paralysed below the chest, Kitty took pride in her hands, and in her brief exeats from the iron lung had been known to file and polish her nails a bold shade of red.

At the stroke of four, Jean rang the doorbell and was greeted by Elsie. She was a plump woman of about her own age with blonde, fluffy hair, pink fluffy slippers and at – and very nearly under – her heels, a white fluffy poodle, which barked excitedly and ran around them in tight circles. Apart from this general impression of fluff, Jean's attention was caught by a large wooden crucifix on the opposite wall, bearing a painted plaster Christ with rouged cheeks and livid red wounds. There were other paintings on the walls depicting Jesus in better days, surrounded by chubby blue-eyed children, or dazzling a cowering Peter, James and John with the whiteness of his robes.

'Thank you for coming,' Elsie said, helping to divest Jean of her wet mackintosh and rain hood, which she hung from a curious pair of carved wooden antlers by the door. 'Kitty's had her nap and she's quite lively.'

She showed Jean into a large, brightly lit day room, in which the 'lively' Kitty lay encased but for her head in the iron lung, a monstrous metal contraption like a coffin made out of an old Morris Minor. It was impossible not to be startled by the sight of a fellow human thus entombed and it took all of Jean's self-control to hide her consternation. But Kitty herself seemed quite unruffled, cheerful even.

Someone had placed a chair near her head at a comfortable distance for conversation, and an angled mirror above her, from which a rosary was hanging, gave a partial view of the room.

'Here you are. Here's your visitor,' said Elsie, withdrawing with carefully planted steps to avoid the wheeling poodle.

'Hello,' said Kitty, turning her neck in its rubber cuff and smiling a welcome.

Her fair hair was curled and set in the latest style, and her cheeks were rouged. She wore a pair of tortoiseshell glasses of powerful magnification.

'I'm so pleased to meet you at last,' said Jean, disconcerted by the mechanical whoosh and gasp of the air pump as it did its work. 'The other girls from St Cecilia's spoke so warmly of you. And all this time you've been under my nose, so to speak.'

'I'm glad to hear that. I've such fond memories of St Cecilia's.'

'Really?' said Jean, staggered by Kitty's fortitude. 'None of the other girls was anything like as positive about the experience, and they surely had far less to complain about than you.'

'We were all more or less immobilised, but I suppose being paralysed I was the only one who wasn't in pain,' said Kitty. 'So in a way I was better off.'

'Do you remember Gretchen in particular?'

'She was a nice girl. The best of the bunch. I didn't get to know her too well because she was at the far end of the ward by the window and I was at the other end nearest the door. But she was a favourite with everyone, because she was so pretty and gentle. Martha was her special friend. The beds were too wide apart for them to hold hands, so they used to hold the ends of a rolled-up towel between them. Isn't that sweet?'

'I suppose so,' said Jean, surprised by this unexpected picture of Martha's vulnerability.

'Sometimes the nuns would get Gretchen into a wheelchair and offer to take her out for a walk, but she always said, "No, just wheel me to the end of the ward so I can talk to Kitty." I've never forgotten that.'

'Were there ever any male visitors on the ward?'

'No, we didn't see any men,' said Kitty with faint disdain. 'Unless you count my angel. Angels are always male, aren't they?'

'What do you mean?' Jean asked with a slight shiver, remembering the religious icons in the hall. She couldn't hear the word without thinking of Margaret.

'I had a visitation one night.'

'You mean some kind of vision?'

'No, it wasn't a *vision*. That's what Elsie calls it, but she's wrong. It was definitely corporeal, because he touched me.'

Jean's heart began to beat faster.

'Do you remember when this was? Was it during the time that Gretchen was a patient?'

'Yes, it was that summer. It was late July. I know that because my cousin had been to Lourdes and brought me back a vial of holy water for my birthday, which is on the fifteenth.'

'So, tell me about this vision – I mean visitation.'

'Every night one of the nuns would come in to say evening prayers with me – usually Sister Maria Goretti.'

'Just you – or were the other girls involved?'

'Oh no. Just me. They weren't believers.'

'Anyway, sorry. I mustn't keep interrupting.'

There was a tightness in her chest of held breath and trepidation.

'Well, one evening I told Sister about the holy water. I didn't know whether I was supposed to drink it, dab it on like TCP or what to do with it. But I'd heard all these wonderful stories from my cousin about the miracles at Lourdes. So Sister took the bottle out of my cupboard where all my personal things were kept and I asked if she could bless it.

'She said she wasn't allowed to give blessings because she didn't have the authority, but it was already holy and she would use it to mark a cross on my forehead. And then she prayed over me to St Bernadette for a sign that I would get well. Then she

284

put my rosary on my pillow where I could see it and I went to sleep, hoping that in the morning I would be healed.

'At some point in the night I woke up and the rosary had slipped off my pillow, and when I turned my head there was an angel standing beside me.'

'What did it look like?'

'It was dark and I didn't have my glasses on, so I couldn't see clearly, apart from the outline of his flowing hair.'

'Did he have wings?'

'I couldn't see.'

'So what made you think it was an angel?'

'Because I felt this tremendous sense of peace come over me as if the Lord had sent him to tell me that everything would be all right, just as we had prayed.'

'And then what happened?'

'He picked up the rosary, which was on the floor, and laid it on my pillow, and his fingers brushed my cheek. So I knew it was real and not a vision.'

At last, Jean thought. It came back to her now, that uneasy half-formed idea that had refused to come into focus at the time of her mother's delirium. There had been a man on the ward, she had said, interfering with her. But it hadn't happened; it was a hallucination. Surely a reverse delusion was equally possible where drugs were involved?

'Weren't you frightened? I'd have been terrified,' she said. A man's hand on her face in the dark . . .

'Not at all. I felt quite peaceful.'

'Did he speak?'

'No, he never spoke. He just touched my cheek – his skin was soft as a child's.'

'And then what? Did he vanish, or fly away, or just slip out of the door?'

Kitty looked offended.

'He seemed to glide away behind me so I couldn't see him any more.'

'Did you tell anyone about it the next day? The other girls or Sister?'

'I didn't say anything to the girls – they would have thought I was making it up. Martha was very scornful of religion – for a clergyman's daughter. But I did tell Sister Maria Goretti and she said it was a sign that St Bernadette had heard our prayers.' She beamed at Jean from her metal prison.

'And you never mentioned it to anyone else?'

'I told Elsie, of course, but she thinks it was just a hallucination. But it wasn't. I was as wide awake as I am now. You don't believe me either, I can tell.'

'I've been called to believe far stranger things lately,' Jean replied with a non-committal smile. There was nothing to be gained by demolishing Kitty's delusion if it gave her comfort. 'Did your condition improve after this . . . visitation?'

'Yes, it did,' said Kitty firmly. 'It did. From that day onwards I no longer felt abandoned by God, and that gave me the strength to accept my condition and live the best life I can.'

Tears of admiration sprang to Jean's eyes. Kitty's bravery and stoicism were a rebuke to her own luxurious troubles.

'I'm studying theology, you know,' Kitty went on. 'With Elsie's help. She reads the books to me and I dictate my essays to her. I'm very blessed.'

After the unnerving whooshing of the iron lung, the silence outside the house was precious as never before. Jean wheeled her bicycle back down the slushy gravel of the driveway deep in thought about this stealthy bedside angel with his gentle hands. Kitty's testimony had unlocked a door now, and Jean felt that only by returning to St Cecilia's and standing in the room where it all took place would she come to a proper understanding of what had happened to Gretchen in the summer of 1946.

Nursing: An emergency table may be made by using an ironing board placed alongside the patient's bed. This makes a very handy lightweight table, and is the right height for drinks and plates.

33

The back door of the ambulance opened and Mrs Swinney, supported by Jean on one side and a walking stick on the other, made a slow and queenly descent to the pavement. She stood for a moment, looking about her as if expecting some kind of reception committee, before allowing herself to be led down the driveway to the house. She had lost weight in the weeks she had been away and her muscles were thoroughly wasted. What remained of her strength seemed concentrated in the fingers of her right hand, which were now digging into the flesh of Jean's arm.

The path and step had been cleared of wet leaves and other hazards, and the house made as clean and welcoming as time allowed. Jean had only received notice the day before that her mother would be discharged and had since been trying to make good on her recent neglect of her housekeeping.

As a homecoming treat she had made a fish pie, with potatoes from Howard's garden, and a queen of puddings, using a reckless half jar of Mrs Melsom's raspberry jam. She had considered making up a daybed in the back room overlooking the garden, to spare her mother the stairs, but it was a cold room, with an unswept chimney and a fireplace that had never been used. The garden in late November was not much to look at anyway, so she had decided against it.

They stood in the hallway, Jean's mother breathless from the journey from kerb to house.

'Home again, home again, jiggety-jig,' she panted and then stopped, her eye caught by the new blue carpet in the sitting room, just visible through the open door. 'What's this, then?'

She approached it tentatively, as though gathering courage to dip a toe into its freezing depths.

'Oh, I bought it. It's rather nice, I think.'

'What was wrong with the old one?'

'Apart from the scorch marks and the bald patches? Hardly anything.'

Her mother gave the merest toss of her head to indicate that the sarcasm had been understood but not enjoyed.

'It's very bright.'

'That's because everything else around it is so old and drab.'

'Ring out the old, ring in the new,' she sighed. 'I see you've moved the furniture around, too. I shan't know where I am.'

'I wanted to make the place look nice for your return,' Jean said, almost believing in her indignation that this had been the chief impetus for change.

'I don't suppose I shall be spending much time downstairs,' came the reply. 'I'm still very unsteady since falling over. I think it dislodged something.'

Jean breathed deeply, drawing on reserves of patience untested these past weeks.

'Of course, you must do whatever is most comfortable. But it would be better for your spirits to be up and about.'

She wondered if one of those fragments dislodged was the memory of the sharp words they had exchanged the last time they were in the house together. She hoped not, because sooner or later she would have to bring up the vexed subject of Howard again, since it was inconceivable that she would be able to keep the relationship a secret under her mother's vigilant eye. And yet, it was still more impossible to imagine that she would enjoy the necessary freedom to see him, much less spend the night with him, now that her mother was an even more resolute invalid. The reaction to the new blue carpet, as an index of tolerance for change, was not encouraging.

After a gruelling ascent of the staircase, requiring a rest stop halfway, which looked as though it might become permanent, her mother was finally helped to bed.

Jean had tried to banish the smell of damp in the room with the electric bar heater, which was only deployed in exceptional circumstances because it was both dangerous and costly. The cable was frayed, exposing bare wires, and the plug rattled in the socket. It gave off a powerful odour of scorched fluff, burned onto the element, which then had to be masked with a squirt of Yardley's Lily of the Valley. The combination was not particularly soothing and triggered a sneezing fit, which left her mother quite weak and begging for fresh air.

At last she was settled, with a cup of tea and some magazines and her prescription painkillers within reach, and only now did she seem to take notice of Jean as an individual with her own separate existence.

'What have you been doing with yourself all this time, anyway?' she enquired.

I have been spending the nights with my married lover, under the nose of his neighbours, leaving the house abandoned and the milk to curdle on the doorstep.

Tomorrow, perhaps, when her mother had settled back in properly, there was a difficult conversation to be had, but not today.

'I've taken down the runner beans and written to Dorrie. And bought some new towels for the bathroom. Nothing out of the ordinary.'

34

The call to Gretchen had to be made, but Jean kept procrastinating, finding ingenious reasons to defer it until some other, less onerous task was done. For as long as a meeting could be avoided, she had no trouble dodging her conscience over Howard, but face to face she would sooner or later have recourse to lies, or evasion, behaviour she despised.

This was not the only reason for her discomfort. Since talking to Kitty Benteen, Jean had a dark sense that something less than holy had taken place at St Cecilia's. Until she had evidence, there was no question of disclosing her suspicion, but it would be there between them, a malevolent spirit, and another barrier to honesty.

In the event, it was Gretchen who rang her, asking if they could meet as soon as possible. She sounded agitated on the phone, the foreignness of her accent suddenly apparent.

'I can come tomorrow, if you like,' Jean offered.

Now that the nettle was grasped there was no point in further delay. It was a workday, but then this was work, and she still had not addressed the problem of leaving her mother alone outside these hours.

'No, it will have to be Wednesday or Friday, because that's when Martha's teaching. We'll have the place to ourselves.'

Jean refrained from asking why Martha's absence was a pre-condition of their meeting, noting only her own relief. Since hearing of her tepid efforts to welcome Margaret into her household, Jean had been incubating a certain hostility towards Martha and had no wish to have it tested by another prickly encounter.

'Could I ask a favour?' Gretchen added when the time and date were settled and the conversation had run its course. 'You can say no if it's inconvenient. I left behind a patchwork eiderdown on my bed at home. I wonder if you could fetch it and bring it with you. It's pink and green.'

'Yes, I know the one you mean,' said Jean without thinking.

'I would ask Margaret to bring it on Saturday, but it's a bit bulky for her to carry.'

'Of course. I'll call in tonight after work and pick it up.'

'Thank you. It gets so cold here in the basement.'

Later, when she remembered this exchange, Jean had a moment of pure panic. How could Gretchen not have noticed her casual familiarity with the furnishings of her bedroom? Perhaps it had been a deliberate trap, into which she had positively sauntered. In matters of duplicity she was an amateur; if she was to survive the forthcoming encounter without giving herself away, she would need to remain watchful.

The missing pane of stained glass from the front door of Luna Street was still unrepaired and had in fact been joined by a fresh breakage, also covered in plywood. In the shared hallway was a bicycle, a twin pram and an umbrella left open to dry. Coats ballooned from the rack of pegs, almost occluding the passage. Jean decided to keep hers on as she fought her way past. It looked as though the weight of one more would bring the whole thing off the wall. It was, in any case, bitterly cold.

Gretchen was waiting for her in the doorway of the flat,

dressed in woollen trousers, thick socks, jersey and a whiskery, hand-woven tabard resembling a pair of hearthrugs stitched together at the shoulders. Her once-lustrous hair was greasy and there were dark semicircles under her eyes. If this was emancipation, she didn't look well on it.

They embraced clumsily across the quilted bedspread that Jean was carrying rolled and trussed up with string. Any awkwardness was forgotten in the warmth of Gretchen's welcome.

'Come in, come in,' she urged. 'I'm so pleased to see you. I've made *spitzbuben*. Do you remember them?'

'Of course,' Jean laughed. 'It wasn't that long ago.'

'It feels like it,' said Gretchen, her face falling. She cheered up on being reunited with her quilt, which she untied carefully, saving the string in a neat skein. 'Thank you for bringing it. It's icy in here. We can wrap it round us on the couch.'

The studio had not changed much under Gretchen's stewardship. It was still dominated by easel, canvases, sketchpads, oils, rags, jars and various scavenged items that might find their way into one of Martha's paintings. In one corner beside the couch and coffee table – the living area – was a small bundle of Margaret's belongings – the limits of her territory, Jean thought with indignation.

'You look very *schick*,' Gretchen said as Jean dared to take off her coat.

Underneath she was wearing the navy shift dress as a gesture of friendship, with a matching cardigan and a red silk scarf round her neck. The same could not be said for Gretchen without doing violence to sincerity, so instead Jean pointed at the tabard and said, 'That's interesting. Did you make it?'

'Oh no, it's one of Martha's. She had a loom once, until she had to sell it. She wears it to paint, because it leaves your arms free. It's lovely and warm, even though it is a horror to look at, so I've borrowed it. I left so many of my own things at home.'

There was the merest hesitation before the word 'home'.

'Perhaps you should call in and collect them some time. I'm sure Howard wouldn't mind. They're no use to him.'

'Oh well, you know.' Gretchen shook her head. 'Let's have tea.'

She went into the kitchen and Jean could hear her clattering about over the gathering shriek of the kettle. When she returned, carrying two chunky pottery mugs and a plate of *spitzbuben* on a tray, Jean noticed for the first time that she was moving stiffly and that her wrists were bandaged with the same leather splints that Martha wore.

'Are you all right?' she asked, jumping up to help. 'You look as if you're in pain.'

'My joints are a bit tender at the moment,' she confessed, turning her hands over and back. 'I don't know why. Maybe it's the cold.' She pointed to a patch of the green marbled wallpaper that was bubbly with damp.

'Is there no way of making it warmer? A paraffin heater or something . . .'

'We have an electric fire, but it's too expensive to use during the day. We put it on for an hour in the evening, but there are so many gaps and draughts in here the heat flies straight out of the windows.'

They were settled on the couch now, with the eiderdown over their legs and mugs of tea warming their hands, and it was almost cosy.

'Are you short of money? I'm sure Howard wouldn't want to think of you like this.'

'He already sends me a postal order every week. But Martha doesn't like accepting money from Howard. She wants to support me herself.'

Jean glanced around. It looked as though she was struggling to support herself before Gretchen even appeared on the scene.

'She works so hard. She's started an evening job too, taking life drawing classes in a church hall in Battersea, but it makes it even harder to paint when she's tired and in pain. I wish I could do my dressmaking to help out, but there's no room here for all my things.'

'Perhaps you'll be able to find somewhere larger?'

'I don't know.' She passed Jean a biscuit. 'These are nice, aren't they? I can still cook!'

'I suppose', said Jean, 'we should talk about the *Echo* and our plans for the story. Dr Lloyd-Jones said you were disappointed about the skin grafts. It was a blow.'

'I don't understand it. I'm not a scientist.' She shrugged. 'I said they could do another graft until it works, but they wouldn't. All it has proved is that their test was no good. Now, Martha is starting to doubt me again and I suppose you do, too.'

'Gretchen, I would have loved to prove your case. Or even to find an alternative explanation. But I haven't been able to do either and I feel that as a failure of mine, not yours. We still want to run the story in some form. As an unexplained mystery.'

Under the quilt Jean felt her hand grasped by the leather splint.

'You are a good friend.'

'So, I'm going to send a photographer round to take some pictures next time you have Margaret. This Saturday? Obviously, we want you to look as similar as possible, so if you could do your hair the same and dress alike . . .'

'We don't have anything matching.'

'Oh, nothing elaborate; just white blouse, dark skirt, that sort of thing. It's a pity you cut your hair.'

Gretchen put her hand up to her bare neck.

'Yes, it was warmer before, too. I could always cut Margaret's the same.'

'Oh no!' said Jean, horrified. 'Her beautiful curls.' She felt quite sick at the thought of any such mutilation. 'And, Gretchen, I have to warn you that once your name is in the *Echo* there is nothing to stop other papers following it up. You may have to deal with some unwelcome publicity.'

Gretchen looked fearful.

'What do you mean?'

'Well, your current domestic situation is not exactly what it was when we first began.'

'But you won't mention Martha's name or anything to do with her?'

'No, of course *I* won't. But others might.' She relented when she saw Gretchen's troubled expression. 'Ignore me. Probably nothing will come of it.'

Outside in the hallway there was a sudden crashing noise and Gretchen started, slopping tea on the tabard. A moment later there was the sound of swearing and clubbing feet overhead and doors banging.

'Just some altercation between Dennis and the bicycle, no doubt,' she said, relaxing again. 'He comes in drunk at odd times and falls over everything. And then his wife throws him out – again – and then a few days later she lets him back in.' She laughed, a catch in her throat. 'Until I came here I would never have believed people could live such chaotic lives.'

'This place isn't really you, is it, Gretchen?' Jean said softly.

Gretchen shook her head, staring into her lap. When she looked up her eyes were swimming.

'Jean,' she said, her face collapsing. 'I've made a terrible mistake.'

'What do you mean?' Jean stammered.

'You were right. You were right all along. I can't do it. I can't do without Margaret.'

'But there's no room for her here. You must see it's totally unsuitable.'

'I know, but I miss her so much when she's not here. The weekend goes so quickly . . . It's not even the whole weekend – it's just one night!'

Jean, who knew exactly how inadequate this pocket of time could be, could only murmur her sympathy. There was nothing to be done about it; Margaret had made her choice. As she tried to find a way of saying this that wasn't too wounding, Gretchen's sobbing intensified.

'Please will you do one thing for me, Jean? I'll never ask another favour,' she pleaded, her voice thick and bubbling.

'What?'

'Please, please will you talk to Howard and ask him to take me back? I know he'll listen to you. I just want to go back to the way we were.'

On the marble-patterned wallpaper, the shadow of a cloud moved across the shadow of the window and the cold room grew colder.

'But I thought Martha was the love of your life. What's happened?'

'It's not like I thought it would be. It's not like when we were in hospital.'

Gretchen pulled a handkerchief from her trouser pocket and ground it into the corners of her eyes.

'Well of course it isn't!' Jean cried. 'You were just a girl then.'

'Martha tries to be kind. She loves me, I know she does, but she's in so much pain it makes her short-tempered. And she hates teaching but she can't give it up because there'd be no money. And she gets so jealous.'

'Of whom?'

'Not even of real people – not people we know, anyway. We never see any other people! If I read a book she is jealous of Carson McCullers or Rosamond Lehmann. Or if I listen to music she is jealous of Schubert.'

'You make her sound quite demented.'

'She admits it. She says she is jealous of the gloves I wear. But that wouldn't matter if only she liked Margaret a little more.'

'And Margaret senses it.'

'Yes, of course. Between the two of them they are pulling me in half. But Martha doesn't understand how painful it is because she's not a mother.'

'But you must have known it would make Margaret miserable. I tried to tell you.' She had to resist the urge to say: 'It's too late. He doesn't want you any more.'

'I thought love could overcome everything.'

'Then you're a fool,' said Jean.

'And so are you,' that stern inner voice, Duty, with its clinging grey skirts and sturdy shoes, reminded her. Hadn't she passed the last few weeks hoping and dreaming much the same thing?

'I can't stay here. I just want to go home.'

Jean felt a pressure in her chest as though something heavy had been dropped on it from a height. Blood pounded in her ears.

'It's easy to say you want to go back to the way things were. But it's like unmaking a cake. Not everything done can be undone.'

'Or you could say it's like mending a torn shirt – it might not be quite the same as before but it's still a shirt.'

'If it's against your nature to feel anything for men, how is that ever going to work – for either of you?'

Jean had to pick her words delicately, without betraying anything Howard had confided about his years of unhappy celibacy.

'I want to be a proper wife to him. For Margaret's sake. I'll do whatever is necessary. Isn't that what you told me when you first came here to try to persuade me to come home? That the most important thing was Margaret? You did.'

'Yes . . .'

'We were happier than a lot of married couples. And we can be again. I'll be a good wife, like I was at the beginning. If you could just tell him how miserable I am and that I ask for his forgiveness. I know he'd forgive me if he could see how sorry I am.'

'Possibly. But wouldn't all this be better coming from you? I can't act as your go-between.'

The idea that she should have to conspire in her own heartbreak struck Jean as the sort of prank invented by an especially twisted deity.

'No, of course I will say all this to his face, if he'll let me. But I can't just turn up if he's going to close the door in my face. If you could tell him how desperately I am regretting leaving him and how unhappy I am without him, I'm sure he'll agree to see me. He's such a good man.'

Yes, he is, thought Jean. It took almost no effort to imagine the scene of reconciliation. The alternative – Howard coldly resistant to his wife's sincere, weeping repentance – was much harder to picture. And weighing heavily in the balance, of course, was Margaret, whose happiness would be complete and wonderful to witness.

'All right.' Her voice sounded strangulated, even to herself. 'Of course I'll tell him. I can't promise it will be today, or tomorrow. Work is very busy and . . . and my mother's just come home from hospital.'

'Oh, I'm so sorry. Your poor mother.' Having achieved her end, Gretchen was very ready to repay her sympathetic dues. 'I do understand. I know it's not always easy to get hold of Howard at the shop.'

'It's not the sort of conversation I can have on the office phone. I'll have to choose my moment.'

'Of course. Thank you so much. And if you do have any news, could you only ring on a Wednesday or a Friday?'

'While Martha's at work.'

'Yes, please.'

In all this time Jean had hardly spared a thought for Martha, another casualty of the whole wretched business, whose feelings would also be trampled underfoot.

'Will you stay for lunch?' Gretchen asked as the clock in the hall struck one with a thud. 'It's only barley soup.'

Jean could tell that this was a piece of mere politeness, a suspicion confirmed by Gretchen's evident relief at her refusal. Perhaps the soup was carefully rationed and any depletion would be noticed. In any case, it was no hardship to decline – even the Swinneys drew the line at barley.

'I must be getting back to work. I shall have to start thinking about how to write your story.'

Jean threw back the eiderdown and stood up, feeling the cold air licking at her legs.

'It's funny,' said Gretchen. 'It hardly seems important now. I went chasing after proof, when the only two people whose opinion really mattered – Mother and Howard – believed me all along anyway.' She gave a sorrowful laugh.

'I forgot to tell you – I had a letter from Brenda the other day,' Jean remembered at the door. 'From South Africa. She sent you her best wishes.' She could not quite trust herself to mention Kitty.

Gretchen's face brightened. 'Dear Brenda. We were so mean to her. For no reason at all.' She caught sight of her reflection in the tarnished hall mirror, peering past the bald patches in the silvering, and winced. 'I look a fright. There's been no hot water to wash my hair for days. I shall have to prettify myself before I go and see Howard or he'll wonder what he ever saw in me.'

35

In an extraordinary case that has confounded
scientists, a woman from Kent claims to have given
birth to a baby in 1947 while still a virgin. Born
in Switzerland, Gretchen Tilbury, twenty-nine, of
Sidcup, was an inpatient at St Cecilia's Nursing and
Convalescent Home in Broadstairs for four months
between June and September 1946, during which
time her daughter, Margaret, was conceived.

Throughout this time, she had been bedbound with
acute rheumatoid arthritis and sharing a ward with
three other young women. The patients were attended
by nuns and nursing sisters. Several of these have
been interviewed and confirm Mrs Tilbury's account.

When the eighteen-year-old Gretchen Edel, as she
then was, went to her doctor in November 1946 with
sickness, fatigue and aching breasts, she thought she
must be suffering from a virus. She was amazed to
be told by the doctor who examined her that she was
expecting a baby.

'I had never even so much as kissed a man,' she
told me over tea and cake in her immaculate suburban parlour. 'I thought, they'll soon realise they've

made a mistake.' But as the weeks passed and the pregnancy became visible, it was clear that there was no mistake.

With the support of her own mother, who never doubted her daughter's story, Gretchen resolved to keep her baby rather than give her up for adoption. Margaret was born on 30 April – a dark-haired, blue-eyed replica of her mother . . .

Jean stopped typing, interrupted by the ringing of the telephone on her desk. She could tell, even from the almost inaudible intake of breath before he spoke, that it was Howard.

'Hello,' she croaked, her throat raw from smoking.

In front of her, the ashtray overflowed with the evidence of her unease. She had been putting off this conversation, but there could be no deceiving him.

'Can you escape?' he asked. 'I've some news.'

From the steady tone of his voice she couldn't be sure whether or not she needed to worry.

'And I have some, too,' she said as brightly as she could manage.

'Oh? Good or bad?'

'Well, that rather depends.'

'I'm outside.'

'All right. I'm on my way.'

'I love you.'

'Yes.'

They crossed the railway line to Willett's Wood and followed the path through the trees. Over the years Jean had often escaped here to eat her lunch, or to clear her head from the fug of the office.

Within minutes they could no longer hear cars or any

man-made sound apart from their own footsteps. It was a beautiful, cold day. A few tenacious leaves clung to the bare branches, scraps of red cloth against the blue sky. Frost had crusted the ridges of mud with silver; puddles of ice crackled underfoot.

'So, tell me,' said Jean, lacing her hand in his and feeling his returning grip.

'I have to go and see Aunt Edie tomorrow,' he said. 'To help her move. Will you come with me? We could stay overnight in one of the empty rooms.'

'I can't. Mother is back home from hospital and she's still very unsteady. I can't leave her overnight.'

'Oh. Well that's good news about your mother. Grim for us, though. How will I survive the weekend without you?'

'With your usual stoicism, I expect. Where is Aunt Edie going? She's not moving in with that Wally chap?'

She stumbled over a tree root and felt his arm tighten to support her.

'No, she's found a hotel in Maidstone that has boarding for long-term residents. They seem to have a few of her sort there already.'

'Does she have a sort?'

'You know – educated gentlewomen of modest means.'

'Goodness – what a title. I thought she was determined to stay in her house and go down in a blaze of gunfire.'

'Thankfully, I think that was an exaggeration. The prospect of another winter in the house was a bit daunting. It's a beast to keep warm and there's no hot water.'

'What will happen to all her things?'

'She can take a little with her. The rest will go to the auction house, the salerooms, jumble. The thing is, she wants to sell the house and give me the proceeds.'

'That's very generous. Are you her only nephew?'

'Yes – she said it's all coming my way eventually, so I might

303

as well have it now so that I can come to some sort of financial settlement with Gretchen.'

There was a loud cracking of twigs, and a dog came bursting through the trees and bounded towards them. It was a large, muscular setter, brown and shiny as a conker.

'What a beauty,' said Howard as it jumped up and planted its front paws on his chest, leaving muddy prints on his tweed jacket.

He stroked its head and ears before gently disengaging himself. The dog wheeled around and plunged back into the woods. Howard laughed and dusted himself down.

'I don't like the idea of Gretchen living in that flat. I've not seen inside the place myself but to hear Margaret, you'd think it was a hovel.'

'It's certainly not what you'd call cosy.'

'So that's my good news. Good for everyone. I'll be able to set Gretchen up somewhere comfortable without having to move from Burdett Road.'

'Aunt Edie's very thoughtful,' said Jean, not quite meeting his eye.

He caught the lack of warmth in her tone and turned to face her, placing his hands on her shoulders and peering at her troubled expression.

'What's the matter? Have I said something to upset you?'

'Not at all.' Jean tried to laugh but it emerged as a sob, which had to be quickly swallowed. 'You haven't asked me what my news is.'

'My God, I'm sorry.' He pulled her towards him and held her tightly; she could feel her ear grinding against his. 'Is it your mother?'

'No, no, that's not it. She took a long breath. It had to be done. 'I saw Gretchen on Wednesday. She wants to come back to you. She realises she's made a terrible mistake.'

Jean relaxed her grip fractionally but Howard did not.

'She said that?'

'Yes, and plenty more besides. She was distraught – begging me to persuade you to take her back. You can imagine how that made me feel.'

'Oh, Jean, I'm so sorry. I don't know what to say.'

'No. I'm sure you don't. It's rather awkward, isn't it?' Her voice was bright with self-command.

'I thought this Martha was the great love of her life. What's happened?'

'Apparently, it's not quite as blissful as she imagined. And not enough to make up for losing Margaret.'

'Ah, so it's Margaret she misses. Not the marriage.'

They had broken apart now and begun to walk again, a little gap – perhaps six inches – between their trailing hands. Jean felt it as an abyss between them, but she didn't have the courage to reach across it. Let him come to her if he wanted to.

'She wants you to be a family again,' Jean said. 'And to be a "proper wife" – her words.'

It was physically painful to plead Gretchen's cause, but she was determined not to withhold anything or twist it to her advantage.

'How is that possible?' Howard exclaimed. 'We both know it's against her nature.'

'That's really down to her to explain. You can hardly expect me to—'

'I suppose I'll have to see her.'

'Yes.'

'Oh, damn. What a mess.'

He patted his pockets in desperation until Jean came to his rescue and offered him one of her own cigarettes. He puffed at it urgently as though he would rather smoke than breathe. Jean could sense his distress at being placed in a situation where he would be forced to disappoint someone.

She had half hoped that he would dismiss Gretchen's pleas without hesitation and proclaim Jean his only love, but this was a fantasy. Howard was the least histrionic of men. He would do the right, sober and generous thing. All the same, his failure to offer her any word of reassurance made her spirit shrivel.

They walked on in silence, their thoughts racing along on separate tracks. If he would only give her some consolation to cling to, she knew she could be brave.

'Gretchen said you can only phone on Wednesdays or Fridays while Martha's at work,' Jean remembered.

'Good grief! I don't see why I need to go in for all this subterfuge just to have a conversation with my own wife!'

Howard flung his exhausted cigarette into the bushes and then changed his mind and went to retrieve it. Even at this extremity he couldn't do something unworthy.

'It depends what you decide. If you intend to take her back and make a go of things it hardly matters whether or not Martha's nose is put out of joint.'

He turned to her in surprise.

'Is that what you think I should do?'

'What does it matter what I think?' she replied, betraying more indignation than she intended. 'It's nothing to do with me!'

'But it affects you, too. And your opinion is important to me. I don't want to hurt anyone.'

'I'm not your conscience,' she said, her voice rising. 'You want me to give you permission to break my heart and go back to Gretchen? Well I won't. Or perhaps you want me to beg you to throw her and Margaret aside for me? I won't do that, either.'

She had never spoken so furiously to him, or anyone. The effort left her breathless. Her face burned.

'You're quite right,' he replied, startled by this outburst.

'I'm sorry, Jean. I didn't mean to upset you.'

He pulled her to him and kissed her hot cheeks and then her lips.

If I fought for him, I could win, thought Jean. I know I could. But it would be Margaret whose face I was grinding under my heel.

'I must get back to work,' she said, disengaging herself from his grasp. 'Perhaps it's just as well we can't see each other this weekend.'

'Can't we?' Howard sounded stricken.

'You're going to Aunt Edie's. And I can't leave Mother overnight.'

'Oh yes. Damn.'

'We'll talk again when you've had a chance to think and when you've spoken to Gretchen, and you can let me know what you've decided. I won't make a fuss, so don't worry.'

She had recovered her composure now, for the moment, and sounded like her idea of a sensible, rational woman. She would collapse later, she promised herself, between seven and seven-thirty, when she had got home from work and done her chores.

36

Jean's last visit to Broadstairs had been in the height of summer. Today, on a wet afternoon in late November, it had that air of melancholy and neglect particular to seaside resorts out of season. The pavements were deserted; the ice-cream kiosks boarded up; shop windows misted with condensation; the sea slate grey.

She didn't like riding her bicycle in the rain, so she had left it at home this time and taken a taxi from the station to Anselm House, formerly St Cecilia's. It was founder's day and the boys had a half-holiday, so the school was quiet.

'You can wander around at your leisure this time,' said Susan Trevor, who had arranged the appointment with just this in mind. The headmaster was attending a memorial service for a former colleague; a few schoolmasters were in the staffroom playing bridge; most had gone home early. 'Pop in when you've finished and we'll have a cup of tea.'

Jean could tell Mrs Trevor was the sort who had plenty to say and relished the opportunity of a fresh audience. Jean thanked her and made her way across the small entrance hall, past the trophy cabinet and the wooden boards displaying the names of past heads of school and house captains and cricket captains, picked out in gilt.

According to the floor plan marked up by Martha, the ward

occupied by Gretchen and the other girls was on the ground floor, now a changing room. There were wire lockers around the walls, containing various balled-up items of sports kit, lone rugby boots and grass-smeared cricket pads. There was a slightly feral smell of unwashed clothes and unwashed boys.

In the middle of the room were benches and coat hooks. The windows were high and barred. It was a long, narrow room and quite a generous space for four hospital beds, Jean thought; Kitty at one end, nearest the door; then Brenda. Gretchen at the other end, with Martha's bed a towel's width away. When she closed her eyes, it was no struggle in the silence to imagine the secret sharing of tangerines; the whispering after lights out; the whooshing breath of the iron lung, and the soft tread of the nuns and perhaps that other stealthy visitor.

A doorway off the window end of the room led to the boys' showers. This would have been the washroom the bedbound girls never got to use. Here, too, were high windows, latched on the inside but not barred. Not the easiest point of entry, Jean thought, but not impossible for someone agile, if the window had been carelessly left open.

She felt a shiver pass through her, as though surrounded by ghosts, and shook it off, annoyed with herself. She didn't believe in the supernatural and, in any case, the girls whose presence she imagined were all still solidly, warmly alive.

In the office, Susan Trevor served tea from a brown china pot with a quilted cosy. It must have been stewing for some time, as it emerged toffee-coloured and not especially hot. Jean drank it quickly, feeling the tannin coat her teeth, while Susan kept up a stream of indiscreet chatter about the eccentricities of schoolmasters; the school's straitened finances; the declining standards of discipline – chiefly lack of respect for authority, answering back, defiance – all those crimes of which age accuses youth.

If only Susan had been a ward orderly at St Cecilia's, Jean thought. Nothing would have escaped her ravenous curiosity and the mystery would have been solved overnight. Her attention kept wandering back to that long room of sleeping girls, until she heard the whispered word 'cancer', which always made her sit up, and realised that Susan had asked her a question.

'I was wondering if you were in touch with Alice Halfyard?' she repeated. 'I was saying she's apparently quite poorly. I heard it from a friend of Mother's who shares the same cleaner.'

'No, I didn't know,' Jean admitted. 'I only met her that once, last time I was here in the summer. I was intending to visit her again today.'

'I hope she's well enough to see you. Poor Alice; she's had such a sad life – and now this.'

Recalling their first meeting, Jean acknowledged that yes, she had sensed an air of spinsterish melancholy about Alice, but it was one that she recognised and didn't therefore trouble to investigate. And it had in any case been slightly overshadowed by those repellent dolls.

'She didn't talk about herself much,' she said. But this was no excuse; she should have asked. 'Why was it sad?'

'Her sister had a baby out of wedlock and then died of peritonitis when it was still quite young. Alice and her mother had to raise the child.'

Jean nodded, remembering the photograph on the windowsill, which Alice had described as her family.

'She showed me a picture of them all together,' she said. 'I didn't realise they were sisters; Alice looked so much older.'

'I think there was nearly twenty years between them. Mrs Halfyard was quite an age when she had her.' Susan lowered her voice, even though there was no one around to overhear. 'Which may account for the girl being a bit peculiar. They do say with an elderly mother the eggs can spoil.'

'Do they?' said Jean, who had never heard any such saying and didn't much care for it.

'Oh yes,' Susan insisted. 'It's well known. Anyway . . .' She poured herself a second cup, the colour of stout, on top of the leaves of the old one. 'That was just the beginning. Alice's sister's child, Vicky, turned out to be not quite right in the head as well, and that's putting it mildly. Had to be looked after at home in the end – under lock and key.'

Jean pulled a face. 'That sounds a bit gothic.'

Something suddenly plucked at her memory – V: *V was waiting for me again today in the rain. Absolutely soaked through like a faithful dog.*

'And once old Mrs Halfyard died there was no one else to help. Alice had an awful time of it.'

'It's a bit ironic that Alice spent her days tending the sick and had this poor child locked up at home. Couldn't she have been looked after at St Cecilia's?'

Susan looked puzzled for a moment and then laughed.

'Oh, you mean Victor? We only called him Vicky as a tease because he kept his hair so long – like a girl.'

37

The once-neat garden on the corner of Wickfield Drive had an air of neglect, which filled Jean with misgivings. Unpruned rose bushes sagged over the wall; the lawn was ankle-high and ravaged by clover and yarrow. Mare's tail had taken over the flower beds and burst through cracks in the paving.

I'm too late, she thought with dismay as she stood on the doorstep, listening to the chimes of the bell as they were swallowed up by the empty house. She rattled the letter box and opened the flap to peer into the unlit hallway, releasing a puff of sour, medicinal air from inside.

There was no reply from the neighbours either side, but in the house opposite she had some success. As she put her hand on the gate there was the sound of barking, growing louder, and the crump of a weighty dog hitting the far side of the door, dislodging some flakes of rendering from the exterior wall. A moment later a harassed-looking woman appeared at the front window.

'What do you want?' she mouthed as the dog continued to batter itself against the wooden panelling.

Jean gestured to the abandoned house behind her.

'I'm looking for Miss Halfyard.'

The window opened an inch.

'She's gone into hospital. Are you family?'

'No. Just a friend. I've tried telephoning a few times.'

'She stayed at home as long as she could but they took her in a fortnight ago.'

She gave Jean directions and closed the window, turning to bellow at the dog. The aftershocks followed Jean up the street.

The hospital for incurables sat on the clifftop, affording the staff and visitors, at least, a glimpse of a dark and wrinkled sea. The patients, confined to their beds on the upper floors, could see only a rolling cloudscape.

Alice Halfyard, a much-reduced version of the woman Jean had met in the summer, was lying in her metal-framed bed, her skin quite yellow against the white of the sheets. Although her limbs were fleshless, under the sheets her stomach formed a swollen dome.

On a trolley nearby lay the remains of lunch: a greenish soup and a pallid blancmange, barely touched. Someone had placed a vase of artificial flowers, blowsy dahlias in paintbox colours, on the bedside cabinet.

Her eyes were closed, but at Jean's approach she opened them. It took her a minute to focus and draw her dry lips into a smile of recognition.

'I thought you might come, sooner or later.' She raised a brittle arm and wagged her fingers towards an empty chair.

Jean, accustomed by now to hospital visiting and the many faces of disease, was nevertheless shocked by Alice's deterioration. The traditional words of enquiry or encouragement – how are you? you're looking well – were wholly useless.

'I'm sorry to find you like this,' was the best she could do.

'I'm glad you're here. Otherwise I'd have had to write you a long letter and I don't think I've got the energy.' She spoke in a low, soft voice, just above a whisper.

'Can I do anything for you?' Jean asked. She glanced at the uneaten meal. 'Do you want me to feed you?'

Alice shook her head. 'I spent my working life in hospitals, but this is my first time as a patient. First and last.'

'What have you got?' Jean knew she would have no time for evasions or false comfort.

'Cancer. Liver and now spine.'

'Is it very painful?'

Alice gave the merest of nods. 'I've learned so much about nursing from being on the receiving end of it. Too late to be any use, though.'

'I'm sure you were very good anyway. I had a letter from Brenda van Lingen a while back. She sent her good wishes. And Kitty, too. She lives almost on my doorstep as it turns out.'

'Kitty? Oh yes. How is she?'

'Physically still very limited. But quite an inspiration, really. Studying theology, with the help of her sister.'

Alice managed a smile. 'A remarkable girl.'

'I thought so, too.'

'Now, tell me about Gretchen's baby. What did the tests prove?'

'Oh. Well, the doctors themselves don't entirely agree. But the skin graft test seemed to suggest that this is *not* a case of virgin birth.'

Alice gestured for a glass of water; it clashed against her teeth as Jean tried to help her to a drink.

'That's a pity,' she said. 'I was hoping for a miracle.'

'Yes. I think maybe we all were.'

'I'm sorry I wasn't more on the ball when you came to see me. I'd not long had my diagnosis and I'm afraid I was distracted by my own woes.'

'That's quite understandable. I suppose you know why I'm here.'

'I can guess.' Alice winced as a sudden pain gripped her.

'Are you well enough to talk?' Jean said, her shame at hounding a dying woman just trumped by dread that the answer might be no and that she would be sent on her way with nothing.

'I'm as well as I ever will be.'

There was still the same sharp intelligence in her gaze as she turned it on Jean.

'I wanted to ask you about Victor.'

'How did you find out?' Alice's voice was a whisper.

'I noticed these references to V in your diary, but none of the patients or nurses had names beginning with V and it set me wondering.'

'I don't remember writing about Vicky in my diary,' said Alice, shaking her head. 'I thought it was only hospital matters.'

'There were no mentions of him during the period while Gretchen was a patient,' said Jean. 'Which is why I didn't come across them at first. Then, when I saw Kitty quite recently, she said while she was at St Cecilia's an angel had visited her one night. Obviously, that made me very suspicious.' She realised that she, too, was whispering.

'I didn't know that. She never said.'

'She'd been encouraged in her belief by one of the nuns, but I don't think she mentioned it to anyone else at the time. And then this morning Susan Trevor told me you had a nephew called Victor and something she said about his long hair made me think of Kitty's angel.'

Alice closed her eyes and a tear trembled at the outer edges of the seams.

'He was my sister's boy. She was a wild one – always in trouble. She wouldn't tell us who the father was – if she knew. But she wouldn't give the baby up; she didn't care what people thought. And the funny thing is, motherhood seemed to be the making of her.

'And then she got peritonitis and died when he was four,

and we brought him up ourselves – my mother and I. He was such a beautiful boy – I've got a picture of him in my purse – everybody loved him. But when he reached puberty he began to change – just like my sister. He became quite withdrawn and started to hear voices.'

At the mention of voices, Jean grew very still, the air trapped in her chest.

'He had these terrible rages. It was the voices tormenting him. We couldn't keep him at school; they wouldn't have him. So we looked after him at home. The doctor gave him some pills to keep him calm, but they made him blow up like a balloon.'

Jean let out a long breath.

'He kept running away and getting into awful fixes. He'd turn up covered in cuts and bruises and with no idea where he'd been. It was so awful. You've no idea.'

The tears were flowing more freely now and her voice was less distinct. Jean had to lean in to catch every word.

'We had to keep the door locked or he'd take off. He wasn't a prisoner,' she added, seeing the expression on Jean's face. 'It was just to keep him safe. If he wanted to go out somewhere, Mother or I would take him. But there was one day when I finished my shift and I came out and he was sitting on the wall outside. He must have got out and followed me.' She plucked a crumpled handkerchief from the folds of her bedclothes and applied it to her eyes.

'Do you think it's possible that he might be . . .' Jean cast about for a form of words that was not too wounding, 'the father of Gretchen's child?'

'When you first came and told me about Gretchen and the baby, it was such a shock, the idea of Vicky didn't even occur to me. Or maybe it did, deep down, but too deep to be faced. But when you get ill like this, and you know you're not going to get better, all sorts of thoughts start to surface.'

'I can imagine,' said Jean.

'But Gretchen would never . . .'

'That's not what I meant. I think she was unconscious. She and Martha used to hoard sleeping pills and take them all at once.'

'You think he forced himself on her.'

Alice's voice was barely audible now, swallowed up in tears.

'I have no proof. I'm asking if you think it's possible.'

'Are you sure you want this?' she asked.

'What do you mean?' said Jean with a now-familiar sense of foreboding.

'Once you've taken it off me you can't give it back.'

'Go on.'

Jean stopped as a ward orderly approached with a trolley and removed the tray of uneaten food. Alice thanked her graciously, watching her progress from bed to bed until they were alone again. When Alice turned to Jean her face was a picture of desolation.

'I wish I could say no. But I can't.'

Her freckly hand reached out across the blanket and caught hold of Jean's. The skin was dry and papery, but the nails, now digging into Jean's palm, were long and almost indecently healthy.

'I woke up in the middle of the night once and he was there in the room, standing beside my bed watching me and, you know, handling himself. I pretended to be asleep. I didn't dare confront him; he was so strong.

'After a few minutes I heard him leave and go back to his room, and then I got up and moved my nightstand in front of the door and slept like that every night from then on.'

'Where is he now?'

'He died six years ago. He seemed to be getting better. I'd

retired by then, so we used to do things together when he felt well enough. He liked to sit on the station platform and watch the trains.

'Then one day I came down and he was gone. I'd got careless and he took my keys out of my handbag and let himself out. He was hit by a train on the level crossing. It may have been an accident – we don't know. He was only twenty-one.'

'I'm so sorry. What a sad story.'

'I felt so guilty, because I was supposed to be a nurse and I'd failed him. But it was also a relief – and that made me feel even more guilty. Mother had passed away by then and there was just me left. I used to wonder what on earth would happen to him when I was gone. For eight years I didn't have a single day without that worry.'

'I'm sure you did everything you could.'

'But thinking what he did to that poor girl – when she was supposed to be in my care. And now there's a child to worry about. Such a terrible, terrible wrong.'

Jean returned the pressure of Alice's fleshless grip.

'Don't torture yourself about what might or might not have happened to Gretchen. We can never know for certain.'

And yet I do, she thought. Everything she had been told confirmed Kitty's story of her strange night visitor. No angel, then, but this troubled boy, standing over Gretchen while she slept her drugged sleep. She could feel the burden, as it passed to her from Alice, pressing down on her, forcing the air from her lungs, as heavy as a grown man.

'Well, you must do as you see fit. He's beyond harm now and I will be too before much longer.'

'I'm glad you told me,' said Jean.

It was a lie of kindness. She felt a wave of nostalgia for her previous anxieties and dilemmas. What comfortable worries they now seemed. Having set out in pursuit of the truth, she had now learned something it would have been better not to know. She would never again be able to look on Margaret with the same innocent delight, unspoilt by fear of what the future might bring.

'Will you pass my purse?' Alice was saying, indicating the bedside unit behind Jean's chair. 'I want to show you something.'

Jean located the red leather wallet from among the few belongings and watched as Alice withdrew a buckled photograph with shaking fingers. It was the size of a playing card and showed a dark-haired boy of about seven holding a cricket bat. He was standing in a garden, in front of a wicket chalked on a wooden fence, and was poised to receive a delivery, caught in a moment of perfect absorption. Jean couldn't help scanning it for any likeness to Margaret, but the image was too small to make any meaningful comparisons.

'That's Vicky, before he got ill,' said Alice. 'He was such a lovely boy.'

'I can see that.'

'Promise me you won't think of him as a monster. He was only a child himself. And whatever he did, he did because he was ill, not evil.'

'I don't.'

'Whatever he may have gone on to do, he was all we had left of my sister and he meant the world to us.'

38

The bell was ringing as Jean climbed the stairs carrying a tray of supper – an omelette with a slice of tinned ham – a glass of milk and Dorrie's letter, which had arrived that morning.

She had thought Mrs Melsom's gift of a little brass handbell a kindness, but after a few nights of jumping up to answer its tinkling summons was beginning to wonder if it wasn't an act of revenge. Since her return from hospital, her mother appeared to have developed quite a taste for a life lived in bed. No amount of hinting, cajoling or stern admonishment could tempt her back downstairs. Her legs were too weak, her balance too precarious; the armchair too uncomfortable. It was as much as she could do to totter along the landing to the bathroom. Steps would be unthinkable.

'This looks nice,' she said, pouring a molehill of salt onto her plate. 'You can't beat eggs,' and then she stopped, realising she had accidentally made a joke and unsure how to proceed.

Jean sat on the dressing table stool, looking at her reflection in the winged mirror – two infinite rows of Jeans with the same hunted expression swooped away from her.

'Are you not having anything yourself?'

'No,' Jean replied. 'I'm feeling a bit nauseous.'

She hadn't eaten more than toast for twenty-four hours and

even that had turned to ash in her mouth. Her visit to Alice had robbed her of all energy and appetite.

'Shall I read to you again tonight?'

She had discovered that it was impossible to think, fret or agonise while reading aloud. Housework, listening to music, reading to herself or any of the other traditional distractions did nothing to quieten the clamouring in her head. They were making great progress with *The Nine Tailors*. Of course, her thoughts could only be held off for so long; as soon as she was quiet they came swarming back.

'Yes, please.'

'What does Dorrie have to say?'

Now, more than ever, she felt the absence of a sister to confide in. It might have helped to talk to someone quite unconnected with the Tilburys, who could listen without judging. In Jean's experience people tended to be divided into two camps: sympathisers and advisers. Dorrie, too much of a hedonist herself to expect much of others, was a sympathiser. She would only listen and comfort. Her mother was firmly in the other camp. Unhappiness had not softened her to the suffering of others; quite the reverse.

Her mother skimmed through the aerogramme, filleting for what she considered to be 'news' – chiefly sickness and health, and the twins' achievements. Matters pertaining to her son-in-law, Kenneth, whom she held responsible for luring Dorrie overseas, were of no interest.

'No. It's all about this new dog. They're all besotted with him. Oh, here we are: Mary's had measles but she's all right now. Peter won a cup for chess. No other news.'

'Shall I read, then?' Jean picked up *The Nine Tailors*.

'I'm still eating.'

'Doesn't matter. You can eat and listen at the same time, surely?'

'Go on, then.'

After an hour her mother begged her to stop; she was drowsy and wanted nothing more than to nod off. Jean closed the book and withdrew, dismissed, dreading her own company. Being left alone with her thoughts was like sharing a prison cell with a lunatic – terrifying and inescapable.

She felt a sort of rage towards Alice for handing her this burden from which there could be no relief. She could never tell Gretchen or Howard that Margaret was the product of rape, her angel voices perhaps a sign of something dark and destructive to come. It would be pointless and cruel and blight all of their lives. And she herself would never be able to look at Margaret's innocent face without the shadow of that knowledge coming between them. She would always now be watchful and fearful.

Another issue – less serious but still a tax on her sprits – was Roy Drake. She couldn't share her discovery about Victor with him – or anyone else – while keeping it from Gretchen. But if she didn't tell him, and proceeded to publish the story as planned, she would be perpetrating a deception against him and the *Echo* and all of their readers. Whichever way she turned it around in her mind, there was no way to make it good.

Two things stood out clearly, though. Margaret was owed every advantage that a united family could bring – all other considerations blew away like straws in a gale. The other certainty: if she spoke out, it must be now; if she kept quiet, it must be for ever.

Jean lay on the couch in the living room as the night deepened around her. She was determined not to move from there until she had decided what to do. The coals in the grate had given up the last of their heat some hours ago and the temperature was dropping rapidly. Through the open curtains she could see a bright sickle moon and a smudge of stars. There was a sort of majesty in the indifference of the universe, but its vastness didn't seem to make her own dilemma any less significant.

The hours passed, marked by the whirr and scrape of the hall clock. At three o'clock she levered herself up, creaking and stiff with cold, and took a sheet of paper and pen from her mother's writing case in the bureau.

Home, 3 a.m.

Dear Howard,

It's only a few days since we were walking in the woods but it seems far longer. I'm sorry I didn't offer much in the way of sympathy or support after springing Gretchen's news on you — I was out of sorts and thinking only of myself. I've had time to reflect now.

Perhaps you have already made up your mind what to do, but in case you haven't, here is my view, for what it's worth. It's no exaggeration to say that the last month with you has been the happiest time of my life. I had thought I was beyond all possibility of experiencing love, but you proved me wrong in the nicest possible way.

As you know, I was always uncomfortable about the effect of all this on Margaret, but while the decision had already been made by Gretchen, it was easy enough to go along with the situation — not an admirable moral position, I admit. But the situation has now changed, and if there is any chance that you and Gretchen can find a way of living together and rededicating yourself to the marriage, putting Margaret's happiness first, then I think you should take it. She is the innocent party in all this and her needs should override all other considerations. I said this to Gretchen when she first left you and I must stand by it now.

It should go without saying that my feelings for you are the same as ever, and unlikely to change soon. It would be nice to think we could still meet as friends occasionally as we used to

*when I was first a visitor to Burdett Road. But I can already
see that might be difficult and painful, and I will understand if
you prefer not to.*

   *Anyway, this was not easy to write and I don't suppose it's
easy to read, but if I know you at all, I know you will accept
what I say is true and do what is best for Margaret.*

   With love,

      Jean

She put it in an envelope and addressed it to Bedford Street, in
case Gretchen might already be installed at home. She hunted
for a stamp – it was essential that she took it to the post right
now while she was resolute and gave herself no chance to
weaken. There in a drawer of the bureau was the collection of
un-postmarked stamps torn from previous correspondence and
saved to be steamed off and reused. A momentary qualm about
this practice – disrespectful to the Queen and almost certainly
illegal – was allayed by her conviction that it was the sort of
shrewd and thrifty thing the Queen would do herself.

   She put on her coat and slipped out of the house, closing the
door slowly and without a sound. It was only a few hundred
yards along the road to the postbox on the corner of Hambro
Avenue. Every house was dark, curtained and hushed. Her
footsteps on the cold pavement chimed in the silence as she
hurried across the road and past the park railings. The trees
stood out black against the velvet sky; she felt exquisitely alone,
the only brave survivor of some apocalypse.

   She hesitated for a second and then, fortified by a tremendous
surge of martyr's joy, thrust the letter into the postbox. A child's
pink woollen glove, dropped on a visit to the park, had been
picked up by a passer-by and mounted on top of the railings.
It gave her a ghostly salute as she passed.

39

'Do you think the religious symbolism is a bit heavy-handed?'

'Yes – and very possibly blasphemous.'

Jean and the picture editor, Duncan, were in his office examining young Tony's contact prints of Gretchen and Margaret. He had taken a reel of naturalistic shots of the pair sitting together on the couch at Luna Street, looking at each other and laughing. Margaret's hair had been clipped back to more closely resemble her mother's and in many of the shots their expressions were identical. He had also staged a photograph of Margaret by herself, mirroring the childhood portrait of Gretchen at more or less the same age.

The little girl had played her part with enthusiasm, mimicking, with a hint of mischief, her mother's uplifted gaze and wistful expression. Young Tony had then overreached himself, having Gretchen assume a Madonna-ish pose with prayerful, downcast eyes while curiously lit to create a glowing halo around her head.

'We can ditch that one right now,' said Jean. Any suggestion of divine intervention made her feel queasy. 'We're not trying to claim it was a miracle. Our line is that it's an unexplained mystery.'

'Is there any other kind?' Duncan wanted to know.

Jean shot him an impatient look.

'It's a great image – very seasonal, too. I can't see why you wouldn't use it.'

'I've got to know this family. They've had a difficult time recently.' She cringed inwardly at the understatement. 'I don't want them to become an object of fascination to religious cranks.'

'If one of the nationals picks it up it will be out of your hands.'

'Yes, I know.'

Jean felt a familiar boiling anxiety in her guts. At the previous week's editorial meeting it had been agreed that it would be a front-page story on the first Friday of December – a considerable coup for Jean but one that gave her no pleasure. Now, she was in the counterintuitive position of hoping that the piece would come and go with as little impact as possible.

'It will be good for you – get your name out there,' said Duncan.

She gave him a weak smile. 'That's what I thought six months ago. A lot has changed since then.'

The urge to confide in someone was almost overwhelming. Duncan gave her a quizzical glance. In all their dealings over the years the conversation had never strayed from the job. If the opportunity to share any detail of their private life had arisen, they hadn't taken or even noticed it. The temptation and the moment passed; Jean collected herself and grew distant and professional again.

They settled on the studio portraits for the front page and one of the informal shots of mother and daughter for the continuation of the story on page 6. Duncan marked the contacts.

'Could I have a copy of this to keep?' Jean pointed to the picture of Margaret. 'This is exactly how I always want to think of her.'

'Gladly,' said Duncan, and if he was struck by the sadness in her voice he kept it to himself.

It was over a week since she had written to Howard and the spirit of righteousness, which had borne her up as she committed it to the post, was diminishing daily. There had been no word of acknowledgement from him, though her letter had hardly merited one, and she had no way of knowing whether or not he had made contact with Gretchen. Having surrendered all claim to him, she now had to accept that she was no longer entitled to any news and that there was every chance she might not hear from him again.

Having done the right thing was nothing like the consolation she had hoped. Without constant congratulation, virtue was a lonely business. She frequently found herself at her desk, halfway through some task like writing up the week's Household Hints or Marriage Lines, when she would lose concentration and gaze into space, transported by some memory of Howard's goodness to her.

This dream state could go on for ten or fifteen minutes until the sound of a ringing telephone or an interruption from one of her colleagues would bring her back to earth. Sometimes, when feelings of sorrow threatened to tip over into despair, she would leave the office and walk briskly to Willett's Wood, where she would follow the path they had taken together at their last meeting and allow herself to shed some restorative tears.

She knew that she was not doing a good job of disguising her unhappiness at work because, having once treated her as one of the chaps, people were suddenly either avoiding her or being uncharacteristically sensitive. Unpopular work that would normally have come her way was being diverted to other departments; volunteers mysteriously came forward to take on jobs that she had started and failed to follow up.

Instead of cadging a cigarette off her several times a day, Larry would bring her a custard tart from the bakery in Petts Wood on his way into work and leave it on her desk. Even the fearsome Muriel stopped her in the washroom, where Jean had gone to splash cold water on her face, and offered to bring in a pamphlet from the School of Yoga, which promoted dynamic breathing and other rejuvenating techniques. People are kind, Jean told herself. I'm very fortunate.

The evenings were a trial, because it grew dark so early and there was too much time to think, but she was kept busy answering her mother's bell. Misery was tiring, so she went to bed early, but it also stopped her from sleeping, so she woke unrefreshed.

She tried to remember what life was like before she had met the Tilburys, just six months ago. The days had passed without great peaks and troughs of emotion; her job and the domestic rituals that went with each season had been sufficiently varied and rewarding to occupy her. Small pleasures – the first cigarette of the day; a glass of sherry before Sunday lunch; a bar of chocolate parcelled out to last a week; a newly published library book, still pristine and untouched by other hands; the first hyacinths of spring; a neatly folded pile of ironing, smelling of summer; the garden under snow; an impulsive purchase of stationery for her drawer – had been encouragement enough.

She wondered how many years – if ever – it would be before the monster of awakened longing was subdued and she could return to placid acceptance of a limited life. The journey into love was so effortless and graceful; the journey out such a long and laboured climb.

One evening, when her mother was settled for the night and the walls of the house were pressing in, Jean slipped out and walked up to the church. She was not religious, but she thought of herself as culturally Christian and had accompanied her mother to services on the major festivals, before the falling-out over the knitted dolls.

Choir practice was just finishing and the singers were leaving, buttoning coats against the chilly night and calling farewells to each other, so Jean hung back in the rectory garden until the last of the footsteps had died away. The heavy wooden door was still unlocked, so she let herself into the cool darkness and sat in a pew at the back, as if prepared to make a quick getaway from God, should He appear.

The only light came from a bright moon through the stained-glass windows. The altar gleamed palely; all was peaceful. She had never been in the habit of praying, for herself or other people, and wouldn't stoop to it now just because she was needy. Instead, she sat contemplating the silence, and the smell of polished wood and candle wax and ancient stone. Minutes passed and she felt her eyes filling with tears, which she allowed to flow down her cheeks, gather at the corners of her mouth and drip off her chin unchecked.

There was a sudden noise – shocking in the stillness – and a shaft of light as the door to the vestry opened. Jolted from her trance, Jean hurriedly wiped her face on her coat sleeve as Mrs Melsom, no less startled, appeared in the doorway.

'Oh my goodness,' she said, clutching her chest and peering into the gloom. 'I wasn't expecting anyone to be here still.'

She was wearing a fur hat that might have done service in the Russian steppes and sheepskin mittens that were somewhat disabling her efforts with the latch.

'Sorry,' said Jean, rising. 'I was just . . .'

'Oh, it's you, Jean,' Mrs Melsom said. 'I didn't mean to alarm you. I stayed behind after choir to sort out the sheet music – it was all in a muddle.' She looked closer. 'My dear, is something wrong?'

Jean blinked hard. She could take the path of denial and hasty departure, or accept the sympathy that was offered. A memory nudged at her – the downtrodden daughter from the hotel in Lymington, refusing her hand of friendship. She had clung to her proud self-sufficiency and they had both been diminished that night. Insight, overdue but dazzling, opened Jean's eyes to the truth that when help is accepted, both parties are enriched.

She gave Mrs Melsom a grateful smile. 'Nothing serious, but the truth is, I was feeling rather low. When I look at the future everything seems a bit . . . bleak.'

A mittened hand rested on her shoulder. 'I'm so sorry to hear that. Things must be very hard for you,' came the reply. 'Why don't we go back into the vestry and I'll put the kettle on.'

'Thank you. You're very kind.'

This encounter led to one practical improvement to Jean's situation. She had not disclosed the details of her recent sorrows with regard to the Tilburys but had hinted at the ending of a love affair, and her feelings of regret and isolation. Her mother's reduced horizons had also come up in conversation, and Mrs Melsom had immediately volunteered to come and sit with her on Saturday afternoon so that Jean might enjoy a little freedom. They would play cards, or chat or do their crocheting together in silence – whatever Mrs Swinney preferred. There were other good sorts at the church who would be happy to do the same on subsequent Saturdays, she was sure. Maybe, by degrees, she might be tempted downstairs again.

For Jean's aching heart, of course, she could offer no remedy and didn't try. There were only the time-honoured methods – endurance, distraction, work – of which Jean was well aware, having had recourse to them once before in the matter of Frank, and recalled now without confidence. Previous experience taught her that the pain would not be unending – but neither would it subside smoothly, incrementally, but rather in a series of crashing waves, some of which might still knock her off her feet.

It was the first Tuesday in December, a few days before the *Echo* was to carry the Strange Case of the 'Virgin Mother' as its front-page story, when Jean was hit by one of these waves as she tidied her desk and filed away all her correspondence and notes. The personal letters from Howard, which had come to her home address, were not included in this archive but remained in her dressing table drawer, awaiting the day when she felt resilient enough to reread them. The sight of Gretchen's handwriting on that first brief note – *I have always believed my own daughter (now ten) to have been born without the involvement of any man* – made her feel suddenly queasy, and she had to go to the window and press her face against the cool glass.

'I'm just going for a walk,' she whispered to Larry, who was talking on the telephone, feet up on the desk, at his end of the office.

He gave her a thumbs up without any interruption to the flow of his speech.

It was that hour in the late afternoon when the winter sun is just above the horizon but giving no heat. Her shadow stretched the length of the path, long, flared legs scissoring as she walked along, kicking through the last spiny chestnut shells and feeling the crunch of twigs underfoot. She could hear the distant shouts of children, playing, and somewhere deep in the trees a dog barking. Her scarf was still on the peg in the office and the cold air drilled into her ears.

As always, she followed the path she had taken with Howard, and at the point where they had abandoned the walk she turned back. In the grey distance, a figure emerged from the mist, a smudge of hat and coat. It was not so much the silhouette she recognised but his walk, as unique as a fingerprint, and she stopped, fixed to the spot until he raised a hand in greeting, and only then hurried towards him.

'I went to the office. Your colleague said you'd gone for a walk, so I guessed it might be here.'

'Why aren't you at work?' Idiotic that this, of all possible questions, was the first to spring to her mind.

'I wanted to see you and I couldn't wait, so I closed the shop. You can do that, you know, when you're the shopkeeper.'

They had stopped about a yard apart on the path, hands in pockets, uncertain what kind of greeting was allowed.

'How are you? How's Gretchen?'

'I don't know about Gretchen. I've been miserable. Your letter just about finished me off.'

Hope, that treacherous friend, began its jabs and whispers.

'It finished me off to write it.'

'I've thought and thought about what you said, and I've tried to see how it could work, because I know you are good and wise, but I can't do it. I can't give you up.'

Jean felt joy flowing through her veins, unfreezing her blood. She had tried to be brave and do the good and decent thing, but she couldn't do it for both of them.

'I thought I could. But it's been awful. Worse than I ever imagined.'

He pulled her towards him and they clutched each other almost fearfully, it seemed to Jean, as though unseen hands would otherwise prise them apart. But he was solid as a tree; strong enough to withstand anything.

'I drove past your house a couple of times, just in the hope of seeing you at the window.'

'I was going to be so strong and dignified, but I've been a wreck.'

'All this unhappiness for nothing.' He kissed her lips, four, five, six times, until she pulled away, laughing.

'Did you speak to Gretchen?'

'Yes, we talked for a long time. I feel for her, but it's nonsense to think we can "patch things up" as if a marriage is just a torn pair of trousers. I couldn't touch her and she couldn't touch me.'

'What about Margaret?'

'Even if there were a hundred Margarets, it would never work.'

'It used to work well enough until Gretchen left.'

She wished she could stop arguing against her own interests, but she couldn't be sure until she had heard her case demolished, point by point.

'Yes, and if she hadn't, *I* would never have left *her*. I would have kept my feelings for you in a sealed box and so would you. But she did, and that released me, and now that I've experienced real love – passion – with you, I can't go back. Do you see the difference?'

'I think so.'

They dared to loosen their grip so they could look at each other. One advantage of being the same height was that their eyes were always level.

'I know that sex isn't *everything*, but it isn't *nothing*, either. It's a part of married love, perhaps the biggest part. And the idea that Gretchen can suddenly bury her feelings of revulsion, and that I could possibly make love to her again, knowing how she really feels, is complete madness.'

'Did you explain this to her?'

'Yes, of course. I think I got through to her in the end.'

'And what will she do? Will she stay with Martha?'

'I think so. She has to have someone.'

'Did you tell her about me – us?'

'No. I didn't know whether there was an "us".' He took off his woollen scarf and wound it around her neck, not needing to be told that without one she must be cold. 'And I've agonised over Margaret, I promise you, but the damage, if that's what you'd call it, has already been done. *Of course* she'd be delighted if Gretchen came back and we all lived together again the way we used to. And imagine how much worse it would then be if a few months on it all fell apart again – as it surely would.'

'I thought my life was over.'

'I know. Everything you felt, I felt, too.'

Happiness flowed and was smooth, but reality had rough surfaces and sharp corners.

'How will we ever manage to be together?'

'With patience and determination. Gretchen will have to be told. And Margaret. And your mother. It will be a bumpy ride, Jean.'

'Yes.'

She quailed at the thought of the turbulence ahead, but he had resolution enough for both of them. The alternative, already sampled, was unendurable. There could be no secrets. Except for that one unsayable thing, which she would keep to herself for ever. Let them believe in innocence and miracles and angel voices; it would be her gift to them all.

'I can't leave Mother. You know I can't.'

'I know. And I can't leave Margaret. So for the time being we may not be able to be together much. But we can still love each other, and if I can only see you once a week, I'd rather that than not at all.'

'Perhaps if I introduced you to Mother it would be easier for her to understand that you're no threat to her.'

With Jean alone she would certainly be difficult, but Howard's presence would be sure to disarm her. She had always taken more notice of men, considering them the superior sex.

'I'd like that. When?'

'Tonight. Now?'

Having accepted that it must be done, Jean wanted it over

quickly, while she was still powered by euphoria.

'I have to get back for Margaret.'

'Of course.'

'Tomorrow, though, she's going to the panto with Lizzie, so the evening is my own.' He sounded hopeful.

'You could come to dinner? Mother doesn't come downstairs anyway. She eats on a tray in her room, so once I've introduced you and we've had a chat, we can escape and be by ourselves.'

It sounded so simple put that way. In reality, however well behaved her mother was in Howard's presence, recriminations would surely follow when the two of them were alone. To prevail, Jean would have to be resolute, obstinate even. Somehow the knowledge that he was out there, emphatically and eternally on her side, shoring her up, gave her strength. Once her mother realised she held no cards, Jean could be generous.

'I'd like that. You're not going to change your mind between now and tomorrow?'

'No. Never.'

She was already there, ahead of him, the anxious hostess in her wondering what she could possibly make that would be worthy of the occasion.

Dusk was falling, a pale lilac glow at the horizon all that remained of the daylight, as they walked back through the woods arm in arm, the trees in their dark suits lining the path on either side.

40

Wednesday, 4 December 1957

Howard stood in the doorway in Bedford Street looking out at a slab of fog. He had been in his workshop all afternoon resizing rings and mending an elegant pocket watch under bright artificial light and had not been aware of its gathering presence. It was thick as custard and glowed a sickly yellow in the lamplight.

On his way into work in the morning visibility had been poor. He had felt a bit chesty as he walked along the Strand, but a cigarette had settled his cough, and he had been able to see well enough to pick up some hothouse roses from the market – at an exorbitant price – for Mrs Swinney. They were now standing in a chipped mug in the washbasin. The stallholder had told him to stir some cigarette ash into the water to preserve the blooms, but Howard wasn't sure if he was pulling his leg, so decided not to risk it.

He took off his twill overall and hung it on its usual hook. The cash box from the till was locked in the wall safe. His tools were neatly put away on their pegs, the cabinets locked. He put on his ulster overcoat and felt hat, and tied a cleanish handkerchief over his nose and mouth. (Freshly laundered linen had been an early casualty of Gretchen's departure.)

In his pocket was a velvet box containing the silver bracelet with moonstones that Jean had picked out as her favourite on that unexpected visit to the shop with Margaret. Already a little in love with her, he had stored the memory away in case there should ever come a time in some unimaginable future when he might be able to make a gift of it. She wouldn't have forgotten, either; he was sure of it. She had spent a lifetime on the sidelines, observing, noting, learning; the little details that other people missed were not lost on her.

He hesitated on the threshold, shuffling the keys in his hand, before stepping out blindly into the milky mass, surprised to find that it offered no resistance. It seemed substantial enough to be carved into chunks. He drew down and padlocked the metal shutters and turned the key in the door, a nightly ritual, the scrape and rattle of locking up tolling the end of each working day.

Progress down Bedford Street was slow, hampered by fear of near misses with other pedestrians. He could hear approaching footsteps but see nothing until suddenly a figure would be almost upon him, when they would apologise and step around each other and move on. Scattered particles of light and the persistent ringing of a bicycle bell alerted him that he had strayed near the kerb, and he stepped back as the cyclist wobbled into view, its headlamp combing from side to side.

He was nearly at the Strand, when he remembered the flowers, still in the sink. Damn and blast. He would miss the 5.18 if he went back and that would make him late. He couldn't decide what would be worse – to arrive late or empty-handed. Unpunctuality – especially on an occasion like this – looked thoughtless, but the roses had been so expensive and the gesture so well meant that he couldn't bear to waste them. No, he would go back. Jean would understand – if the weather was anything like as bad at Hayes, she would have had a difficult journey home herself and might well be glad of a little extra time to prepare.

He turned and floundered up the street the way he had come, holding his arms out in front of him as though warding off an assailant and apologising to left and right. Now that he had no chance of making the early train there was no point in trying to rush. In spite of his handkerchief mask, the metallic taste of the fog filled his mouth. He was glad to reach the temporary refuge of the shop once more for a few breaths of relatively unpolluted air.

His decision to return was vindicated by the discovery that he had left the tap on at a rapid drip and the plug in the sink. By morning there would have been a flood to deal with.

He put these lapses of concentration down to preoccupation with seeing Jean rather than the absent-mindedness of age. Inside, he felt no different from the young man who had jumped into the Thames at Battersea and swum across to the opposite bank just to impress the sister of one of his school friends. It was only when he was forced to look at his reflection while shaving that he was confronted with evidence of the hungry years.

He wrapped the bouquet of roses in newspaper, forming it into a sealed parcel, to protect the blooms from the murky atmosphere, and restarted his journey, keeping close to the buildings and feeling his way along the wall. On the corner, he passed the pub where he had recently whiled away the evenings with a pint rather than return to the empty house. The windows were lit up, and the interior of polished wood and shining brass was bright and welcoming. A few solitary drinkers were defying the weather, or sitting it out, but Howard pressed on, untempted, thinking only of Jean waiting and wondering as his promised time of arrival came and went.

On the Strand policemen with whistles were attempting to negotiate a safe passage for pedestrians at the traffic lights. Howard could hear rather than see the shuddering bulk of buses and taxis panting out clouds of diesel, and feel their hot breath on his legs as he crossed in a shuffling mass to the other side.

At Charing Cross a great press of people was waiting in the concourse, weary office workers and Christmas shoppers laden with carrier bags. A group of half a dozen schoolgirls in uniform snaked past arm in arm, shrieking noisily, confident in their little gang. Swirls of ghostly mist had penetrated in here too, through the open archways, giving it a curious atmosphere of being both inside and outside.

He was elated to discover that the 5.18 to Hayes was still on the platform, its departure delayed, congratulating himself on having made the right decision to go back for the flowers and imagining his disgruntlement if he had left them behind for nothing. Sometimes the cards just fell right.

Drawn along with the curious urgency that makes people speed up as they approach a train, Howard hurried through the barrier. A flurry of movement, whistles and the slamming of doors suggested that departure might be imminent, so he jumped on one of the rear carriages and found a space to stand between the seats.

He laid the newspaper parcel of flowers gently in the overhead luggage rack and unwound the handkerchief from his face, grimacing at the sooty particles trapped in its fibres. The train gave a lurch and a tug. Howard's fellow passengers exchanged smiles of relief and raised eyebrows. At last. He patted his pocket, feeling the hard shape of the velvet box, and imagined Jean's look of recognition and pleasure when she opened it. He would not be so very late, after all.

Afterword

The Lewisham train crash of 1957, described in the opening chapter, was at the time the second worst peacetime rail disaster in British history. (The Harrow and Wealdstone crash five years earlier being the worst.)

A total of 90 people lost their lives and 173 were injured. The driver of the Ramsgate steam locomotive, which had not stopped at the danger signal and collided with the stationary Hayes train, was prosecuted for manslaughter but acquitted after two trials, the original jury having failed to reach a verdict.

In a landmark case – *Chadwick v. British Railways Board, 1967* – which became a precedent for thirty years, the British Railways Board was successfully sued by the widow of a member of the public who had assisted at the scene for damage caused by 'nervous shock'. Henry Chadwick, who had climbed inside the crippled carriages to help the injured and dying, was unable to work again until his death (from unrelated causes) in 1962.

An unduly observant reader might notice that the account of the crash appears in the (fictional) *North Kent Echo* on Friday, 6 December 1957, thereby knocking Jean's virgin birth story off the front page.

The seed for this book came from an interview broadcast on BBC Radio 4's Woman's Hour towards the end of the last millennium with journalist Audrey Whiting. The *Sunday Pictorial*, for whom she worked in 1955, ran a competition to find a virgin mother, prompted by research by Dr Helen Spurway, a geneticist at the University of London.

Dr Spurway had observed that a species of fish (*Lebistes reticulatus*) was capable of spontaneously producing female progeny. It had also proved possible to obtain parthenogenetic development in rabbits by freezing the fallopian tubes. This led to speculation about whether or not spontaneous parthenogenesis might be provable in other mammals – most notably the human female.

The competition was launched, inviting women to present themselves for research. Of the nineteen who came forward, all were gradually ruled out for various reasons – including confusion as to what virginity actually involved – apart from a Mrs Emmimarie Jones, who had been bedridden in a German hospital at the time of 'conception'. She and her daughter, Monica, were subjected to various blood and serological tests, which seemed to validate her claim, but the final skin graft test eventually failed in both directions.

Details of the tests and their outcomes were reported in *The Lancet*, Vol. 267, issue 2934, 30 June 1956, pp. 1071–2 and Vol. 268, issue 6934, 21 July 1956, pp. 147–8. Even the doctors running these tests disagreed as to their significance. Their correspondence in *The Lancet* makes interesting reading.

Having caught the tail end of this interview on the radio, I sensed its potential as the basis of a novel but at the time I was writing (in my view, at least) humorous fiction, and this story didn't lend itself to light comedy. I therefore left it hanging at the back of my mind for well over a decade, like a piece of flypaper, to see if anything stuck to it.

I had been living in Hayes, Kent, for more than twenty years and used to commute daily on the Charing Cross line without ever having come across a mention of the Lewisham rail crash. It was only when researching the local history of the area in 2015 to see whether or not it might do as the setting for what I now thought of as the virgin birth novel that I came across a reference to it. This was the fly that stuck.

I have had to do some violence to history to unite these two strands. The facts of the rail crash are, as far as I can manage, accurate; the virgin birth story – apart from the seed described above and the medical tests detailed in *The Lancet* – is fiction. The characters, events and conversations are all mere invention. There is, I understand, a chapter about the case of Mrs Emmimarie Jones in *Like a Virgin: How Science Is Redesigning the Rules of Sex* by Aarathi Prasad (London: Oneworld Publications, 2012), but I didn't dare to read it in case it contained something that derailed my plot.

All the household hints are taken from issues of the *Hayes Parochial Magazine* and the *Hayes Herald*, published between 1953 and 1959.

I did some enjoyable reading to steep myself in the flavours of a period that I am just too young to have lived through. The novels of the 1950s are too numerous and too well known to need listing here. Of the non-fiction, the most useful were:

The diarists of the mass observation project collected in *Our Hidden Lives: The Everyday Diaries of a Forgotten Britain, 1945–1948*, edited by Simon Garfield (London: Ebury Press, 2005).

Family Britain 1951–1957, David Kynaston (London: Bloomsbury, 2009).

For a frank and illuminating account of extramarital love and sex, long before such things were formally invented in 1963, I was glad to have found *Diary of a Wartime Affair: The True Story of a Surprisingly Modern Romance* by Doreen Bates (London: Viking, 2016).

London: Portrait of a City 1950–1962 by Allan Hailstone (Stroud: Amberley Publishing, 2014) provided photographic inspiration.

For the local history of the Hayes area I am indebted to Jean Wilson and Trevor Woodman's *Hayes: A History of a Kentish Village: Volume 2: 1914 to Modern Times* (J. Wilson, 2012).

Acknowledgements

When I was first published in my twenties, I used to think acknowledgements were a sign of weakness and I pitied those writers who seemed to need a whole village to raise their book. I feel rather differently about the matter now and ashamed that some extremely helpful people went unthanked.

In that spirit, I am indebted to the following: Judith Murray of Greene & Heaton, who is everything a writer could wish for in an agent; Federico Andornino, my editor at W&N – his suggestions have greatly improved the book and it has been no small pleasure working with him; Claire Pickering for thoughtful copy-editing.

Thanks are also due to Ken and Sylvia Truss for their encyclopaedic knowledge of the era and area in which the book is set, and very much overdue to Esther Whitby, my mentor for the past three decades.

Last in this list, but the first in importance, is my husband Peter, for his unwavering support.

About the Author

Clare Chambers was born in south-east London in 1966. She studied English at Oxford and after graduating spent the year in New Zealand, where she wrote her first novel, *Uncertain Terms*, published when she was 25. She has since written eight further novels, including *Learning to Swim* which won the Romantic Novelists' Association best novel award and was adapted as a Radio 4 play, and *In a Good Light* which was longlisted for the Whitbread best novel prize.

Clare began her career as a secretary at the publisher André Deutsch, when legendary editor Diana Athill was still at the helm. They not only published her first novel, but made her type her own contract. In due course she went on to become an editor there herself, until leaving to raise a family and concentrate on her own writing. Some of the experiences of working for an eccentric, independent publisher in the pre-digital era found their way into her novel *The Editor's Wife*.

She takes up a post as Royal Literary Fund Fellow at the University of Kent in September 2020. She lives with her husband in south-east London.